PIETRO

Titles available in this series

Yannis
Anna
Giovanni
Joseph
Christabelle
Saffron
Manolis
Cathy
Nicola
Vasi
Alecos
John
Tassos
Ronnie
Maria
Sofia
Babbis
Stelios
Kyriakos
Monika
Emmanuel
Theo
Phaedra
Evgeniy
Ludmila
Pietro

Greek Translations

Anna

published by Livanis 2011

PIETRO

Beryl Darby

JACH

ISBN 978-1-9997176-67

Printed and bound in the UK by
Print2Demand
1 Newlands Road, Westoning,
Bedfordshire MK45 5LD

First published in the UK in 2020 by

JACH Publishing
92 Upper North Street, Brighton, East Sussex, England BN1 3FJ

website: www.beryldarbybooks.com

Author's Note

There has never been any evidence of illegal burials taking place in the area. All the characters are fictitious and this book is entirely the product of my imagination.

My thanks to Carla who gave me invaluable information about Italy and to Rhonda who arranged for the cover photo to be taken.

.

January 2016
Week One

Ludmila sat and thought about her impending deportation. At present she had not been given a date, but she needed to speak to Mr Propenkov and ensure that arrangements were made to her satisfaction. She would be relieved to be back in her native Moscow as she no longer felt safe in Crete, unsure if she was being watched if she ventured out of the apartment. Having attempted to leave Crete earlier with her brother, although not in possession of her passport, she knew the authorities would be aware that she might try to do the same again.

It was cold in Heraklion now and would be even colder in Moscow. She eyed her fur coat that hung in the wardrobe, running her hands lovingly over the soft fur and feeling with satisfaction the padding she had placed in the cuffs and beneath the fur collar. She still had her insurance.

She pressed the phone number for Mr Propenkov's office into her mobile 'phone and hoped she would not get the recorded message she had heard the previous week saying he was on leave until the New Year. He finally acknowledged her call with a curt 'Yes?'

'Mr Propenkov, it is Ludmila Kuzmichov here.'

'I know. I recognised your number. If you are planning to appeal against the deportation order I can tell you that it will not be rescinded.'

'I will be very relieved to be back in my native country, but there is a problem that I need to speak to you about. I am willing to come to your office or you could visit me at my apartment, whichever is most convenient for you.'

Propenkov sighed. He did not want to have anything more to do with the woman. 'I can spare you half an hour tomorrow, no more. Be with me at ten.'

The line went dead and Ludmila smiled to herself. At least he had not refused to meet with her.

Ludmila made sure she was at the Russian Consulate well before ten and having spoken to the woman on the reception desk and confirmed that she had an appointment with Mr Propenkov she took a seat on the uncomfortable plastic chair as far away from the other people who were waiting as possible.

She resisted looking at her watch when her name was finally called and she was led down the corridor to Mr Propenkov's office, although she was sure it was already after ten. She would make a very obvious point of checking the time when she sat down in front of him. If he was thinking of curtailing the interview before her allotted thirty minutes he was going to be wrong.

Mr Propenkov rose as she entered and apologised for keeping her waiting.

'Please take a seat and tell me as briefly as possible the problem you are envisaging.'

Ludmila removed her coat and settled herself on a chair that was no more comfortable than the one she had left a short while earlier. 'It is a financial question. At present you have been good enough to arrange for me to have a small sum to enable me to buy my food and other necessities from the hotel. When I reach Moscow what am I supposed to live on? When I arrive I will need a taxi from the airport to my apartment and money for food. As you know, life is expensive in Moscow.'

Propenkov frowned. 'You have no income in Moscow?'

'You know I do not. My husband kept the bank account in his

name and gave me a generous allowance. The apartment is in my husband's name so I am unable to approach the bank in Moscow and ask if I can have a loan and guarantee it against the apartment. It is likely they will want to repossess the apartment and sell it. I will then be homeless. My husband is still the legal owner of the hotel and I feel I should have some of the capital transferred to me so I can cover my living expenses.'

'The hotel is up for sale as your husband claims not to have sufficient capital that he can use to cover his legal expenses.'

Ludmila nodded. 'That is a problem that I am sure he will be able to deal with. It does not help my current situation. Until such time as the sale of the property is completed he is still the legal owner and as such I feel I should be entitled to an adequate sum to ensure I am able to live decently rather than having to beg on the streets.'

'What about your current apartment in Heraklion?'

'Again it is owned by my husband. If the deeds were transferred to me I would be able to sell it or rent it out and that would give me sufficient income to live on after the sale of the hotel.'

Propenkov nodded. The transfer of the property into her name would be sensible if Kuzmichov agreed. He was surprised that the business man had not made his wife a joint owner in his property.

'I will need to speak to my legal advisers and also speak to your husband. I agree it seems to be a practical solution to your financial predicament.'

'How long will this procedure take?'

Propenkov spread his hands. 'I cannot possibly say. Legal matters move slowly.'

'I will appeal against any deportation date until the matter of my income has been settled. I cannot be expected to leave the country without a rouble in my purse.'

'I understand and I am sure that a satisfactory arrangement can be agreed upon.'

'And in the meantime am I still able to receive the allowance

I have been allocated from the hotel?'

'I see no reason why that should be discontinued at present, but I will need to speak with Mr Iliopolakis. He is in charge of the administration at the moment. I will contact you, Mrs Kuzmichov, should there be any problem regarding the allowance, and again when I have received the advice from my legal advisers to see if your husband is willing to come to an arrangement regarding transferring the apartment in Heraklion into your name.'

Ludmila nodded. She was satisfied that she would not be left without any money whilst she was in Heraklion and if Evgeniy agreed to sign the apartment over to her it would be a bonus. Once she was back in Moscow she knew her financial worries would be over.

'There is one other thing, Mr Propenkov. I would very much like to visit my brother to see that he is keeping well.'

Mr Propenkov shook his head. 'I will have to request permission for you through the various legal channels. If a visit is refused then I will press for permission for you to make a telephone call.'

'I see no harm in me visiting my brother whilst he is in prison.'

'At present he is not in prison. He is in the Remand Centre and security is strict. If you were given permission to visit or speak on the telephone your conversation would be monitored the whole time.'

Ludmila shrugged. 'That would be no problem. I can assure you our conversation would be completely innocent.'

Mr Propenkov looked pointedly at the clock in his room. 'Is there anything else, Mrs Kuzmichov? I do have another appointment.'

Ludmila looked at her watch. She had received her allotted half an hour. 'Thank you for your time. I will hope to hear from you very soon regarding the apartment and speaking to my brother. Shall I telephone in a couple of weeks if I have not heard from you?'

'There will be no need for that. I will contact you when I have any news to impart, whether it is good or bad.'

Ludmila gathered her fur coat from the chair and allowed Mr Propenkov to help her on with it. She gave a little smile to herself. All the time she had her coat she had plenty of security.

Evgeniy shook his head when Mr Propenkov suggested that he should sign the apartment in Heraklion over to Ludmila so she could sell or rent the property.

'There is no way I would even consider it. She is already receiving money from the hotel that I do not consider she has any entitlement to. How am I supposed to be able to pay the expenses you say are being charged to me?'

'Mrs Kuzmichov claims she will have no income when she returns to Moscow. Surely it is your responsibility to provide for your wife from your assets.'

'She will not suffer. She has plenty of friends in Moscow. The apartment and all the contents belong to me. I bought it from Mr Iliopolakis and the furnishings were part of the agreement. I am not prepared to hand everything over to my wife.'

Mr Propenkov had anticipated Evgeniy's reaction. 'Very well. Do you wish to sell the apartment once your wife has left Crete?'

'That would be most practical and one less thing for me to worry about.'

'What about the contents?'

Evgeniy shrugged. 'I bought it furnished. It can be sold furnished.'

Mr Propenkov rose. 'I will prepare the necessary documents and bring them in for you to sign. Did you have an itemised list when you bought the contents from Mr Iliopolakis? That could help me when I draw up a prospectus.'

'It should be around somewhere. Ask Ludmila.'

Mr Propenkov telephoned Ludmila Kuzmichov. 'Good morning, Madam. I have some information for you.'

'Yes?' answered Ludmila eagerly. Had Evgeniy agreed to sign the apartment over to her?

'I have spoken to your husband regarding the apartment and he will not sign the title deeds over to you. He says he needs the money from its eventual sale to cover his own legal expenses. He told me there should be an inventory of the furniture that was included in the purchase price, I would be very grateful if you could let me have that information.'

'Why do you need that?'

'It would enable me to assess the value as a whole and the apartment would then be advertised as being a fully furnished property for sale.'

'I'll have to look for it,' replied Ludmila sulkily. This was not what she had expected. 'Suppose I cannot find it?'

'I feel convinced that the document is somewhere safe in the apartment. Your husband would not have been so foolish as to destroy it. Should a dispute regarding the ownership of an article arisen he would have needed to prove that it belonged to him. If it really does not come to light within the next two or three days I will ask Mr Iliopolakis for his copy. I feel sure he will have kept it. It is quite urgent as a date for your deportation has been arranged for two weeks time.'

Ludmila's mouth felt dry. 'That does not give me very much time to make arrangements.'

'The Cretan government has been very lenient and understanding but your departure can no longer be delayed.'

'What about my possessions? I will not be able to carry everything that I am taking back with me.'

'I suggest you get as much packed as possible and I will arrange for them to be collected next week and sent on to Moscow.'

'I don't have my passport.'

'I will escort you to the airport and hand your passport to the authorities who will be expecting you. You will be accompanied on the flight and upon your arrival in Athens they will then arrange for your supervised departure. Once you are on board the flight to Moscow your passport will be returned to you.'

'What about my money? I cannot be expected to arrive in Moscow without any money.'

'I will have that with me when I collect you from the apartment and that again will be handed to you when you are on board the Moscow flight. Please make a note of the date of your departure and I will advise you of the time of your flight as soon as I have the information. If you have any queries feel free to telephone me. In the meantime I would like you to call me as soon as you have found the inventory.'

'May I visit my brother before I leave Crete? '

'I will see if I can arrange for you to visit the Remand Centre. You will be able to see your brother and have a telephone conversation. Please restrict yourselves to the Greek language. Remember it is very likely it will be recorded and if the guard who accompanied you has any suspicions about the content of your conversation the recording will be replayed before you are permitted to leave.'

'That is no problem. I only wish to ascertain that my brother is keeping well and tell him that I am to return to Moscow.'

Ludmila was given permission to telephone her brother, but warned that a security guard would be listening to their conversation.

'It will be necessary for you to be at the Centre before two for the security checks to be completed. If you are late and the call is not placed promptly you will not have the opportunity again,' Mr Propenkov advised her.

'I understand. Can you tell me if my request for a quantity of roubles to be put at my disposal has been agreed?'

Mr Propenkov shook his head. 'I am waiting to be informed about the proposed meeting between Mr Iliopolakis and the bank manager. Have you found the inventory for the apartment as I requested?'

'I am still looking for it,' replied Ludmila. She knew exactly where the document was but she was not prepared to hand it to Mr Propenkov until she had decided which items she was going to take back to Moscow with her. She would amend the condition of a number of items on the inventory and claim they were damaged at the time of the purchase and had subsequently been thrown away. There was also the dinner service, cutlery, linen table cloth and bedding that had been purchased on Evgeniy's credit card. She would make sure she packed those to go to Moscow along with any other items that she thought would not be missed.

The conversation with Mr Propenkov left Ludmila with mixed feelings. Although it would be considerably colder in Russia than it was in Crete she was prepared to face that. She needed to return to Moscow as soon as possible so she was able to make contact with the friends who would be able to help Ivan, but she also needed money for her initial expenses.

Mr Propenkov looked after her as she left his office. He did not trust the woman and he would pass her details on to the Supreme Commander at the Ministry of Internal Affairs. Groshenkov was a man he could trust to keep a discreet eye on her activities. On a secure line Mr Propenkov spoke with the Commander and apprised him of the people smuggling operation that had been taking place in Crete and the subsequent arrest and sentencing of the organisers.

Mr Groshenkov listened carefully. 'We have had our eye on Evgeniy Kuzmichov and his wife for a number of years but have never found enough proof to convict them of anything. I have to congratulate you on your success. I will arrange for a reliable agent to rent a room opposite Ludmila's apartment and report on her activities.'

'She claimed she had acted under duress from her husband.'

'Well if that is true she will be leading a blameless life when she returns to Moscow.'

'I will arrange for her to be escorted from Crete to Athens

and then on the plane to Moscow and advise you of her time of arrival. Alert the passport authorities that she has 'DEPORTED' stamped throughout her passport and she should be questioned but not detained.'

'It will be interesting to know what excuse she gives them for the deportation. I'll have a man waiting to follow her when she leaves.'

Ludmila Kuzmichov arrived at the Remand Centre well before two, gave her name to the guard on duty and informed him that she was able to have a telephone conversation with her brother, Ivan.

The guard consulted his list. 'I understand this has been arranged by Mr Propenkov. I will have to ask you to wait until we have the video link established. Your brother will then be brought up and you will be admitted to the room where you will be able to see and speak to him.'

Ludmila was escorted to a small room and was disconcerted when she heard the door locked behind her. Why was she being locked in? She was a visitor, not a criminal. She sat on the hard wooden chair disconsolately and shivered. There was no heating and despite wearing her fur coat she felt completely chilled. How must Ivan be suffering if there was no heating in the Remand Centre cells?

After what seemed like an interminable amount of time she heard the key in the lock and the guard reappeared.

'Please follow me, Madam. Make sure you have all your possessions with you as you will be unable to return to this room.'

Ludmila followed the guard down a brick corridor until they reached a room at the end. Once more a door was unlocked and she was led into a brightly lit room, the only furniture being a long table with a chair behind it where another man was sitting. The guard stood in front of the door and waited.

'Please place your bag on the table and empty the contents in front of me,' he ordered.

'There is nothing illegal in my bag,' protested Ludmila.

'I will be the judge of that. Please empty your bag as requested.'

From her bag Ludmila removed a pack of paper handkerchiefs, a notebook and pen, her keys, lipstick, compact mirror, nail file, purse, comb, hair spray and mobile 'phone. The guard immediately picked up the 'phone, hair spray and nail file and placed them to one side. He examined the other items and then turned the bag inside out and felt it carefully. Finally satisfied that she had nothing hidden in the lining he pushed the bag back across the table towards her.

'You may replace your belongings. The items I have removed will be returned to you when you leave.'

Ludmila opened her mouth to argue and then thought better of it. If she caused a scene she might be refused the promised telephone call. Sulkily she pushed the items haphazardly back into her bag.

'Please remove your coat, Madam.'

'Remove my coat? I am too cold to be without my coat.'

'It is necessary for our visitor requirements that your coat is examined along with your other items of clothing.'

'I am only having a telephone conversation with my brother,' protested Ludmila. She had not had to endure such strict security when she visited Evgeniy. Her bag had been searched and she had been instructed to walk through a detector machine the same as was in use at the airports

'Rules have to be obeyed.' The guard stood and looked at her as she unwillingly removed her fur coat.

He felt in the pockets, around the hem, cuffs and collar and threw it on his chair. 'Please stand a short distance away from the table on that line, Madam, with your feet apart and your arms outstretched.'

'If I am to be subject to a body search surely that should be done by another woman.'

'We do not have any women on our staff. Please stand as I have requested.'

The guard patted down Ludmila's body quickly and efficiently. His attitude was totally impersonal and she would be unable to complain that he had taken any liberties. She wondered if Mr Propenkov had been subjected to the same intensive searching when he had visited her when she was in gaol.

'Thank you, Madam. Here is your coat.'

As the guard handed her coat to her she heard a distinct click and looked up. The eye of a camera looked down and she realised that the whole episode had been recorded. No wonder the guard had not taken any liberties when he gave her a body search.

Ludmila followed her original guard along another passage to a grilled security gate and pressed a bell at the side. Another man appeared and unlocked the grill, permitting them both to walk through and into a small room, with the guard taking up a position in front of the door. There was a table, chair and telephone with the cord linked through a sheet of glass to a replica arrangement on the other side.

She waited anxiously for Ivan to appear and when he did so she gave a sigh of relief. He looked well and there were no signs of brutality on his face. She heard the guard switch on the tape recorder and give the date, time and the names of her and her brother.

'Please lift the telephone receiver now, Madam, and you will be able to speak to your brother.'

'Hello, Ivan. Are you well? I've been given permission to speak to you today as sometime soon I am going to be deported to Russia.'

Ivan nodded. 'I'm well enough. Bored and hoping I will be freed soon.'

'Is that likely?'

Ivan shrugged. 'It will depend upon the immigration authorities. At present they are trying to decide whether I should be returned to Russia or Syria. Syria is very unsettled and dangerous at present, so I hope it will be Russia. Not stopping as ordered when trying to out run a storm at sea is hardly a crime.'

'It was very frightening. I was thankful that you are such an accomplished sailor.'

'Where is Evgeniy?'

'In prison. He was given ten years.'

Ivan raised his eyebrows and whistled through his teeth. 'You were fortunate to only be given a deportation order.'

'I was innocent, as you know. It was Evgeniy who arranged everything.'

Ivan grinned. 'Yes, he was the master mind. We had no option but to do as he said. What are you planning to do when you return to Moscow?'

'I haven't decided yet.'

'Will you have sufficient money to live on?'

'I believe so. Mr Propenkov is arranging for me to have a sum of money drawn from the hotel each month.'

Ivan nodded. His sister had obviously been able to persuade the representative from the Russian Consulate that she was penniless.

'When you return to Moscow don't forget to visit Mother.'

Ludmila understood the message Ivan was giving her. 'Is Svetlana still looking after her?'

'They appear to be quite compatible.'

'I hope Mother will be understanding about your predicament.'

'I'm sure that once you have explained the situation there will be no problem.'

'I will do my utmost,' promised Ludmila. 'Is there anything that you want or need that I can send in for you?'

'Nothing I can think of at present. I am not being badly treated. The food could be better, but I have access to newspapers and I am allowed on a computer once a day for an hour, but not permitted to receive or send messages.'

'Could you ask for that rule to be relaxed when I am back in Moscow? I would obviously like to be able to keep in touch with you regularly and a written letter can take a long time to arrive.'

'I'll ask if it's possible. In the meantime, take care, Ludmila, and don't forget to visit Mother.'

Ivan replaced the receiver of his 'phone and indicated that he was ready to leave. Ludmila waved as he exited the small room and also rose to go. If the recording of their conversation was played back there was nothing incriminating in it at all, but she knew she had the information that she needed to proceed once she was in Moscow to help her brother.

'Will you be helping Saffron with the lunch for the workers when they are picking the olives?' asked Vasilis.

'I've not been asked, but I think it is expected of me as I went last year.'

Vasilis nodded. 'I'm pleased to hear that. I have to go up to Heraklion and see the bank manager about the finance for the hotel. I hope he has some news of a prospective buyer. I don't want to be responsible for the administration of the hotel any longer than necessary. Unless you want to come up to Heraklion with me I'll arrange to go whilst you're with Saffie.'

'I have no desire to go up to Heraklion and sit around whilst you and the bank manager have long discussions. I'll be far happier here making up the rolls.'

'I'll obviously take you up there and collect you when I return. I'm planning to 'phone Vasi and ask him to have a discussion with me. Would you like to come up with me or prefer that I asked him to come down here?'

'I really do not mind. Whichever arrangement suits you both best.'

Cathy joined Saffron in the kitchen whilst Vasilis and his son sat in the lounge.

'I'm looking forward to being in London next week,' smiled Saffron, 'but I hate having to fight my way through everyone at the airport and hanging around for the flight. At least the olive picking should be completed. You'll come and help with the lunches, won't you?'

'Of course,' nodded Cathy. 'You don't ever have to ask. I enjoy it and Vasilis has to go up to Heraklion and it is a good excuse for me not to have to accompany him.'

'Hotel problems?'

'I'm not sure. He has to meet with the bank manager and he's hoping a buyer has come forward for "The Central". What do you and Vasi plan to do in London?'

'Probably some theatre visits and just general sight seeing and a bit of shopping. I love seeing Marjorie again but two weeks in London is more than enough for me nowadays.'

'She wouldn't consider coming over here to live permanently?'

'I have suggested it to her and said we could rent an apartment for her down by the town, but she says she would be bored during the winter and the summer would be far too hot for her to go out until the evening. She also said that she would miss her friends. She does have quite an active social life, enjoys the theatre and cinema and a meal out in company.'

'It does sound as though she is happy where she is,' agreed Cathy.

'I know, I understand how she feels. I would not want to return to living in London. I just feel somewhat guilty about being so far away.'

'I'm sure she would not want you to feel guilty. If it was necessary you could be with her within a day.'

'Provided she realised that she needed me and didn't think she was being a nuisance. After all she has done for me during my life I would hate to let her down or for her to think I didn't care. No one could have had a better step mother. It was such a shame that Dad died. They were so happy together.' Saffron brushed a tear from her eye and Cathy squeezed her hand.

'It isn't like you to be depressed and feeling low. When did you last 'phone her?'

'This morning. I 'phone her every day.'

'Then you have no need to feel guilty. She knows you care or you wouldn't call every day. Cheer up. Shall I help you to carry the plates through to the dining room?'

Vasilis explained to Vasi that he had been requested to meet with the bank manager regarding the "Central Hotel".

'I'm hoping he has a prospective buyer. I'm not enthusiastic about continuing indefinitely as the administrator for the hotel. I had expected it to only be for a few months. I certainly can't afford to buy it back, not that I want to. I've spent the capital I received from the sale on the apartment in Elounda and building the new house will take all that is left over. I'll be drawing on my savings for the furnishing.'

'How is the house progressing?'

'Nothing going on at present. The builders obviously took time off for Christmas and the New year and I expect most of them will be involved with olive picking. I can't expect any work until that has been completed.'

'What about your idea of making the hotel a consortium and offering shares to the staff?'

'That's still a possibility. Would you be interested in having a share in "The Central"?'

Vasi shook his head. 'I don't want to become involved. You know we've discussed turning this big house you built for Cathy into a business premises. The conversion will cost a considerable amount and I'd also like to buy the apartment where you are living at present. That would be ideal for Saffie and myself.'

'You're really going ahead with that idea?'

'Unless you want the house back. It does still belong to you after all.'

Vasilis considered carefully before he spoke. 'I was far too ambitious when I built this house and did not take into account the fact that Cathy might be unable to live here as her arthritis progressed. I think it would be more practical if you just moved to the apartment without purchasing it. That would release money for whatever alterations you have in mind for the house. The only condition is that I receive a percentage of any profit you make when you turn it into a business.'

Vasi nodded. 'I was obviously going to offer you a share and I'll not make any drastic alterations without consulting you. If we move to the apartment I can pay you rent.'

'We can discuss that later.'

'Have you thought about approaching Uncle Yannis and asking if he would be interested in an investment?'

'Not yet, but I think it unlikely he will be interested. He's far too occupied with trying to get rid of his stock of pots to turn his mind to anything else at the moment. I think he's worried that when anything happens to him all his beloved stock will be thrown away.'

'I'm sure that wouldn't happen. It might take time for all of it to sell, but John seems to know his way around selling on the internet. Cathy has said she wants some large pots for the new house. She may change her mind of course when she sees how it is laid out.'

'We'll buy some, of course, for when we have completed the alterations to this house, but that will not be this year. Won't she want to take the ones she has at the apartment with her?'

'Maybe, but the house isn't likely to be finished until June. By then she will have planted the current ones and they could be too heavy to move.'

'Why don't you ask her to wait until she has seen the new garden?'

'I don't want her asking to visit until it is finally completed. I even avoid driving that way with her so she cannot see the front elevation. I'd like it to be a complete surprise for her.'

Yannis shook his head when Vasilis approached him and suggested that he might like to be a shareholder in the Heraklion hotel if it became a consortium.

'I haven't any spare capital. When you bought the hotel I used the money to build this house and also to develop Plaka. I know I have rents coming in, but maintenance has to be considered. Besides, I'm too old to think about speculating now. Any surplus cash I have is from the sale of my ceramic stock. Make the offer to Giovanni. He might be interested.'

Vasilis did not believe for one moment that Yannis was as penniless as he was making out.

Giovanni smiled when Vasilis approached him. 'I have no capital to invest. Uncle Yannis owns the land where the self catering units are built. Although we received insurance money after the fire it was insufficient to rebuild completely and we had to borrow from the bank and repay the loan. They are giving us a good income now during the season, but we have to live during the winter months and spend that time doing the necessary maintenance and refurbishment. We all have a small salary and thanks to Uncle Yannis we are able to live here without having to pay the utility expenses. Once Marianne and I have contributed to our weekly food and I have paid for petrol for the vehicles there is not a lot left over. I've also had my mother in law staying here for weeks now, and although I am happy to have her here I cannot ask her to pay for her food. She is a guest. That is an added expense. Fortunately my mother contributes a small amount from her pension which is a help.'

Vasilis nodded understandingly. He had not expected Giovanni to be willing to invest in the hotel, but he did not believe that the man was as poor as he was claiming.

'I'm hoping that when I meet with the bank manager he will tell me there is a buyer interested.' Vasilis sighed, 'I thought once I had retired I would not have to concern myself with running a hotel again.'

Vasilis was surprised to see Mr Propenkov already in the bank manager's office as he entered.

Mr Tanakis rose and shook Vasilis's hand. 'I hope you don't mind, I asked Mr Propenkov to be here for part of our meeting as the discussion will involve both Mr and Mrs Kuzmichov.'

Vasilis nodded and took a seat. 'I thought Mr Kuzmichov had agreed that I would become the administrator for "The Central" until such time as a buyer was found. Has he retracted that idea or has someone come forward with an offer?'

'Neither, Mr Iliopolakis. Mrs Kuzmichov has spoken with Mr Propenkov and he would like to be able to reassure her that the allowance she has been granted will continue for the duration of her time in Heraklion.'

'I thought she was being deported?'

'She is, but these formalities take time. Her departure is due in nine days time,' explained Mr Propenkov. 'She obviously needs money to enable her to live whilst she is still here. She has also requested that a sum of money, from the hotel, is given to her for when she finally arrives in Russia and in the following months.'

Vasilis raised his eyebrows. 'How much?'

'One hundred thousand roubles. That is not as unreasonable as it sounds,' continued Mr Propenkov hurriedly when he saw the shocked look on Vasilis's face. 'It is the equivalent of about one thousand three hundred Euros. The cost of living in Moscow is far greater than living in Greece and she has no access to any money in the country. Everything is in her husband's name. She had suggested that her husband signed over the deeds of the Heraklion apartment to her and so would then be able to sell or rent it out to give her either a one off lump sum or a regular monthly income. She would then not be requesting any subsidy from the hotel and it would just be the interim period that would need to be covered. Unfortunately her husband refused as he says he will need the capital from the apartment to cover his own costs.'

'And how long would this interim period last? If Evgeniy

Kuzmichov has refused to make her the owner of the apartment the situation could continue for years. I cannot envisage that any prospective buyer of the hotel would want to have such a drain on his financial resources for an indeterminate amount of time.'

'Quite,' agreed Mr Tanakis. 'It would be unreasonable to expect.'

Mr Tanakis looked at Mr Propenkov who spread his hands. 'The sale of the hotel is not my affair. Kuzmichov knows that it is necessary for him to sell to cover his legal expenses and has agreed to that. I will leave you now, unless you have any other questions regarding the Kuzmichovs. I am sure you prefer to have a financial discussion in private. Please contact me at my office when any decisions have been reached.'

Vasilis looked at Stavros Tanakis when Mr Propenkov had left. 'Is Mr Propenkov being honest about the amount of money he says Mrs Kuzmichov needs when she returns to Moscow?'

'I believe so. I have looked at the conversion rates along with various everyday items and compared with the prices in Crete they are almost double the amount you would pay here.'

Vasilis shrugged. 'I don't see how the money can be refused to her whilst her husband is still the legal owner of the hotel.'

'I have a proposition, Mr Iliopolakis. You suggested that the hotel be floated on the stock exchange with the current employees being given the first opportunity to purchase shares. How about yourself, Mr Iliopolakis? Would you not want to be the majority shareholder?'

Vasilis shook his head. 'I am quite happy being retired. I agreed to become the administrator for the hotel on a temporary basis to prevent closure and the staff losing their jobs. I will be more than happy to relinquish that position as soon as possible.'

Mr Tanakis nodded. 'So if the bank was willing to step in and become the major shareholder you would have no objection?'

'Provided the bank was not proposing to close the hotel and leave it derelict or tear it down and build an apartment block. My only concern is with the employees. Many of them have worked there for years and could find it difficult to find an alternative position. Before making a final decision I would like to discuss your offer further with my financial adviser.'

'Of course. I had not expected an immediate decision from you. Contact me when you have had time to discuss the proposal and if you have any queries please contact me. If you agree in principle we can discuss the fine details of the contract later.'

Vasilis nodded. 'It galls me to think that she will be receiving more money from the hotel each month than I deduct each month in administration fees.'

'Maybe you should increase your fees?'

'I don't think I am entitled to more. Dimitra does most of the work, checking that staff wages and invoices are correct. I simply check her figures and authorise the payments. If I run out of money and ask you for a bank loan to help pay for my new house I hope you will look sympathetically at me.'

Mr Tanakis smiled. It was extremely unlikely that Mr Iliopolakis would ever run out of money.

Vasilis drove back to Elounda. He was aggrieved that Ludmila would still be receiving an allowance from the hotel, although he had to admit that the property still belonged to Evgeniy. He hoped that the bank would move swiftly and make the hotel into a consortium so he could relinquish the responsibility. It was sad that no one had come forward to make an offer for the profitable business.

January 2016
Week Two

Vasilis examined the hotel accounts and drew up a simple balance sheet for the year before he had sold the property to Evgeniy. It showed a healthy profit and continued to do so even when Evgeniy became the owner. Once Evgeniy had been arrested the report became more complicated and showed the establishment had run at a loss for some months and was only just beginning to show a small profit again. If he deducted the compensation that had been paid to clients whose holidays had been disrupted, the expenses claimed by the other hotels to accommodate visitors at short notice, along with the allowance that was given to Ludmila and his own fees as the administrator, then the accounts showed a profit.

He drew another sheet of paper and calculated the approximate amount of profit that could be expected for the coming year. He felt sure that Mr Tanakis had employed virtually the same procedure and this had influenced his decision to agree to the hotel becoming a consortium with the bank as the major shareholder.

Wanting to ensure that his figures were correct and also wishing to ask Vasi if he wanted to become a shareholder he 'phoned and asked if it was convenient for him to visit.

'I thought you might be interested to know the outcome of my visit to the bank.'

'Of course. Bring Cathy up with you and stay for lunch. She'll be company for Saffie whilst we talk.'

'Are you sure? Saffie is probably busy getting ready for your visit to England.'

'She's so well organised that we could leave at a minute's notice. She keeps asking me if I'm sure there there is nothing more I want to take. It's unsettling. I keep thinking I must have forgotten something vital.'

'I'm sure you haven't. We'll be there about eleven. That should give us plenty of time to talk before lunch. Tell Saffie not to go to any trouble. Bread and cheese will be quite sufficient.'

'I'm sure Saffie can do better than that.'

Leaving Cathy with Saffron in the kitchen Vasilis followed his son into the lounge where he was presented with a glass of wine.

'Is there a problem?' asked Vasi.

'Since visiting Mr Tanakis I've been working on some figures from the hotel and I'd like you to have a look at them. Make sure I haven't added or missed any zeros. When I arrived to see Mr Tanakis I found Mr Propenkov was with him. Apparently Mrs Kuzmichov wanted to be assured that she would have her allowance from the hotel whilst she remained in Heraklion.'

'Reasonable,' nodded Vasi.

'Yes, but what is not so reasonable is that she is also asking for the allowance to be continued when she finally gets deported to Russia.'

'Hasn't she got any money she can access when she returns?'

'Apparently not. She claims that everything was always in her husband's name. According to Propenkov the cost of living in Russia is considerably higher than in Crete. She is asking for one thousand three hundred Euros a month.'

'So why does that worry you if the money is coming from the hotel all the time it belongs to Evgeniy Kuzmichov? It is him that is paying it, not you.'

'I know, but Mr Tanakis is suggesting that the bank becomes the majority shareholder with shares being offered to the staff.

That would mean that Kuzmichov no longer owned the property so why should his wife expect to have any income from it?'

'Does she know about that proposal?'

'No, Mr Tanakis and I discussed it after Propenkov had left.'

'Did you agree?'

Vasilis shook his head. 'I said I had no objection to the bank becoming a majority shareholder provided this did not mean that the hotel was closed down and the site sold so a block of apartments could be built. I told him I wanted to consult with my financial adviser before making a final decision.'

Vasi frowned. This was the first he had heard of his father having someone to advise him regarding his investments. 'Who is your financial adviser?'

'You are. What do you think?'

'Me!'

'We've always discussed the ownership and management of the hotels together so I think you are in a far better position to advise me than Mr Tanakis. He only sees the balance sheets and a profit for the bank.'

'I don't think we can discuss that profitably at the moment. We need to have all the facts and figures before us, how much profit the hotel is making before Mrs Kuzmichov has her allowance; how much would the selling price be now? Evgeniy Kuzmichov was eager to buy at your asking price as he thought he was going to make a good deal of money running the illegal immigration scheme from there. An honest hotelier would expect to pay less than the asking price as one always asks for more than one expects to receive so that negotiations can take place. How much would the bank want to invest?'

'I don't know exactly but I have calculated all the figures for the income of "The Central" for the previous eighteen months and also a projection for the future. Mr Tanakis said the bank could be the majority shareholder if it was made into a consortium.'

'Do you have a figure in mind that should be asked for the purchase of the hotel?'

Vasilis shook his head. 'I've looked on the internet but there is nothing of a similar size for sale. I need to work out a realistic asking price. I don't want Evgeniy Kuzmichov to end up making a vast profit.'

'Then it would be most practical to ask the same price as he paid you for it. You have nothing to lose and that way he does not gain financially.'

'Would you come up with me? He'll probably take more notice of you.'

'I doubt that, but I can't possibly visit him until we return from England. Why don't you ask Marianne for some advice?'

'I have all the financial records that Dimitra has forwarded to me each week, along with all the figures I have worked out. I can send her copies.'

Vasi nodded. 'It wouldn't hurt for her to have a look at them before you present them to Mr Tanakis. Can I leave that with you? I need to look at the accounts for 'The Imperia' before we go away. It has become very popular with the locals during the winter months and Yiorgo has asked if we can employ an additional person for the evenings.'

'What about the hotels?'

'Redecoration is progressing well and the bookings are coming in. I'm expecting them to be full during the height of the season. How is your house coming on?'

'The men were working when I went down yesterday. They're pleased to be able to work indoors, unlike the poor archaeologists who are still pulling bones out of the earth next door.'

'Provided your house is finished in June as you hope Saffie and I can move into your apartment and we should be able to consider the alterations to the house to make it into a self catering establishment.'

'Do you think that project will be successful?'

'I'm certain of it. Not everyone wants to lie on the beach all day.'

Wishing to be certain that his figures were correct and that it would be reasonable for the bank to repay Evgeniy Kuzmichov his original purchase price for the hotel for he called Marianne and asked if he could visit and ask her opinion.

'Of course you can. Will you bring Cathy and stay for a meal?'

Vasilis shook his head. 'I don't want to impose on your hospitality. I'd just like to explain the position at "The Central" and ask you to look at the figures I've come up with. I can drop everything in to you and I'd be grateful if you would check them to make sure that I haven't made some silly computer error. There's no immediate rush but I ought to make an appointment with Mr Tanakis for next week. I won't be happy until everything is finalised.'

'Bring everything up to me and I'll have a look and get back to you. We'll arrange then for you and Cathy to come up and stay for a meal.'

Yannis was feeling depressed. 'I've not had a single sale since before Christmas.'

'I'm not surprised. People will have spent any spare money they had on presents and festivities. Since then they've all been involved with picking olives. Once the season starts up again I expect your sales will increase. '

Yannis shrugged. 'Maybe. '

'I'll try to think up a new advertising strategy. I'll investigate similar sites on the internet and see if one of them gives me inspiration. Leave it with me. I'm bound to come up with an idea.'

'What do you think, Nick?' asked John some time later.

'It's a difficult one. Museums and individual collectors will look at the internet for items they want, but most of Uncle Yannis's sales were to the tourists. They need to see a display as they walk past.'

John looked at his wife in delight. 'You're a genius, Nick. That's what we need – a display. I'll go and tell Uncle Yannis.'

'I've had an idea.' John sat down beside his uncle.

Yannis looked at him suspiciously. Usually John's ideas needed money spent on them to bring them to fruition. 'What's that?'

'Why don't you hold an exhibition?'

'Exhibition? What do you mean?'

'One of your tenants is bound to give notice and say they don't plan to rent a shop from you in the season. We could move some of your pots in there; print up a pamphlet and advertise it as an exhibition of classical pottery.'

'What about the ceramics that we're advertising for sale?'

'No problem. That continues. I can easily make up a pamphlet from the details we have on the web site describing the different pots and tourists could buy them directly from the exhibition. I wouldn't include the large pithoi as they would not be practical for a tourist to take home.'

'I closed down the shop in Plaka as I was getting so little business,' remarked Yannis dolefully.

'This will be different. It won't be advertised as a shop. A lot of visitors will go to an exhibition, particularly when they see that it is free entry.'

Yannis looked at his nephew suspiciously. 'So who is going to be in attendance at this 'exhibition'? You can't just have people wandering in and out as they please. Some of them will help themselves to anything they fancy.'

'You could be up there and they would be able to ask you for any further information.'

'I don't want to spend all day sitting up in a shop again.'

'You wouldn't have to be open all day. Late afternoon as people are returning to their accommodation or early evening as they are going out to find somewhere to eat. Just three or four hours.'

'Suppose the ceramics that I have advertised for sale on this web site that you have organised for me are sold?'

John shrugged. 'No problem. If the last of a particular design sells on the internet we simply remove it from the exhibition and mark it as sold in the pamphlet. That might be quite a good idea anyway. We could mark a few as 'sold' or 'under offer'. That always makes people think they have missed a bargain. It also works the other way. If the last design sells from the exhibition we remove it from the internet site.'

'I'll think about it. At the moment I don't know of anyone who isn't planning to continue to rent. Pity I allowed Monika to have my original shop. That was ideally laid out to display the pots at their advantage. Why didn't you come up with this idea earlier?'

'Nicola suggested it to me,' admitted John. 'You could try it for one season.'

Yannis shook his head. 'I don't think I would sell enough to cover the lost rent from a shop.'

'Then we won't have them in a shop. You could have two or three tables up in the square at Plaka. There are hundreds of people up there every day.'

'And what will I do with them when they aren't on display? I don't want to keep carting them backwards and forwards from the house.'

'You'll only have the smaller items. I'm sure Theo would be willing for you to store them in his taverna. He always closes when the last boat returns from Spinalonga.'

'That still means packing and unpacking them and moving them around.'

'I'm sure one of us will be available to help you with that.'

'I'll think about it.' reiterated Yannis.

'Don't think for too long. I'll need to see Theo and put some notices around the town. Tell me at the end of the week if you want to go ahead and decide which pots are the most practical to display; then I can make a start on the pamphlet.'

Ludmila telephoned Mr Propenkov to advise him that she had

packages ready to be transported to Moscow and that she had also found the itinerary of the items that had been purchased with the apartment.

'Unfortunately not all the items are here now.'

'Why is that?' asked Mr Propenkov.

'We had only seen them in situ. When we actually examined them carefully some were found to be damaged and we threw them away. I'm sure none of them were of any particular value. As they belonged to us and rather than cause arguments with Mr Iliopolakis and asking for refunds we thought it simplest to dispose of them and amend the inventory accordingly.'

Mr Propenkov frowned. It seemed logical that anything that had been found to be damaged should have been thrown away, but he was not sure he believed the woman. It would hardly be worth his while to ask Mr Iliopolakis for his copy and check with him the value of each item. Having paid Vasilis Iliopolakis Ludmila was correct when saying that everything belonged to them.

'I understand. The current inventory will be useful to me when the apartment is advertised. I trust none of the fixtures or fitting are damaged in any way?'

'Certainly not.'

'Then there should be no problem. I will arrange for your packages to be collected and they will be waiting for you when you arrive in Moscow.'

'Has my allowance been agreed?'

Mr Propenkov sighed. 'Yes, Madam. You will receive an allowance until such time as the hotel is sold. Once a sale has been completed you will no longer have any entitlement to the finance.'

Ludmila smiled. She hoped the hotel did not sell for a long time, but even so she knew that she had sufficient savings in Moscow and the allowance was just a bonus. Many of the items she was taking back with her would be sought after on the black market and sell for inflated prices.

Elena mopped at the trickle of blood that was running down her shin. She held the tissue firmly on it but it was still oozing blood when she took it away. She would have to ask Marianne for a plaster and explain how she had banged her leg.

'How did you do that?' asked Marianne.

'I was putting my tights on and just hit my leg against the bed.'

Marianne placed a plaster firmly over the graze. 'That should at least stop it from sticking to your tights or you'll pull it open again when you take them off. I don't know why you don't wear pop socks like Marisa. They are more practical and save you from struggling.'

Elena wrinkled her nose. 'They often show your legs between your skirt and where they end.'

'So wear trousers. There's no need to wear a skirt in the winter. I'll get you some when I go into the village. Do you want flesh coloured or black like Marisa wears?'

'I don't really mind. Maybe a few pairs of each. Then I'll have some to take back with me.'

Marianne raised her eyebrows. 'Does that mean you're planning to return to New Orleans?'

'Eventually. Andreas is arranging to go to New York in two weeks time for an appointment with his agent. He has asked me to fly back with him. It will be company for both of us and he is going to arrange for us to stay in a hotel at Heathrow over night. He's invited me to visit his agent with him. If his agent thinks the performance we gave at Christmas could be enlarged upon and staged as a play Andreas wants me to help him re-write some of the women's parts.'

'And if his agent turns the idea down?'

'Nothing will happen immediately whatever the decision, and I will have plenty to do back in New Orleans. I've decided I am going to sell my house so I will have to pack up my belongings and get rid of a lot of the unwanted items I have stored there. I don't need such a large place. Andreas is happy in his small cottage. I could be happy in a one bedroom apartment.'

Marianne looked at her mother in surprise. 'Are you thinking of buying an apartment out here?'

'No, all the time you are willing to have me I don't need an apartment of my own. I'll be happy to pay rent to stay here with you. I should have paid you for this extended stay. I don't want Giovanni to think I am taking advantage of his hospitality.'

'You don't have to think about paying us for staying here at the moment. If it became a permanent situation we might have to make a financial arrangement just to cover the cost of your food, the same as we have with Marisa.'

'It will all take time,' sighed Elena. 'I plan to begin looking for an apartment as soon as I return to New Orleans. I can also make a start on turning out and packing the belongings I want to keep. Once I know where I am going to live I can put the house up for sale. If no one has bought it by the time I am ready to move I can leave it in Greg's hands. I know he will deal with it efficiently.'

'I thought Helena wanted to move into your house with Greg?'

Elena shrugged. 'She thought that was an easy way of getting a larger house in a better area without having to pay for it. If she wants my house she must buy it from me at the going rate.'

'I can't see her being very happy with that.'

'It will be up to her. If she persuades Greg to buy it then it becomes theirs to do as they please with. The money they pay me will be sent to you and Giovanni. That would be only fair. If I keep the house myself it will have to be sold eventually and the proceeds divided between you.'

'Oh, Mamma, you don't have to give us anything.'

'You and Helena will have equal amounts.'

'What about Andrew?'

'Andrew will have his share. I have money put aside for him. I'm hoping I might be able to see him whilst I'm in New York with Andreas.'

'I've never discovered exactly what work he does.'

'I understand that it's confidential and he had to sign the

secrets act. I know it involves him travelling a good deal to all parts of the States.'

Marianne gave a little giggle. 'I remember how cross Helena was when he was able to get a flight home when we had the volcanic dust problem.'

'I'm afraid Helena thinks herself highly important and expects preferential treatment. I'm afraid she had to wait like all the other ordinary people who wished to fly.' Elena looked down at her leg. 'Well that seems to have stopped bleeding, thank you. Don't forget my pop socks, such a silly name, when you go into town, will you?'

Having collected Skele from Dimitris and taken him for a walk up on the hill John returned home feeling pleased with himself. He left the dog sitting outside with a bowl of water whilst he went in search of Nicola.

'Do the girls want to say hello to Skele before I take him back to Dimitris?'

'I expect they would be most annoyed if they were unable to see him. Now they are back at school they only see him at the weekends. It will have to be a quick 'hello' or they'll be late for school. Marianne is taking them down as there is some shopping she needs.'

'They can come with me when I take him for his walk on Saturday,'

'It's too cold for them to be out for any length of time. You're usually gone well over an hour and they'd be frozen by then.'

'I found something when I was out today.'

Nicola looked at her husband with interest. 'What did you find?'

'Well, Skele found it really. He was nosing around in the grass and I thought he might have found some poisoned meat to eat so I went over to move him away.'

Nicola looked concerned. 'If people are putting poisoned meat out again for the dogs to eat it would be better if you didn't take him up on the hill again.'

John shook his head. 'There wasn't any meat around, he was just investigating smells, but I found a Euro.'

'Big deal. We'll have to decide what to spend it on.'

'I thought it could go into Yiannis's money box, but it made me think. Someone must have dropped it from their pocket. How many people drop coins when they are up there or on the beach in the summer?'

'I'm sure the beach cleaners find any coins that may have been dropped.'

'Very likely, but not if they've been covered by sand or gone in between the pebbles, so I'm going to buy a metal detector.'

'That will cost you a good deal more than the Euro that you found. It will probably take you years to find enough Euros to cover the outlay.'

'I've watched some programmes where metal detectors have been used and some people have found a small fortune in gold or silver. I thought I'd take it over to Spinalonga.'

Nicola looked at him sceptically. 'Are you expecting to find a horde of gold hidden there by the Turks?'

'You never know. They may have stashed some of their valuable belongings there before they left.'

'I doubt that. If you were planning to leave somewhere you're going to take your money and jewellery with you, not leave it hidden over there for someone else to find, you big Palooka.'

'I'm not actually expecting to find hidden Turkish gold,' smiled John. 'I just thought that if I wandered around over the grassy areas I might find some coins that had been dropped. Visitors often sit down for a rest and a coin could have dropped from their pocket.'

'Are we that hard up?' asked Nicola.

'Not at all. I'm just interested to find out exactly how the device works and see what turns up.'

'You're more likely to find the pull rings from drink cans than coins.'

'Very likely, but I want to give it a try. I'll start by walking up over the hill and later go over to Spinalonga early in the mornings before any tourists arrive.'

'Will you take Skele?'

'No, when I've finished I'll sail down to Elounda and collect him from Dimitris and sail back here.'

'Is that wise? I suppose you could tie him to something to stop him from falling over board.'

'No, if he was tied and did fall he'd probably strangle himself. He can swim. All dogs can. I'd just stop the boat and go over the side and haul him back in.'

'Have you made a decision, Uncle Yannis?' asked John.

'What about?'

'Having an exhibition of your pots.'

'I'm not sure that having my ceramics displayed on a table at Plaka is a good idea. You know how windy it can be and how many people congregate up there going to and from Spinalonga. The tables could be bumped and the items knocked over.'

'What about down in the car park? The coaches and the little train stop there so you should have plenty of interest.'

'That would mean packing them up and bringing them home every day.'

John gave an exasperated sigh. 'Alright, let's think about the hill leading down to the boats. I'm sure we could construct a shelter of some sort with polythene windows so the items were not blown over. It could be moved around so that the back panel was always against the wind.'

Yannis shook his head. 'You can't build a shelter in the middle of the main thoroughfare.'

'It wouldn't be a permanent structure. Unless there was a real gale blowing it could be safely anchored with sand bags and just folded up each night and stored along with the pots. It would give you some protection whilst you were sitting there.'

'I wouldn't want to sit there for hours on end.'

'I'm sure we could find someone who was willing to man the stall and you would only need to be there for an hour or so.'

'I'll think about it.'

'You said that the last time we discussed the idea. If you do want to go ahead I need to speak to Theo about overnight storage and also get a pamphlet prepared. Then there is the construction of a shelter. I'm sure Marcus would be willing to help with that.'

'You'd still have to find someone willing to be there for most of the time.'

'There are plenty of people who would like a part time job during the summer.'

'That would mean I had to pay them.'

'Of course,' agreed John. 'If you sold four or five pots a week that would cover their wages. Any more that were sold would be a profit to you, once you had paid for the materials for the shelter.'

'I wish you'd stop referring to them as 'pots'. They are ceramics, museum replicas, not just a piece of cheap pottery,' remarked Yannis irritably.

'So could we give it a try? I'll make a bargain with you. We'll give it a month and if you don't have sufficient sales to cover someone's wages I'll not charge you for the materials used to make the shelter. I'll have printed the pamphlet and not charged you for that so you really have nothing to lose.'

'Suppose I sell something and someone else wants the same item? I can't keep coming back to the house.'

'You just 'phone the house and one of us can come down with it. I can make a list of where the items are stored so that whoever takes the call knows where to look.'

'I'd be pleased to get them out of my bedroom.'

'Good. That's settled, then. I'll speak to Theo about the

overnight storage. There isn't really anywhere else suitable as the shops and Monika stay open later for the visitors who come to the area to have a meal in the evening.'

Marianne telephoned Cathy and invited her and Vasilis for an evening meal. 'Come early as I want to talk to Vasilis about some accounts he asked me to look at.'

'Is there a problem?' asked Cathy anxiously.

'Not that I can see. In fact I think Vasilis should be quite pleased with my conclusions.'

'I'll be so relieved when he no longer has anything to do with "The Central". He says he'll have to go up to see Mr Tanakis again next week.'

'Come and spend the day with us. You don't want to be at home for hours on your own. We will be taking my mother and Uncle Andreas up to the airport on Wednesday so any day apart from that one is good for us. If he arranged the visit to the bank on Tuesday it would you give you both the opportunity to say goodbye to them.'

'I don't want to be a nuisance, you're obviously busy. I really do not mind being alone, but I do worry when Vasilis is a lot later home than I had expected.'

'You are certainly not a nuisance. Ask Vasilis to bring you here on his way up to Heraklion and he can collect you on his return.'

'Are you sure? I know Vasilis likes to know I am with someone if he is away for any length of time. He's worried that I'll fall over.'

'I'm quite sure,' replied Marianne firmly. 'I wouldn't ask you otherwise. I'll be happier to know that you are safely with us should you have an accident than on your own in the apartment.'

Marianne handed Vasilis the sheaf of papers with the accounts he had worked out for "The Central".

'You have made it look a very viable proposition,' she commented.

'The figures are accurate.,' Vasilis assured her. 'I haven't falsified anything.'

'I'm sure you wouldn't. I also feel quite sure that Mr Tanakis has looked at the trading figures and expenses and come to the same conclusion. He obviously realises that it could be a very profitable investment for the bank. Once the money for Mrs Kuzmichov no longer has to be paid the hotel should show a healthy profit each month, increasing further in the summer.'

'Do you think it reasonable that Evgeniy Kuzmichov should be paid the price he originally paid me?'

'I think you are being more than reasonable. I don't know how Mr Tanakis feels but if it were me I would want more as compensation for the my time and the trouble I had been to.'

'I have been drawing an administrator's fee,' admitted Vasilis.

'I'm pleased to hear that, but you probably withdrew far less than the recognised rate for such services.'

Vasilis shrugged. 'I just wanted to do my best for the staff and keep the hotel afloat. That's something else I would like your advice on, Marianne. If the bank becomes the main shareholder and it is agreed to offer shares to the current employees we need to agree on a price for each share and then compose a covering letter to all of them.'

'I can draft the letter for you easily enough, but it will be up to Mr Tanakis to decide on the individual purchase price of a share and the amount of dividend that will be offered at a later date. You also need to ask him if there is a limit on shares. Would someone have to buy at least ten, but not be allowed to purchase more than one hundred? Would they have to hold them for a certain amount of time before selling? Only Mr Tanakis can answer those questions and then you can insert the details into your letter.'

'I thought I would just have to write to everyone and tell them the shares were available.'

Marianne smiled. 'People want to know exactly how much they are spending and what they are buying. Some people would be greedy and want to buy a large number with the idea of selling them on within a few days if the share price rose. I'm not saying it is wrong for them to speculate, but this is a rather different scenario. It's possible that the bank will take up all the remaining shares. If there are a shares left over once transactions have been agreed they can be placed on the open market for the speculators. Be guided by whatever Mr Tanakis says in that respect. He will have access to stock brokers and know whose advice he should take.'

Vasilis shook his head. 'I thought it was going to be so simple.'

'It can be. Why don't you ask Mr Tanakis to set out the legal conditions for purchase and subsequent sale and just enclose a copy of that document in each letter that you write to an employee.'

'Can I do that?'

'Provided you state that the information comes from the bank, that it has your approval, and you are only sending it through to the employees for their consideration. You should add that there is no obligation for them to buy and their decision does not affect their employment.'

'Marianne, you're a marvel.'

'I'll get your letter drafted out so you can take it with you when you go up to Heraklion. Provided Mr Tanakis does not see a problem you can then start addressing envelopes ready for when he sends you through the purchase details. It will just be a question of photocopying the papers and inserting the name of the employee on your letter. You can even sign one so your signature is copied rather than you having to sign each one individually.'

Vasilis shook his head. 'I will have to sign them. I would be suspicious if I received that kind of letter and the signature had been photocopied.'

'Up to you,' smiled Marianne. 'I'm just trying to save you from writer's cramp.'

January 2016
Week Three

Vasilis duly deposited Cathy with Marianne whilst he drove on to Heraklion. After his conversation with Marianne he had used the draft letter she had e-mailed to him as the basis for his communication with all the staff at "The Central". He felt cautiously optimistic about his impending meeting with the bank manager.

Mr Tanakis greeted him genially and asked his secretary to bring them coffee. Once settled Vasilis withdrew the sheaf of papers from his briefcase.

'I have given considerable thought to the proposal that the bank becomes the main shareholder in the hotel consortium. I have also looked at the balance sheets for the previous years and to date. Due to the compensation that had to be paid out last year saw a loss overall. At present the hotel is making a marginal profit, but if the amounts paid to Mrs Kuzmichov were deducted the profit margin would increase considerably.'

Mr Tanakis nodded. 'I have examined the figures and if I was not confident that the financial position was basically secure and the profit margin would increase during the coming months I would not be in a position to recommend that the bank becomes the majority shareholder.'

Vasilis gave a sigh of relief as Mr Tanakis continued.

'The bank will have to buy the hotel back from Mr Kuzmichov, that will appear as a loss, of course, but once completed there should be no more excessive expenditure. Have you any idea how much Mr Kuzmichov would be willing to sell for?'

'I have no idea, but I would not want him recompensed with more than he paid me for it originally. If it was on the open market I would expect a purchaser to offer him less than that amount.'

Mr Tanakis nodded. 'I agree and I am hoping we will be able to settle for a figure that is less than his original purchase price. The compensation and the allowance that has been made to his wife will be taken into account.'

'Suppose he does not agree?'

'Mr Kuzmichov is not actually in a position to refuse. I understand that he owes a considerable amount in legal fees and the only way he can clear that debt is to sell the hotel. The offer will be made to him and the circumstances explained. You can leave that safely in our hands. If necessary we can ask Mr Propenkov to assist us with the negotiations.'

'So it will be nothing to do with me?'

'Nothing at all, Mr Iliopolakis.'

'How long will all of this take?'

'It will be in the interest of the bank to act as speedily as possible. I hope you will still be agreeable to act as the administrator until such time as the formalities have been finalised.'

'Of course, but the sooner I can relinquish the responsibility the happier I will be.'

'Have you considered becoming a shareholder?'

Vasilis shook his head. 'No. That could mean that I still had some involvement with future decisions and I want to wash my hands of the whole business. I do want to ask about the purchase of shares, though.'

Vasilis drew out the letters that Marianne had prepared for him. 'Obviously I would like the employees to be given the first opportunity to purchase shares. If insufficient numbers take up the offer then, of course, the proposal could go to the open market.

I need to know from you the price of each share and if there are limits to the number able to be purchased.'

'That is not my department. I will consult the share investment department and take their advice.'

'How long will that take?'

Mr Tanakis shrugged. 'I should have the answer within a week.'

'Once you have that information would it be possible for you to set it down in writing for me? I can then send a copy to all the employees with a covering letter. That is permissible, isn't it?'

'As you are the administrator there is no reason why you should not be privy to the information and the details must obviously be made available to any prospective purchaser.'

'I would not give any recommendation regarding purchase in my letter. Here is the draft I have prepared.' Vasilis handed the letter to the manager who read it swiftly.

'I see nothing I could object to in that. You have simply informed them of the current position and assured them that their employment does not depend upon them taking up the share offer.'

'So I can start running off copies and signing them?'

'No reason why you should delay. You will then have everything ready to send out when our investment bankers have calculated a reasonable price. I trust you will not disclose the amount Mr Kuzmichov will receive from the bank.'

Vasilis smiled. 'I would be very interested to know, but it is no business of the employees. I did not tell them how much I paid originally or the amount Mr Kuzmichov paid me.'

'I am sure you made a healthy profit.'

'Property prices rose over the years,' replied Vasilis non-committally. He was certainly not going to tell the bank manager how much profit he had made. Before he knew it the tax man would be demanding a large proportion of back tax.

Giovanni and Marianne drove Elena and Andreas to the airport and helped them with their luggage.

'Have a safe journey and call me when you have arrived at Heathrow.' Marianne kissed her mother goodbye. 'It's going to seem strange without having you at home.'

'Don't get too used to being without me. I am planning to be back. I'm going to miss the girls and Yiannis dreadfully.'

'Marisa is going to miss having you for company. I feel guilty that we all tend to neglect her during the day whilst we're working. I'm hoping I can manage to get her to agree to visit Evi and Maria. When the weather is better one of us can take her up and collect her later. If that can be established as a regular routine they could then be asked to come to the house.'

'I'm sure they would love that. They would certainly have something new to talk about and tell their neighbours. When I called on them briefly last week they were still talking about the visit they made last year. I think they were a little over awed by the size of the rooms. You could put both their cottages into your lounge area and have space for another.'

'You're certain you want to sell your house and have a one bedroom apartment? You could feel very cramped and claustrophobic.'

'If that was the case I would have to sell again and buy a larger two bed apartment,' replied Elena philosophically. 'Don't worry about me, Marianne. I'll not do anything rash or without due consideration. Just expect to have Helena on the 'phone to you telling you that I am being a foolish old woman and must be stopped.'

'Are you planning to tell her that you will divide the proceeds of the sale of your house between us?' asked Marianne.

'Certainly not. I will give her the opportunity to buy and if she refuses and I sell elsewhere the money can come as a surprise to her.'

Marianne pursed her lips. She could imagine some very acrimonious conversations between her twin sister and her mother.

'If there are any problems let me know. You are always welcome to come back here.'

Elena hugged Marianne. 'I can't thank you enough, Marianne. Those brave women who stood up to the Germans and Italians made me realise that I am capable of dealing with Helena and knowing I can come over here and spend time with you makes me feel even more confident.'

'You have to go, Mamma. Giovanni is signalling that your flight has been called.' Marianne tried to hide the tears that had come to her eyes.

Marianne and Giovanni stood together watching Elena and Andreas as they walked through the security check and on to the departure lounge.

Marianne gave a deep sigh. 'I wish I could be with Mamma. I have a feeling that Helena is going to be most unpleasant.'

'If your mother is offering her the house she really has nothing to complain about.'

Marianne shook her head. 'Helena will not expect to have to buy it. She will expect it as a gift. Why do you think she had been trying to get Mamma to agree to have her and Greg living there? Once established she would claim it was her house when anything happens to Mamma.'

Giovanni looked at Marianne in surprise. 'You really think Helena is that devious?'

Marianne nodded. 'She would claim that it was her right as she had looked after Mamma whilst I was having a luxurious life in the sun without any responsibilities.'

Giovanni frowned. 'I suppose the day will come when your mother does need to be looked after.'

'Of course,' agreed Marianne, 'But having looked after my grandmother, Aunt Anna, Uncle Yiorgo and now watching over Uncle Yannis and your mother I think we are better qualified in that respect than Helena ever will be. I just hope it will not happen for a long time.'

Ludmila's passport had been returned to her and she was disconcerted when she saw that there was a large black stamp saying 'DEPORTED' and written beneath was 'no future admission to any area of Greece'. She hoped this would not cause her any inconvenience when she arrived in Moscow. At least Mr Propenkov had kept his word and handed her an envelope with a large quantity of roubles enclosed before he bade her farewell. He had not told her that she was going to be under continual surveillance once back in Moscow.

Arriving at passport control she handed over her passport. A frown crossed the face of the official.

'I will have to ask you to wait, Madam.'

Giving a deep sigh Ludmila smiled at him. 'I hope I will not have to wait too long. I have had a long journey and I am very tired. I'm planning to go to a hotel and catch up on my sleep.'

She received no answer as the official spoke to someone via a telephone link. Her passport still being retained she had no option but to stand there and wait for someone to appear.

After what seemed to be an interminable amount of time a senior official arrived and asked her to follow him. Once inside his small office he indicated that she could sit. He examined her passport minutely, continually glancing up at her to ensure that her photograph was a true copy of her face. Finally he sat back.

'Why were you deported from Greece?' he asked.

'It was a misunderstanding. As you know there is little love lost amongst the Greeks and the Turks. I was on a sailing trip between the islands and we were caught in a storm and blown off course. Unfortunately we ended up in Turkish waters and were accused of violating their border laws. They complained to the Greek authorities that we had been trying to enter Turkey illegally. That was quite untrue. To avoid antagonising the Turks further the harbour master arranged for our boat to return to Crete with the proviso that once we arrived I would be given a deportation order.'

'Rather a harsh sentence for an unfortunate infringement of the Turkish laws. What about the other passengers? Were they also given deportation orders?'

'Everyone else on the boat was Greek. They could not be deported from their own country.'

The official looked at Ludmila suspiciously. 'You realise that we can check this information with the Greek authorities?'

'Of course. Do I have to wait here whilst you do that? I really am exhausted after my long journey.'

'Where are you planning to go now, Madam?'

'I told you; to a hotel to get some rest.'

Without answering the official rose and took a photocopy of every page in her passport. 'You appear to have travelled widely and visited Turkey in the past.'

'They were business trips on behalf of my husband. I was granted an entry visa each time and I never over-stayed my allotted time.'

'The name of the hotel where you are planning to stay and the proposed duration of your visit there.'

Hoping the hotel whose name she plucked from her memory had not been closed down she gave it to him. 'I only plan to stay there for a short while and then I will return to my apartment in Moscow.'

'The address of your apartment.'

Again Ludmila gave a fictitious address and watched whilst it was recorded. 'May I leave now? I need to collect my baggage.'

The official nodded and handed her passport back. 'Should your deportation be for anything more serious that accidentally straying into Turkish waters we will be contacting you and investigating your activities.'

Ludmila rose. 'I am sure you will have no need to contact me again.'

Feeling annoyed that she would have to change her plans Ludmila hurried to the baggage collection area and picked up her case which was sitting at one side of the carousel. At least it was still there and had not been taken to the area where unclaimed baggage was investigated. She then asked directions to where the boxes that Mr Propenkov had sent to Moscow on her behalf were stored. She would have to collect them now, rather than having them sent on to her.

She showed her passport to the man on the counter and asked for her belongings to be brought to her. He did not question the deportation stamp, satisfied that as she had been allowed into the country there was no problem.

Having signed her name to acknowledge receipt of the boxes she looked at them in consternation. 'I will never be able to manage those on my own. Could they be taken to the taxi rank for me?'

'Do you have no one with you who can help?'

'I am travelling alone.'

Grudgingly the man lifted his telephone and asked for a porter to come to Ludmila's aid. She smiled sweetly at him when he arrived.

'I really do appreciate your help. I need to go to the taxi rank so I can return to my apartment.'

Without a word the porter loaded the boxes onto his hand trolley and with a curt 'Follow me,' he set off across the concourse and out to where the taxi rank was situated. He walked to the first cab and pointed to the boxes. The driver alighted and opened the boot. The lady would be paying extra to him if she expected him to unload them at her destination.

'Where to?' he asked and this time Ludmila was forced to give her correct address.

It was snowing quite heavily and although the roads were reasonably clear of traffic they crawled the thirty three kilometres to the centre of Moscow. Upon arrival the driver placed her boxes on her doorstep.

'I am terribly grateful to you. I do have a small favour to ask.

Should anyone ask if you brought me here please do not tell them the address. I have left my violent husband and I know he will be looking for me.' Ludmila took the taxi fare from the envelope containing her roubles and added considerably to the amount. 'I trust I can rely on your discretion.'

The driver nodded. For a tip that large he would deny ever seeing the woman.

Zavinalov had been waiting at the airport for Ludmila to arrive. He watched for her to leave the area where she had claimed the boxes Propenkov had sent in advance and followed her and the porter to the taxi rank. Zavinalov stood with his hand on the door of the taxi that was next in line and waited until all Ludmila's luggage had been loaded.

'I need you to follow that taxi,' he ordered the driver and flashed his official badge at him.

Ludmila shivered when she entered her apartment. It felt icy cold. She dragged her boxes inside and then turned the heating up as far as possible. She sat huddled in her fur coat in an arm chair, too tired and cold to move. She dreaded a knock on the door and finding that the police were there to question her about her deportation from Crete. She would have to plan her next movements carefully as she did not wish to draw attention to herself in any way.

John unpacked the parcel carefully when it arrived in the morning and read the assembly instructions. When he used it he would need to have a trowel with him along with his camera. Should he unearth anything of real value or of archaeological interest, although he thought that unlikely, he would need to have a proper record of the find.

'Do you fancy coming with me and trying this out?' John asked Nicola.

Nicola shook her head. 'I have to collect the girls from school.'

'That's no problem. You get Yiannis ready and I'll come in the car with you. We don't need to go far or be out for long. Once we reach an area where there is a grass bank I'll turn my back and ask you to place a coin somewhere amongst the grass. You walk away from the area and I'll see if I can find it.'

Nicola smiled. 'You're worse than a child with a new toy, you big Palooka.'

'It is a new toy, and I can't wait to see if it works.'

'Now, I'll stand and look towards the sea and you place the coin somewhere. When you've done that walk back down the hill and don't give me any indication of where you placed it. Tell the girls it is like hide and seek and they mustn't help me.'

Nicola put her finger to her lips and shook her head at the girls. 'You are not to say anything at all to your Pappa or make any signals to him. It's a game he's playing.'

'Why can't we play?' asked Joanna.

'He's not sure how it works yet. I'm sure he'll let you play another day.'

John gazed steadfastly out to sea until Nicola called to him. He placed his headphones over his ears, switched on the detector and began to swing it backwards and forwards over the grass. Within seconds he leant down and straightened up with a wry grin.

'It's a bottle top.'

Nicola laughed. 'Try again.'

A ring pull from a can came to light, another bottle top and a small piece of metal that looked like the end of a zip fastener before John finally found the one Euro coin that Nicola had placed in the grass.

He switched the detector off and removed his headphones. 'At least I know it works.'

'Can I try, Pappa?'

'Let them have a go, John.'

'Alright, but one at a time. Come and stand by me whilst your Mamma hides the coin and I'll show you what to do.'

Obediently the girls stood beside their father and waited until Nicola said they could turn around. John placed the headphones over Joanna's ears and held them in place. 'These are a bit big for you. Now lift up the detector and swing it around above the grass until you hear a noise.'

'It's heavy,' complained Joanna.

'That's because it isn't a toy for children. It's meant for grown ups.'

Joanna swung wildly and John finally held her hand to control the movement, relieved when she shouted 'I heard it.'

'Stand still and bend down to see if you are right.' John relieved her of the headphones and the detector as Joanna scrabbled amongst the grass, finally finding the coin and holding it up triumphantly.

'Now your turn, Lisa.' Again John helped his daughter to manage the machine until she also found the coin that he had placed on the bank.

'Do you find a coin every time?' asked Lisa.

John shook his head. 'No, you saw what I found first of all. Your Mamma placed the coin for me to find and I placed it there for you to find.'

'Oh,' Lisa looked disappointed. 'So if you don't find a coin every time why do you bother to look for them?'

John smiled. 'Well, sometimes people have buried their money in the ground to keep it safe. If you happened to find that it could be very valuable.'

'Why would they bury it?' asked Joanna. 'It would be safer in their purse.'

'There could be a lot of reasons. I'll explain to you about hidden money once we're back in the warm.' John held out his hand for the return of the coin. 'Where's my Euro?'

Lisa closed her fingers firmly round the coin. 'I found it,' she declared with a determined set to her mouth.

'It's not yours. I gave it to your Mamma to place in the grass.'

'But I found it.'

'I found it first,' declared Joanna. 'It should be mine.'

Nicola suppressed a smile. 'I think you will have to give in and find another Euro, John.'

With a sigh, John took another Euro from his pocket and handed it to Joanna. 'There you are, one each. I don't think I will take you two treasure hunting with me again. You take all the treasure. Come on, let's get you home and have a hot drink.'

'So are you pleased with your new toy?' asked Marianne when they were sitting at the kitchen table with mugs of hot chocolate.

John nodded. 'It's obviously working as promised, but I'll not be taking these two girls with me in future. They're too expensive. I placed a coin for them to find and then they insisted on having one each. At least if Skele finds a coin he doesn't expect to keep it.'

Joanna and Elisabetta exchanged smiles. They knew they had managed to persuade their father to give them some extra pocket money.

'I wonder who they have inherited their devious ways from?' smiled Marianne. 'I think you only have yourself to blame, John.'

Elena phoned Marianne to tell her that she and Andreas had arrived safely at Heathrow. 'We're spending the night here and catching the New York flight tomorrow. Once we're there Andreas has said I can stay in his apartment. It will only be for about a week, just whilst he visits his agent and I am able to arrange to see Andrew.'

'Have you 'phoned Helena to tell her you're in New York.?'

'There's no need for me to do that. As far as she is aware I am still with you in Elounda. If I said I was in New York she'd probably want to come up and collect me. Makes me feel like a parcel.'

Marianne giggled. 'I do hope she won't 'phone here and ask to speak to you.'

'If she does tell her I am with Andreas on important business and cannot be contacted at the moment.'

'Suppose she calls your mobile?'

'It will be switched off most of the time. I can check who has called me and answer them if it is necessary. If Helena's number comes up I will ignore it until it suits me to reply.'

'You really are quite wicked, Mamma.'

'No, I just want a quiet life and not be hassled by Helena. I'll let you know when I am flying on to New Orleans and 'phone Helena then so she knows where I am.'

Marcus was surprised when he woke up in the night. He had seemed more tired the previous evening than usual although he could not put that down to any extra exertion. He felt vaguely uncomfortable and tried to shift his position carefully so as not to disturb Bryony. As he turned he dribbled slightly and gave a little smile. Only old men drooled and he was not yet sixty. He wiped it away with his hand and his face felt strange beneath his touch, almost numb, as if he'd been to the dentist and had an injection. He must have slept in the wrong position or had his pillow too high, he decided. He smoothed the pillow out and lay on his back. The change of position did not seem to help and he turned back onto his side and tried to will himself to go back to sleep until the sun would begin to come through their window.

When he awoke he heard Bryony in the shower. It was unusual for her to be up before him. He must have gone back into a deep sleep after his short period of wakefulness. He stretched and swung his legs over the side, shuffling his feet into his cloth slippers as he did so. He sat there, waiting for Bryony to emerge from the bathroom and was surprised when a drop of moisture dripped off his chin. Where had that come from? Marcus lifted his hand to his face and a tremor of fear went through him. He knew he was touching his face, but could not feel his fingers on his skin. Had he suffered a stroke in his sleep?

Tentatively he touched the other side of his face and realised with a feeling of relief that there was no numbness there. He lifted both his arms and flexed his legs. The rest of his body appeared to be reacting normally, that didn't happen if you had a stroke.

He stood up and went over to the bathroom door. 'Bryony, are you nearly finished? I need the bathroom.'

Bryony emerged, a towel wrapped around her. 'Go on in. I can finish drying off in the bedroom.'

Marcus looked at himself in the mirror above the basin, rubbing at it with a towel to remove the condensation. He looked alright. He rubbed more moisture away and looked again. Actually he did not look quite right; his eye lid was drooping slightly and one side of his mouth was drooping also. He touched his face again and could not feel his fingers on his skin. It must be a stroke.

'Bryony, come here a minute. I want you to look at something.'

'What's that?' Bryony looked around the bathroom door where her husband was still looking at his face in the mirror. 'Am I supposed to be admiring how handsome you are?'

'No,' Marcus shook his head and turned towards her. 'Look at my face and tell me if anything seems a bit strange to you.'

'Strange? How do you mean?'

'Anything out of the ordinary that you haven't noticed about me before.'

Bryony eyed him critically. 'Your eye doesn't look quite right. Have you got something in it that's irritating you?'

'I don't think so. Anything else?'

'Well, your mouth is a bit droopy on that side. Oh, Marcus, have you had a stroke?'

'I don't know. I woke up in the night feeling a bit odd, and now I can't feel my face if I touch it on that side.'

Bryony swallowed down the knot of fear that had developed in her stomach. 'Get dressed, never mind about having a shower, and we'll ask Marianne or Giovanni to drive us to the doctor. If it is a stroke you need treatment as soon as possible.'

'It can only be a very mild one. My arms and legs are fine.'

'I don't care how mild you think it is, we're going to the doctor. Get dressed now.'

'Can I at least have a cup of coffee?'

Bryony shook her head. 'Better not to until you've seen the doctor.'

'That could be hours away.'

'You'll have to make do with a glass of water. Can you manage to dress yourself or do you need me to help?'

'I'm quite capable of getting dressed.'

'In that case I'll go and find Marianne or Giovanni and ask them to phone the doctor and tell him to expect us.'

'He may not be there.'

'In that case we will go into Aghios Nikolaos to the hospital. You need a medical diagnosis as quickly as possible.'

Doctor Spanakis looked Marcus up and down as he entered the surgery. 'You appear to be walking alright. Do you have any pain in your left side? Mr Pirenzi was concerned that you may have had a stroke or mild heart attack.'

'I haven't any pains anywhere.'

'Good. Take a seat and I'll listen to your heart and take your blood pressure.'

'Do you think I've had a heart attack or a stroke?'

'That's what I intend to find out,' Doctor Spanakis smiled. 'Once we know the cause of the problem we can start on the remedy.'

His heart sounded healthy and his blood pressure was normal, which was a relief to Marcus.

'Now stand up and move your legs as if you were running on the spot.'

'Good,' observed the doctor, 'Now raise your arms above your head.'

Marcus did so with ease. The doctor wheeled his chair closer and looked intently at Marcus's eye and mouth.

'It's my belief that you have an attack of Bell's Palsy.'

'Not a stroke?'

'There are no signs that you might have suffered a stroke, but I want you to go to the hospital in Aghios Nikolaos for the specialist to check you out, just to be on the safe side.'

'So what is Bell's Palsy?'

'It's a condition that attacks the facial nerves. That is why your eyelid and one side of your mouth is drooping.'

'Will I wake up tomorrow and find I'm back to normal or will it be worse?'

Doctor Spanakis shrugged. 'I can't say, but you must be prepared for it to get worse before it gets better. Some people respond quickly; in others it takes a while. You will just have to be patient. The only remedy is rest, complete rest. I am not talking about an afternoon siesta. Once you have visited the hospital you need to go back home and retire to bed. Sleep as much as you can and do nothing.'

'How long will I have to do that?'

'Until there is a noticeable improvement. I cannot put a time limit on it. Once you begin to recover you will not feel so exhausted.'

'Am I infectious?'

'No. Bell's Palsy is usually the result of you having had a virus at some time in the past and it has lain dormant in your system until now. Something must have triggered it. Have you felt unwell?'

'No, I'm never ill.'

'Do you sleep well?'

'Usually. Last night was an exception. I woke up and did not really know why.'

'Are you stressed?'

'Not at all, at least nothing that I'm conscious of.'

'No financial worries?'

Marcus shook his head. 'No, nothing.'

'Then I expect you will make a rapid recovery. In the

meantime, do not worry about the condition. It is not life threatening. Provided you obey my instructions regarding resting it should not worsen after a day or so. You will probably find that you sleep for the best part of each day and night and that is the only remedy. You may also find that certain foods affect you adversely. Once you begin to recover you will not sleep for so long and be able to continue with your daily life, but you must not do too much. Becoming over tired could delay your recovery. What work do you do?'

'Whatever Mr Pirenzi asks of me; decorating, maintenance, shopping, gardening, driving.'

'Well you won't be doing any of that for a few months. Your body won't let you. You'll have to ease back in slowly, a couple of hours light work at first and increase the hours gradually. Definitely no driving for at least four months. Once you realise you are recovering limit yourself to a just a few hours at a time for the first month or so. Once you become tired you will notice your eyelid and your mouth beginning to droop. That does not mean it is getting worse. It is a signal that you need to get some rest.'

'So why do I need to go to the hospital?'

'I would like the specialist to have a look at you to confirm my diagnosis. I would not have wanted to miss a symptom of any other underlying cause. Assuming he agrees with me, come back again in two weeks time and I will assess your progress or lack of it. We will then proceed from there.'

Giovanni chauffeured Marcus and Bryony to the hospital and promised to meet them inside once he had found somewhere to park the car.

'Don't worry if you are kept waiting. My time is my own. I can spend all day here if necessary.'

'I certainly hope I won't be here that long. I even wonder if it's worth my while seeing the specialist.' Now Marcus had been reassured by Doctor Spanakis that his condition was not serious he was anxious to get home. He did actually feel incredibly tired.

'The doctor said you were to see the specialist and has telephoned him to expect you. How would it look if you did not arrive? Doctor Spanakis might refuse to treat you in future,' Bryony warned him.

'Quite right,' agreed Giovanni. 'Go on in and let them know you are here.'

With a resigned sigh Marcus climbed out of the car.

'How are you feeling, Marcus?' asked Marianne as they returned to the house.

'Well, I'm very relieved that I haven't had a stroke or heart attack, but I feel a bit odd..' Marcus wiped the side of his mouth. 'Apparently I have Bell's Palsy.'

'Did the doctor say how long it would be before you would recover?'

'He couldn't say. He said it depends upon the individual. I have to go to bed and rest, do absolutely nothing except sleep. I have to go back to see Doctor Spanakis in two weeks time. He seems to think that if I comply with his instructions there should be an improvement by then.'

'Where did you catch it?' asked Marianne.

Marcus gave a lop sided smile. 'Apparently I have had a virus at some time. Don't worry, the doctor assured me that I am not infectious. I can carry on as normal and be with people, although I feel a bit of a fool dribbling.'

Marianne patted his shoulder. 'There's no need. We understand and will explain to the others. There's no need for you to see anyone outside of the family.'

'I think you should go and rest,' advised Bryony. 'You know what the doctor said about rest and sleep. You've had a bit of a shock and you said you were awake in the night.'

'I would like a cup of coffee and then I promise I will go to bed.

Can you make sure my book is within reach. If I can't go to sleep I can always read provided I can see well enough.' He closed his unaffected eye and squinted at Marianne. 'Seems alright.'

'You go on up. I'll bring you some coffee and make sure your book and a glass of water are beside you. Maybe we could fix up one of the alarms that we used for Grandma. You'd be able to contact us if you wanted anything then.'

'I don't think I'm quite at that stage of dependence yet. You heard what the doctor said; it's not life threatening.'

Bryony gave a weak smile as Marcus left to go up to their rooms.

'What's wrong, Bryony?'

Bryony looked to ensure that Marcus had actually gone up the stairs and was not standing at the far end of the room listening.

'You don't think he has the start of Motor Neurone Disease, do you?'

Marianne and Giovanni looked at Bryony in both horror and amazement.

'Did the doctor mention that?' asked Giovanni.

Bryony shook her head. 'No, and I didn't want to ask in front of Marcus. I know he's saying he's fine, but he's putting on a brave face. I have never known Marcus to be ill and I can tell he is worried.'

'Of course he's worried. He has no idea how long his current condition will last and if it might become worse. Try not to let him see how concerned you are.'

Giovanni patted Bryony's shoulder. 'Leave it with me. I'll have a look and see what is says on the internet.'

'And tell me honestly what you find?'

'Of course. Take Marcus his coffee and settle him down. You can then sit beside me and read all the information I find for yourself.'

Giovanni trawled through the internet looking up Motor Neurone Disease and Bell's Palsy, ready for Bryony's return.

Bryony returned with the untouched cup of coffee. 'He was already asleep,' she explained.

'Just as the doctor ordered. Come and sit beside me and I'll go through slowly so you have time to read each section for yourself.'

'Well,' he said finally. 'I could see nothing there that made any reference to the two conditions being connected in any way. Bell's Palsy appears to only affect the facial muscles, whereas Motor Neurone seems to start with mobility problems and becomes progressively worse as all the muscles in the body are affected.'

'That's a relief,' admitted Bryony, 'But they don't always put all the information on the internet.'

'Ask the doctor when you visit him again. He should be able to put your mind completely at rest.'

John took Nicola's hand. 'You know we planned to go to New Orleans in February or early March?'

Nicola nodded. 'Have you decided which weeks yet?'

'I'm sorry Nick, I can't go. We don't know how long Marcus is going to be ill and unable to do anything. I can't leave Dad here to get everything up and running for the season on his own and expect Mum to look after the children. You can go. I'll stay here and work with Dad as necessary and help Mum with the children.'

Nicola bit her lip. She had been looking forward to the visit to her parents. She knew John was right. It would be unreasonable of them to both go away just when they would be needed most.

Nicola squeezed her husband's hand. 'I understand, John, but I'm not prepared to go away without you. We can always make a visit at the end of the season or they can come here again to visit us.' She hoped he would not realise how disappointed she was.

January 2016
Week Four

Ludmila kept the heating in her apartment turned up as high as she could. It seemed impossible for her to get warm. She had made a quick visit to the nearby shops and purchased some essentials, slipping and sliding on the packed snow. It would be on the ground for a considerable amount of time and she would have to become used to walking on it again.

Sitting in her armchair she carefully unpicked the stitching in the collar of her fur coat and withdrew a woollen stocking packed tightly with dollar bills. She drew them out carefully and finally retrieved the small key that was hidden amongst them. Hanging the key on a chain around her neck she repaired the collar and turned her attention to the cuffs, removing further accumulations of dollar bills.

Whilst she was at the bank she would ask to inspect her strong box where she had deposited her jewel cases holding her expensive rings, earrings and necklaces. Evgeniy had given her those as payment when she had managed to deliver contraband goods to Turkey and hand them over to her brother or one of his agents. It was gratifying to know that she had them as additional financial security.

The bank manager greeted Ludmila cordially. 'We have not seen you here for a considerable amount of time, Madam.'

'I was very fortunate in being able to secure some work in

America. My contract ended a few weeks ago so now I am back home. I do have a small problem. I was paid in cash, American dollars, and I would like to deposit those on my account so I can have access to them in roubles.'

'Of course, that will be no problem. How much do you wish to deposit?'

'Twenty thousand dollars.'

'Twenty thousand?'

'Yes, is that a problem?'

'To add that amount to your account I would need authentication from your employer that they indeed paid you for your work. We have to be very careful when accepting large amounts to ensure that it has been honestly come by.'

Ludmila rested her arm on the counter and leaned forward. 'Suppose I only deposited ten thousand dollars today and came back in a week or so and deposited the remainder?'

'I would still need the paperwork from your employer. I am sure you have come by the money honestly and it is rightfully yours, but when our accounts are examined by our head office they will demand to see a copy of the paperwork. This is a regulation whenever any large denomination of foreign currency is deposited.'

'I see.' Ludmila shrugged. 'I will have to contact them. When I have done that I will return.'

Feeling furious Ludmila left the bank without asking for access to her strong box. Now she would have to go to a money exchange and they would give her a much lower rate of exchange than she would have had at the bank. She should have realised that she might be asked for proof to show how she had come by the money.

She also needed to arrange a new account in her married name and send the details to Mr Propenkov so her allowance from Crete could be paid in. Once the arrangement ceased she would close the account. It was not wise to have too much personal information available to the authorities.

Ludmila looked around her living room. She needed somewhere to hide her accumulation of dollars rather than placing them all in the safe. There was nowhere suitable and she walked into her bedroom and looked around. A thief always looked underneath the mattress so it was not an option to hide them there. Nowhere in the kitchen was suitable, but in the cupboard beneath the sink was a box that contained a few tools for immediate running repairs. She rummaged amongst the screw drivers, hammers, pliers, a chisel and a miscellany of odd screws and nails. Finally she selected a hammer and screwdriver hoping her idea for a safe hiding place would be practical. Ludmila upended the stool that sat before her dressing table mirror and prised up the tacks from the backing material that covered the piece of wood that formed the base and then worked on undoing the screws that held it in place.

She counted out the dollars carefully, keeping two thousand aside to be changed into roubles. She would place them in the safe, keeping them for her current living expenses and changing small amounts into roubles as she needed.

From a drawer she took a pillowcase and placed the remaining dollars inside, evenly spaced, and then placed another pillowcase over it. It fitted snugly between the top and bottom padding. It was unlikely that a common burglar would look there for any valuables. Having discovered the safe they would assume they had taken everything of value. Before she screwed the piece of wood back in place she sat on the seat and it was as comfortable as previously, giving no hint that there was anything hidden inside. Feeling satisfied she re-tacked the backing material over it.

Ludmila pulled the small bookcase away from the wall and spun the dial to press in the security number before using the key from the chain around her neck to open it. She removed the passport that was in her maiden name; she would need that when she went to the bank along with the small key that was inside. Placing most of the dollars inside she closed and reset the security code and pulled the bookcase back into place.

Ludmila placed the passport in her maiden name of Kolmogorov safely in her handbag along with the four hundred dollars. Once she had arranged the bank accounts she would contact Svetlana and arrange to visit Mother.

Zavinalov reported to Groshenkov that he had obtained a room opposite Ludmila's apartment that looked down into her front room and reported on her activities since her arrival. She had spent the majority of her time in her apartment and no one had called on her. He had followed her when she visited the nearby shops and the bank, but there was nothing suspicious about the activities.

'Do you want me to continue to watch her?'

'Keep up the surveillance for a few more weeks. She must have suspected that she would be watched and thought she was being clever when she first arrived and gave the airport authorities a false address. Why would being watched worry her? Propenkov is sure she has some scheme in mind. She was so insistent that she should meet with her brother but did not ask for the same concession to be granted so she could visit her husband.'

'Do you want me to speak to the bank manager?'

'Not at this stage. He could make her aware of our interest. Just keep me informed of all her activities however innocent they may appear.'

Marcus spent all night and most of each day asleep in bed. He had never felt so tired in his life. When he did get up he looked at his face but could see no discernible improvement, but nor did it appear any worse. Bryony continually checked on him to see if he wanted anything and when he was up she would change the bed so that his sheets were fresh for his return. She eyed his face surreptitiously, anxiously looking for any sign that he was recovering.

'He should give it a rub with some raki,' advised Yannis. ' That would help.'

'It might make it worse,' demurred Bryony.

'Rubbish. Raki never did anyone any harm. You don't see people here walking around with a paralysed face.'

'I'll see how Marcus feels about it,' promised Bryony.

'If it doesn't improve his face he could always drink it.'

'Marcus doesn't drink alcohol,' Bryony reminded Yannis.

'It would be for medicinal purposes. He would need the good stuff, not that watered down liquid they serve to tourists. I'm sure Giovanni will have some stored away. Shall I ask him?'

'Not yet, Uncle Yannis. I'll ask the doctor when we visit him next. If he says it would be beneficial then I'm sure Marcus will agree to try it as a cure.'

Doctor Spanakis looked at Marcus's face critically.

'It's no better, is it,' said Marcus despondently.

'It is certainly no worse. As I told you, recovery can take time. The facial nerves are affected. Think of it as being like cramp. When you have an attack of cramp the muscles have gone into spasm. Usually you stand up, walk around and the muscles right themselves within a few minutes. This just takes longer for the facial nerves to recover and return to normal.'

'Is there anything I can do to hasten the process?'

Doctor Spanakis shook his head. 'You will just have to be patient and wait for the improvement to happen. Are you still having plenty of rest?'

Marcus nodded. 'I never seem to be awake.'

'Sleep is the best and only cure. Obviously if you think the condition has worsened then do come back and see me and I'll send you to a specialist in Heraklion.'

'Would it help if I saw a specialist now?'

'Not really. He would tell you the same as I have at this stage and recommend the same treatment. You say you have no other worries so my advice is for you to try to forget about it, stop looking in the mirror and touching it. Tomorrow or in a few days time, when you wash your face you will suddenly realise that you have some semblance of feeling back.'

Bryony listened to Doctor Spanakis. It was all very well him telling Marcus not to look in the mirror, but she would look at her husband's face regularly and if she thought it was getting any worse she would tell Marcus immediately and insist they visited the doctor. She did not mention Yannis's idea that Marcus should rub his face with raki.

Marianne received a telephone call from her mother. 'I just wanted to let you know that I am flying to New Orleans tomorrow. Andrew is going to take me to the airport and arrange for a car to meet me and take me home so I won't have to bother Helena and Greg. I have 'phoned Helena and asked her to get some fresh food in for me and turn the heating up.'

'How has your time been with Uncle Andreas?'

'Somewhat boring. He has been involved with discussions with his agent most days, and then spent the evening telling me the details. I don't think anything has been decided yet about a possible production so at the moment he certainly doesn't need me here. I'll be able to go home and start turning out and packing up.'

'Have you mentioned your plans to Helena yet?'

'No, there's plenty of time for that. If I start sorting things out upstairs she won't know my intentions until I am ready to tell her. I did speak to Andrew and in his opinion I am being very practical. He's offered to help in any way he can, but his work commitments have to take priority and I understand that. I would only ask him to help with any legalities that I didn't fully understand.'

'You could always ask me,' suggested Marianne.

'I know, but you already have enough to deal with. I'll keep you updated and not make any hasty decisions.'

John removed his waterproof coat. 'That was not a pleasant walk,' he remarked to Nicola

'You weren't gone long and you didn't take your detector with you.'

'Far too wet to stay out there and play around with that.'

'I would have expected a real treasure hunter to go out whatever the weather.'

'There will be plenty of other dry days. It was Skele's choice to cut the walk short. We had only gone a short distance up the hill and then he came back to me and began to walk back down and sat by the car door. He made it pretty clear that he had had enough.'

'Where is he now?'

'I've returned him to Dimitris. It's no day for a dog to be sitting outside. I know Dad tolerates him coming in to see the children but he doesn't want him in the house permanently. I don't see the problem. He could stay in our rooms.'

'I don't think Dimitris would be willing to give him up even if your Dad did agree to that idea. Skele is as much part of their family as he is ours.'

'Dimitris spoils him. He allows him to sleep beside his bed at night on a large cushion.'

'There's nothing wrong with that. You should be pleased to know he's warm and comfortable.'

'I suppose I'm just a bit jealous. It's almost as though Skele is Dimitris's dog and I just take him for walks.'

'That's only in the winter. Once the taverna is up and running during the season he'll be up there with you every day. Stop fretting. You're just fed up because you couldn't go and use your metal detector today.'

'I had planned to call in on Theo and ask about the storage of Uncle Yannis's pots. I suppose I could sit at the computer and make a start on a pamphlet.'

'That's a good idea,' Nicola encouraged him. 'You could show it to Theo when you do visit him so he would have some idea of the amount he would be asked to store.'

'There's also the shelter that I have promised to make. If Theo isn't willing to store that I will have to ask Saff or Monika to put it in one of their shops overnight.'

'Provided it folds down it would be possible to bring that home and you'd only have to ask them to store the sand bags that will hold it upright.'

'I can't see either of them being very willing to store anything. Saff's shop is crammed to the hilt and Monika only has that little back area,' replied John despondently.

'I'm sure you'll manage to sort something out. You usually do. Has the rain eased off at all? I'd like to take Yiannis out for a little while if so.'

John sat at his computer and brought up the file that contained the photographs of Yannis's ceramics. He copied it and then went in search of his uncle.

'I need your help with the pamphlet, Uncle Yannis.'

Yannis frowned. 'I don't know anything about computers.'

'You don't have to. All I want is your help to describe the pots you will be using in the exhibition.'

'I thought you already had all that.'

'I need you to tell me which ones you plan to display and a short description of how they would have been used. Were they drinking vessels, plates, libation vessels or just ornaments? What is the scene on them? Is it a party, a war scene, a funeral?'

'I also need to know the price you will be asking for each one.'

Yannis frowned. 'The same price as we agreed earlier that you put on the internet.'

John shook his head. 'Those prices also included packing and postage. We're not planning to send them anywhere, but I think you need to increase the price of the individual pieces. There's the cost of the materials I need to buy to make you a shelter. We still have to work out the dimensions. I haven't spoken to Theo yet but if he agrees you may have to give him a storage fee.'

'Why should I have to pay anything to Theo? They won't be in his way over night.'

'I'm only saying you may have to pay him. I won't suggest it to him.'

Yannis sighed. 'When do you want to do this?'

'Now.'

'I've not finished reading the newspapers yet. Why don't you take that dog of yours for a walk and come back later?'

'I've already taken Skele. Your newspapers won't go away, but if Dad sees me hanging around doing nothing he's bound to find a job for me to do. Now is a good opportunity. Another week or two and Dad will want to start doing any necessary work on the self catering apartments. With Marcus unwell and unable to help I'll be expected to do more; then I'll have the taverna and shop to sort out.'

Reluctantly Yannis rose and followed John to his room.

John spent the remainder of the morning sitting at the computer with his uncle. It was a tedious business. Yannis would describe in detail the scene displayed on each vessel, along with the age and where it had been discovered.

'Do we really need to say quite so much about each item?' asked John as page after page was filled. 'It's going to be a pamphlet, not a book.'

'People need to know what they are looking at.'

'I agree, but if they have too much information they are going to become bored. I think we ought to restrict the pamphlet to just a few words about the scene; something like 'Trojan War', and 'various designs available' and add the price. We could write a separate description of the item and that could be given to the purchaser.'

'They might want that information before they buy.'

John sighed in exasperation. 'So we have two copies. One we can give to them to read at the table and another that can be given to them if they buy the item. Not everyone is interested in where they were found; some people will buy just because they like the illustration.'

'They always seemed to want me to tell them all the details when they came to my shop.'

John sat back and stretched. 'You say you don't want to be sitting up there all day so you won't be able to give them a sales talk with all the minute details. If I'm there I'm quite good at talking people into making a purchase, but I don't have your knowledge and I'm pretty sure that anyone who agreed to relieve you for an hour or so would be as ignorant as I am.'

'Do it your way,' agreed Yannis sulkily. 'I'll want to see everything before you start making copies. I don't want to have to explain away mistakes.'

'Don't worry. I'll check everything thoroughly with you. Let's see if we can finish the rest of the work after lunch. I need a break and I'm sure you do as well.'

'I'll need my rest after lunch.'

'Fine. You can have a couple of hours siesta and I'll work on an information sheet for one or two of the items. You can then check that and if you're happy I can do some more tomorrow. Once I know how many pots you plan to display I can start to work out the dimensions of the shelter.'

'Ceramics,' muttered Yannis.

John grinned. 'Alright, ceramics, but I will still need to know the quantity and work out if you need two tables or two dozen.'

'I don't think I'll need that many.'

'I'm glad to hear it. I'm thinking of five, three in a line at the front and then two more behind them leaving you a space to sit in between.'

John began to wish that Nicola had never thought of the idea of an exhibition and he had not encouraged his uncle to hold it. There was far more work involved than he had anticipated. He also had an idea that Yannis would continually ask for changes to be made each time he read an information sheet.

'Come on, then. Let's go and see what Mum has prepared for our lunch. I have an idea that Nick will ask me to go and collect the girls from school if it's still raining. It will save her from having to get Yiannis dressed up. I could look after him for her, of course, but I certainly couldn't concentrate with him around.'

Ludmila changed four hundred dollars at the local exchange centre. She claimed to have been visiting America and this was the money she had brought back with her.

'I over estimated the amount of cash I would need for hotels, but they seemed to prefer that I used a credit card. Now I have to repay my card and I need money on my bank account to be able to clear it.'

The counter clerk was not interested in why she would need the money. American dollars were always in demand and he would make a profit in exchanging the notes for her and again when he sold them on. He counted out the roubles and pushed the notes across the counter to her.

Ludmila gathered them up and placed some inside her purse and the others in an envelope. Now she needed to go to the bank and deposit them in the account she held in her maiden name. Opening a second account in her married name could be more difficult. She would have to produce her passport and hoped that the deportation order it contained would not mean she was refused. She needed that account so she could advise Mr Propenkov of the details so he could pay her allowance. Once the hotel was sold and the arrangement discontinued she would close the account.

John drove up to Plaka and looked for Theo. His taverna was firmly locked and the shutters in place. He had no idea where the man lived and banged on the door in the hope that Theo would be inside. He scrolled down his mobile 'phone and pressed the number for the taverna. It rang four times and then a recorded message cut in to say the taverna was closed until April. He tried the other number he had for Theo and was told that the number was no longer in use. He turned away dispirited. Seeing that Monika was in her shop he thought she might know where Theo lived or at least when he might next be at the taverna.

Monika looked up as John entered. 'Oh, nice to see you John. Have you come as a customer?'

'Not really, although if you have two suitable books for the girls and a picture book for Yiannis I'll buy them. I really came to ask you for some information.'

Monika perched on the side of her desk. 'I may not be able to help you unless it's a literary question.'

'I wondered if you know where Theo lives. I want to speak to him and the taverna is closed.'

Monika frowned. 'I could take you there, but I'm not sure of the street name or his number. Haven't you got his 'phone number?'

'I think he may have changed his mobile number. When I called it the line went dead. I tried phoning the taverna and received a recorded message to say it was closed until the start of the season.'

'I'll 'phone my mother and see if she can help. What is so urgent about you talking to Theo?'

'I'll explain in a minute.'

John waited patiently whilst Monika talked with her mother and wrote a number on a piece of paper and handed it to John. The conversation finally ended and Monika smiled.

'You were quite right. Theo has bought a new mobile. My mother had his phone number. She said he plans to go away next week. She disapproves terribly that he goes off to shoot rabbits in the season.'

'Good job I came here now, then. I really want to ask him for a favour. It was Nick's idea originally and I'm working on it with Uncle Yannis.' John explained the idea of having an exhibition in the square.

Monika nodded. 'Thank goodness I changed most of the shelving or he would probably have wanted his shop back.'

'He doesn't want to have a shop any more. He'll only be there for a few hours each day, but he would like to store his pots each night with Theo once the taverna closes.'

'You'd have to ask Theo about that. I know he closes about an hour after the last boats return from Spinalonga. Just don't offer to let Uncle Yannis store his stock with me. I've hardly enough space as it is.'

'There is one item I thought you might be willing to look after for him. I'm going to make him a shelter. It will only be a simple affair, a frame with polythene windows and the structure held in place with sand bags. I'll fix the sides with hooks and put hinges on the back panel so it can all be folded up.'

Monika eyed John suspiciously. 'How big is this 'simple structure'?'

'Well, about the size of your big central counter.'

'And where are these pots going to be displayed? On the ground?'

'No he would have five tables with his chair in the centre.'

'So you are really asking me to store the structure, five tables and a chair.'

'And the sand bags,' added John cheekily.

Monika shook her head. 'No way. I only have that little back room for storage and it's always full. I can't have items like that cluttering up my shop in the evenings.'

'It was worth asking. I'll see what Saff says.'

'I think you'll find she says the same as me. Why don't you put everything on the back of the truck? You could leave them there ready for the following day.'

'It's a possibility, I suppose. Have you got the books for the children? You have more idea than I do of the kind of stories they like and they're both quite good readers.'

John drove to the outskirts of Elounda and joined Theo in a taverna where he had a glass of red wine in front of him.

'I hope I haven't interrupted your plans for the day,' apologised John as he took a seat opposite.

'Not doing anything important at the moment. What are you drinking?'

'I'll only have a frappe, thanks. I'm driving and although there's hardly anyone around I wouldn't want to take a chance. When it's quiet people seem to take less care when crossing a road than during the season when there's traffic everywhere. Monika tells me you're off shooting rabbits next week.'

Theo smiled. 'I like to keep my eye in. You never know when being a good shot will come in useful.'

John nodded in agreement, remembering how Theo had pinned Emmanuel to the floor by placing a bullet close to him when he was about to attack Monika.

'Actually I want to talk to you about an idea that Uncle Yannis has.'

'Not going to put the rents up I hope.'

'No, nothing like that. It's more a favour.' John explained the idea of having a shelter in the square where Yannis could display his pots and sell them to visitors. 'Would you be willing to store the shelter and his pottery in your back room when you close each day? We don't want to keep taking everything back to the house each night.'

Theo shook his head. 'I stack the tables and chairs that I use outside in there each night and if it is very windy or wet I use the area for customers. I'm sorry, I can't help. I'm not sure if Yannis would be allowed to have a shelter in the middle of the square. It would have to be quite a large affair and would obstruct the way to the boats. It becomes congested enough as it is. The shop traders could complain and ask him to move or even call the police and ask for him to be arrested for causing an obstruction.'

'Do you think the police would arrest him?'

'They could if he didn't have a street trader's permit. Is it worth taking a chance? Items could be knocked over and broken. Why doesn't he open a shop?'

'He doesn't want to be committed to sitting in a shop all day. If it was in the open air he could call it an exhibition and if visitors were interested they could purchase items.'

'John, has he really thought this through? Suppose I did agree to him using my back room for storage when I was closed what would happen if he did not come up one day or decided to close his exhibition early? I would be falling all over his boxes. Monika has a few examples in her book shop and Saffie has some of the smaller items, can't he be content with that?'

'He has them all advertised on the internet, but sales have been slow since Christmas. He was hoping this would be a way of improving his trade.'

Theo shook his head. 'It isn't practical. Why don't you ask your father if you can have the exhibition there if Yannis is so set on it.'

'Dad wouldn't want people tramping through the house.'

'I'm not suggesting that. Once you are through your gates you have a large space that you only use to park your vehicles. You could have the shelter that you are talking about and the pottery on display there. If you had a notice at the entrance saying it was an exhibition people would stop and come to have a look. All you'd have to do would be to move the boxes in and out of the house.'

John drank some of his frappe and wiped the froth from his lip. 'I hadn't thought of that. I suppose it's a possibility if Dad will agree.'

'Only one way to find out. You'll have to go home and talk to him.'

John nodded. 'Actually the more I think about it the more practical it seems. Uncle Yannis likes to have a siesta each afternoon so one of us would be around to relieve him then. I could suggest to Dad that we give it a month's trial. If it doesn't work out then we'll have to forget it.'

'I'm sorry I can't help you,' apologised Theo.

'I understand. There's no need to be sorry about it. In fact, I think the idea you have given me of having an exhibition at the house is really good. All I have to do is twist Dad's arm. Enjoy your shooting.'

John drove home thinking about Theo's idea. It was more practical than having a stall of any kind up in Plaka. It could even save having to make a shelter. The more he thought about it the more enthusiastic he became, but before he approached his father he would speak to Nicola and ask for her opinion.

'I think it's a far better idea provided your Dad is willing. You could place two of the large pithoi down by the gate with a sign saying the times the exhibition was open. Provided you filled them with earth or sand no one would be able to run off with them.'

'I could get a plant and place it in each one. That would make the entrance look attractive and inviting. It would certainly save having to cart boxes and a shelter up to Plaka each day as Theo cannot store them.'

'There's another bonus,' added Nicola. 'We don't know how long Marcus is going to be ill. Provided he is well enough by the summer he could sit out there whilst Uncle Yannis has his siesta.'

'I'll go and talk to Dad and provided I can get him to agree I'll then go and talk to Uncle Yannis.'

Giovanni listened and frowned. 'I'm not sure. I wouldn't want people coming round to the patio or into the house.'

'They wouldn't.' John assured him. 'I've looked at the area that is wasted space when all our vehicles are parked. There would have to be sufficient room left for them to back out or drive in.'

'We wouldn't want them using our parking space.'

'We can have a notice by the gate that says 'No Parking inside the Gates' along with the opening hours. If we find the hours are inconvenient we can always change them. There could be a rope up one side making a safe walk way to where Uncle Yannis would have his display and there would be another rope across the path that leads round to the patio. That one would have a notice saying 'No Entry'.

'I can't see people wanting to stop here to look at a pottery display.'

'I'd make up some posters and put them around the town. I would make sure it said free entry and people always go for that idea.'

'Uncle Yannis won't want to sit out there all day in the sun.'

'He could have a large sun umbrella, even two to keep him shaded. Nick had a good idea. We don't know how long Marcus will be unwell, but Bryony says he will still have to rest once his face has recovered. I don't know that he will be much help to you, but he could sit out there whilst Uncle Yannis has his siesta or a break. It would help Marcus to feel that he was being useful.'

'Let me talk to your mother before you say anything to Uncle Yannis. If she agrees I'll go along with the idea.'

Yannis sighed in despair when John told him that Theo would not be able to store anything for him. 'That's it, then. I can't cope with packing it all up and bringing it back here each day.'

'You won't have to. Theo came up with an even better idea. I've spoken to Dad and he's willing for you to have a display here.'

'Here? What in the house?'

'No, outside where we park all the vehicles. I've discussed the details with him. We place two of your big pots.....'

'My pithoi, you mean?'

'Yes, the really large ones, down by the front gates. There will be a notice saying there is a free exhibition; people won't be allowed to park inside as that could be inconvenient when we need to go in and out. We'll rope off an area for the visitors to walk to where you will be sitting. You can have the five tables as we discussed, but I won't need to build you a shelter. You can have two large sun umbrellas so you can be in the shade.'

Yannis considered. 'I suppose it's possible.'

'I think it's a good idea. Mum has agreed that the pots can all go back into the room that Grandma Elena occupied. I'll make sure they are sorted out into the different kinds and you can check that I've got them right. It won't take long to set it up each day or take down at night. If you need more items they are on hand. We won't have to make a special trip up to Plaka. Theo also pointed out that with the congestion that occurs up there you could easily find that your pots get knocked off the tables and broken. I know that concerned you.'

'I wish you'd stop calling them 'pots'. They are ceramics, museum replicas.'

'There's an additional bonus,' John continued ignoring his uncle's protest. 'Marcus will probably be unable to work properly for a considerable amount of time. Apparently he will have to rest a good deal even after his face has recovered. He can relieve you when you want to have your siesta.'

'Marcus doesn't know anything about ceramics.'

'He'll have all the information there, the pamphlet and the description of each item. If someone is really keen to know more he can ask them to come back later when you will be there.'

Yannis nodded slowly. 'I suppose it might work. How long will I be expected to be open each day?'

'I suggest something like ten until two and then five until seven. That way you should be able to attract the people who are just out for a drive in the morning and those who are returning to their accommodation in the early evening. If those hours don't work we can always change them.'

'I shall want to see the posters before you start placing them around the town. I don't want them referring to a 'pottery display'. People will think they are ones I have made myself from a lump of clay.'

John grinned. 'I know, they are museum reproductions of ceramics.'

February 2016

'So how was your visit to London? Is Marjorie keeping well?' asked Vasilis.

'We enjoyed three visits to theatre performances with Marjorie. Her friend Mr Goldsmith came with us. He seems pleasant enough. We had some meals out which made a change from eating Greek food. I just missed having a salad every day. The English seem to think it is only a summer meal, not an essential accompaniment to your main course. Saffie and I also went to the Tower of London. She wanted to see the Crown Jewels. Marjorie didn't come with us as we had been to Hampton Court the previous day and she said she had done more than enough walking then. What have you been up to whilst we were gone?'

'I've been busy composing the letter to go to the staff at "The Central". I can't finish it until I've heard from Mr Tanakis. He has to negotiate with the department at the bank who deal in stocks and shares. Once they have agreed on a share price and the amount that will be available to the staff I can complete the letters and take them up to the hotel.'

'Will there be a limit on the number that any one person can purchase?' asked Vasi.

'I'm not sure. I am relying on Mr Tanakis for the financial details. I imagine it could depend upon the number that the bank are willing to put on the market.'

'It would be a bit unfair if one or two of the employees were able to buy vast quantities and stop the others from buying just a few.'

Vasilis shrugged. 'To tell you the truth, Vasi, I no longer care. I just want to be done with the whole business and able to think about the interior decoration of the house.'

'Won't Cathy want to be involved in that?'

'Of course, but I don't want to take her down to the house until the lift is installed. I want that to be a complete surprise for her. Once the plastering is finished it will look more attractive to her than it would at present. It's just bare walls and doorways.'

'You're still expecting it to be finished so you can begin to live there in June?'

Vasilis nodded. 'Once the decoration is finished it will just be a question of ordering furniture. I may take Cathy over to Athens so she can see the items for herself once she's trawled the internet and selected some possible furniture.'

'You won't be taking the furniture from your apartment?'

'It wouldn't really be suitable. The rooms in the house are twice as large as in the apartment.'

'Well, that's a relief,' smiled Vasi. 'By June Saffie should be busy up at the shop and I'll be dealing with the hotels. I wouldn't want to have to think about buying furniture.'

Ludmila pressed in the number cautiously. She would have to be careful with her choice of words as she could not be certain that her mobile 'phone calls were not being recorded.

'Hello, is that Svetlana?'

'Yes, who's calling?'

'It's me, Ludmila. I wanted to ask after Mother.'

'Mother is fit and well.'

'I'm pleased to hear it. I'd like to visit. When would it be convenient?'

'Friday, about eleven would be suitable.'

'Thank you. I'll see you then.'

Ludmila closed her 'phone. She would take an underground train to the area and have a taxi to a road nearby. That way she should be able to ascertain if she was being followed as she walked to the address. Mother needed to know about Ivan and find a way of having him released from the Detention Centre before he was either deported to Syria or sent to Russia to be incarcerated in a prison.

Ludmila walked down the road hoping she was inconspicuous. The area was almost deserted and when she turned the corner she stood in a doorway and watched as the man who had been behind her shambled past. Feeling more confident she walked on and rounded the next corner where the road was once again empty of pedestrians. A car passed by and did not slow or give her a second glance, but she waited until it had almost reached the far intersection before proceeding.

Acting confidently Ludmila mounted the steps to a large front door, pushed it open and stood in the hallway. She pressed the intercom that said Svetlana and waited to be answered.

'Yes?'

'It's Ludmila.'

'Come up. I'll hold the door for you.'

Swiftly Ludmila mounted the two flights of stairs and entered into the apartment where Svetlana was holding open the door. She closed it behind Ludmila and shot the bolts into place.

'Mother's waiting,' she announced.

Ludmila followed her down the hallway to a room at the front where Svetlana tapped deferentially on the door before opening it and allowing Ludmila to walk in.

'Nice to see you, but I imagine you are only visiting because you want something.'

'I know you like your privacy and do not welcome unsolicited callers.'

The man sitting in the chair at the far side of the room smiled, showing his yellowed teeth. 'The only way I can work successfully is by protecting my privacy. What do you want?'

'Ivan asked me to come to see you.' Ludmila stood where she was just inside the doorway. She knew it was unacceptable to sit down unless invited.

'What trouble has he got himself into this time?'

'It was not his fault,' said Ludmila insistently. 'It was all Evgeniy's idea.'

The man frowned. 'You'd better sit down and tell me.'

Ludmila sat gratefully on the hard chair. At least the man who was known in select circles as Mother had not refused to listen to her.

'It's quite a long and involved story.' Ludmila began to explain that Evgeniy had sold most of his company's assets in Russia and then invested in a large hotel in Crete and also bought an apartment for them to live in. 'I thought he had finally decided to live a quiet and blameless life, but he then persuaded Ivan that it would be profitable to bring refugees from Syria over to the hotel where a safe passage to England could be arranged.'

The man raised his eyebrows. 'Continue,' he ordered.

'I had to drive to a secluded cove and meet them when Ivan brought them ashore. I would then drive to Heraklion and Evgeniy would take them to the hotel.'

'Was that all?'

'No, I had to change their money into Euros and sterling and take them to book their flights to England. Nothing more than that.'

'And being an innocent lady to the scheme you thought nothing amiss?' he asked. Ludmila detected the sarcasm in his tone.

'Of course I knew there was something illegal taking place but I had to do as Evgeniy told me and it all went well until a nosy policeman noticed that I was arriving at regular intervals at the arranged pick up location. He alerted the authorities and they kept watch, finally raiding the hotel as Evgeniy arrived with his passengers.'

'So where is Evgeniy now?'

'He's serving a prison sentence in Crete.'

'And Ivan?'

'He's still at a Detention Centre waiting to hear if he is going to be deported to Syria or sent back to serve a prison sentence in Russia.'

'And you were allowed to go free?'

'I was arrested, but they believed me when I said I had only complied with my husband's instructions. I was deported back to Moscow.'

'So what is it you expect me to do?'

'You have – connections – in the right places. Are you able to get Ivan released? It would not be safe for him to return to Syria but he could go to Turkey. I also need a new passport. Mine has 'DEPORTED' printed all over it.'

The man tapped his fingers together. 'Both your requests might be possible, but they would be expensive. Do you have any money?'

'A certain amount and I have some jewellery,'

The man raised his eyebrows and a flicker of smile touched his lips, but the amusement did not show in his eyes. He tapped his fingers together.

'Jewellery. I may be interested, but I doubt if I would be able to pay you the full value. I would have to pay a commission to others to dispose of it on the open market.'

'I could try to sell it.' said Ludmila eagerly.

'Of course. You may find you are offered a higher price than I am able to pay you. I will contact you when I have a new passport for you. Once a satisfactory arrangement has been made for Ivan I will expect three quarters of the cost to be paid immediately and the remainder when Ivan is safely out of Greece.'

A smile of relief crossed Ludmila's face. 'How long do you expect it to take?'

The man shook his head. 'I cannot give you a time limit.

Delicate negotiations have to proceed gradually. I should be able to give you a progress report in about two months. Should it be impossible to release Ivan you will still be liable for the expenses that have been incurred. You understand?'

Ludmila nodded. She had every faith in the man who was called Mother to arrange the release of her brother. 'I'm sure you will be able to make a satisfactory arrangement.'

'Let us hope so. Svetlana will see you out now. You are only to visit me here again when Svetlana telephones to say your passport is ready. Make sure you bring sufficient with you to cover the payment.'

'Of course. I understand. I'm sure I'll have enough to pay your bill.'

Mother smiled to himself. She might not be so confident when he finally told her the sum that would be involved.

Zavinalov reported the visit to Groshenkov. 'She took a somewhat devious route to get to the address, using the underground and a taxi and then walked the remainder of the distance. She stayed about twenty minutes and I was unable to follow her when she left as she called a taxi. I took a note of the number but by the time I had managed to find a taxi it was too late to catch up with her. When I arrived back I called the taxi company and asked to speak to the driver of the taxi she had used. I said I thought I may have left something in the car.'

Groshenkov listened patiently as Zavinalov continued. 'I gave him an address from further down the road and the time. He said the only visit he had made to the area was when he collected a lady and took her to her apartment. I apologised and said I must have made a mistake in the registration number of the cab.'

'Give me the address where she visited. I'll find out who lives there.'

Vasilis read the e-mail from Mr Tanakis through carefully. He must not make a mistake in the letters he sent to the hotel staff.

He tapped his teeth pensively. Should he take a copy and ask Marianne for her advice and opinion or make an appointment to visit Mr Tanakis?

'Why don't you 'phone Mr Tanakis?' suggested Cathy. 'He should be able to clarify anything you're unsure about. It would save you the drive to Heraklion.'

'I'll still have to go up and sign the papers to release me from being the administrator.'

'Surely if the letters to the staff are completed by then you could drop them in at the hotel after you've been to the bank?'

Vasilis nodded. 'That would simplify matters. I'll read this through again and make some notes and then contact Mr Tanakis.'

Vasi drove down the road towards his hotel and was surprised to see the road was blocked with police cars. He drew to a halt and lowered his window.

'What's wrong? Has there been an accident?'

Panayiotis stepped forwards. 'Sorry, sir, the road is temporarily closed.'

'I need to get to my hotel.'

'Not just at this moment, sir. Later maybe or tomorrow.'

'What's happened? Has there been an accident at my father's house? Have one of the workmen been injured?'

'Oh, you're Vasilis's son. I should have realised when you said you were going down to your hotel.'

'So now you know who I am may I continue?'

Panayiotis shook his head. 'I'm afraid not. The road has to remain closed for the time being.'

'Why?'

'I'm not at liberty to tell you that, I'm afraid. Please turn back now.'

Vasi realised that he would not be allowed access however much he argued. He reversed his car back along the road until he could turn easily and then drove onto the waste ground that was used as a car park by visitors in the summer. He pulled his mobile 'phone from his pocket and pressed in the number to call his father.

'Pappa, what's happening? Is your house falling down? The whole road is cordoned off and there are police everywhere. Your workmen are sitting in the taverna nearby. I'm not allowed to drive down to the hotel and Panayiotis won't tell me what is going on.'

'What do you mean? There was no problem yesterday. I was down there checking the progress of the builders.'

'Well you'd better come down here now. Panayiotis might be willing to tell you more than he would tell me.'

'I was just about to 'phone Mr Tanakis. I've had an e-mail about the shareholdings and I just wanted to check with him that I understood it properly.'

'That can wait. I think it more important that you come down here right away. I'm parked on the waste ground at the beginning of the road.'

Vasilis sighed in exasperation. 'Very well, if I must.'

Vasilis drew in next to his son's car and climbed out. 'So what's going on?' he asked as he saw the number of police cars in the vicinity of his house and the road was cordoned off.

'I'm hoping Panayiotis might tell you. It's obviously nothing to do with the hotel or the police would be further down the road. If it was your house that is causing a problem I would expect Panayiotis to have contacted you. Maybe someone has been trying to dig up some of the remaining graves on the waste land.'

'I can't think why anyone would want to do that,' remarked Vasilis

Vasi shrugged. 'Probably hoping to find some gold buried in there with them.'

Vasilis looked at his son in horror. 'I hope it's nothing to do with John.'

'Why should it be?'

'Nicola told Monika that John had bought a metal detector

and he was searching the banks up and down the road for coins dropped by tourists. She told Cathy who told me.'

'Surely he would not be so stupid as to expect to use the contraption on this land without permission. If he has been down here at night he'll end up in prison.'

'Let's find Panayiotis and see if he can tell us anything.'

As Vasilis and Vasi walked down the road two of the police cars drove past them and up to the main road. Two cars still blocked off access and Vasilis looked for Panayiotis. He was deep in conversation with the archaeologist in charge of the excavations and in a small area at the back a tent had been erected.

'Maybe someone was camping there,' suggested Vasi.

'There are better places to camp than there and it's illegal.'

'That could be why the police are down here, but that would be no reason to close off the whole road.'

As Vasilis and his son approached a man emerged from the tent dressed head to foot in a white protective suit. He pushed back the hood and went to the archaeologist and Panayiotis.

'You don't think someone has died there, do you?' asked Vasi.

'It's possible, I suppose. Someone walking home from work could have had a heart attack and fallen down there. That could be why there's a tent up and that man dressed in white has been examining the body.'

'That's not Doctor Spanakis.'

'The police may have called in their own doctor.'

Vasilis and Vasi watched as the man in white peeled off his gloves. Panayiotis took out his mobile 'phone and made a quick call whilst the archaeologist stood there looking perplexed.

The police cars did not move and Vasilis approached the officer nearest to one. 'Can you give me any idea how long it will be before I am allowed access to my house? My workmen are sitting over there waiting to work.'

'Shouldn't be much longer now, sir. Forensics have pretty

much finished. We're just waiting for the transport to arrive.' The officer walked away and Vasilis looked at Vasi.

'Why would they need Forensics rather than the ordinary doctor?'

Vasi shrugged. 'Don't ask me. I just want to get to the hotel. We might as well sit in the car. There's little point in us standing here getting cold.'

Vasilis rubbed his hands together. Now Vasi had mentioned it he also felt cold. 'I'll just go and have a word with my workmen.'

It was a further half an hour before a black vehicle drew up and two men climbed out, removed a stretcher from the back and were admitted through the police cordon. One police car drove away and the two men from the remaining vehicle began to place yellow tape across the frontage forbidding people access. They waited until the men bearing the stretcher returned, then attached the tape to the final two metal stakes.

'Don't know why they're doing that,' remarked Vasilis. 'There's already tape across saying "no access". The archaeologists put that there.'

The black vehicle departed and Panayiotis and the archaeologist shook hands. Panayiotis walked to the waiting police car and after a brief conversation the car drew away towards the hill leading to the main road.

'I'll go and get my car. Ask Panayiotis if he'd like to go to your hotel for something to warm him up. The poor man looks frozen. I'll tell my men they can go and start work.'

Vasi grinned. It was true that Panayiotis did look cold, but he thought his father had an ulterior motive and was hoping to get information from the man by offering him some sustenance.

Panayiotis accepted the invitation, left his own car at the site and climbed into Vasi's car for the short drive to the hotel.

Vasi unlocked the main door and indicated that Panayiotis should take a seat whilst they waited for Vasilis to arrive.

'What would you like? I can offer you coffee, hot chocolate, whiskey. What would you prefer?'

'A coffee with a shot of whiskey would be welcome. I'm off duty now and one whiskey won't put me over the driving limit.' He yawned. 'It's been a long night.'

'Have you been there all night?' asked Vasilis as he sat down opposite Panayiotis. 'You should have been home hours ago.'

'I know,' remarked Panayiotis ruefully. 'Just as they were finishing up work the previous evening another grave was discovered. It was too dark to start excavating properly then so Tomas was called out to keep watch until it was time for me to come on duty. The archaeologist arrived at first light and I was expecting to be told I could go home at the end of my shift. I was sitting in my car when he called me over. He wasn't happy with his latest discoveries.'

'Why was that?'

'Didn't look like the others.'

'In what way?'

Panayiotis lowered his voice although there was no one around. 'I can't say except that it did not look as old as the others.'

Vasilis and Vasi both looked at him in amazement.'

'You mean it was a recent burial?'

Panayiotis shrugged. 'I can't say. I'm not a specialist in skeletons.'

'So what happens now?'

'The archaeologist called the discovery in to the police and I was ordered to stay on duty. The police took one look and called up Forensics. They had to come from Heraklion so they cordoned off the road until they arrived and had completed their initial examination. They'll continue to investigate the actual site more thoroughly during the day.'

'That poor archaeologist must be as cold as you. Would he be able to join us?' asked Vasi.

'I don't think so, but he might well appreciate a coffee like mine.'

'I'll take him one.'

'It will probably be in the newspapers or on the news later but until it becomes public knowledge keep the information to yourselves.'

'Of course,' agreed Vasilis. 'I'll tell Vasi not to talk about it. What about the workmen? They'll be curious and probably jump to their own conclusions.'

Panayiotis sighed. 'I'll have a word with them and tell them to keep quiet. I'll threaten them with prosecution if I find they've been talking to all and sundry.'

'Can you do that?'

'I can make the threat. They're not to know that I cannot carry it out.' Panayiotis drained his mug. 'That was very welcome. Thank Vasi on my behalf. I'll speak to the workmen as I go back to my car and then I have to go home to write up my report. When I've done that I'll be able to go to bed and get some sleep. I'll be back on duty again tonight.'

'Come in and have a meal with Cathy and I this evening,' offered Vasilis. 'Save you having to cook.'

'I'd appreciate that. I mustn't have too much to drink as I have to be back down here at two in the morning."

'Come whatever time suits you. I'm sure Cathy will have something that can be served within minutes of your arrival.' Vasilis was hoping that once in the privacy of their own home Panayiotis would be able to tell them more about the body that had been unearthed.

'It's nothing elaborate,' smiled Cathy when Panayiotis arrived. 'I made a moussaka so if you were later than expected I could just heat it up. There's a salad to go with it and I bought some baklava. I tried once to make my own and it was a disaster.'

'I'm sure it will be delicious.' Panayiotis sat at the table and Vasilis poured him a glass of wine. 'I mustn't have too much. I'm on duty tonight.'

'I'll not force it on you. I saw a mention of the excavations on the local news tonight. They said that another body had been found but it was not as old as the previous skeletal remains. How do they know that?'

Panayiotis took a mouthful of his wine and smiled. 'From what I saw of the other skeletons they were just bones with an occasional piece of cloth attached from their original shroud. This body did not have a shroud, but there were remnants of clothing.'

'Maybe they didn't have a shroud available and just buried the person in their clothes.'

'From the scraps I saw the clothes looked reasonably modern.'

'From the scraps I saw the clothes looked reasonably modern along with Western style walking boots. Could have been army boots. I'm not breaking confidentiality when I tell you that this was not an ancient burial. I can't say how long it has been there. Certainly not days or weeks; more like a number of years as the clothing was badly disintegrated.'

Vasilis frowned. 'Correct me if I'm wrong, but if he was from the military he should have had dog tags giving his identity. That could also account for him wearing Western style boots.'

'Forensics have spent the day down there making a thorough investigation of the site. They may have found some tags or something else that will positively identify him. It's likely that there will be a short report in the newspapers eventually.'

'Could someone have had a heart attack and fallen down there?'

'I've never heard of a dead person managing to bury themselves.'

'I suppose he could have committed suicide and his family didn't want the village to know,' suggested Cathy. 'They could have buried him and told the villagers that he'd gone away somewhere.'

'It's a possibility,' admitted Panayiotis. 'I just hope no more like that come to light.'

Vasilis shook his head. 'How could anyone dig a grave without being seen? It would have taken a considerable amount of time. Even if they had worked at night the hole would have been visible during the day.'

'Originally olive trees grew on the hill and down to where there was a collection of sheds that had been used by those who worked on the salt pans to store their equipment. When the pans were no longer in use the sheds were left there. The grave may have been inside a shed originally. No one would have seen a hole and it's unlikely that someone working during the night would have been spotted.'

'Who does the land belong to?'

'It's been in the same family for years. An area was purchased by the government when they built the road down to Elounda, but the family own the land both above and below the road.'

Cathy touched her lips with her napkin. 'They must have had a shock when they were told that a body was buried there. Could he have been killed during the war and buried there?'

'If he was a soldier killed by a villager they would have wanted to hide the evidence. That would make the body over seventy years old and the scraps of clothing did not look like the remains of a uniform.'

'I wonder if his identity will ever be known,' mused Cathy.

By the end of the week Vasilis had finally completed the letters for the staff at "The Central". He had needed to make numerous calls to Mr Tanakis and then he had the onerous task of adding the figures to the draft letters that he had prepared. It had taken him far longer than he had anticipated and then he had had to sign each one before placing it in a named envelope. He gave a sigh of relief as he sealed the last one. Tomorrow he would drive up to Heraklion, visit Mr Tanakis and sign the necessary papers relieving him of his duties as administrator and then take the letters on to the hotel and leave them at reception.

He had all but forgotten about the discovery of the body on

the waste ground next to his house. After the first report that a body had been discovered there had been nothing more in the newspapers or on the local news.

'Put your coat on, Uncle, and come outside with me. I can then show you my ideas for your exhibition.'

'I'm not sure this is going to work.'

'Of course it will,' answered John positively. 'It just needs a bit of thought and organization.' John held Yannis's overcoat as he pushed his arms into the sleeves and waited whilst he buttoned it up.

'Do I need my scarf?'

'Might as well have it round your neck, but I'm not planning to keep you out long. Have you got your stick?'

Yannis followed John out through the patio doors and down to where John had placed a chair on one side of the driveway.

'You sit there and watch me.' John walked down to the gate and pretended to be looking at a notice. He then walked up the side of the drive to where his uncle was sitting.

'That's the way the public will come in. There will be a cordon up to keep them off the drive. Now, I'm a customer. I'm looking first at the table down here, then I look at my pamphlet and look again at the display. I lean over a little and look at the display at the back and back at the pamphlet. I move up gradually and finally I point to a pot that I'm interested in. You pick it up and hand it to me so I can examine it. I hand it back to you and agree to purchase. From beneath the tables you take the appropriate box and pack the item carefully, making sure you put the correct information sheet inside. You accept the money, hand the box over and that is it. The man returns to the front gates and later tells all his friends about your exhibition and recommends they come and see you.'

'Is that all you wanted me out here for?'

'No, are you happy with the position or would you prefer to

be further up and have the tables across the cordon that closes off access to the house?'

'If I'm sitting here it doesn't give people a lot of space between the cordon and the tables. It might be better if I was further up. The area of grass up there is larger. People shouldn't need to jostle each other when coming or going. It wouldn't be so far to carry the items either.'

'Fine,' said John. 'I'll take the chair and we'll go further back and see what you think then.'

Yannis sat down heavily on the chair John placed for him. 'This is better. I can see who is coming in.'

John stood beside him. 'I agree. You'll have two umbrellas behind you so you won't have the sun on you or the pottery. I don't know how stable the colours are but I wouldn't want you to find that one side had faded.'

Yannis looked at his nephew in horror. 'That would be a disaster.'

'One that we should be able to prevent. You'll have your mobile with you and if the umbrellas need to be adjusted you can call the house and one of us will come and move them. You don't want to struggle with them yourself. They're quite heavy.'

'Suppose it's raining or there's a strong wind blowing?'

'We can put a notice down at the gate saying the exhibition is closed temporarily due to the weather.'

'What about when I have my break? I don't want to have to pack everything away and then get it all out again.'

'When you decide you've had enough we'll padlock the gates so no one can get in. We all have keys so if we need to take a car in or out we can open them.'

Yannis nodded. 'It might work, I suppose, but what am I supposed to do with myself if no one comes? '

'You can read your newspaper. Marisa would probably sit with you some of the time. She's lonely now Grandma Elena has gone home. We'll give it a try for a month. If you don't get any sales then we decide that it isn't worth the effort. You won't have lost any money by having to pay rent and you'll still have the internet sales.'

'I hope you're right. Can we go back in? I'm beginning to get cold sitting here.'

John shook his head at Nicola. 'I'd never noticed that Uncle Yannis was such a fussy old man. What happens if it rains or the wind blows? Suppose the pots fade in the sun? How will we stop people coming in when he has his break? What will he do with himself if no one comes? He can think up all manner of problems.'

Nicola smiled. 'His pottery is so precious to him. He loves all the different designs.'

'I know. I can see I will have a problem stopping him from displaying everything he has. I'm going to move all of them into the spare bedroom and try to have some sort of order. I'm going to sit at the computer and take duplicate copies of all the photos of the items we have placed for sale on the internet. I need to get on with it as Dad is going to be asking me to help with decorating the apartments soon as Marcus won't be able to help this year. When I go into Aghios Nikolaos to the Cash and Carry for Dad this afternoon I'll pick up some paper and print them off.'

'What do you need to do that for?'

'Think, Nick. A customer buys an item and the next person in the queue says 'I wanted that pot.' Provided there is another one identical Uncle Yannis will tell them it is no problem and contact the house. Will whoever takes the call know exactly which pot it is and the design? I know they all have their names written on the boxes but that means very little to me. If I stick a photo on each box and label it as a K1 or K2 anyone will be able to find them quickly and easily.'

Nicola frowned. 'What will that mean?'

'The K will stand for kylix. I'll do the same for the amphora by putting an A in front of each number and so on.'

'That is a really good idea, John.'

'I'll have to do the same in the pamphlet. Provided Uncle Yannis doesn't want a full description of each item put on the box it shouldn't take me too long.'

'Can't you lift that information from the sheet you have already prepared?'

'That might work for some of them, but I haven't actually finished those sheets yet. I have to bring up a photo of the pot and then ask Uncle Yannis to find it for me and tell me what he wants me to write. It can take a considerable amount of time.'

'You must be gaining a lot of knowledge about his pots.'

'Ceramics, Nick,' replied John solemnly. 'Museum replicas. You need to know the difference between an amphora, libation cup, drinking cup, kylix, plate, pithoi and the historical or mythical designs that are depicted. After that you have the marine designs like the octopus pot that Monika has in her shop, but smaller. I have to admit that I begin to find it quite interesting. There's such an amazing variety of shapes, colours and designs.'

'Don't you start or you'll become as obsessed as Uncle Yannis. Do you think this project will finally get off the ground?'

John nodded. 'I know Uncle Yannis has appeared unwilling but I'm sure if it was cancelled now he would be bitterly disappointed.'

March 2016

Marcus had noticed some improvement in his face. It no longer felt so numb and he asked Bryony to look at him and give her opinion.

'Does my eye lid droop as much?'

Bryony eyed her husband critically. 'I don't think so. Does it feel better?'

'A little. What about my mouth?'

'It's hard to say. I'm used to it and take no notice now.'

Marcus patted the corner of his mouth with a handkerchief. 'I don't think I'm dribbling quite so much.'

'Then that's a good sign. Why don't I telephone the doctor and book an appointment to ask his opinion?'

'Maybe we should wait a day or two. I don't want to keep bothering him with something so trivial.'

'It's not trivial, Marcus. You're self conscious about it and worried that you may have the problem for ever more. You need to see him and be reassured.'

'I'm not as tired as I was, so that must be a sign of recovery. I thought I might join all of you for the evening meal tonight.'

Bryony looked at Marcus, doubtful that he would be able to stay up so late. 'If you want to do that you'll have to sleep all afternoon. You know the doctor said that you were not to overdo things and continue to have a good deal of rest until you have made a complete recovery.'

'I can at least give it a try.' Marcus gave her a lop-sided smile.

Vasilis drove up to Heraklion and went straight to the bank where Mr Tanakis was expecting him. He signed the papers relieving him of his responsibility of acting as the administrator for the hotel with a flourish.

'I'm not expecting to have any further involvement now,' he smiled. 'How does Mr Kuzmichov feel about the bank taking control?'

'He really has no choice. According to Mr Propenkov if he does not pay his debts to the Russian Consulate once his sentence is completed they will demand his extradition to their country and will be imprisoned there until the debt is cleared.'

'Not a pleasant thought.'

'I will contact Mr Propenkov and arrange for the debt to be repaid gradually. I will make it clear that the bank is not prepared to pay the full amount immediately. I also need to ask him to advise Mrs Kuzmichov that she will no longer be receiving an allowance.'

Vasilis drove to "The Central" and handed all the letters except one to the manager, briefly explaining the contents.

'Any investment needs careful consideration,' he advised him, 'But as the bank is acting as the main shareholder there should be no risk involved. If there is a shortfall in the number of staff who take up the offer the remaining shares will then be placed on the open market. Should the price of them escalate any shares held by the employees could be sold and they would make a profit. I have explained all of this in the letters to each person and checked my information with Mr Tanakis.

I would be grateful if you would ensure that every member of staff has a letter. If they have any queries they should contact the bank. I no longer have any involvement with the hotel, so I have also come to say goodbye and thank you for your help.'

The manager shook Vasilis's hand. 'I am so sorry that you will no longer be in control. You saved the hotel and all our jobs. We are very grateful.'

'I'm sure all will go smoothly in the future. The main responsibility will be with you and I am sure you are quite capable. Just before I leave I will pay a quick visit to Dimitra and give her the letter personally. I would not want you to think I had missed her out or you had mislaid it.'

Dimitra opened the envelope that Vasilis handed to her fearfully. This was obviously going to be her notice. She would not only have lost her job but also the hotel room on the top floor that she now considered her home where she felt safe and secure. Although she had tried to rekindle her previous relationship with Alecos after her traumatic experience she found it impossible. She did not want to be touched. Even standing too close to anyone made her feel uneasy.

Before she read it she looked at Vasilis apprehensively. 'I suppose Mr Vasi would not be willing for me to work at one of his hotels and allow me to have a room there?'

'Why? Do you wish to leave "The Central"?'

Dimitra shook her head. 'The new owner might not want me and then where would I go?'

'At the moment you need have no fear of that. If you read the letter you will see that you are being offered shares in the hotel. If you accept the offer that will make you one of the owners.'

'I don't know. I have hardly any savings. I wouldn't be able to buy sufficient shares to be able to influence the owners to keep me employed and allow me to live here if they decided I was not needed.'

'You don't have to decide immediately. Read the letter and consider the offer. If insufficient staff take up the offer the shares will be offered to the general public. According to the bank manager he is expecting the share price to increase and you would be able to sell them to another employee or on the open market and make a profit.'

'What would you do, Mr Iliopolakis?'

'The hotel will be nothing to do with me as from today. I am not in a position to advise you in any way. Consider the offer, speak to your bank manager and ask his opinion before you make a decision if you are uncertain. If you do not buy any shares it does not mean that you will lose your job here, but the accounts for the other hotels will have to be taken away from you. It would be unethical for you to stay here as an employee and also be working for Vasi.'

'You and Mr Vasi have been so good to me. I'll never forgive myself for being so taken in by Alecos.'

'That's over and done with, Dimitra. It taught us a lesson at the same time. You have proved your worth and your loyalty since then. If you do decide you would prefer to leave I can speak to Vasi.'

Dimitra still held the unread letter in her hand. 'I'll think about it. May I let you know?'

Elena had started at the top of the house. The rooms up there had not been used since her children had left home and as such had become a dumping ground for unwanted items. There was a box of soft toys that Helena had said her children did not want as they could afford to buy them new ones. She had suggested that her mother kept them for John with the snide remark that Marianne would probably be grateful for any hand outs she received as she was a single mother. Although Marianne had never returned from Crete the box of toys had sat there untouched ever since.

Elena placed all the boxes to one side. She would sort through all of them gradually and ensure she did not dispose of anything she might want later or that had a sentimental memory. The bedding could certainly go, but she ought to give it a wash through. It would have been stored away clean, but no doubt it could do with a freshen up.

She looked at the beds and mattresses. They could stay there. If Helena and Greg did buy the house they could find them useful for when their boys came to stay. When she was ready she would contact the local refugee centre and ask if they would be willing to collect everything if it would be of use to them. Once the rooms were completely empty she would clean them thoroughly and close the doors. That way they would only need a quick dust and hoover at a later date.

Elena sat on the bed each morning for three days and spread the contents of the boxes out. It really was rubbish. Old paper back novels, travel brochures, out dated maps, a piece of material, some postcards sent by friends from the places they had visited, none of it was of any use or wanted. She placed the items into a rubbish sack and by the end of the week she had five sacks of rubbish and a number of empty boxes ready for the weekly trash collection.

Moving down to the back room that Matthew had used as his office she felt a sad nostalgia. All the files that had related to his patients had been removed by the medical authorities and sent on to his successor, but there were his books and papers still sitting on the shelves. The medical papers he had received on a regular basis would be well out of date and she placed them in an empty box for disposal. The books that sat neatly on the shelves she was unsure about. Medical books were expensive and she would not want to throw them away if they could be of any use to current students. She would have to take advice.

Leaving the books untouched she turned her attention to Matthew's desk. She should have turned it out properly long ago, but having had a cursory glance in the drawers she decided there was nothing of any importance in there. Now she had no excuse not to empty it completely.

In the drawers she found odd paper clips and fasteners, tags for files, a miscellaneous collection of pens, pencils and erasers, and scraps of paper with notes on them that meant nothing to her, along with a nail file. She picked it up and smiled. Matthew had always been so particular about his hands and nails. She put it safely in her pocket; she would certainly keep that.

As she emptied each drawer she pulled it completely out and upended it to get rid of dust and residue that had collected in the bottom, then wiped it with a duster. When she reached the bottom there were two stacks of letters there, the rubber bands holding them together had disintegrated, and when she picked up the top one she saw it was from Marianne.

Curiously she lifted the next and then realised they were all the letters that Marianne had written to them whilst she was studying in England and visited Crete with Elizabeth. Elena's tears began to flow. Marianne and Matthew had always been close, but for him to have saved every letter made her realise just how much he must have missed her. It was so sad that he could not see her now, happily married, with a son to be proud of and a thriving business. She was unlikely to read the letters, but she would certainly not throw them away. At the appropriate moment she would tell Marianne that she had them.

Marianne had a telephone call from Helena and before she had a chance to ask after her sister's health Helena cut in and spoke over her.

'Mamma is turning out and sending all sorts of items to the local refugee centre. She says she is planning to sell her house and move to a small apartment. Who put that crazy idea into her head?'

'Well, you did.'

'I didn't suggest that she sold. We wanted to move in there with her and give her a home with us so we could care for her.'

'Mamma wants to be independent. She doesn't need to be looked after.'

'Not yet, maybe, but the time will come.'

'Then when that day arrives we'll have to think again. What else did Mamma say about selling her house?'

'She said she wanted to talk to Greg and I thought she would be asking his advice, but not at all. She offered to sell the house to us for the current market price. She ought to be giving it to us.'

'If she gave you the house where would she get the money to buy an apartment?' asked Marianne reasonably.

'Well she would only need half the price of the house to buy an apartment. Why should she expect us to pay an extortionate amount?'

'You say she has offered to sell you the house for the current price. I think that's fair, not extortionate. Property prices are bound to rise and you and Greg will be able to make a handsome profit when you decide to sell. Maybe she has other plans for the rest of the money.'

'Surely she's not going to buy a hovel in Elounda like Uncle Andreas.' Helena sounded horrified at the idea.

'Uncle Andreas has made his cottage very nice. He has a thoroughly modern kitchen and bathroom. Many of the villagers have done the same. They have kept the facades and the old features inside and modernised as practical. They no longer need a toilet outside and a tin bath in front of the fire once a week.'

'You would take Mamma's side, of course. You live out there in that big house and it has given you grandiose ideas.'

'No, Helena. I do not have grandiose ideas. We are a family living here. We all work and contribute to the business and the upkeep of the house. We could not afford to all live separately and you seem to forget that I looked after Aunt Anna, Uncle Yiorgo and Grandma. That would not have been possible if we had all lived in separate houses.'

'That's exactly what I mean,' exclaimed Helena triumphantly. 'When Mamma needs to be looked after she needs to be living with us.'

Marianne sighed. 'When that day comes we'll discuss the problem. Mamma may want to go into a Care Home as Grandma did. She was quite happy there until Hurricane Katrina struck. In the meantime I suggest that you ask Greg to decide about buying the house. You would probably get a better bargain if she sold directly to you. Once it was on the open market the price would probably go up.'

'It would be ridiculous for Mamma to go into a Care Home rather than live with us.'

'That would have to be her decision, Helena. If Greg wants to 'phone me and ask my opinion he's welcome. I don't think there is any point in you and I discussing it further at the moment. Goodbye.'

Marianne closed her mobile 'phone. So Helena had expected to be given the house with no concern for her sister and brother having a share. Marianne was pleased that her mother had not told Helena that she planned to divide the amount she received for the sale of the house between her twin daughters and had money put aside for Andrew. Those decisions would not go down well with Helena.

Marcus was convinced that he was recovering from his attack of Bell's Palsy. He was not so deathly tired and able to join the family each evening for their meal. He certainly did not attempt to stay up late, once having eaten he would retire to bed. By the time Bryony joined him he was asleep.

She woke him each morning with a cup of coffee, a bowl of fruit salad and a croissant, sitting beside him whilst he ate it. Marcus would then have a shower and shave and sit on the sofa in their room with the intention of reading. He never managed more than two or three pages before his eyes closed and the book dropped from his hand. After finding him like this day after day Bryony finally persuaded him to return to bed after his shower.

'You only need to stay there a short while. You know you'll be more comfortable sleeping in the bed rather than the chair. When you wake up you can get up again when you feel ready.'

'I feel like a weak old man,' he complained. 'Uncle Yannis has more energy than I have.'

'You know what the doctor said. It will take time. If you don't have sufficient rest you'll delay your recovery.'

'I'll need to be well enough to help Giovanni get the apartments ready for opening by Easter. He'll be relying on me.'

'No he won't,' replied Bryony firmly. 'He has John to help him and if necessary I'm sure Dimitris would come up and give a hand. He'll be coming up anyway to do the electrical checks and give Giovanni the safety certificate. Giovanni understands that you cannot think about work for quite a while.'

'John will be busy getting the taverna and shop open,' argued Marcus. 'He can't be expected to do that and an airport run when necessary.'

'Marianne or I can always go up to the taverna. Stop worrying yourself about it. Accept the fact that you have to behave like an invalid for a while. If you start to worry you could easily delay your recovery.' Bryony spoke more positively than she felt. She did not want to spend her time in the taverna and be unable to work for Saffron in her gift shop.

Marcus sighed. He hated to be treated as an invalid, but he still did not have sufficient energy to do anything physical for very long. Just having a shower, shaving and getting dressed sapped him of energy.

John had finally produced photographs of all the items that were now stored in the spare bedroom, numbered them and stuck them to the outside of the boxes. The posters had been approved by his uncle and each time he went into Elounda to collect or return Skele he would take a few with him and ask the hotels and tavernas to display one prominently for their expected visitors. The pamphlets were printed and the ropes to cordon off the grounds had been purchased. Now John had to spend most of his day up at the self catering establishments or in the taverna making sure that all was in readiness for the coming season. Having spent so long on the pamphlets, posters and sorting out the pottery he had rarely been able to go out with his metal detector and on the few occasions when he had the opportunity he had found no more than one Euro and a few cents amongst the grass. He hoped that once the tourists arrived in the area his searches would be more fruitful.

He took a poster up to Theo and asked if he would display two, one inside and the other outside. 'It was a good idea of yours that we changed the venue to the house. It certainly simplifies everything. I didn't have to build a shelter and the pots only have to be brought out of the house each day.'

'I'm glad I was helpful to you. I'll come along myself one day and have a look although I've no intention of buying anything.'

'You never know. When you see them you might change your mind.'

Theo shook his head. 'I'm happy to recommend a visit to my customers but they are not the kind of items I would want around as decoration.'

Mr Propenkov called Ludmila and told her that her allowance would no longer be paid as the hotel was now in the hands of the bank.

'How am I supposed to live without any income?'

'Mrs Kuzmichov, that is not my affair. I am sure a lady of your abilities will be able to find some work. You were fortunate that Mr Iliopolakis was willing to make the arrangement when he was the administrator.'

'When will I receive the final payment?' she asked.

'It was transferred to you yesterday when the completion papers for the handover of the hotel were signed.'

'Is there no way you can help me by speaking to the bank and explaining my dilemma?'

'The only way the bank would be able to help would be to give you a temporary loan. I think it most unlikely that any Cretan bank would do that. I suggest you speak with your bank in Moscow and see if you can come to some arrangement with them.'

Ludmila closed the call feeling annoyed. She knew she had plenty of money to live on, but not knowing how much she would have to give to Mother to arrange for her brother's release was a worry. She would have to visit the bank and remove the jewellery she had in her strong box and begin to sell the items.

She made her coffee and sat down to think. First she would withdraw all the money from the bank account where her allowance had been paid and close it. She would then visit the bank where she had the account in her maiden name and ask to have access to her strong box. She would remove one item and photograph the remaining collection. In the first instance she would take the item to a jeweller to be valued and say it was for insurance purposes. Having taken out an insurance policy for everything she would remove items gradually from the strong box, She realised she would eventually have to declare to the insurance company that she had moved the items to her apartment, but having the small safe installed in her apartment she would tell them that she considered the jewellery perfectly safe now she was back living there permanently and it was no longer necessary for her to pay the bank for a strong box.

Pleased that she had thought of a solution and knowing that she would eventually have sufficient funds at her disposal to pay Mother she felt calmer. She would obviously claim that it would be necessary for her to pay in instalments as she would be unable to draw such a large sum from the bank without questions being asked.

Provided she sold the jewellery gradually she could eventually stage a break in at her apartment and claim that they had been stolen. That way she should be able to receive almost double the value.

Vasilis spoke to Vasi regarding Dimitra's suggestion that she might be able to be employed at one of Vasi's hotels and also allowed to have a room.

Vasi shook his head doubtfully. 'I'll consider it, but the hotels are not large enough for her to have a permanent room.'

'I have told her that the accounts for your hotels will have to be taken away from her. She cannot expect to be employed at "The Central" and also work for you.'

'They shouldn't be too difficult for me to deal with.'

'I did have another idea. Obviously I have not mentioned it to Dimitra. If you go ahead with your plans to make the house into a self catering establishment you could probably do with having someone on site. Provided Dimitra was willing to organise the catering and cleaning she could be useful and she would still be able to deal with your hotel accounts.'

Vasi nodded. 'That's a possibility. I'll discuss it with Saffie and see how she feels. We know we would need someone to check the guests in and out. I suppose a full time house keeper could be a practical solution.'

'Did you have anyone in mind?'

'Not really. The people who live in Kato or Pano Elounda either have full time jobs during the summer or they are too old.'

'I'll leave the idea with you. If Dimitra does decide that she wants to leave "The Central" we can discuss it further then. I don't think anything will be decided by the bank until they see how the hotel runs under the current financial arrangements.'

Ludmila visited the bank and requested access to her strong box. She was escorted to the vault and the grilled door unlocked. Whilst she waited for the guard to locate the box that corresponded with the number that was recorded against her name she looked around. There was no sign that the area had any security cameras. The guard placed the box on the bare table in front of her and stood back against the grilled door. Ludmila took off her gloves and removed the key from the chain around her neck. Once unlocked her jewellery lay there, carefully protected in padded cases. She spread a piece of black velvet onto the table and opened the leather jewellery boxes one after another and placed each item on the material.

'Am I permitted to take a photograph of my belongings?' she asked the guard.

He shrugged. It was nothing to do with him what she did with her possessions provided she replaced everything or signed for any item she removed.

Carefully she photographed each item separately and then as a whole collection. She had three diamond brooches, two necklaces, one with rubies and the other with amethysts, a bracelet with sapphires and pearls, a gold chain, a number of pairs of earrings, all set with gems of various value, along with a large emerald ring. After careful deliberation she selected one of the diamond brooches.

'I would like to take this away with me.'

The guard placed a form in front of her. 'You will need to complete that, Madam and I will need a witness to the removal and your signature.'

Whilst Ludmila filled in the information required of her on the form the guard spoke over his radio.

'I would like someone to come to the bank vault. A customer wishes to remove an item from her strong box. She is completing the necessary form at this moment.'

Whilst waiting for the second employee to arrive Ludmila replaced all the jewellery into its respective cases and returned them to the strong box.

The second guard scrutinized the form carefully and also the brooch, checking that the number on the tag attached to it corresponded to the number she had entered. Finally he nodded and signed the form witnessing her signature and that of the other guard. He took a heavy ledger from the shelf and turned to the page that was in Ludmila's name.

'Please check that the item you are removing corresponds with the deposit number and description. When you are satisfied please sign there,' he placed his finger on a line, 'and I will witness your signature and delete the item from your inventory.'

Ludmila did as she was asked and returned the pen to the guard.

'Thank you,' she smiled. 'You may replace the box now. I just wanted the one item. I have been invited to rather an important gathering and I would like to wear it.'

The guard nodded. Provided the strict security measures were followed it was none of his business why a customer would want to remove anything from their strong box.

Ludmila placed the brooch into its case and then put it in the pocket of her coat. As she hurried home she kept her hand in her coat pocket. Should anyone witness her leaving the bank and decide to snatch her handbag expecting it to contain a large amount of cash they would be disappointed. The keys to her apartment were in her other coat pocket and her hand bag held only her small camera and the piece of black velvet material. Once home she connected her camera to the computer, printed off the photographs and placed them inside a folder. She took a copy on a flash drive before deleting the information and placed it along with the brooch into the safe. Tomorrow she would take the brooch to a jeweller to be valued.

She walked into the jewellers with a bright smile on her face. 'Would you be kind enough to value this item for me?'

'Do you wish to sell it?'

'Oh, no,' said Ludmila in mock horror. 'It has been left to me by a relative. I think the stones are diamonds, but I would like you to confirm that. If they are I will then need to insure it. I wouldn't dare to wear it until I had done that.'

The jeweller scrutinized the stones and the setting through his eye piece. 'You are planning to wear this brooch?'

'If it is paste I will wear it at any time, but should the stones be diamonds I will only wear it on very special occasions.'

The jeweller shook his head. 'It is hardly worth insuring. The stones are Cubic Zirconium. Imitation diamonds. If you wished to sell it I would be able to offer you about one thousand roubles.'

'It is of sentimental value. I do not wish to sell it however worthless it may be. Thank you for your time.'

Ludmila took the brooch back. The jeweller was a crook. She knew the stones were genuine diamonds. He was obviously hoping that she was ignorant of its true worth and he would be able to purchase it for a fraction of its value.

Zavinalov telephoned Groshenkov. 'Something a bit more interesting at last. The lady visited her bank yesterday and asked to inspect her jewellery that they hold in their vault. Apparently she took some photographs, removed a brooch and completed all the necessary formalities.'

'How did you find that out?'

'Most people are willing to give me information when I give them a handful of roubles,' replied Zavinalov nonchalantly. 'Today she visited a jeweller. Apparently she was hoping to sell the item but was not satisfied with the amount he offered.'

'You found that out in the same way, I presume. Did she go to any other jeweller?'

'No, she returned to her apartment. I need someone else to be here. I had to go back later to question the jeweller and she could have gone anywhere during the time I was away.'

Groshenkov frowned. 'Have you anyone in mind?'

'I thought Daria Lashenkova could be suitable.'

'A woman?'

'Why not? She's proved herself efficient in the past and if she did have to follow the woman anywhere she could be less conspicuous than me.'

'Very well.' Groshenkov had an idea that Zavinalov wanted the woman in the apartment with him so he would not have to cook and clean for himself.

April 2016

John was feeling pleased with himself. He had completed the photographs and labelling of all his uncle's boxes of pottery along with helping his father to redecorate some of the self catering establishment rooms ready for their first visitors.

'I'm going to have a few days to myself before our first guests arrive,' he announced to Nicola. 'I really have had to work hard to please both Dad and Uncle Yannis.'

'I thought Ronnie and Kyriakos were moving in this week to their usual summer apartment,' remarked Nicola.

'They are, but they're no trouble. Ron will probably help Akkers to get his taverna up and ready before she starts to paint. The following week we only have three apartments booked. Easter in Europe was at the end of last month so many people will have taken some holiday then. Most things don't really open or start up until after our Easter and it's late this year. Regular visitors know that. Give it another month and we'll probably be turning people away.'

'The weather will be more settled by then,' agreed Nicola. 'Do you think you'll be able to cope with the taverna and shop if you have to do airport runs for Dad along with helping Uncle Yannis?'

John grinned. 'I can't expect you to go up to the shop and taverna with little Yiannis but I thought you could probably help out with Uncle Yannis.'

'Me?'

'You could help him set up or pack up if I'm not around. You could ask Mum to look after Yiannis for a short while. By then Marcus should be able to be some help. He is improving.'

'I wouldn't want to ask Marcus in case it was too much for him. I know he wouldn't refuse to help, but I'd hate to be responsible for making him have a relapse and that doesn't solve the problem of the taverna if you have to do an airport run.'

'I'll ask Bryony. I'm sure she wouldn't mind looking after it for a few hours.'

'Bryony works for Saffie, remember. I can't see her wanting to be in the taverna rather than Saffie's gift shop.'

John sighed. 'I'm sure a solution will present itself if necessary. I'm not going to worry over it now. Tomorrow I'm going out with my metal detector. I've only been up on the grassy banks by the side of the road and not found very much. I thought I'd have a scout around some of the tavernas before they open up. Last season's customers may have dropped a few coins and the owners not found them yet.'

Nicola looked at him sceptically. 'I think that most unlikely. You'll probably only find a few bottle tops.'

Whilst John swung his detector over the areas close to the tavernas that had not yet opened for the season he thought about the problem that had arisen. Marcus was not permitted to drive at present and usually retired to rest for an hour or so during the afternoon. Depending upon the times of aircraft arriving and departing it was often necessary for two drivers to be responsible for transferring passengers. Departures must not be late for their flights and arrivals did not appreciate being kept waiting.

His mother spent most of her day on the computer dealing with bookings and queries from customers, along with being responsible for ensuring that Uncle Yannis and Grandma Marisa had a light meal in the middle of the day. Nicola had the children to look after although she was more than willing to help whilst the girls were at school and Yiannis was having a rest. If Bryony was going back to her part time work in Saffron's gift shop she could not be expected to run the taverna and shop at the same time. Trips to the Cash and Carry would be necessary along with general shopping, although it should be possible for either him or his father to fit them in amongst their other commitments.

Now they were going to be one helper short it would definitely be a problem. In the past he would have suggested that Dimitris was employed but now he was a successful electrician and busy most days.

The whine of the metal detector stopped John's train of thought and he bend down to investigate the cause of the signal. Almost hidden by the grass he could see a glint of gold and put his hand down expecting to draw up a Euro. To his surprise he found a gold bracelet hanging from his fingers.

John examined it carefully. It was untarnished which should mean that it was gold and did not just have a thin covering over a base metal. It did not appear to be damaged except for the small clip that should have held the safety chain in place. Elated John placed it in his pocket, sure it was worth more than all the Euros combined that he had found earlier.

He swept the area carefully, but no more signals came from the metal detector, and he moved further around towards the rear of the building A series of signals came but when he investigated them they were either metal bottle caps or ring pulls from cans. This must be where the rubbish sacks were stored and these items had fallen out and been ignored. Although disappointed John felt that the discovery of the bracelet more than made up for his lack of further success.

'Do you want to see what I found?' he asked Nicola.

'A two Euro coin?'

John shook his head. 'Far more interesting and exciting than that.' He took the bracelet from his pocket and held it in front of her.

117

'Did you really find that?'

'It was up by Akker's taverna. I think the safety chain needs repair, but apart from that it's perfect.'

Nicola took the bracelet in her hand and examined it. 'It's very attractive and quite heavy. I think it's what they call a 'gate' bracelet. You say you found it close to Kyriakos's taverna; do you think it could belong to Ronnie?'

John frowned. 'I hadn't thought of that. I suppose it could be hers and she lost it when she was up there. Shall I call her or wait until they come down to the apartments next week?'

'I think you should call her now. If it's something she was given by her grandmother she could be quite devastated to think she had lost it.'

Ronnie sounded quite breathless when she answered her 'phone. 'Yes,' she gasped.

'Ron, it's John here. Are you alright?'

'Fine. I've just been chasing away the goat that decided to come into my poor little garden and eat anything it could find.'

John laughed. 'Do you know who owns it?'

'Yes, I chased it back home and asked him to make sure it was kept fenced in properly in future. I'm not just thinking of my garden, there's a considerable amount of traffic up here during the season and I'd hate the poor thing to be run over.'

'You should have caught and kept it. Easter is coming.'

'I couldn't possibly do that. I don't mind eating meat that I buy from the butcher but I couldn't look after an animal and then cook and eat it.'

'You're too soft hearted. Good job Akkers isn't a farmer.'

'I've also never been truly hungry in my life. If I had I'm sure I would eat anything regardless.'

'That's true. When I remember what the locals ate during the war just to keep themselves alive the mere thought makes my stomach churn. Snails, insects, snakes …..'

'Stop it, John. You're making me feel really ill. Why did you call me?'

'I wanted to ask if you had lost anything.'

'I don't think so.'

'I'm not talking about today, but towards the end of last season.'

'No.'

'Did you have a gold bracelet? Nick says it a 'gate' design.'

'No. I don't wear jewellery. I'm not one of those artists who wears flowing robes, bangles and beads. Why?'

'I was out with my metal detector today and happened to find a bracelet up by Akker's taverna. It was probably lost by a tourist, but I wanted to check that it didn't belong to you before I gave it to Nick.'

'That was kind of you, John, but it certainly never belonged to me. Give it to Nicola by all means. Did you find anything else exciting?'

'Well I know where Akkers stores his rubbish bins. I found bottle tops and can rings.'

Ronnie laughed. 'I'll tell him he must be more careful about putting them in the sack in future.'

'Is Akkers planning to employ anyone at the taverna on a casual basis?'

'Not that I know of.. Why? Are you looking for a job?'

'Definitely not. I'll need someone to look after the taverna and shop for me if I have to do an airport run.'

'I thought Marcus and your father did the airport.'

'Oh, I forgot. You don't know of course.' John proceeded to explain that Marcus had suffered an attack of Bell's Palsy. 'He's not allowed to drive at the moment and still becomes incredibly tired after any exertion. Uncle Yannis is going to have an exhibition of his pottery at the house in the hope of selling some of it and the most we can ask of Marcus at the moment is to look after that when Uncle Yannis needs a break.'

'That sounds interesting. I'll tell people about it when I'm back painting in Plaka.'

'I'll let you have some pamphlets and there are going to

PIETRO

be notices all around Elounda and Plaka. It's been quite a job organising everything to Uncle Yannis's satisfaction and I just hope it will be a success for him.'

'Incidentally, do you have a street trader's licence?'

'No. I don't need one. Officially I am just an artist sitting there painting the view. Why do you ask?'

'Originally we thought about setting up a stall on the hill that leads down to the boats and Theo told me that we could be prosecuted if we did not have a street trader's licence.'

'I sell a few to customers, but the bulk of the paintings are in Saffie's shop. I do hope Marcus is back to full fitness soon. It sounds a miserable complaint to suffer from. If I hear of anyone who is looking for part time work I'll let you know.'

Ludmila took the diamond brooch to an insurance company and showed it to the middle aged man across the desk from her.

'How much do you wish to insure the item for?'

'The current market value.'

The man raised his eyes. 'I will need to have it authenticated with our resident jeweller.'

'I am not prepared to leave it here,' replied Ludmila firmly.

'Of course not, Madam. I will make another appointment for you when the jeweller will be in attendance and able to give you an accurate estimate of its worth.'

'I do have some other pieces, probably of similar value. Will I have to bring them all in?'

'We will need to see them and have proof that they belong to you.'

'I keep them in the strong box at my bank. I have only taken out this one item. Would it be possible for the jeweller to meet me at the bank? That way he could value the items and it would also prove that they do belong to me.'

The man nodded. It was a sensible suggestion. He lifted the telephone and spoke rapidly to someone on the other end.

'If you would care to wait for a short while the jeweller will come here and inspect the brooch you have brought with you. Should it not be of any value he will tell you. If that is the case it is likely the other items you have are also worthless and would not be worth insuring.'

Ludmila sat and waited. If this jeweller also said the stones were Cubic Zirconium she would be furious. She had been with Evgeniy when he had purchased the gift for her and he had certainly paid for genuine diamonds.

The jeweller examined the brooch minutely. 'It is, as you claim, Madam, a gold brooch set with genuine diamonds. I will have to consult my manuals regarding the cut of the diamonds and the setting before I can put an exact value on it. May I photograph it?'

'Certainly. I know you are a reputable company but I would not be happy leaving it with you, particularly if a photograph will suffice.'

'It will initially. I may have to make a more thorough inspection at a later date. Where do you normally keep it?'

'In the strong box at the bank along with the other items.' Ludmila opened her bag and took out the folder containing the photograph of her other jewellery.

'And you wish to have the complete collection valued and insured?'

Ludmila nodded. 'I would like to wear an item, just occasionally, for a special occasion and I would not dare to do that if it was not insured.'

'Very wise, Madam. I suggest we make an appointment for one morning next week and I will accompany you to the bank and inspect the other valuables.'

'Certainly. I am free whenever it suits you.'

Ludmila left the insurance office with mixed feelings. At least once her jewellery had been valued and insured she would know if Mother was offering her a fair price to help her to settle her bill to him.

As Vasilis was about to leave his apartment in Elounda he saw Panyiotis arriving and stopped to speak to him.

'Is there any news about the modern skeleton?' Vasilis asked.

Panayiotis shook his head. 'Still with Forensics as far as I know. Unless they can identify the remains it will likely just be listed as an unsolved murder case.'

'Surely someone must have a missing relative.'

Panayiotis shrugged. 'It's possible, but people do go missing for different reasons. It does not mean they have been murdered. Thankfully no more have turned up and the archaeologists have declared the ground is clear. At least I don't have to sit down there at night any more to make sure no one goes onto the land and disturbs anything.'

Vasilis drove down to where the builders were finishing the exterior cladding for his house. He parked across the road and admired the work that had been completed. There was still a considerable amount that needed to be done, but provided the area where the lift was to be installed was ready he could arrange for that to take place.

He walked up the steps to the front door and along the paved front area to where Achilles was working. The man placed his tools on the ground, wiped his hands down his trousers and indicated the cladding.

'It's beginning to look good, Mr Iliopolakis.'

'It is indeed.'

'The side wall still has to be finished, but the back is rendered.'

'I would like to go inside and see the progress that has been made there. I also need to know if the housing for the lift is completed. Once that is installed I can bring my wife over and she can start to think about the internal decoration and choose the fittings she wants in the kitchen and shower rooms.'

'Would you like me to come with you or should I continue working here?'

'Come with me, Achilles. I can then consult you about anything that comes to mind as we go.'

Ludmila walked from the underground station to the open market. Despite it being cold most of the snow had melted leaving only a few icy patches to be avoided. She ignored the stalls selling food and made her way to where the household items were displayed.

'Good morning, Oleg.'

The man looked at Ludmila in surprise and then smiled. 'I haven't seen you in a long time Mrs Kuzmichov. How are you and your husband?'

'We're both well, thank you. And your family?'

'Likewise. What can I do for you?'

'Mr Kuzmichov is still abroad. We are thinking of moving from Moscow and I have begun to sort out our surplus belongings. I have some items, towels and bedding, that I would like to sell. Would you be interested?'

'I feel sure that your household goods are of far better quality than those I have on my stall.'

'Quite true, Oleg, but I also know that you have contacts who would be willing to purchase them from me at a fair price and would know where to sell them to make a profit. If I return next week with a list and some photographs would you be able to assist me?'

'It's possible. Bring me a sample at the same time. I will be unable to ascertain the quality from a photograph.'

Ludmila nodded and moved away, threading her way through the various stalls until she reached the nearby metro. She knew there was a small money exchange establishment close by and this was a good opportunity to exchange some more of her dollars into roubles.

Vasi parked in the centre of the village and walked to the "Imperia" where Yiorgo was consulting with the chef about the evening menu.

'Finish your discussion,' said Vasi. 'I'll help myself to a drink whilst I wait.' He selected a can of lemonade, pulled the ring and inserted a straw. He knew that his contemporaries laughed behind his back about him using a straw rather that drinking straight form the can, but Cathy had been most insistent that he always used a straw or a glass, impressing upon him that the cans held germs.

Yiorgo, having finished talking to the chef, walked over and joined him. 'Any problems?' he asked.

'Not that I'm aware of. I just wanted to confirm that I will be closing down the "Imperia" at the end of next week. That should give you time to get the boat ready for the Spinalonga trips.'

A broad grin crossed Yiorgo's face. 'I can't wait to get back to sea. I've appreciated working here throughout the winter, much better than being an odd job man on a building site for my father.'

'You've been an excellent manager. The locals appreciate having the "Imperia" open when the other tavernas have closed down. The job will be here again for you at the end of the season.'

'Thanks. It's a shame we can't stay open all year.'

'You can't be in two places at once. When my hotels are busy I don't have the time to continually check that the "Imperia" is being run efficiently. If the standards slipped word would soon get around.'

'How is your father's house progressing?'

'He seems happy with it and hoping it will be finished in June so he and Cathy can move in.' Vasi did not mention his plans for turning the house where he and Saffron lived into a self catering establishment. He trusted Yiorgo, but knew he would tell Barbara and the information would be spread around the whole village.

'I believe he is going to ask my father to work on the inside decoration.'

'He knows how meticulous your father is and he insists that your brothers and sons work to the same high standards. They've just about completed the work I asked for at the hotels.'

Yiorgo nodded. 'I know they're planning to go up to Kastelli and do some more work on Miss Ronnie's house. Did you know that Blerim has asked if he can go back to work with them?'

'I thought he wanted to have a job with the council?'

'He's not happy working as a refuse collector. It grieves him to see some of the furniture that is put beside the bins for disposal. Most of it could easily be repaired instead of being crushed and taken to the dump. He says he has managed to save some money and would rather work with my father and risk not having a regular income each week.'

'I know which job I would prefer,' agreed Vasi.

'Pappa has agreed and with an extra worker, depending upon how much they are asked to complete for Miss Ronnie, they should be finished in time to start work for your father.'

Vasi nodded. The necessary work on his hotels ready for the new season was complete and if his father was going to have Mr Palamakis and his employees work on his new house there would be plenty that Blerim was capable of undertaking. He would obviously ask them to do the alterations that would be necessary to turn the big house where he and Saffron lived into self catering accommodation.

'There was another thing I wanted to discuss with you regarding the Spinalonga trips. Do you think we could increase the price?'

'How much would you be asking? It can be quite expensive for families now as they have to pay to walk around the island.'

'I though one Euro would be reasonable provided the other boatmen also increase their prices. We don't want to find they are taking away our business because they are cheaper.'

'I'll keep my ears open when I'm working on the boat and see if I can find out their plans. We could put the price up for adults, but offer a group price for families with children.'

'That's a good idea, Yiorgo. Let me know what you find out and we'll make a decision later.'

John hammered the iron stakes into the ground along the side of the driveway and looped the rope between them.

'That looks ugly,' commented Giovanni. 'If we get people walking up and down there they'll wear the grass out.'

'I agree, but can you think of a better idea? The grass can always be resown if necessary. At least you won't be able to see it from the house. I'm going to put a notice at the bottom that says 'Exhibition Entrance' and another on the gate saying 'Private. No Parking'. Would you be able to help me down with two of the large pithoi? I want to place some bricks in the bottom for stability and then some plants in the top.'

'You're going to a lot of trouble for Uncle Yannis,' remarked Giovanni.

John shrugged. 'I'm just trying to keep him happy. He loves his pots and hates having them stored in boxes around the house.'

'So do we! I wish he'd kept his shop in Plaka.'

'That had become just a liability to him and he wasn't happy up there without Aunt Ourania. The internet sales are a bit slow and I hope having an exhibition will encourage some of the tourists to buy souvenirs. I can put some information on the advertising site we use for the self catering apartments and say that is it an added attraction to the other amenities in the area.'

'Will you have the time? I shall have to rely upon you for some of the airport runs until Marcus is well again.'

'I'm sure I'll manage. We just need to find someone reliable to run the taverna and shop when I am unable to be up there.'

Ludmila decided there was no need for her to wear her fur coat any longer as the snow had melted and the spring sunshine made it pleasant to be out. As she was going to the market it was better not to look too well off or the stall holders raised their prices. She selected the linen and lace tablecloth she had brought back from Crete and placed it in a large shopping basket along with photographs of the towels, bedding, dinner service and cutlery.

She made sure the labels proving their provenance was showing. Russians loved anything that was from abroad knowing it was usually of better quality than those produced in Russia.

Oleg looked at the photographs and shrugged. 'Hard to say. I would need to see examples.'

'I have brought a table cloth with me'

Oleg spread the table cloth out on his stall and examined it carefully. There were no stains or pulled threads visible.

'How much do you want for it?'

'Four thousand five hundred roubles.'

Oleg shook his head. 'I'll not be able to sell it for that price. I can give you two thousand.'

'Four thousand.' Ludmila knew that she was expected to haggle with him.

Oleg pretended to consider. 'Two thousand five hundred.'

'It's worth twice as much. I'm sure I'll get a better price elsewhere.'

'Three thousand. I can't go any higher.'

'Three thousand five hundred. I can't afford to go any lower.' Ludmila stood her ground.

Oleg felt the linen between his finger and thumb. He knew he had a regular client who would pay him at least eight thousand roubles for such a high quality table cloth.

With a deep sigh he nodded. 'Three thousand five hundred, although I am robbing myself.'

'I doubt that,' remarked Ludmila. 'I'd like it in cash now. I have a bill to pay.' She was not prepared to leave it with the trader without him paying her for it.

'I haven't got that amount with me. I'll need to go to a bank. Can you come back later?'

Ludmila shook her head. 'I need the money immediately. Ask your neighbour to keep an eye on your stall whilst you're gone. I'll wait here until you return and make sure he pays you for any sales from your stall.'

Oleg glared at her and shrugged. He called to the man who had the stall next to his and explained that he had to go to the bank and needed to have his stall supervised. Ludmila moved back from the main thoroughfare and stood as if she was the owner of the stall. She held up the table cloth for inspection by the passers by until one stopped and asked the price.

'A bargain at six thousand roubles. It is from America. See, there is the label.'

The woman frowned. 'That is a lot of money for a tablecloth. Will you accept five thousand?'

Ludmila shook her head. 'Five thousand five hundred is the best price I can offer.'

The woman hesitated. 'Very well.' She pulled a roll of notes from her bag and counted them out whilst Ludmila folded the table cloth carefully and looked for a suitable bag to place it in.

'Is there anything else here that I could interest you in, Madam?'

'I can't afford to buy anything else. I don't know what my husband will say when I tell him how much this cost.'

Ludmila smiled and looked around, hoping Oleg would not return until the woman had moved on. If it was this easy to sell American goods she might ask if she could rent a stall for a few days. It could be more profitable to her than selling to Oleg.

Oleg returned, breathing heavily from where he had run part of the way. 'I have your money,' he said.

Ludmila shook her head. 'I'm sorry. I changed my mind and decided not to sell it after all. I should have thought about it more carefully before I troubled you.'

'What about the bill that you said you needed to pay?'

'I'm sure I can come to some arrangement with my bank. A small loan for a week or two should be sufficient until my husband sends me some more money.'

Oleg glared at her retreating form as Ludmila walked away. He would not do business with her again. He had spent time explaining to the bank that he needed the money immediately and they had reluctantly agreed to him having an overdraft. He would now have to return the money and try to avoid paying the bank charges.

Zavinalov reported that Ludmila had visited an insurance firm and arranged to have her jewellery insured for a very sizeable sum.

'I would have thought she would already have had it insured,' mused Groshenkov.

'Probably thought that as it was in the bank vault insurance was unnecessary. Now she has taken out a brooch she probably feels it is a wise precaution. She visited the local market and Lashenkova and I followed her. She spoke to a stall holder and showed him some items she had brought with her. The stall holder disappeared off and left her to look after his stall. Whilst he was gone she sold one of the items she had shown him and when he returned she left. Lashenkova followed her and I spoke to the stall holder. He was not very pleased. He had offered to buy an expensive table cloth from her but when he returned from the bank she had changed her mind about selling it. I didn't tell him that she had sold the item in his absence, but the roubles I gave him seemed to mollify him somewhat.'

'Money in his hand for nothing. What did Lashenkova have to report?'

'Nothing. Kuzmichov walked back from the market, called in at the supermarket and returned home.'

To Groshenkov's frustration Borovich continued to report that the only movement he had seen at the Asimenikov apartment had been when the woman went out shopping.

May 2016
Week One – Monday

John gave his customary smile to the man who entered the shop. 'Good morning. What can I get for you?'

The man seemed to consider. 'Speak English?'

'Of course. How can I help you?' replied John.

A look of relief crossed the man's face. 'I do not speak Greek. I know little of the English so that would be easier for me. Your dog is friendly?'

'Perfectly friendly unless he thought you were threatening me. I couldn't answer for his actions then.'

The man eyed Skele dubiously. 'I am not planning attack. You have rooms?'

'Self catering apartments.'

'I want room. How much?'

'We charge you for the night. How long do you want to stay?'

'Three, four days.'

'I'll call my mother and ask. She is in charge of the bookings.'

John phoned Marianne and spoke rapidly to her in Greek, finally turning back with a smile. 'My mother will be here in a few minutes and be able to show you the accommodation. Can I get you anything whilst you wait?'

'Bottle water please. I will go out.'

John placed a large bottle of water on the counter along with a pamphlet advertising Uncle Yannis's exhibition.

The man shook his head. 'No. Small.'

John replaced the bottle into the fridge and withdrew the smaller size. 'Here's my mother now.

She'll get you settled in and be able to answer any queries you may have.'

The man put his hand into his pocket and pulled out a handful of small change. John waved it aside. 'You can pay me for the water later.'

Marianne returned from the apartments. 'Seems like a nice man. He says he's Italian.'

'Really? He said he didn't speak Greek and his English is limited. Had he told me he was Italian it could have been easier for both of us.'

'I gained the impression that he is just touring around the area.'

John nodded. 'I gave him a pamphlet about Uncle Yannis's exhibition.'

'As I left there were two people at the gate obviously wondering whether to come in.'

'That would please Uncle Yannis if they did. He'd probably keep them there talking for so long that eventually they would buy something just so they could escape. One way of clearing his stock,' grinned John.

'If they are still there talking to him when I return I shall begin to believe that you're right. I may have to rescue them.'

John shook his head. 'Not a good idea. Uncle Yannis would blame you if he lost a sale.'

Marianne parked her car and as she walked up to the house Uncle Yannis called to her.

'What do you want, Uncle? Some more water or would you like me to ask Marcus to come and relieve you or a while?'

'I have sold a vase,' announced Yannis proudly. 'I need one from the house to take its place.'

Marianne frowned. 'How will I know which one you want?'

'John has labelled them all. This is the one I need. There should be two of that design.' He pointed to the pamphlet. 'I believe they are in the bedroom where your mother stayed.'

'Can I take this with me?'

'Bring it back to me when you have found the vase. I also need a pad of paper and a pen. Ask Marisa if she is going to come down to sit with me soon. I have nearly finished reading my newspaper.'

'I'll try not to be too long.'

Marianne was pleased that Uncle Yannis had made a sale, but to have to spend time finding the vase, speaking to Marisa and then going back to him was annoying. She had been busily composing an e-mail to a travel agent when John had called her. Bryony was up at Saffron's shop and Nicola had taken Yiannis for a walk. Everyone would be expecting her to have a light lunch ready for them and also the evening meal. If she could find the vase without a problem she would ask Marisa to take it down so she could then finish the e-mail and continue with her preparations for the food.

Thanks to John's labelling system Marianne found the required vase quickly, but Marisa refused to go down to sit with him.

'I'll go down in about half an hour. I want to finish the letter I'm writing to Angelo. He and Francesca want to come over to visit me.'

'Where do they want to stay?'

'Here, of course.'

'Have they said when they want to come?'

'They mentioned early July.'

Marianne nodded. 'As soon as you know their dates tell me and I can get a room ready for them.' This would mean moving all the boxes of pottery from the spare bedroom and dispersing them around the house again. 'I'll take this vase down to Yannis and tell him you'll be down soon.'

'How can I help you?' John asked in Italian when the man arrived at the taverna an hour later.

'Why did you not tell me you spoke Italian?'

'I didn't know you were Italian when you arrived. It would have been no good me speaking to you in Italian if you had been Spanish or Portuguese. How can I help you?'

'I would like something to eat, please. I understand you serve snacks.'

John placed a menu on the table. 'I'll give you a few minutes to decide and then come back.'

'An omelette with some salad will be sufficient.'

'And a drink?'

'A frappe,' he added as he spread a map and notebook out on the table before him and began to study it carefully.

'Are you looking for anywhere special?' asked John.

The Italian sighed. 'I do not know where to start.'

'There are plenty of interesting villages nearby. Have you visited Crete before?'

'No.'

'Then I can recommend going across to Spinalonga by boat from Plaka, driving up a short way into the mountains and returning via Aghios Nikolaos.'

'I have been there and visited the nearby villages. You speak very good Italian,' observed the customer.

'My father is half Italian and I was brought up speaking the language. I'll have your meal ready for you in a few minutes.'

The man nodded and proceeded to make more notes whilst he waited. If the young man's father was half Italian he might be able to help.

John came over and cleared away the empty plates. 'Would you like anything else?' he asked as he placed a small dish of melon cubes and grapes on the table.

'I would like to talk with you if you can spare the time.'

'My time is my own unless a customer arrives,' smiled John and slid into the seat opposite.

'Where are you planning to visit today?' asked John curiously.

133

'I have to return to Elounda and look for the cemetery. I think I may have passed it without realising. If I do not find what I am looking for there I will drive on to Plaka. I believe there is a cemetery there also.'

'Why are you interested in cemeteries? Are you writing a book about burial customs?'

'No, I am looking for someone.'

'If you went to the main church in Elounda and spoke to the priest I am sure he would be able to help you. There should be a record of the burials.'

'I tried that approach when I was in Aghios Nikolaos, but the priest there was not very helpful. I was unable to give him an exact date and he said he did not have time to look through all his records that covered those years.'

'So if you are returning to Elounda I suggest you spend some time there. A walk across the Causeway where the old salt pans are can be interesting. On a clear, still day you can see the ruins of old Olous beneath the sea. There is a good taverna over there with a Christian mosaic. Also, on the road leading from Elounda to Plaka there is an exhibition of ceramics that are museum replicas.'

The man shook his head. 'I am not here to visit the tourist attractions. Would your father know of any Italian families living locally?'

'He might. I don't know of any.'

'Did none of them make a home here after the war?'

John shrugged. 'It's possible. Who are you looking for?'

'It is a rather delicate subject.'

John raised his eyebrows. 'You are looking for a certain young lady?'

'No, oh, no, nothing like that. I am looking for a grave.'

'A grave?'

'A grave from the time of the war over here and another from a later date.'

'Start at the beginning. Why are you looking here for a war time grave? Surely the obvious place to look would be at Souda Bay? That is where the big cemeteries and memorials to the fallen are.'

The man sighed. 'My grandfather was with the Italian army when they occupied this end of the island so it is unlikely his grave would be at Souda Bay. My father looked there and also asked for burial details of any Italians buried in the area. My grandfather's name was not among them.'

'Are you sure your grandfather died?'

'He did not return. My grandmother was notified that he was missing, presumed dead.'

'There are graves there for soldiers whose names were unknown,' John reminded him.

'I know, but my grandfather was never in that area. He was stationed in Aghios Nikolaos. My grandmother had letters from him, describing the area and the people.'

'I don't want to sound rude, but would he by any chance have met a Cretan woman and decided to stay here?'

'I do not think that was likely. He was devoted to his wife and also to my father who was a young boy at the time. They had not been married that long. I feel sure that if he preferred to stay in Crete with a woman he had met he would have done the decent thing and written to my grandmother.'

'It's possible that a letter went astray or he asked the woman to post it and she destroyed it,' suggested John. 'Where exactly have you looked?'

'My grandfather was just an ordinary soldier under orders. I understand from his letters that they were expected to visit the villages and search for any resistance workers who might be hiding there. From Aghios Nikolaos I have travelled to all the nearby villages along the coast as far as Sitia and also those inland as far as Kritsa and Neapoli. I've explored all the outlying villages in those areas. Now I have come down here and I plan to visit all the villages between here and Malia.'

The Italian placed his finger on the map and traced his journeys.

'By now my grandfather would be aged ninety eight. I have looked at all the old men in the villages I have visited. I have even asked them if they knew my grandfather and shown them his photograph. I have been visiting the local churches and speaking to the priests, asking if they have any records of an Italian being buried there. It is very difficult and time consuming. I am now visiting the cemeteries that serve those villages in the hope of finding a tomb stone or memorial of some sort that the priest is unaware of. I was going to ask you to direct me to the cemeteries in this area. They are often difficult to find.'

'If you do not speak Greek how will you know if the tombstone belongs to one or other of your relatives?' asked John.

'I have their names written down in the Greek lettering. Pietro Rossi was my grandfather and Lorenzo Rossi my father. I am also Pietro.'

'I think your chances of locating a grave in his name is slim. We have a system here. A family can purchase a tomb and then all their relatives are buried there initially. Their names are inscribed on the tomb. After someone has been buried for three years they are removed, the bones are washed and they are placed in an ossuary. If the tomb belongs to the family the ossuary is placed inside. If it does not belong to them the ossuary is removed to a storage facility. The name on the tomb is removed and someone else uses the tomb.'

Pietro sighed. 'It is the same system in Italy. It appears I could be wasting my time looking for a sarcophagus or gravestone.'

John shrugged. 'I don't know. It's possible that if he stayed here and lived with a Greek woman he would have had the same burial rites. If the family owned a tomb he could have been buried there and his name added to list of occupants or there could be a plaque on the cemetery wall in his memory.'

'My grandmother contacted some of his compatriots and they confirmed that he had never shown any interest in the local women. They said he went out one day and never returned.'

'It's possible that he met with an accident; fell into a ravine, broke a leg and was unable to reach help.'

'Possible, yes, but his company searched for him and found no trace. They asked the local people and they denied having seen him.'

'As this area of Crete was occupied mainly by the Italians at that time I doubt if the locals would have felt very friendly towards them and been willing to help.'

'I understand. Why should they help those they considered to be their enemy? I know it is many years ago now, but the memories remain. No one was unfriendly towards me, but they also claimed to know nothing that could help me in my search.'

'As far as I am aware there were few battles around here that resulted in the deaths of soldiers; many of them were billeted out in peoples' houses to ensure there was no resistance movement formed. That was how my grandparents met.' John smiled. 'My grandfather stayed in a local farmhouse and he and the daughter fell in love. My grandfather died some years ago, but my grandmother is still alive and lives with us. I could ask her if she has any information that could help you.'

'I would be grateful if you could ask her, but that is not the end of the matter. My father came to Crete to see if he could find any trace of his father. The war had been over for more than thirty years and the Cretans showed him no animosity or ill feeling. He wrote to my mother when he was in Aghios Nikolaos and said that the people were friendly, but he was still unable to find out any information. He went to the Town Hall and asked to see their records and he found nothing. They suggested that he searched in some of the outlying villages as some of the elderly inhabitants might have some information.'

'Did he speak Greek?'

Pietro smiled. 'He taught Classical Languages at the University. Unfortunately I did not inherit his linguistic ability. I tried going to evening classes to learn. I can ask a question but I cannot always understand the reply.' He spread his hands in resignation. 'I am the manager of tile manufacturers. A business man.'

'Did your father have any success?'

'My father also disappeared without a trace.'

'What! How could he have disappeared?'

'That is what I would like to find out. My grandmother is no longer alive but my mother needs to know what happened to her husband.'

'If you father was taken ill whilst he was here there should be records in the local hospital. In the event that he died the Italian Consulate would have been informed and your mother contacted to ask her about returning his body to Italy for burial.'

'Exactly. I asked at the hospital in Aghios Nikolaos and they searched their records for that year without success.'

'What about Heraklion? If he was seriously ill he may have been transferred there.'

'Surely there would be a record at the hospital in Aghios Nikolaos if that had happened?'

John pulled a paper napkin from the holder. 'Tell me the exact dates that your father was here. I know the doctor in Aghios and I could make some enquiries. He could be more forthcoming to me.'

'I would appreciate that.'

'I'll do whatever I can, but I still think it is far more likely that once in Crete your relatives found a woman they wanted to stay with and decided it convenient not to return to Italy.'

'Not the kind of news I would want to take back to my mother, but at least she would know what had happened to him. I, too, would like to know.'

'I take it you are not superstitious.'

'No, why do you ask?'

'They say things happen in threes. Two men from your family have disappeared. Are you not concerned that you might also disappear?'

The man shrugged. 'My day comes when it comes. I cannot

prevent that, but I am not expecting anything ill to befall me whilst I am here. I certainly do not believe in curses or spells of any kind. How late do you stay open?'

'The shop is open from eight in the morning so people can buy anything they want for their breakfast. The taverna opens at eleven for those who want a snack lunch and both establishments are then open until five thirty. Most visitors prefer to go to a local taverna in the evening for a meal unless they are catering for themselves. I can recommend the one that Kyriakos runs. It is at the bottom of the hill in Plaka.'

'Thank you. How much do I owe you?'

John calculated the bill and the Italian paid adding on a large tip. 'I will return tomorrow and let you know how I got on.'

As John arrived to open up the shop he found the Italian waiting outside.

'I'm sorry to be so early,' he apologised. 'I should have thought yesterday and bought some coffee for this morning.'

'No problem. Someone has to be first.' John unlocked the door and Skele settled himself down in a patch of shade.

'I was a bit concerned that your dog would be on guard when I arrived.'

'Skele comes home with me and stays the night with a friend. I bring him back up in the morning. When we first had him he was not allowed to live at our house as my aunt had a cat. We no longer have my aunt or the cat, but Skele is used to the routine and Dimitris would be most upset if I did not allow Skele to spend the night with him. Would you just like a tin of coffee or would you like a breakfast to go with it?'

'I thought your taverna did not open until eleven.'

'I can always make an exception to the rule. How about sausage and bacon or would you prefer just to have yoghurt and fruit?'

'You've tempted me with the sausage and bacon. That would certainly set me up for the day.'

'I'll cook an extra sausage and you can give it to Skele. He'll be your friend for life. Have a seat and I'll bring you a coffee. When you've had your breakfast you can tell me where you went yesterday and if you had any success.'

'I enjoyed that,' commented Pietro as John collected his empty plate. 'I found that the outlying hotels and bed and breakfast establishments in the villages were unwilling to accommodate me for one night. Most of them asked me to pay for a full week. I ended up spending some nights in my car and when I've wanted a breakfast I've usually been offered only fruit and cereal.'

'You were fortunate not to have been found by the police. It's against the law to sleep rough over here.'

'I had little option until I based myself in Aghios Nikolaos. I was trying to visit the villages that would have been accessible on foot from Aghios Nikolaos. If the soldiers were sent out on patrol from there surely they would have been expected to return in the evening so there would be a limit to the distance they could travel.'

'Not necessarily. They could have been transported to an area in the morning and expected to walk back to their base later. It's also possible they may have been ordered to stay in the area over night if resistance activity was thought to be taking place there.'

Pietro shook his head. 'Being unable to communicate properly the villagers probably had no idea what I was asking them.'

'Did your father mention the names of any villages that he had visited when he was here? If he found no trace of your grandfather in those you could cross them off your list. Anyway, where did you go yesterday when you left here?'

'I drove back to Elounda and took the road that leads to the small villages higher up. I had to leave my car and walk, of course. I spoke to everyone I saw and showed them the photograph but no one had any knowledge of either man. From there I drove through a place called Pines. Most of the houses there appeared to be modern buildings and there were no old people around. I saw a sign that said Kastelli and found another small village down in the valley. I stopped there for some lunch and asked around as usual before driving on to Kastelli. That was more encouraging. I happened upon a couple who were outside in their garden and asked them for directions to the cemetery.'

'How did you manage that?' asked John curiously.

'I heard them speaking in English. I admired their house and garden and they began to tell me the history. Apparently it was used as a hospital by the Italians.'

John nodded. 'I know where you mean. I met a man who had been treated there.'

'An Italian?'

'No, a Cretan.'

'They treated local people?'

'Just because the Italians were an occupying force it did not mean that they were all bad. They helped many of the villagers. Were they able to help you at all?'

Pietro shook his head. 'No, they have not lived there long enough. They took me to the local church and I spoke to the priest. He was unable to help me as he has only been there for the past fifteen years. They directed me to the cemetery and I spent a long time walking around there but could not find any name that even resembled Rossi. By the time I returned it was too late to go anywhere else so I will drive back to Elounda again today. Did you speak to your grandmother and ask if she knew anything?'

John shook his head. 'I had no opportunity last evening. My great uncle was excited having sold two pots at his exhibition. He could not stop talking about it. No one else had a chance to say anything. I'll see what I can do this evening, provide he hasn't sold any more. There is a limit to the number of times we want to hear him describe the decoration on them and how he convinced the customer to make a purchase. Where are you planning to go today?'

'First I need to drive back towards Elounda and look at the

cemetery at Mavrikiano. I understand there is a small cemetery at Plaka. When I have looked there I will follow the road that goes up the hill to some more small villages. I can ask the villagers if they have any knowledge of my father or grandfather and visit their cemeteries.'

'Sometimes there is a cemetery that serves a number of villages in the area. There is one at Vrouhas. It is on a grassy headland and you reach it by driving down a lane. Look for the word "necropolis" and follow the directions on the signpost. That way you can't miss it.'

'I'll remember. Thank you for your help. I'm afraid I ate both my sausages. I was supposed to save one for your dog.'

'I have one for Skele. You can take it outside and give it to him. He loves sausages. When we found him he had been scavenging on the beach and the only food we had here to give him were sausages.'

Pietro smiled. 'Not surprising that he loves them. I hope he eats proper dog food now.'

'Usually. A sausage is a treat on special occasions. I'll wrap it for you to take outside so you can give it to him.'

Skele sat obediently and waited until Pietro placed the sausage on the ground before him. He looked at it longingly until John gave him permission to eat.

'He's very well trained.,' observed Pietro. 'Most dogs would have snatched that up.'

'He's a dog in a million. He's wonderful with my children and no trouble up here with the customers, he never begs. He even knows who he can trust and lets me know if they are any threat to me. I hope you have a successful day and I'll try talking to my grandmother this evening.'

Before John had a chance to speak with his grandmother Yannis began to tell him about his day.

'I had a strange man visit today. He showed no interest in my ceramics at all. I think he wanted souvenirs from the war.

I couldn't understand most of what he was saying. Said he was Italian. He kept asking me about a soldier and saying the same name over and over again and showing me a photograph.'

John smiled. 'I know who that was. He's staying at the self catering establishments. I was going to speak to you yesterday evening but you were too busy telling us about your sales.'

'I haven't made any today,' remarked Yannis sadly.

'There's always tomorrow. I'm sure word will get round and you'll have more customers. I wanted to speak to you about this Italian man. He's told me that he is looking for his grandfather's grave.'

'Why is he looking for it down here? He should be up at Souda Bay.'

'Apparently his grandfather was stationed in Aghios Nikolaos and listed as missing, presumed killed. He's looked at Souda and there was no record of him there so he's wondering if he was buried locally.'

'I've never heard of any Italian soldiers being buried locally.' Yannis shook his head.

'If Victor was still alive I'm sure he would know,' interrupted Marisa. 'He knew all the soldiers who were in Aghios.'

'Did you ever hear him speak about a soldier called Pietro Rossi?' asked John.

Marisa frowned. 'Not that I recall, but I didn't take an awful lot of notice. We had Victor and Mario staying with us and I remember Ourania's mother had Umberto with her. She didn't like him. She was convinced he had designs on Ourania.'

'Do you remember the names of any of the other soldiers?' asked John.

'I think there was one called Julius,' said Yannis.

Marisa nodded. 'And another was called Emmanuel, but I can't remember any other names.

'Not to worry. I told him I would ask you so I've done what I can. He'll just have to keep on looking.'

'Did you have any success?' asked John as Pietro sat down at a table outside the taverna.

Pietro shook his head. 'I walked around the cemetery on the Elounda road. I found the graves of the men who lost their lives when the Imperia Seaplane crashed, but nothing that I could trace back to my family.'

'I asked my grandmother and also my great uncle last night. They neither of them knew of a soldier called Pietro Rossi. I can't say I was surprised. My grandmother was only interested in Victor and my great uncle was younger. He was trying to keep the farm going as well as taking messages to the local resistance who were hiding locally. If Aunt Anna was still alive she may have known more.'

'Do you think if either of them saw me they would see a family resemblance that would jog their memory? I could show them his photo.'

John shook his head. 'I think it very unlikely. I believe you met my great uncle yesterday; the man with the ceramics exhibition. He speaks only a little English and all he could understand was that you were asking for a soldier. He thought you had mistaken his exhibition for one of war time souvenirs. Cretans have a remarkable memory for faces and I'm sure if you resemble your grandfather and he had known him he would have seen the likeness.'

'So I am no further forward,' sighed Pietro.

'I'll call my mother and ask if you can visit us. It's possible that my grandmother may see a resemblance. She is older than my great uncle. He was little more than a boy at the time.'

'I would be grateful for any help.'

'Hi, Mum, I'm at the taverna with the Italian man. I know it's a bit of a long shot but could he come to the house and meet Uncle Yannis and Grandma? He's hoping they might recognise his grandfather from a photo he has.' John listened to Marianne's reply and smiled. 'Thanks, Mum. I'll tell him.' John turned back to Pietro. 'Mum says you're welcome to come up to the house this evening, about eight. You can join us for our evening meal.'

'That would be an imposition.'

'Not at all. I think the rest of the family would be interested in your story.'

Pietro shook his head. 'It is beyond belief that two soldiers could be sent out on patrol and never return.'

'There were two of them? What happened to his companion?'

Pietro shrugged. 'As I understand it he never returned either.'

John frowned. 'There were andartes in the area. I suppose they could have been ambushed and taken prisoner. When their captors realised they were only foot soldiers and not officers for whom they could have demanded a ransom they may have been taken further into the hills and killed. They would not have killed them close to a village or suspicion would have fallen on the locals and they would have suffered reprisals.'

'True, but if I accept that both men were killed by the resistance or fell into a ravine surely their remains would have been discovered by now. They could have been identified by their dog tags.'

'That would depend where they had been taken. If they had been placed in a ravine there could have been a rock fall or land slide since then that buried them. It's also likely that their dog tags were taken from them and thrown away somewhere else.'

Pietro sighed. 'In that case I am unlikely to find any trace of my grandfather, but what about my father? The war was over and he was a civilian when he came here in 1980. Someone must know what happened to him.'

Pietro arrived at Yannis's house shortly after eight. He had driven past twice to make sure he had the correct location. The house, standing back in its own grounds, looked far too grand for a taverna owner even if he also had self catering apartments to supplement his income. He rang the bell hesitantly, hoping he was truly expected.

John called to him from the patio. 'Come round this way, Pietro. We only open the front door on formal occasions. Come and have a seat and what would you like to drink?'

Petro sat down in a chair and looked at the elderly couple who were sitting a short distance away. He recognised the man whom he had seen on his previous visit to the ceramics stall. They both nodded to him and then continued with their own conversation in Greek.

'Right,' said John, as he handed Pietro a glass of wine. 'I'll introduce everyone. The elderly couple are my Grandmother and Great Uncle Yannis. Uncle Yannis has lived in this area all his life and Grandmother lived here until she married and went to Italy. Here is Giovanni, my father, he speaks Italian, of course, and you've met my mother. This is her cousin, Bryony, and her husband, Marcus who live here and help to run the business.' John indicated Bryony and Marcus. 'This is my wife, Nicola. I'm afraid that only my grandmother, my father and I speak Italian. I will have to relate your story to everyone else in Greek.'

Pietro nodded and took a mouthful of his wine. He hoped it would not go to his head as he had not eaten since a snack lunch at midday.

'Help yourself to a plate of food. Everyone is being polite and waiting for you to serve yourself first. Then it will be every man for himself. Mum's bound to have plenty more in the kitchen so don't worry about taking the last item from a plate.'

Still Pietro hesitated and finally took a small cheese pie.

'Don't be silly,' Marianne spoke sternly. 'That is not enough for a big man like you.' She placed two chicken kebabs on his plate along with a generous helping of rice and salad.

John grinned. 'Mum will be most offended if you only nibble at the food. She is used to us all clearing the table for her. Eat your fill and then we'll talk.'

Pietro watched as everyone else loaded up their plates to capacity and began to eat with relish. He was obviously expected to do the same. Finally, as the large dinner plates were cleared away and bowls of fruit took their place, the family began to look at him expectantly.

'Right,' said John. 'Anyone want their glass refilled before I start?'

Pietro was amused to see that it was only the elderly couple who held out their empty glasses and John duly obliged by filling them up.

Briefly John outlined the story that Pietro had told him about his grandfather's disappearance followed by his father's disappearance when he looked for him, thirty five years later. He turned to his Grandmother and Yannis.

'I know I asked both of you about the Italians who were stationed in this area during the war and the name Pietro Rossi meant nothing to either of you. Pietro has a photograph of his grandfather and is hoping you might recognise him even if you do not recall his name.'

John held the photo out and both Yannis and Marisa peered at it closely before shaking their heads.

'Does Pietro remind you of anyone?'

Yannis and Marisa eyed him up and down intently and then shook their heads.

'I remember him coming to view my ceramics the other day, but I don't think I had ever seen him before then.'

'He tells me he resembles his grandfather in his looks. It was just a chance that one of you might remember a face from the past.' John turned back to Pietro. 'I'm so sorry. They are unable to help. Do you know the name of his companion who went missing with him?'

Pietro shook his head. 'I'm afraid not.'

'Companion?' asked Nicola. 'You mean two soldiers went missing?'

'Apparently.'

Nicola swallowed. 'I'll talk to you later, John. Something has occurred to me.'

John raised his eyebrows. 'Tell me now.'

'No,' replied Nicola firmly. 'Later. I could be wrong.'

Giovanni answered his mobile and frowned. 'That's annoying. The people who are arriving tomorrow have been given a change of flight time. I'll have to ask you to do an airport run tomorrow, John.'

'What about the taverna?'

'Bryony?' Giovanni looked at his sister in law.

'I've promised Saffie I'll be at the shop tomorrow.'

'It will have to be you, then Marianne and Nicola will have to look after things here. John can do the early run so he should be back here by the time the Cash and Carry open. When he's deposited the guests he can return there for the supplies we need. He should be finished by twelve.'

'So what were you going to tell me?' asked John as he undressed ready for bed.

'I need to check up on something first. I promise I'll tell you tomorrow evening.'

No amount of persuasion on John's part would make Nicola divulge the idea that had occurred to her whilst Pietro was there. Finally she turned her back on him.

'I'm going to sleep. You have to be up early tomorrow and I'll have my hands full getting the girls ready for school and dealing with Yiannis. Whether I am right or wrong it will keep until tomorrow.'

Frustrated, but accepting that Nicola would tell him in her own good time, John placed his arm around her waist and pulled her close.

May 2016
Week One – Tuesday

Pietro arrived at the taverna and was surprised to see Marianne there.

'Where John?' He selected a bottle of water from the fridge and placed the money on the counter.

'Driving to the airport. Collecting visitors.'

Pietro nodded. 'I forget. I thank you very much for good evening.'

'I'm just sorry that we were unable to help you at all.'

Pietro shrugged. 'I look still. Thank you.'

Vasilis drove down to his house. There was no sign that the waste land next door had ever been disturbed by the archaeologists. It actually looked more respectable than previously. To help them with their work the archaeologists had moved odd timbers, stones, car tyres and general rubbish to one side. He wondered if the family who owned the land would be willing to clear it up completely and make it look more presentable or would be willing to sell it to him so he could remove the eyesore. He also wondered what their reaction had been when they were told that a body had been found on their land. If Panayiotis was at home that evening he would ask him.

He stood and looked at the facade. The front steps were completed and led up to the large front door. A wall had been built at the side and there was no access to the patio. The terraces still needed to be planted and he could see the men gathered around the area where the lift was to be installed. Feeling a frisson of excitement he parked his car and walked through the gate towards them.

'Just about ready to try it out,' announced a man who appeared to be in charge. 'We have it in place and the machinery connected. I've sent Stelios up inside to switch on the electricity at the mains and ensure it's working properly.'

'What happens if it doesn't work?' asked Vasilis anxiously.

'We have to find out where we've gone wrong and put it right. Don't worry. We've installed lifts before.'

Vasilis nodded. There was nothing he could do except stand and watch whilst the men pressed various switches and finally the door closed and the lift began to ascend.

'What happens if the upstairs door doesn't open?'

'No reason why it shouldn't. If it's stuck Stelios will be able to sort out the problem.'

'I don't mean just now, but in the future? I would hate my wife to be stuck in there for hours.'

'If there is a power outage and the electricity fails you can switch to the generator and that will take over. In the unlikely event that both fail the door can be opened from the inside but make sure you switch the power off first. If it came back on the lift would move either up or down with the door open. That could be dangerous.'

Vasilis nodded. He had hoped that Cathy would be able to use the lift even when he was not at the house. She would not be able to cope if there was a power outage.

'Will a mobile 'phone work if you are in the lift?'

'Depends upon the signal locally.'

'Is there an alarm in the lift? If my wife did get stuck in there and her mobile did not work no one might know she was there for hours.'

The engineer gave a sigh. 'Once we are happy that all is in perfect working order you can try it out for yourself. Why don't you go and have a drink somewhere and come back in about an hour?'

Reluctantly Vasilis turned away. 'I'll be at the hotel down there if you need me.'

The engineer grunted. He would have no need of Vasilis who obviously had no idea about the machinery for a lift.

It was a little over the hour when Vasilis returned to the house and saw that the men were preparing to pack their tools away and leave.

'Is it working properly?' Vasilis asked eagerly.

'Perfectly. We've tested every component. Do you want to have a ride?'

Vasilis hesitated. 'What happens if I'm unlucky enough to get stuck inside?'

'If you don't get out upstairs in the house we'll know where you are. Before we leave I'll go through the electrical settings with you. No need to have them on all the time when you're not living here.'

'Will my mobile work when I'm in there?'

'Give it a try.'

Dubiously Vasilis stepped inside the lift. 'What do I press?' he asked.

'That one is to close the doors and the other to open them. They have arrow symbols on them. To go up you press the "up" arrow and to come back down you press the "down" arrow. If you don't close the doors or if you press the press the wrong button the lift won't move.'

'What about the other ones?'

'That one is to activate the generator and has "G" on it. The other one is for the alarm – see the bell on it?'

'I'd like to test that before you leave.'

'All in good time. Now, close the doors and press the arrow

to take you up inside the house. Open the doors to the lift and get out; then get back in and come back down.'

'I'll want to try my mobile before I get out.'

'Whatever.' The engineer was becoming thoroughly impatient. Had the man never been in a lift before?

To Vasilis's intense relief the lift moved up slowly and smoothly. He opened the doors and stepped out into his spacious hallway. With a nod of satisfaction he stepped back inside, closed the doors and called Cathy on his mobile 'phone before pressing the "down" button.

'Hello, Cathy. Can you hear me?'

'Perfectly, Vasilis. What is the problem?'

'No problem. I just wanted to test my 'phone. I'll be home shortly.'

Vasilis pressed the "down" button and the lift descended to the ground floor. He opened the door and smiled at the engineer.

'That all appears to be perfect and my mobile 'phone worked successfully.'

'I'll just run through the controls with you, then we'll be off.' He unlocked a small door set into the wall. 'Make sure you keep this locked. You don't want anyone fiddling around in there. This is the lever to put the electricity on. It's a separate supply from the house so even if the lift power is turned off you still have electricity everywhere else. If you have a power outage and need to use the lift you use that switch there and it will start up the generator. That is in the cupboard next to the lift and I suggest that you also keep that locked unless you need to use it. Make sure you do not lose the keys. There's no access to the generator from the house.'

'Thank you,' said Vasilis humbly. 'I hope I'll not have to trouble you on a regular basis.'

'You ought to have a maintenance check annually, but if you have a problem with the power a local electrician should be able to sort that out. It's really only the lift mechanism that needs specialist knowledge.'

Vasilis drove home feeling both excited and relieved. After lunch he would take Cathy for a drive and bring her down to the house. He was longing to show her the lift and be able to take her inside to see the layout of the rooms now they were ready for the fitments and decoration.

As Vasilis drew up outside the house Cathy's face fell. 'I thought the access would be at ground level. I'll never be able to manage those steps.' She turned distressed eyes to her husband.

'You'll have no problem.' Vasilis assured her as he took her wheelchair from the boot. He opened the car door and helped Cathy to get settled in her chair.

'You cannot possibly pull me up all those steps. You'll put your back out.'

'I wouldn't attempt such a thing.'

He led the way down to the entrance to the lift and unlocked the door to the electricity cupboard and switched on the power before he opened the door to the housing of the lift.

'You won't need to use the steps. I've had a lift installed. It's large enough to take your wheelchair. Go in and make sure you can reach the control panel and understand the symbols. Once you're happy with them give me a few moments to go up and unlock then press the "up" arrow. When you arrive upstairs open the doors and I'll be waiting for you.'

'Suppose we have a power outage and it gets stuck?'

'I've discussed all that with the engineers who installed it. There is a switch that connects to the generator but you only touch that if it is necessary.'

Cathy looked at Vasilis doubtfully. 'What happens if I am here on my own?'

'If you become truly stuck you can use your mobile to call me or Vasi. There is also an alarm bell. We tested it this morning and Vasi came running out of the hotel to see what was going on. I'll go through all the controls with you properly later. It is no different from any other lift. Once you've been up and down a few times you'll be fine.'

Cathy nodded. She trusted Vasilis and knew that he would not ask he to use the lift unless he was convinced it was safe. She stretched out her hand to the control panel which was exactly at the right level for her.

'Make sure you close the doors before you press the arrow to go up,' he reminded her.

Vasilis hurried up the steps and pressed in the code to unlock the large front door. As he entered he could hear the sound of the lift arriving and he stood and waited until Cathy opened the doors.

'So what did you think?' he asked.

'I was relieved when a light came on inside as I closed the doors. I would hate to be in there in darkness. What happens if the electricity does fail? I won't be able to see which button I press for the generator or the alarm.'

Vasilis frowned. He had not thought to ask the engineer about that possibility. 'I'll speak to the company who installed it. I can put a torch in there that you can us in an emergency.'

Cathy wheeled herself out and looked around. 'After our apartment this looks enormous.' She rose from her wheelchair and picked up her crutches.

'That's because there are no furnishings anywhere. Look, this will be our bedroom with the bathroom en suite. All the doors are wide enough to accommodate your chair. There's even sufficient space in the bathroom so you can use it in there. The shower will be fitted with hand rails, a hoist and a seat so you should have no problem. All you have to do is decide on the tiles that you want.'

Cathy nodded. 'You've thought of everything.'

'Come and see the kitchen.'

Vasilis led the way into the spacious room. 'This appears large at present, but once you have all the kitchen equipment in here it will look considerably smaller, but there will still be sufficient space for a centre island where you can sit. Some of the cupboards will be a little high for you to reach from a chair, but they can have items stored in them that are hardly ever used. I can always get them down for you. From the patio doors at the side you have access to the back patio and garden area. There is a very low step and I can have a ramp fitted later if necessary. Do you want to come outside and have a look? It's nowhere near finished out there yet.'

'What do you plan to do?' asked Cathy as Vasilis helped her down the step and she stood and looked at the area of rough ground.

'Most of it will be paved and down there will be a garden area. We can have some seating out here and umbrellas with a large table so we can sit out here for our meals during the summer and also entertain.'

Cathy nodded enthusiastically. 'What about in the winter?'

Vasilis smiled. 'Come back inside and I'll take you through to the dining and lounge area.' He helped her back through the door and steered her to the side of the room away from the patio windows that ran across one wall. 'This will be the dining area. Plenty of space for a large table. Over there will be a large open wood fire. That we will only use occasionally as it will be for effect. There is the air con for the summer and that will act as central heating for the winter.'

He waited until Cathy had looked her fill, envisaging the dining area in the future. 'Now you can tell me what you think of the lounge.'

Cathy gasped as she looked through the windows. 'The view. It's amazing.'

Vasilis smiled, pleased at her reaction. 'This is why I built the living area at a higher elevation. I didn't think you'd want to sit and look at the road and parked cars.' Vasilis pushed open one of the patio doors. 'There's a small step, but again a ramp can be fitted. There will be plenty of space for garden furniture so we can sit out here in the summer.'

'Will that area be paved?' asked Cathy as she looked at the large hole some feet away from them.

'That is where your swimming pool will be,' he announced.

'My swimming pool?'

'I know how difficult it is for you to use a beach. Here you can swim whenever you please.'

'Oh, Vasilis, you've thought of everything possible to make me happy.' There were tears in Cathy's eyes. 'I did miss the pool at the house when we lived in Heraklion.'

'I know and our present apartment has nowhere suitable for one to be installed. Once we live here it will be much easier for you to go out. You can use your wheelchair to go over the Causeway or along the waterfront to the square and into the town for your shopping. People will always hold the traffic up to allow you to cross the main road.'

'I can't wait to move in? I don't mind if the pool has not been installed or the garden finished. I have enjoyed living in our little apartment, but this is magnificent.'

'You need to decide upon the decoration and the fitments for the kitchen. Some furniture might be quite nice so we have a bed to sleep on and some chairs. I think it will be another month before it is truly habitable.'

'I wasn't suggesting tomorrow. I'm so excited. Can I ask Ronnie and Saffron for their ideas?'

'Of course. The house is yours to decorate and furnish however you please.'

'I want you to be happy with it also.'

Vasilis smiled at Cathy. 'If you are happy, then I am happy.'

John returned from the airport run and his visit to the Cash and Carry. Marianne was relieved to see him and be able to leave the taverna.

'I've four messages on my laptop asking for accommodation dates. I need to get back home and double check that your father hasn't booked anyone else in on those dates whilst I've been up here.'

'Have you been busy?'

'Not particularly. Pietro came looking for you this morning.'

'Did he want anything special?'

'I don't think so. He was just surprised to see me here instead of you. He thanked me for yesterday evening and bought a bottle of water.'

'He probably didn't understand when Dad said about the airport run and the shopping. I've dropped off the bits you asked for back at the house and I'll bring in everything we need for up here. Don't tell Dad; I collected Skele from Dimitris's. I made him sit on a piece of newspaper in the front foot well and had the windows open all the way. You take the decent car back. Tell me if it smells at all, won't you? I'll use your old one to come home as I'll need to give Skele a run.'

'So that he can make my car smell as well,' remarked Marianne.

'Skele doesn't smell, well, only occasionally. Charcoal biscuits don't agree with him.'

'I hope you haven't given him any today then. I'll give the car a spray with air freshener just to make sure.'

Cathy could hardly wait until she knew that Ronnie would have finished painting for the day and Saffron would have closed her shop so she could 'phone both of them. She wanted to show the house off. She would ask Ronnie her advice regarding the decoration and Saffron to recommend the furnishings.

Ronnie was almost as excited as Cathy. 'That's wonderful. I'd love to help with the decor. When can I visit?'

'Tomorrow?'

'I'll be there as soon as I've finished my early morning painting. I can tell Kyriakos that I won't be back before he goes up to the taverna so he won't be hanging around and wondering where I've got to. I'll call you when I get to Elounda. Where do you want to meet me? At your current apartment or at your new house?'

'I think here at the apartment would be best. Vasilis can take us both up in his car.' As she was talking to Ronnie Cathy realised that she did not have keys to access the lift or to unlock the front door. She could see Vasilis outside talking to Panayiotis and she would interrupt him and ask about keys immediately.

Panayiotis smiled at her. 'I hear you have been to view your new house. What did you think of it?'

'Wonderful. Beyond my wildest dreams. I had expected the rooms to be at ground level. It was such a surprise when I went up in the lift and saw the view. It is magnificent.'

'I was sworn to secrecy about the elevation. I saw how the building was progressing when I was down there on duty but Vasilis impressed upon me that I must say nothing to you as it was to be a surprise. I didn't know about the lift and I did wonder how you would manage those outside steps.'

'I've been asking Panayiotis about the body that was found. Apparently there was nothing on him to provide identification.'

'So what will happen to him now?'

'He will stay in the mortuary until all enquiries regarding his identity are completed.'

'How long will that take?' asked Vasilis.

Panayiotis shrugged. 'No one can say. The parish records are being examined and any man that cannot be accounted for is being investigated. They may have moved away from the area, even gone abroad, but we need to make sure that the body does not belong to a man who appears to be missing. It takes time to contact the various towns and then the countries to try to trace an unknown man. All we can do is give them a description of the body, height and approximate age at the time of death.'

'Under the circumstances do you think the owners of the land would be willing to sell?'

'What would you want it for? Would you build another house?' asked Cathy.

'No, I was planning to approach the owners and ask if they would clean the area up a bit. It is just a rubbish tip at the moment. If they want to sell to me I'd make sure it was properly cleared and the olives could be added to my own crop each year.'

Cathy shook her head in despair. 'You are supposed to be retired, Vasilis. Stop trying to find work for yourself. Panayiotis, would you like to come in and have a celebratory drink with us? I'm still so excited. I've 'phoned Ronnie and she is coming tomorrow to look at the house. Oh, that's what I came out for,' she exclaimed. 'Vasilis, I have no keys to access the lift or open the front door.'

'Don't worry. I'll give you a set of keys along with the code for the door. You don't need the code to open it from the inside. Come on, Panayiotis, let's have a drink together to round off the day.'

John managed to curb his impatience until Yiannis had been settled down for the night, the girls had been fed and bathed and were watching a cartoon on the television.

'So, tell me, Nick. I'm eaten up with curiosity.'

'So you remember the performance we gave just before Christmas?'

'Of course.'

'Think about when the women were relating how they had suffered and also resisted the Italians.'

'Yes?'

'I unearthed the script again today and had another look. There are a few lines that describe a mother and her daughter shooting two Italian soldiers and burying them in their olive grove.'

'What? Where? Let me look.'

Nicola handed John the script. He read the information twice and looked up at her with a broad smile. 'You're a genius, Nick. I'd forgotten this. Where did the information come from?'

'Uncle Andreas, I suppose.'

'Then I must 'phone him and ask who actually told him. If the family are still living locally we could ask them what they know about the incident.'

'We can't 'phone him now. It's the early hours of the morning in New Orleans. You'll have to wait until tomorrow.'

Ronnie arrived with a sketch pad tucked under her arm. 'What do you want me to do?' she asked.

'Vasilis is going to take us up and we'll meet Saffie there. I'd like both of you to discuss the most practical layout for the kitchen and then for you to give me ideas for the colour scheme of the kitchen and bathroom.'

'What about the rest of the house?'

'I'd like to get the bathroom and kitchen sorted out first; then I can think about the lounge. I wouldn't want the decoration in the lounge finished before the fitments arrived in case it suffered damaged as the items were brought in.'

'Have you any ideas in mind?'

Cathy shook her head. 'Not really. I only saw the house for the first time yesterday. Obviously I'll need a fridge and freezer, washing machine, tumble dryer, oven, hob, microwave and cupboards.'

'You'll also need a sink and drainer along with worktops.'

'The kitchen area is quite large. I expect everything will fit. Vasilis says there should still be sufficient space for me to have a central preparation area.'

'Ready, ladies? I'll take you along and wait until Saffie arrives. Once she's there I'll let you in and take myself off to Vasi's. You won't want me around.'

'I'll want you to agree to my ideas,' said Cathy.

'That we can discuss later. You know the equipment you need in the kitchen. Make a list and we can have a look on the internet. If you can't see what you want in Greece we can see what's available in England or the States.'

'I'm sure I'll be able to find everything I want locally,' Cathy assured him. 'It would cost an enormous amount to have things imported and their electrical wiring does not always comply with ours.'

'These things can be fixed.' Vasilis waved his arm airily. 'I have placed your wheelchair in the boot and we should go or Saffie will think we are not coming. You have your keys, Cathy?'

Ronnie looked at the house as they drew up. 'How do you manage all those steps, Cathy?'

'Quite easily,' smiled Cathy. 'Vasilis has had a lift installed. It's wonderful. I just sit inside, press a button and it takes me up to inside the house.'

'What a superb idea. Do you have any steps inside?'

'Just two very shallow ones that lead out to the patios and Vasilis has said he will have ramps made for those. I can be completely independent.'

'Can visitors use the lift?'

'No,' said Vasilis very definitely. 'Everyone except Cathy has to use the steps.'

'So what do we do now?' asked Ronnie as she climbed out of the car and Vasilis took Cathy's wheelchair from the boot.

'We wait for Saffie and then we will all go inside.'

'I can't wait. This is really exciting.'

'How is your house progressing?' asked Cathy.

'Slowly. I'm hoping the Palamakis boys will be able to work up there during the summer.'

Vasilis frowned. 'I am relying on them working down here for me. Ideally I would like us to be able to move in by the end of July.'

Ronnie shrugged. 'I expect we can work something out. Here's Saffie now.'

Cathy showed her first visitors around her house. 'I thought I'd have brushed stainless steel for the appliances, a black granite work top, terracotta tiles on the floor and walls and the cupboards painted grey. What do you think, Ronnie?'

'I'll make up some sketches for you and paint them the way you describe and you can make a final decision then on your colour scheme. Have you had any ideas for decoration elsewhere?'

'I've not really thought about more than the kitchen. I'm hoping you and Saffie can come up with some ideas for me.'

'Uncle Andreas, this is John 'phoning from Crete.'

'What is wrong?'

'Nothing. All is well here. I just wanted to ask you about something. You know when we did the play last year…..'

'Yes, I am working on a production and we are hoping to have the first performances ready by September. I know you suggested that I wrote something about Spinalonga. I have not had time to think about that. Once my current work is complete I will think about the idea again.'

'I'm pleased to hear that there will be a professional production. That was what I wanted to speak to you about. The Spinalonga idea can wait until you have more time.'

'All the actors will be professional. I cannot invite you to have a part.'

John smiled. He had no desire to become an actor. 'No, I want to ask you about some information. In the production we gave Monika said that she and her mother shot and killed two Italian soldiers and then buried them in their olive grove. Who told you that?'

'Your grandmother. Why does it matter?'

'There is an Italian over here looking for information about his grandfather. He was a soldier in this area and he and a fellow went out on patrol and never returned. Who told Grandma about the missing soldiers?'

'I've no idea. One of the women that she talked to I expect. You'll have to ask her. Sorry I can't help.'

'No problem. I'll call Grandma. Hope all goes well with the production.' John closed his mobile feeling disappointed. He hoped his grandmother would remember who had given her the information.

Twice during the day he called his grandmother in New Orleans only to be asked to leave a message. The second time he decided he should say something. If Elena found she had two missed messages from Crete she would be very worried that something was amiss with the family.

'Hi, Grandma. John calling. Just hoping you are keeping well. We are all fine. I'll give you a call another time. I just want to ask you something, but it isn't urgent.'

May 2016
Week One – Wednesday

Ludmila checked that she had the slip of pink paper that allowed her to sell goods in the market safely in her purse along with sufficient change should she be offered a large rouble note. The market organiser had been unwilling to allow her to be there for only three weeks and tried to tell her that she had to pay for six months. Ludmila argued with him that she only needed the stall for a short while as she was only selling her surplus household goods as she was moving from Moscow to St Petersburg. Finally he had relented and sold her the permit allowing her to trade for three months.

'I cannot do better than that. If I give you weekly rates soon all the stall holders will be asking for the concession. Instead of having a full market every week it would soon be half empty as they tried their luck at other venues. You pay for a three month permit or nothing.'

Grudgingly Ludmila had paid him. She had no wish to become a regular market trader. She only wanted sufficient funds to be able to pay Mother to arrange for the release of Ivan.

Ludmila loaded up two suitcases with towels and bedding. They were heavier than she had expected and she would not be able to manage to walk to the metro and then to the market with them. She ordered a taxi and waited impatiently for its arrival.

The driver looked at her in surprise. 'You want the market? You do not want the train station?'

'The market,' replied Ludmila firmly. Having managed to secure a stall there she did not want to arrive late and find that affluent customers had already made purchases and it was only the poorer people who were looking for cheap items who were still there.

She consulted the slip of paper that had the number of the stall printed on it and began to walk along the first row, dragging the cases behind her. Curious looks followed her. When she had finally walked down three rows of stalls she decided that she had to ask for directions. She stopped beside a stall that was selling clothing and asked where she would find her stall only to be told that it was in row six.

Ludmila dragged her cases to the end of the row and crossed rows four and five. As she made her way up the row of vendors she could see an empty table and assumed that must be hers. Having checked the number she looked around. This was not where she had expected to be. On one side was a woman selling cheap toys and on the other the man had vegetables. She had wanted to be in the area where better quality household furnishings were sold.

Not having any choice she opened her cases and placed the contents on the table. People passed by but hardly glanced at her towels and bedding. The vegetable man was shouting out details of the produce he was selling, but Ludmila did not have the courage to start calling out to passers by. The woman selling the toys moved over and fingered her towels.

'Nice,' she remarked before returning to her own stall.

For three hours Ludmila stood there, feeling conspicuous and over dressed compared with the other traders and their customers. Although one or two people looked at her items before moving on she sold nothing. Deciding she was wasting her time she repacked her cases and went in search of Oleg.

Oleg scowled as she approached him. 'If you've changed your mind I'm not buying your table cloth,' he announced.

Ludmila shook her head. 'I told you, I've decided to keep it. I have some towels and bedding with me. I'm not asking you to buy them. Please will you put them on your stall and if you sell them you can keep some of the money for yourself.'

'I'll expect half of the selling price.'

'They're good quality. I'll expect them to fetch a decent price.'

'I'll be the judge of the price. Let me have a look.'

Ludmila opened up the cases and Oleg riffled through the contents. 'Not bad,' he observed. 'Doubt if I'd get more than two thousand roubles for a pair of towels and three thousand for a set of bedding.'

'Is that all?' Ludmila had expected twice as much.

'Take it or leave it.' Oleg closed the cases.

Ludmila hesitated. She knew her goods were worth considerably more but she had already wasted her money in renting a stall for three months. Oleg's offer was better than nothing.

'I'll take it. Can I leave them with you now and come back next week? I have some cutlery and a dinner service that I want to sell.'

'I don't deal in those items. Have a word with Vlad.' Oleg pointed to a stall on the other side. 'Tell him I sent you. He'll probably want to see the goods before he makes any agreement with you.'

'They're good quality. The cutlery is silver and the dinner service is bone china with the stamp of the manufacturer on the base of every piece. I also have some Waterford glasses.'

Oleg shrugged. 'That means nothing to me. I only deal in textiles.'

Ludmila opened up the cases again and began to hand him the contents. He placed them in a pile at one side and she knew he would not lay them out and try to sell them until she had left.

'I'll see you next week. I'll speak to your friend Vlad now.'

Oleg nodded. He wanted her to leave as soon as possible so she would not see the prices he was planning to ask.

Vlad shook his head when Ludmila suggested that he accepted her dinner service, glasses and cutlery to sell on his stall.

'I can't do that. People who come to the market are looking for bargains, but the kind of price you'll be expecting for those items they couldn't pay. Plates sell at around a hundred roubles depending upon their size. It would be no good me asking more for them. They would sit here for ever. The same with the cutlery and glasses.'

'Do you know anyone who would be willing to buy them at a reasonable price?'

'I suggest you advertise them privately or go to one of the shops that sell second hand goods. I'm sorry, but I can't help.'

Ludmila walked away disconsolately. She was sure that Oleg would sell her towels and bedding for a good price and only give her a fraction of the money and now Vlad had refused to help her. She would have no choice but to ask Mother if he would accept the items and sell them on to cover some of the expenses incurred for her passport and Ivan's release. He would surely have an outlet for them as she knew he would for her jewellery.

Mr Zavinalov contacted Mr Groshenkov. 'Mrs Kuzmichov visited the bank today and removed all her jewellery from the strong box and cancelled the facility. Do you think she has decided to sell some of it and use the money to live on,' suggested Zavinalov. 'She could be in financial difficulties as she hired a stall in the market. It was not a success and she asked another stall holder to sell goods on her behalf.'

'That is the most likely solution and having the items insured was a safety precaution.'

Groshenkov tapped his teeth with his pen. He did not believe that Ludmila was penniless. He knew the balance on her bank account. She was obviously intending to sell her jewellery for a reason. Propenkov had been correct when he said he was sure she was up to something devious.

John finally spoke to his grandmother in New Orleans. He listened patiently as she told him about the various apartments she had looked at locally.

'I've not seen anything suitable yet. They're either in a run down area which has still not recovered from Hurricane Katrina or on a third or fourth floor. I don't want to be dependent upon an elevator in case it breaks down. It could be out of commission for weeks.'

'I'm sure you'll find somewhere suitable soon. I spoke to Uncle Andreas and asked him a question about the production we gave in Elounda. He told me I needed to ask you.'

'Me! I only passed the information on to him. He did all the compiling and writing.'

'It's the information that I'm asking about. Who told you about the soldiers who were shot and buried in the olive grove?'

'Goodness, I don't remember.'

'Is there any way you could find out? It could be quite important.'

'Is the family proposing to sue you for misinformation or defamation of character?'

'No, nothing like that and it may not be relevant.' John told her about the Italian who was trying to find out what had happened to his grandfather. 'Nick remembered that Monika had said the lines and I'd like to find out who told you. If some of the family are still alive they may be willing to talk about the incident now as it happened so long ago.'

'Well, I'll do my best. I'm not sure where my notes are. I've been so busy turning out that I may have thrown them away.'

'I do hope not, Grandma. I'm relying on you.'

'I'll start looking for them later and let you know if I find anything.'

Ronnie spent the day looking up kitchen equipment on the internet. She had taken the dimensions of the kitchen and hoped she would be able to arrange a large fridge freezer, the dish washer and a washing machine on the back wall and still leave sufficient space for a double sink to be placed beneath the window. No one wanted to look at a blank wall whilst they were using the sink.

She sketched out the plan and then concentrated on the return wall to the patio doors. That would be the ideal place for an oven, microwave and hob. There would be sufficient space on the worktop to remove dishes when they were cooked and also place the plates there. That would leave the rest of the room free to have a large centre island that could be used for preparation, serving or eating.

Bearing in mind Cathy's ideas regarding a colour scheme, once satisfied that the equipment she had selected would fit, Ronnie made three copies of her kitchen design. In one she shaded the equipment grey to represent brushed stainless steel, coloured a terracotta section as tiles on the wall beneath the window and above the cupboards and along the other wall before adding black granite worktops. She painted the cupboards that would fit above the worktop grey.

Having painted the cupboards grey Ronnie was not happy. It gave the room a heavy look. In her next attempt she left the equipment white, but she was still dissatisfied. Finally she made two more copies, using her original ideas for the stainless steel or white fitments and the terracotta tiles but leaving the cupboards as light natural wood and changing the black granite work top to grey. To her eyes having light wood cupboards was the answer. If Cathy was not happy she would just have to start again and have some other ideas.

When Kyriakos returned from the taverna that evening he looked at her designs critically and shook his head.

'Definitely not grey cupboards and drawers. I'm not sure if the terracotta tiling is right. I know terracotta goes well with grey but will it make the room look dark?'

'It is a very large room and light comes in from the window, the patio door and the lounge area.'

169

'But black granite will also make everywhere darker. What colour tiles do you envisage for the floor?'

'Cathy said terracotta.'

Kyriakos shook his head. 'If you have terracotta tiles on the floor and walls it will make the room look smaller. Why not have a look and see if you can get a floor tile that has a faint grey or fawn vein in it? You could then get the same wall tiles instead of the terracotta. I would then say that the area above the cupboards and the wall should be left painted white. Maybe Cathy would prefer to have white marble for the work tops.'

Ronnie shook her head. 'Marble is not practical. If something really hot or cold was placed on it the area could crack. Granite is far more hard wearing and amenable.' She looked at her designs again. 'I think you're right about having the wall and above the cupboards left white. Of course, we only discussed the kitchen. I don't know her ideas for the dining and lounge area. The colour she chooses will have to blend in, one complimenting the other.'

'I would say that the area should be white. She can then have whatever colour upholstery and curtains she wants to brighten it up.'

'Kyriakos, you are a genius. I'll show Cathy my sketches for the terracotta tiles and grey cupboards as she seemed to want that colour combination and then show her the others. You have a far more discerning eye than I have.'

Kyriakos shrugged. 'You are the artist. You know the colours to put together. I just look at it and say the colour scheme I would prefer to live with.'

'And you always come up with the correct solution. I still view it as a picture that I am painting to make it look as attractive as possible.'

'None of your sketches are unattractive, but although I have not seen inside the house I know which colour scheme would suit me, although Cathy and Vasilis may have other ideas.'

John waited impatiently for his grandmother to telephone him with the information he had requested. He was loath to keep calling her. If she became annoyed with his persistence she might just say she had thrown away the original papers and not bother to look any further. It could have been any one of a number of village women who had told her about the Italian soldiers.

'Will you tell Pietro?' asked Nicola.

John shook his head. 'No, I'll have to wait until Grandma contacts me and then talk to her informant. For all we know it could have happened miles away and is just a story that has been passed down through the villages.'

'It could take you weeks to find out.'

'I know,' sighed John. 'I'll ask Pietro for his address before he leaves and promise to write and tell him if I discover anything. I wouldn't want to get his hopes up.'

Ludmila was surprised when she received a short message from Svetlana on her mobile 'phone. "Come for coffee on Thursday morning."

Ludmila read the message a second time and then began to feel excited. Did this mean that Ivan was about to be released? She opened her safe and counted the money she had stored in there. It would not be sufficient. She would take all the cash along with the diamond brooch and hope Mother would be satisfied.

Elena searched through the brochures that had been sent to her describing apartments that were for sale in the vicinity. The ones that seemed most suitable were also grossly overpriced in her eyes. She drove past them and around the area and narrowed the choice down to three that she felt it could be worth her while to make an appointment and view. There was no rush for her to make a decision. She would not be placing her house on the market until she had received a decision from Helena and Greg. If she had not found anywhere suitable she could always reverse her decision and stay in her house indefinitely.

She still had plenty to keep her occupied. She had placed Matthew's medical books in a box and telephoned the local University asking if they would like to take them off her hands. They refused and said that as they were such old editions the information would be out of date.

'I realise that,' replied Elena. 'I thought the diagrams could be useful and although tremendous strides have been made in the field of medicine probably some aspects have remained the same.'

Finally, after considerable persuasion from Elena, they did offer to display their details on a notice board that was used by the students.

'I doubt that you'll get more than a couple of dollars for each one,' the secretary warned her.

'Money is not the reason why I am wanting to dispose of them,' replied Elena frostily. 'I am planning to move from the area. My late husband bought the books and if they can be of any use to the current medical students I would be only too pleased to give them away. If you would put my 'phone number on the notice and ask anyone interested to call me I'd be grateful.'

Elena continued to go through the notebooks, pamphlets and papers that were in Matthew's office. She tried to disassociate herself from the task. For years she had left the room untouched as if Matthew was going to return. If she began to think of the items as being personal to him she would never dispose of any of them. Although she had sent his clothes to a homeless charity years ago they had no sentimental attachment for her, but his stock of medical information that he had collected over the years seemed far more intimate.

Ludmila rang the bell at Svetlana's and was admitted to the room where Mother sat. She could hardly disguise her impatience.

Without any prior formalities Mother asked 'Have you brought some money?'

Ludmila nodded. 'I wasn't sure how much you would want. When will Ivan be released.'

'Ivan? This is not about Ivan. You asked me for a new passport.'

'Oh,' Ludmila felt totally deflated. 'Of course. I had hoped you had news of Ivan for me.'

'These things take time. Do you want the passport?'

'Of course.'

Mother handed her a brown envelope and she withdrew her new passport from it. The cover was worn as if by use and inside there were the dates she had entered and left Russia, Turkey and Syria. There was no mention of her entry and ignominious departure from Crete.

'Thank you, Mother. How much do I owe you?'

'Thirty eight thousand roubles.'

Ludmila gasped. She had not expected it to cost more than ten thousand. 'As much as that!'

'A considerable amount of work had to be done.'

'You used my old cover and photographic details.' she protested.

'Of course. I saved you money by being able to insert new pages rather than have to make a completely new document.'

'I haven't that amount of cash with me.'

Mother took the passport from Ludmila's hand. 'Come back when you can pay for it.'

'I have brought a diamond brooch with me. That should be worth more than thirty eight thousand roubles.'

Mother raised his eyebrows. 'Show me.'

Ludmila withdrew the box from inside her bag and opened it to show the brooch.

Mother looked at it suspiciously. 'Is it real?'

'Of course.' She placed it in his hand and he tested the weight and scrutinized the stones carefully.

'I believe you,' he said finally. 'I will accept the brooch in exchange for your passport.'

'It is worth more than thirty eight thousand. Evgeniy paid seventy five thousand.'

Mother raised his eyebrows. 'I'm sure he did, but it is second hand now. The value has halved. I will be lucky if I am able to sell it for thirty eight.'

Ludmila did not believe him, but she was in no position to argue. If she wanted the passport she must pay his price. She handed him the box so he could place the brooch safely inside and received her passport in exchange.

'When will Ivan be released?'

Mother shrugged. 'These things take time to arrange. You have to be patient. Svetlana will see you out.'

After Ludmila left Mother used a disposable 'phone to call an acquaintance.

'I have a job for you.' He outlined the plan he had formulated for Ivan's escape from the Detention Centre. 'Update me on progress and call me on this new number.' Having given the details he handed the 'phone he had been using to Svetlana 'Destroy it,' he ordered.

Zavinalov reported on the visit to Groshenkov. 'She has paid a further visit to Svetlana's apartment but stayed only a short while.'

Groshenkov had received the same information from Borovich. He consulted the file he had on the Asimenikov couple. According to his information they were father and daughter and the man never left the apartment. He spent most of his time making telephone calls, using throw away 'phones that Svetlana purchased regularly from the supermarket. When he tried to have the calls traced he was only able to ascertain the area where they had been received and not the recipient. That in itself was suspicious.

Elena sat and thought. She had returned from Crete with her brother and they had spent some time in New York. She had not fully unpacked whilst she was there so the notes should still be amongst her belongings. Upon returning to New Orleans she had emptied her case and either washed her clothes or sent them to the dry cleaners. The notes John wanted would not have been amongst them so they could not have been washed or thrown away. She had no recollection of putting them anywhere for safe keeping. She had told Andreas all the relevant information she had gathered and he had incorporated it into his play. She racked her brains – had she left the papers with him in New York in case he needed to refer back to them? She did not remember doing so. Surely she had not thrown them away whilst she had been turning out the house? She had kept the letters Marianne had written to her father, but thrown away the Christmas and birthday cards that only had a brief, conventional message inside. Had the notes become mixed in with those and sent off with the garbage?

Elena spent a disturbed night turning the problem over in her mind. It was obviously important to John that he should know who had given her the information and could be even more important to the Italian who was searching for his grandfather. She tried to conjure up the faces of the various elderly ladies she had talked to about their memories, hoping that would help her recall who had given her the information, but nothing was forthcoming.

When Elena woke late, having finally fallen asleep in the early hours, her first thought was of the notes she had made. She showered, dressed, ate her breakfast and made her bed, trying to empty her mind whilst she went through the mundane daily routine. She must forget about them and then the whereabouts of their location would come to her.

To Elena's annoyance Helena arrived unannounced and sat down in the kitchen.

'What are you doing today, Mother?'

'The same as I have been doing most days, sorting out my belongings and deciding what I would like to take with me.'

'Where are you going?'

'I don't know yet. I have three apartments to look at that seem quite attractive.'

'Well, let us know when you have decided. Greg has agreed that we purchase the house from you so we need to get the formalities sorted out as quickly as possible. We have a prospective buyer for our house.'

'If I am unable to find anywhere suitable I will stay here indefinitely. I will not be rushed out of my home to suit your convenience even if you have a prospective buyer. I suggest you wait until I tell you I have made a decision about an apartment and can give you a moving date. Then will be the time for you to put your house on the market and I'm sure you'll have no trouble selling.'

'The current prospective purchaser has offered us a good price. We want to accept it.'

'Then do so, but be prepared to stay in a hotel or rented apartment until I have decided where or when I will be moving.'

'Mamma, that is most unreasonable,' protested Helena.

Elena shook her head. 'I am not the person being unreasonable. I could have put my house on the open market and I would have probably sold it for considerably more than I am asking you and Greg to pay. The choice is yours; you either wait until I am ready to move or you withdraw your offer to me. It will be up to you if you wish to sell your house and move elsewhere.'

'But we want to live here, in this house,' wailed Helena.

'Then you will just have to be patient,' replied Elena firmly.

'Couldn't we have a more reasonable discussion over a cup of coffee?'

Elena looked at her watch. 'I really need to get on. I have an appointment to view the apartments I am interested in. If one of them suits me I will let you know.'

'You never used to be like this. Marianne must have influenced you when you were in Elounda.'

Elena shook her head. 'It was nothing to do with Marianne. It was the women that I talked to about their war time experiences. Hearing how they had stood up to the invading Germans and Italians made me feel embarrassed that I was so weak willed. I determined that in future I would do as I pleased, no matter who I upset or offended.'

'Well you've certainly managed to upset and offend me.' Helena stood up. 'Call me when you have any positive news for me. Of course, by then, Greg and I may have changed our minds.'

Elena shrugged. 'That will be up to you.'

Helena glared at her mother and picked up her bag. 'I can see myself out.'

Elena sat back with a sigh as she heard the front door close behind her daughter. She felt so aggrieved that she was tempted to call Greg and say that she had withdrawn her offer and was going to put the house on the open market and if they wanted it they would have to negotiate with anyone else who was interested.

She made another cup of coffee and sat trying to relax. Helena always had the effect of unsettling and stressing her. Maybe she was being unreasonable. She would call Marianne and ask her opinion.

Marianne listened sympathetically to her mother. 'You did quite right, Mamma. Helena was just trying to bully you. Take your time making a decision.'

'I do feel a bit guilty. Maybe I should not have mentioned the house to her and Greg until I had somewhere to go.'

'You can always come over here and stay with us, you know that. I'm sure Uncle Andreas would allow you to live in his little house if you wanted a bit of peace away from everyone here.'

Elena gave a deep sigh. 'Thank you, Marianne, but I'm sure that won't be necessary. I just wish I could find my original notes from when I was talking to the ladies in the villages. John was asking who told me about the burials during the war.'

'I'm sure you'll find them. Whether they will be of any help to the Italian man I don't know.'

'They must be somewhere. I know I haven't thrown them away.'

177

'Did you leave them in your suitcase? You may have left them there so they were at hand if Uncle Andreas asked you to go up to New York.'

'My suitcase! Of course. Thank you, Marianne. That would have been the last place I would have looked.'

'Go and see if they're there and stop worrying about Helena. If she dares to 'phone me and complain I'll tell her exactly what I think about her badgering you.'

Elena was suddenly anxious to end the 'phone call and check her suitcase. 'If I find them I'll call John.'

'I won't tell him. I wouldn't want to get his hopes up.'

May 2016
Week One – Thursday and Friday

Cathy looked at the sketches Ronnie had prepared of the kitchen area and nodded. 'I like the lay out. It's practical and everything is within reach for me.'

'What about the cupboards? They can't all be low level, you'd never have sufficient storage space.'

'I can arrange them so that the items that I use frequently are on the lower shelves. Vasilis can always reach things down from higher up. I plan to have a storage cupboard in the dining area for the decent dinner service and glasses. Vasilis and I usually use the same ones when we eat alone. The cupboards that I do need to be able to reach will be the ones with my packets and jars of ingredients that I need for cooking each day along with the saucepans.'

Ronnie nodded. 'In that case I suggest that there is a cupboard at the end of the worktop by the sink. It can have all your cooking ingredients in there. Beneath the worktop you can have a drawer for all the cutlery and beneath that you can keep your saucepans.'

'That should work well. I won't need all these other cupboards around.'

'I think you should keep them in mind. Once you have actually moved in and start to use the kitchen you will probably find that you need more storage space. They can always be put in situ later. You need to decide whether you want white fitments or brushed stainless steel. You could have coloured ones, of course.'

Cathy shook her head. 'I've decided white would be preferable. They are easy enough to keep clean. The brushed ones often show finger marks every time you open the door and they have to be polished out. I've also noticed that if the sun shines directly on them it can be quite blinding. If the finish is white you only need a damp cloth to remove any marks.'

'That brings me to my next question. Are you set on having the terracotta and grey for the walls and cupboards?'

Cathy hesitated. 'Have you thought of something you think would be more suitable?'

'Well, I did a sketch with terracotta tiles over the sink area and grey cupboards, but when I showed Kyriakos he said he thought that would make the room look dark, particularly if you had black granite worktops.' Ronnie passed the coloured sketch across to Cathy.

'I like it and I don't think it would make it look dark, but it might make it look a bit gloomy, particularly in the winter.'

'Do you still want terracotta floor tiles?' asked Ronnie.

'I think so and have them just above the sink area as well, but not on the other walls.'

Ronnie smiled. 'Kyriakos suggested that you had floor tiles that had some fawn or grey in them. You could then follow that colour scheme through to the tiles above the sink. Look, I produced this after I had spoken with him.'

Cathy looked at the sketch and compared it with the previous ones. 'Oh, yes, I really like that. It makes the whole area look brighter. Leaving the cupboards as light wood stops them from looking too heavy. If I had white tiles with some grey in them over the sink I'm sure I could find some tiles near enough the same for the floor and have a grey granite worktop rather than black. What do you think?'

Ronnie shook her head. 'I'm not sure. Everywhere may begin to look a bit grey again then whereas the black will break it up, but it's your kitchen and it must be the way you want it.'

'I'll talk to Vasilis this evening and ask his opinion.'

'Have you thought about the décor for the rest of the house?'

'Not really. I think the lounge and dining area should be white then we can add whatever colour we fancy in the way of furnishings and curtains. I'm rather fond of my bedroom and bathroom here and would be happy to repeat the turquoise wall and tiles.'

Pietro sat with John beneath an umbrella outside the taverna. 'I've written down my address for you and how I can be contacted should you find out anything that you think might be relevant. I know I have to return to Italy tomorrow morning and in all honesty I don't think there would be any point in me staying any longer. I've visited every churchyard and cemetery in the vicinity and not found out anything at all.'

'You're absolutely certain that your grandfather was stationed in Aghios Nikolaos?'

Pietro nodded. 'In the last letter my grandmother received he described the town. I know it will have changed drastically by now, but he mentioned the lake and said he had walked down there when he was not on duty.'

'After sending that letter he may have been transferred elsewhere,' John reminded the Italian.

Pietro sighed. 'I know, but I had to start somewhere. People cannot just disappear off the face of the earth.'

'This may sound rather hard hearted and unfeeling of me, but he could have been blown to bits and his body unrecognisable.'

'Of course, but you also say there were no full scale battles down in this area. If two soldiers had been sent out on patrol together and they had been blown up their Commanding Officer should have known the vicinity where it happened and be able to name them and record the manner of their death.'

'I still think it most likely that the soldiers met with an accident and due to a rock fall they were never found or they could have been considered deserters and not worth bothering about.'

181

'That doesn't explain the disappearance of my father.'

'The same accident could have befallen him,' suggested John.

Pietro eyed John sceptically and shook his head. 'That would be too much of a coincidence. Have you managed to speak to the doctor that you know?'

'Not yet. We've been short staffed at the apartments due to my uncle's illness. I need to have time to talk to the doctor and persuade him to give me access to the archived records. They may not even be here; they could be in Heraklion or Athens. Even if they are available I'll have to search through all of them for the relevant year and that could take hours.'

'I'm very grateful for the help you have given me. If you do find out anything from the medical records please let me know.'

'Of course. Any relevant information that I discover I will impart to you.'

Pietro shook John's hand. 'I would appreciate that and I hope we will be able to meet again. I'll settle my bill now, if that is convenient, as I have to make an early start tomorrow. I am not able to be absent from my work any longer.'

John listened carefully to his grandmother as she read through her notes to him. 'I'm almost certain it was Evi who told me. She arrived whilst I was talking to Maria and they became involved in an argument about who did what, each trying to take the credit. Finally Evi went back to her house in a huff. When I left Maria Evi called me over and said she knew far more than Maria as she was two years older. I don't know if that is true.'

John was about to comment that their ages were irrelevant when his grandmother continued. 'Now I cast my mind back I can hear Evi talking. She lowered her voice and I had to bend down close to her. She said that as the soldiers were seen coming over the hill the woman told her daughter to hide. She took her father's hunting rifle from beneath the bed. She may have been trying to frighten them off, but she hit one and he fell down. His companion bent down to help him and she shot him also. He drew his gun and pointed it at her so she shot him again. When neither of them moved the enormity of the situation dawned on her. She called her daughter and they went out into their olive grove and dug a pit large enough to put both the bodies in. When the soldiers came looking for their lost men she denied ever having seen them.'

'Grandma, how would Evi know so much? I'm sure the woman who committed the crime did not go around boasting about it.'

'I'm only repeating what she told me. You'd have to ask her.'

'Do you think Maria knows any more about it?'

'She never mentioned it to me. It may have happened miles away and a rumour circulated and Evi embellished the facts.'

'That's possible. Thank you, Grandma. At least you've given me somewhere to start. I'll have to talk to Evi and see if she has any further information.'

John repeated the conversation he had had with his grandmother to Nicola. 'From what Grandma said Evi appears to know a good deal about the incident. We could arrange to go up and speak to her tomorrow. There's no airport run. Bryony will be at the house all day with Marcus. Provided Dad is willing to be up at the taverna for an hour or two I'm sure Mum won't mind looking after Yiannis.'

'Why do you need me with you?'

'From what Grandma and Uncle Andreas said the women were more willing to talk to a woman rather than a man. We can take some biscuits with us and call on Maria as well so that she doesn't feel left out.'

'And if Evi confirms that the event was local what do you plan to do? You can't go around digging up everyone's olive groves.'

John grinned. 'I have a metal detector, remember. If the story is true the women may have taken their boots and guns, but it's highly unlikely that they would have undressed the soldiers before they buried them. Their uniforms would have had metal buttons and they should also have been wearing dog tags. If Evi can give me a rough location I can run the detector over the ground and see if it indicates that there is any metal below.'

'I still don't think the owners will be very pleased if you dig holes all over their land.'

'I'll fill them in afterwards. They'll not know I've been there.'

'Suppose you do find some uniform buttons what do you plan to do then?'

'I suppose I'll have to confess that I've been metal detecting and ask the police to investigate.'

'You won't try to dig the bodies up yourself?'

'Certainly not. I may dig around a bit to see if I can find more evidence to take to the police, but I doubt if there's anything left of them except bones by now.'

'We'll have to approach Evi carefully. What are you planning to say?'

'I'm going to say that we're helping Uncle Andreas with research for the film that's in the pipeline about war time Crete.'

'John! That's an outright lie.'

'Well,' John shrugged, 'I'll dress it up a bit, say it's background information that his publisher is asking for.'

'That's better, but it's still not the truth. If you do find anything and it becomes public knowledge Evi will know we lied to her.'

'Can you come up with anything better?'

Nicola frowned. 'I'll think about it.'

'So have you come up with any idea how we can ask Evi for the truth?' asked John as they drove up the hill towards Pano Elounda.

'Leave it to me. We'll make some small talk and then I'll broach the subject. If she clams up we could then try asking Maria if she knows anything.'

Leaving the car in the car park Nicola and John climbed the steep hill to where the road led to Pano Elounda.

'I'm sure it would have been quicker if we had parked below

Mavrikiano and walked through,' remarked Nicola.

'I doubt if there is much difference. Whichever way you go to these villages you always have a steep climb. There are some superb views from up here, but I'd far rather be down on the coast.'

'Imagine having to climb this hill every day in all weathers if you worked down in Elounda.' Nicola wiped her face. 'I'm dripping and we're only half way there.'

'They were probably used to it having done it since they were children. I do wonder if Uncle Andreas will continue to live at Kato Elounda. He's not getting any younger. Have you thought how you will ask Evi for information?'

'I think so. I'm going to say Uncle Andreas needs the information.'

'That was what I was going to say and you said I would be lying,' protested John.

'My lie will not be as blatant as yours and will basically be the truth.'

Evi was sitting outside when they reached Pano Elounda and waved to them. 'I haven't seen you for a while. Go and get some chairs from the front room and come and sit beside me. You can tell me all your news.'

'We haven't really got any news,' smiled Nicola. 'We've been rather busy as our uncle has not been well.'

'What? The old one?'

'No, Uncle Yannis appears to be fit enough. He's busy selling his pots. John thought of the idea of holding an exhibition in the garden area of the house. John's father was not best pleased with the idea, but his mother was delighted. There are pots stored everywhere in the house and she would love to be rid of them.'

John placed the chairs on the uneven paving in front of Evi's house. 'So how have you been, Evi? Keeping well and not finding it too hot?'

'I don't sit out when it's hot. I go inside where it's cool. That's the beauty of these old houses. They keep the heat out in the summer and the heat in during the winter. No need for any of your machines that need electricity.'

'You have got electricity, haven't you?' asked Nicola anxiously.

'I have electric for the light when it gets dark and my television. That's all I need.'

'We've all been spoilt,' agreed Nicola. 'We use electricity to cook by, do our washing, run our computers and watch television.'

'Not much of interest on the television. It all seems to be for young people or sporting events. I only put it on so I hear the voices and see people. It's a bit of company.'

'So how do you amuse yourself otherwise?'

'I sit with my neighbours sometimes.'

'You don't read?'

'Only a newspaper occasionally. Not much in there to interest me either.'

'I couldn't imagine not reading,' smiled Nicola. 'You remember our Uncle Andreas who wrote the Christmas performance? He's talking to his publisher in America about turning it into a book about life in war time Crete. You told him that a woman had shot some soldiers and she and her daughter buried them in the olive grove. He's a stickler for accuracy and wants to know if that happened here or in another village.'

'Here, of course. How else would I know about it?'

'Whereabouts?'

Evi waved her hand in the general direction if Elounda. 'In those days Despina's olive trees went right down to the coast.'

Nicola frowned. 'I can't think of anywhere that olive trees go down to the shore.'

'They went down to the path that leads to the Causeway. Despina was an only child so when her father and mother died all the land was inherited by her. She's been dead for years now. She and her daughter were regarded locally as Resistance heroines at the time.'

'Do the family still own the olive grove?'

Evi shrugged. 'As far as I know it still belongs to them.'

'Whereabouts do they live? In Elounda?'

'The younger ones may have moved down there for convenience.'

'So after Despina died who inherited the olive grove? Did she have a son?' asked Nicola.

'Only a daughter. Despina's husband didn't return after the war so the land eventually went to Adonia.'

'And she married and had a family?'

'Adonia married after the war ended, but the man was a waster. The olive grove provided a good income, enough for all of them to live comfortably on, but he gambled. His mother in law finally gave him a strip of land down by the seafront where she paid for them to have a house built. She hoped that having a home of his own would make him more responsible. He ran up debts and wanted her to sell more land, but she refused. It led to arguments between them and finally he left. Sold the house he had been given and went to Heraklion and didn't bother about his wife and daughter. Adonia and Despina went back to live with her mother.'

'I'm becoming really confused,' smiled Nicola. 'Despina was still alive and when Adonia had a daughter she was called Despina after her grandmother.'

'That's right; Despina Maria and her daughter was called Adonia Evangelina.'

'What about their husbands?'

'Despina Maria's husband was ill and died just a few years after they were married. Adonia Evangelina's husband was killed in a traffic accident. Their daughter was just a babe at the time.'

'How sad. The whole family appears to have suffered tragedies over the years. Was their daughter also called Despina?'

'Eleni Despina.'

'Is she married with children?'

'I don't know. I haven't seen any of them for years.'

'You were friends?'

'Of course. Despina was my husband's aunt. I used to visit the family occasionally when I went down to Elounda, but they aren't inclined to come up here to see me. They probably think I'm dead by now.'

'That's sad. If you tell us exactly where they are I'd be willing to call on them and offer to bring them up to visit you.'

Evi shook her head. 'Things are best left as they are. I have nothing to say to them. Are those biscuits for me?' She reached out her hand and grasped them firmly. 'I'd appreciate you taking the chairs back inside for me. The sun is coming round and I won't be able to sit out any longer.'

John rose promptly and carried his chair back inside and returned for Nicola's. 'Would you like me to carry yours inside also, Evi?'

'Of course. No point in having a strong man around if you can't make use of him. I can manage my biscuits. I see you have another pack. Are they for me as well?'

'No,' smiled Nicola. 'We are going to call on Maria. We can't visit one of you without seeing the other and she would be hurt if we gave you biscuits and did not have any for her.'

Evi sniffed. 'I hope she appreciates them.'

John squeezed Nicola's hand as they walked away from Evi's small house. 'You did really well, Nick. You managed to get so much information from her.'

'I hope you were taking note of the names. I was getting completely lost with the relationships.'

'I'll write them down as soon as we get back home. We can always come back and check them with Evi.'

'We're really no further forward about the site of the olive grove.' Nicola shook her head in disappointment.

'I think we are. We know the olive grove stretched down to the Causeway. We'll drive around on the way home and see where there are still olive trees growing on the hill. I've never taken much notice of them as there are olive trees all over the place.'

John drove back down to Elounda and up the hill towards Aghios Nikolaos, drawing into a parking place that had been designed for visitors to take photographs of the view.

'There are olive trees up there on the hill, but there are houses and apartments built up there also. Some of them have olive trees bordering their driveways,' observed Nicola as she squinted up at the hill.

'Another day we could drive up some of them and see if we can find the house where the Despina relatives live.'

'What excuse can we make for being there?' asked Nicola.

'We can say we've visited Evi and she asked to be remembered to them. What about down the hill from the road and along the Causeway? There seem to be a few olive trees around.'

'They probably belong to whoever owns the property.'

John nodded. 'But who did they belong to before the land was built on? That could have been some of the land that was sold by the gambler.'

'Where could we find out?' asked Nicola.

'We could conduct a land search at the Town Hall in Aghios Nikolaos, but that could be time consuming and probably wouldn't show where the trees actually were, only the area of the land that was sold off.'

'They may not have kept any records at that time if it was a private transaction unlike the government purchasing the land to build the road.'

'So have you got a better idea?'

Nicola nodded. 'We ask the occupants of the properties down by the Causeway who they purchased the land from.'

John pursed his lips. 'We could try, but I expect some of them have been sold on since they were originally built.'

'Those records should be available.'

'Even if we can obtain that information we might not be able to track down the original purchasers. They could be anywhere now.'

'Don't be so pessimistic. We start by asking Vasilis. He bought the land down there to build his hotel and he bought that other plot of land to build his new house. He has to know who the original owners were.'

John turned to Nicola with a delighted smile. 'Brilliant! Why didn't I think of that?'

'Because women have a more logical mind than men. Come on, we can't stand here admiring the view. We said we'd only be gone about an hour and it's nearer two.'

'I'll call Mum and say that we are going to pay a quick visit to Vasilis and ask if she wants us to pick anything up from the village.'

Vasilis looked surprised to see John and Nicola when they knocked at the door of the apartment in Elounda.

'What brings you down here? Nothing wrong, is there?'

'Nothing at all. We would like to ask you a few questions if you have the time. As we were passing we thought it would be easier to ask you in person rather than over the 'phone.'

'Come on in. I'm sure Cathy will be delighted to see you. I expect she will want your opinion on the décor for her new house.'

Cathy looked out from the kitchen area and smiled. 'Lovely to see you both. Have you brought Yiannis?'

'No, we had some chores to do and Mum agreed to look after him for a while.'

'Well, sit yourselves down. What would you like? Coffee, beer or some fresh lemonade,?'

'I'd like a beer' agreed John and Vasilis nodded.

'Lemonade for me, please, Cathy.'

Vasilis walked into the kitchen and collected the beer from the fridge, returning to bring in some glasses and a jug of lemonade whilst Cathy followed with a plate of biscuits.

'I made these this morning. It's a new recipe I've tried so tell me what you think.'

Nicola bit into one and nodded. 'They're lovely. You'll have to give me the recipe for Marianne.'

'They're very easy. Just your basic biscuit mix and then I added orange and lemon juice. I grated a bit of the rind and added that.'

'That is what makes all the difference.'

Cathy smiled with pleasure. 'I'll give you some to take back with you and Marianne can give her opinion.'

'I don't want to rob you of your stock.'

Cathy shrugged. 'I can easily make some more. I have nothing else to do this afternoon except look for floor tiles on the internet.'

'For your new house?'

'Ronnie has drawn up some designs for me. The layout is perfect, but I need to decide on the tiles. Would you like to have a look?'

'Of course. I'll leave John and Vasilis to talk. They don't need me.'

'So what did you want to ask me?' asked Vasilis.

'It's about land purchase.'

'Are you thinking of buying some?'

John shook his head. 'I couldn't possibly afford to buy any. Three children to clothe and feed take more than enough money. I wanted to ask the name of the person you purchased the land from to build your hotel.'

'It was already built when I bought it. Only a small place, but there was plenty of land available so I could expand.'

'Who owned it originally?'

'I'm not sure. It was years ago. I'd have to look up the purchase agreement.'

'Do you have that here?'

Vasilis shook his head. 'My lawyer holds all my legal documents. I can ask him to send me a copy if it's important.'

'I'm trying to track down who owned the olive groves during the war. I understand they stretched all down the hillside as far as the pathway to the Causeway.'

'A number of people owned them I believe. When the price

191

of land along there rose they decided that they could make more money from property than olives.'

'Who owned the land you bought to build your new house?'

'Mr Lucanakis.'

'Does he also own the plot of land next to you?'

'No, I'm planning to find out who does own it. It's been used as a rubbish tip for years and is a perfect eyesore. I'd like either to get them to clear it up or let me buy it so that I can make it look respectable.'

'Wouldn't Mr Lucanakis know?'

'Possibly, but he has gone to Australia to visit relatives and I have no way of contacting him.'

'I'll just have to ask around then. It's possible Uncle Yannis might know.'

'What's your interest in it?' asked Vasilis.

'Just something I'm looking into for an acquaintance. I'd rather not tell you the details at present.'

Vasilis raised his eyebrows. 'Meaning?'

'That I'm planning to do something that could be classed as illegal by the landowners and I could be prosecuted. As your neighbour is a policeman it's better that you have no knowledge of my activities.'

'I wouldn't tell him your plans,' Vasilis assured John.

'I'm sure you wouldn't, but you could be accused at a later date of withholding information. I'll only ask you to contact your lawyer and ask who owned the land originally where your hotel is built. If I find out what I'm looking for I'll tell you and I may need to speak with Panayiotis and ask his advice.'

John sat at the table and waved his Uncle away as he approached. 'I'm a bit busy at the moment, Uncle Yannis.'

'This is important.' Yannis ignored him and sat down in the chair opposite. 'You'll have to go to Rethymnon tomorrow.'

John raised his eyebrows. He was obviously not going to be

able to continue with writing out the details of Despina's relatives whilst he remembered their names until he had dealt with his uncle.

'Why do I have to do that, Uncle Yannis?'

'I've sold three Attic Ware vases to the museum shop there. They want them as quickly as possible.'

'I'll have to check with Dad. I may have to do an airport run and someone will be needed at the taverna whilst I'm gone.'

'If you have to go to the airport you could go to the museum first.'

John shook his head. 'That would depend upon the flight times. I couldn't expect the museum to be open before ten and it will take me near enough an hour to drive there from Heraklion and the same coming back. By the time I have delivered them and returned to the airport it will be nearly mid-day. If visitors are arriving at eleven I can't expect them to hang around at the airport for an hour or so.'

'Then you'll have to do a special trip. I don't want to lose the sale just because it's inconvenient for you to deliver them.'

John sighed. 'I'll speak to Dad. You get the pots packed up ready and I'll let you know when I can take them.'

'I'll need you to help me.'

'Me? Why?'

'They are in one of the boxes stacked in the spare room, but there are some other boxes in front of them and I can't move those. They're too heavy and you told me I was not to ask Marcus to do anything more than sit at the table to give me a break.'

'I'll help you get them out tomorrow.'

'I need them now. They have to be properly packed and if you can go up tomorrow morning they need to be ready for when you leave.'

'Can I finish what I'm doing and then I'll help you.'

Yannis nodded and continued to sit at the table, drumming his fingers impatiently. John placed his pen to one side.

'Alright, I'll come now. I can't concentrate with you sitting there banging away. It doesn't mean that I'll be delivering them tomorrow. I'll still need to speak to Dad.'

Having satisfied his uncle's request John returned to writing down the names of people Evi had given to him and Nicola. He should have asked for the family name of the younger members; it would have made them easier to trace. When he and Nicola had put their children to bed he would sit down with her and ask her to check if he had recorded the names correctly.

Nicola read the list with a frown on her face. 'This doesn't help an awful lot, John.'

'Why not? I'm sure I have their names correct.'

'We don't know how old any of them were or are now. If old Despina shot the soldiers in 1942 how old was her daughter at that time? She can't have been a child or she wouldn't have been able to help her mother dig the grave.'

'Alright, let's say that her daughter was twenty. According to Evi, Despina was widowed in the war and her daughter, Adonia had been deserted by her husband. Unless the daughter, Adonia, married again she must have already had a child. The girl was another Despina. We give her another twenty years and that takes us to 1962.'

'Why are you assuming they all had their children when they were twenty?' asked Nicola.

'Because I have no idea how old they were. They probably didn't know for sure as accurate records of the population only started after the war. Even then it was a bit haphazard. If a farmer had a child in the winter months he would not have made the journey to town until the spring. By then it would be doubtful if he remembered the exact date. Adonia's husband died but they already had a daughter, Despina Eleni. We need to find out if she married and has any children.

Nicola was writing down the names and dates on her own sheet of paper.

'How does this look?' she asked as she passed the page to her husband.

1920	Despina inherited olive grove married – has daughter – widowed in war
1942	Despina and soldiers now aged 40 ? Daughter Adonia – 20 ? married gambler – deserted by husband
1944	Adonia had daughter Despina Maria now aged 92 Alive?
1962	Despina Maria had daughter Evangelina Adonia – husband died. Now aged 74. Alive?
1982	Evangelina Adonia – husband killed – now aged 54 Daughter Despina Eleni born in 1980 Despina Eleni now aged (36) – married ?

'If that time line is correct and we work on your assumption of twenty years between each generation then Despina Eleni should be about thirty six now and her mother in her mid fifties. It's quite likely that Despina Maria is still alive. She would only be in her seventies. If the family still live locally they must be known. Did you ask Uncle Yannis? I saw you talking to him earlier.'

'He only wanted to talk about a pottery delivery to Rethymnon. Insisted I moved some boxes so he could get to the ones he wanted and then disappeared off to pack them up. We can ask Uncle Yannis and Grandma Marisa tomorrow if they know of the family.'

'I have had another idea,' continued Nicola. 'If the olive groves originally stretched down the hill to the coast some of them must have been cleared to make way for the road. There should be a record of the negotiations and the name of the land owner. Where would they be held?'

'Probably the Town Hall in Aghios.'

'Couldn't we ask them to do a search?'

'We could try, but I'd rather try to contact the family first. It could save us a visit to the town and a considerable amount of time.'

May 2016
Weeks Two and Three

Ludmila was feeling depressed. She had visited Oleg and he had given her six thousand roubles for the bedding and towels he had sold on her behalf. She was convinced that he would have sold them for three times that amount. She had taken specimens of her china to the second hand shops and asked if they would purchase the whole dinner service from her and how much they would pay.

Three of them had said they would only pay her if the dinner service sold and two others offered a price that she immediately refused. That left only her jewellery that she could raise money on. She trailed around the jewellers with the emerald necklace and asked them for a valuation. The quote was reasonable but when she asked how much they would buy the necklace for the price dropped dramatically and she refused to accept it. Although she knew that Mother would not pay her the full value she decided that any offer he made would be offset against the cost of arranging for Ivan to be released and returned to Moscow.

Mr Zavinalov reported to Mr Groshenkov that Ludmila had been visiting money exchange bureaus regularly.

'On one occasion Lenishkova was able to stand close enough to see that she was changing American dollars into roubles. Surely it would be easier for her to pay them into the bank and she would not lose money on the transaction?'

'The bank would want proof that she was legally entitled to the money. I doubt if the dollars were honestly come by, but there is no reason why she shouldn't change a small amount into Russian currency at a bureau. Anything else of importance?'

'She visited the market and one of the traders there gave her some money. I don't know how much and she did not seem particularly pleased. She has also been to various second hand shops and a number of different jewellers.'

Mr Groshenkov raised his eyebrows. 'I am intrigued by these visits. According to the information I have from the bank she has sufficient money to live on. Why is she trying to raise more capital?'

Mr Zavinalov shrugged. 'Maybe she is trying to get the value of her jewellery decreased so she has to pay less insurance money.'

Mr Groshenkov nodded. 'It's possible, but I'm convinced she has some underhand scheme in mind.'

The crash that Marianne heard sent her running from the kitchen into the hallway. Bryony was sitting on the floor surrounded by broken crockery.

'Goodness, what's happened? Are you alright?'

Bryony looked at her and gave a weak smile. 'I think so. I was collecting the breakfast trays from Marisa and Yannis and turned my ankle. I'm sorry, I've made an awful mess.'

'That can be cleared up.'

Marisa opened the door of her room and looked out. 'What's going on?'

'Bryony dropped the trays she was carrying. Nothing to worry about. You go back in and get dressed.'

Marianne began to collect up the pieces of broken china and place them on the tray as Bryony struggled to get to her feet, wincing with pain.

'I think I've twisted my ankle.'

'Stay where you are. I'll clear this up and ask Giovanni to come and help you to stand.'

Giovanni placed his hands beneath Bryony's shoulders and helped her to her feet. As she tried to place her weight on her foot she gave a groan and her face went white.

'I think I'm going to faint,' she muttered.

Giovanni allowed her to slide gently back down onto the floor. 'Put your head between your legs. When you feel better I'll help you up again.'

'I'll get a chair. I think you've done more than just twist your ankle.'

With Giovanni's help Bryony managed to stand and sit down in the chair that Marianne pushed beneath her. 'Let me have a look.'

Bryony's ankle was already swelling and Marianne touched it gently. 'Where does it hurt?'

'There mostly.' Bryony leaned down and pointed to the area just below her ankle bone.

Marianne nodded. 'You're not to move and I'll fetch you a cold compress. If there's no improvement in half an hour Giovanni will take you into the hospital in Aghios for an X-ray. Is Marcus up yet?'

'He was in the shower when I came down so he should be dressed by now.'

'I'll go and ask him to come down and sit with you. I'll get the cold compress first.'

Bryony let out a yelp of pain as Marianne placed her foot on a cushion and laid the bag of ice on top. 'Apart from the pain how are you feeling?'

'A bit shaky, but I don't feel faint any longer.'

Giovanni looked at his watch. 'I can't take Bryony to Aghios. I'm meeting guests at the airport in just over an hour.'

'Then I'll take her. Marcus can come with us and stay there if she's going to be any length of time. He can call me to collect her. I'll ask Nicola to take any 'phone calls and keep an eye on Uncle Yannis and Marisa whilst I'm gone.'

'She has to take the girls to school,' protested Bryony. 'I'm sure I'll be better in no time.'

Marianne shook her head. 'You are not to move for the next half an hour. I'll tell Nicola and I'll look after Yiannis whilst she takes the girls. If your ankle is still swelling and hurting when she gets back then you are certainly going to go for an X-ray.'

'I'm being such a nuisance.' Bryony's eyes filled with tears. Her ankle was so painful.

'Not at all. Accidents happen. I'm going to ask Marcus to come down now.' Marianne went into the spare bedroom and returned with a wheelchair. 'If you can sit in this I'll wheel you through to the kitchen. You don't want to be sitting in the hallway.'

The X-ray confirmed that Bryony had broken her ankle and once her leg was encased in plaster up to her knee Marcus phoned Marianne.

'She mustn't put her foot to the ground for twenty four hours to let the plaster set. I'm sure I can get a taxi. There's no need for you to drive over.'

'Don't be silly, Marcus. You have the wheelchair there that she arrived in so I'll meet you at the front entrance in about twenty minutes. I'll tell Nicola that I'm leaving now.' Before Marcus could protest Marianne closed her mobile.

Marianne discussed the current situation with Giovanni when he returned from the airport run. 'We can manage provided both you and John don't have to go to the airport on the same day. If that happens then I'll have to go up to the taverna and have to rely on Nicola to deal with whatever happens here. She can always call me if there is a problem. Once Bryony has recovered a little she can always sit in the kitchen and prepare vegetables whilst I spend time on the computer and do the cooking.'

'What about Marcus? He claims he's feeling considerably better. Can't he help?'

'He's been told that he mustn't get over tired. He can relieve Uncle Yannis as necessary and do a few other odd jobs. He'll have to help get Bryony up and down the stairs if you and John are not around. She's far too heavy for Nicola and I to manage. At the moment she's concerned about letting Saffie down by not being able to go to the shop.'

Giovanni grunted. 'In that case Saffron will just have to manage without her. She did in the past.'

'True, but you have come to rely on Marcus to do odd jobs and an occasional airport run. Now you can't do that you're working far longer hours. You know how tired you are in the evenings. I'm sure Saffie has her life arranged so she can cater for Vasi and spend some time with him rather than being at the shop until late each evening.'

'Bryony should be able to walk on her ankle now it is in plaster. She'll only be inconvenienced for a few weeks.'

'It will be at least six weeks before Bryony's plaster is removed and we don't know how strong her ankle will be then. We will be going into the height of the season. You know how hectic it can be; airport runs often twice a day and the visits to Cash and Carry; also Angelo and Francesca are coming to stay and we'll have to spend some time with them.'

Giovanni frowned. 'They're coming to see our mother. They can always hire a car and go out and about. They don't need us to amuse them. I'm sure that once Bryony has got over the shock and becomes adept at manoeuvring around with her leg in plaster she'll be able to go to Saffie's shop. She can sit down up there most of the time. If both John and I have to do airport runs Marcus should be able to look after the taverna and shop for a couple of hours if it's still impossible for Bryony to cope. He could probably deal with the Cash and Carry in June as well as relieving Uncle Yannis for an hour or so.'

Marianne sighed. When Giovanni was in a belligerent mood there was no reasoning with him. 'We'll see how it goes. No point in worrying about it at the moment.'

'Well,' sighed John, 'That puts our plans on hold for a while now Bryony is out of action.'

'She didn't hurt her ankle on purpose,' remonstrated Nicola.

'I know that and I am truly sorry for her. It's just that we cannot expect Mum to look after Yiannis and the taverna whilst we go off hunting down land owners.'

'They'll still be there later. We could try looking on the internet to see if we can find any information about the road.'

John nodded. 'I suppose so, and Vasilis may have spoken to his lawyer and found out who originally owned the land where the hotel is built.'

'We've still not asked Uncle Yannis or Marisa if they remember a family with the names Despina and Adonia. We ought to ask them this evening. If they could tell us the family name we could try to find their address in Elounda.'

Both Marisa and Yannis shook their heads when John asked if they knew of a Despina or Adonia who lived locally and owned olive groves.

'How would I know them?' asked Marisa. 'I was in Italy for years.'

'I thought you might remember them from when you lived at Plaka.'

Marisa frowned. 'You say they lived in Elounda. I didn't know anyone who lived there. I don't remember ever leaving Plaka except to walk on the hills with Mamma Anna to look for herbs.'

'What about you, Uncle?'

'I didn't leave Plaka until after I'd married Ourania. I have no knowledge at all of ever having met ladies of either name.'

'Why do you need to know? Is it important, John?' asked Marisa.

'Not really. Nick and I were going to give them a quick visit and send Evi's regards. She's a distant relation apparently.'

'So why didn't she tell you where they lived?'

'The nearest to an address that she could give was that they had a house amongst an olive grove and the olive trees went down as far as the seafront road.'

'They wouldn't have all that now.' Yannis shook his head. 'The road has been put through.'

John nodded. 'That's why it's a bit difficult to know exactly where she meant. Not to worry. It was just a chance that you might know them. When we visit Evi again she might be able to be a bit more explicit.'

'Well, that was a disappointment.' remarked John to Nicola later. 'I had thought they might have known the ladies when they were young.'

'I would have been very surprised,' answered Nicola. 'People didn't move around then like they do now. They might have gone down to the market every week but apart from that they would have been busy at home, looking after the house and children; even working out in the vineyards and definitely harvesting the olives. I suppose Uncle Yannis could have helped with the olive harvest.'

'He would have been unlikely to have walked into Elounda to pick olives. There would have been other olive groves nearer who would have employed him for a few drachmas, and you have to remember he was only a boy at the time we are interested in.'

'If Yiannis is happy playing with his cars tomorrow I'll try to have a look in the internet and see what I can find out about the road.'

'Lucky you to have the time. I have to clean the windows at the taverna tomorrow and sweep all the paths around the self catering units. I will be so pleased when Marcus is able to do that again.'

'He does say he is not getting so tired now and his face looks much better. His mouth is no longer drooping at one side and he isn't dribbling.'

'Once Bryony doesn't need him to help her up and down the stairs I'll suggest that he begins to do some of the jobs we relied upon him for in the past. I'm sure he'll be pleased to get back into a useful routine again.'

Two days later Bryony claimed that her ankle was no longer hurting her when she walked around. 'I can manage the stairs on my own and there's no reason why I can't go back up to Saffie's shop. I'll just have to ask someone to drive me up there and collect me later.'

'I'm sure I could do that,' said Marcus. 'It isn't very far and if I have a problem I promise I'll tell you and we'll have to make a different arrangement.'

Bryony looked at her husband doubtfully. 'Are you sure you should be driving?'

'I have to get back to normal at some time. Giovanni has been very understanding and John has coped with some of my usual maintenance work but I can't expect to sit around for ever and do nothing. I'd like to try to get back into a work routine as I'm becoming extremely bored. I'm nowhere near as tired as I was even a month ago.'

'You don't want to overdo things and give yourself a set back.'

'I'll be sensible. If I go up to the self catering units in the morning and do any necessary jobs I can always come back in the afternoon and have a rest before I go and sit with Uncle Yannis. Marisa often spends time with him in the morning so he won't be dependent upon me. I'm not sure if I ought to drive at night for a week or so, but I'm sure Giovanni or John would be willing to collect you. I'll talk to Giovanni when he returns from the airport run.'

'You won't offer to do that, will you?' asked Bryony anxiously.

Marcus shook his head. 'Certainly not at the moment. I'm sure I'll be fit enough in another month to make the drive there and back.'

Marcus enjoyed driving Bryony up to Saffron's shop. After his months of enforced idleness at last he felt he was being useful again. He gave her strict instructions that she was to call Saffron if her leg began to give her any pain and insist that the shop closed early.

'I'm sure that won't happen. I have no pain at all in my ankle now. I'm becoming quite used to having the extra weight to carry around with me. I'm far more concerned that you will do too much.'

'John is going to sort out some outstanding jobs up at the self catering units whilst I sit in the taverna and deal with any customers. If there are any jobs he cannot do then I'll have a look and see if they are within my current capabilities. I promise I will be sensible provided you are also, Bryony.'

'Don't worry. Saffie has said that I can close early if I find it becomes too much for me later today. I only have to 'phone and let her know. John has offered to collect me this evening and if I did have to leave early I'm sure either Giovanni or Marianne would collect me if he was not available. Drive back carefully.' Bryony kissed her husband on his cheek and he gave a delighted smile.

'That's the first time I've been able to feel anything in my cheek. It just shows what a kiss from you can do.'

Bryony gave a giggle. 'Don't be silly. It just means that you are getting full feeling back again.'

She climbed carefully out of the car and picked up the stick she was using to aid her balance as she walked. Marcus watched her anxiously as she negotiated the paving slabs and she waved to him as she reached the shop doorway. Fortunately he did not see her catch her foot on the doorstep and clutch wildly at the door frame to keep her balance.

Saffron hurried forward. 'Are you alright? You haven't hurt yourself?'

Bryony smiled sheepishly. 'I just didn't lift my plaster quite high enough. No harm done.'

'You're sure? You don't have to be up here, you know.'

'I want to be here. Everyone is running around after me at home as if I was an invalid. I've only got a broken ankle.'

'Yes, and I used to be a bone specialist,' Saffron reminded her. 'How many people did I see who insisted that their fracture was nothing to worry about and then aggravated it so it didn't set right? It's no fun to have a bone broken and re-set.'

'I am being careful,' Bryony assured her. 'I just misjudged the step. It won't happen again.'

'Have you got Monika's 'phone number on your mobile?'

'Of course.'

'Then make sure you have your mobile in your pocket the whole time. If you did fall over, and it's easily done when you have a plaster upsetting your balance, you'd probably have quite a job to get back on your feet again. You could 'phone Monika and she could come in to help you.'

'I'll remember, but I'm sure it won't happen.'

Saffron rolled her eyes. 'How many times did I hear a patient say that to me!'

'Do you miss being a doctor?' asked Bryony.

Saffron shrugged. 'Not really. I did at first and if I had been able to speak Greek I would have asked to retrain to their standards. Now I'm happy to be here in the shop and not inside a hospital room all day.'

'I know what you mean. I was happy working in an insurance office until I came here. Now I would hate to go back to that. Every day I was doing the same monotonous job.'

'Most people find they are doing routine work each day It's fortunate that they are willing to do the mundane jobs or everything would grind to a halt. I'm going to leave you now, but remember, if your leg begins to ache you make arrangements to be collected and close the shop. Put your mobile in your pocket before I go out of the door and make sure it stays there in case of an emergency.'

'Yes, Saffie,' agreed Bryony meekly. 'Please don't worry. I'll be absolutely fine.'

Marcus felt quite exhilarated. It was the first time that he had been able to feel Bryony's lips on his cheek for over three months. He was definitely recovering. Having spent three hours up at the taverna and shop whilst John checked the self catering units that would be occupied the following week he had driven back to the house and had a leisurely lunch before taking Bryony to Plaka. Now as he drove back to the house he felt the familiar tiredness overcoming him. By the time he had parked the car it was all he could do to walk into the house and up the stairs to his bedroom where he collapsed on his bed fully clothed.

He was awoken three hours later by a knocking on his door and Marianne stood there. 'Are you feeling alright, Marcus? I was becoming concerned as you came straight up here after taking Bryony to Plaka.'

Marcus smiled shakily. 'I didn't realise how much it had taken out of me to concentrate on driving until I arrived home. Now I've had a sleep I'm sure I'll be fine for the rest of the day.'

'You didn't do too much at the taverna this morning?'

'Hardly anything. No one wanted a breakfast and only a few visitors came in for shopping. It was no more tiring than sitting with Uncle Yannis.'

'If you're planning to take Bryony up to Plaka again tomorrow it might be as well if you didn't go to the taverna.'

Marcus shook his head. 'I'm considerably better. I even have some feeling back in the side of my face. I want to be able to get back into a proper routine as quickly as possible.'

Marianne looked at him suspiciously. 'You must say if you find anything too much to cope with at present. We understand.'

'You can't make allowances for me forever. I promise I'll be sensible and tell you if I need to rest. I'll have a quick shower now to freshen up and then I'll be down and sit with Uncle Yannis for a while.'

Mr Groshenkov reported back to Mr Propenkov that he had

managed to arrange for a colleague to gain entrance to the apartment where Svetlana lived.

'Having become interested in this address I am arranging to gain more information about the occupants. The man I sent claimed he was from the electric company and needed to check her meter reading. He spread out an array of tools and took his time messing around. When he decided he could not stay any longer he knocked on the living room door and opened it before she had a chance to answer him. He saw a man standing and looking out of the window. He apologised for disturbing him and said he had finished checking the meter and the fault that had been reported to him must be in another apartment. The man nodded and walked back to the table where there were papers spread about. The bogus electric man then asked if there was anyone else living there who might need extra heating or electrical appliances. The man shook his head and Svetlana confirmed that they were the only occupants.'

'Interesting. So if Ludmila is visiting Svetlana as a friend why does she stay such a short time?'

'I will arrange for a listening device to be installed so that we can hear what is going on there.'

'What excuse are you going to use?'

'The technician will say that the other apartments have been checked and a fault is still being recorded in their apartment. It has to be either in their appliances or the wiring That should enable him to poke around in the living room. If he can plant a bug in the rooms we should be able to find out what goes on when Ludmila or anyone else visits.'

Mr Groshenkov arranged for a technician to visit the apartment and plant a listening device so the conversations that took place could be monitored.

'I need the work done immediately and it will have to be connected to a monitoring station that is manned continually. I don't want to find that night time meetings are taking place that I do not know about.'

Two days later Mr Anikov reported back that he had completed installing the listening device and arranged for monitoring to take place.

'It was quite straight forward as I had expected,' he explained. 'There is no telephone. They only use mobiles so any conversation that is picked up will be from their end only. Before I entered I fixed one just outside the doorway. I managed to install two bugs in the living room. One is next to the man's chair. I had to ask him to move it so I could get to a power point where he had a standard lamp plugged in. I was able to install a bug under the shade of the standard lamp when I was supposedly checking the wiring. The other one is across the room by the window. I found a junction box and told them that one of the wires was loose and making a contact when they walked across the floor. I bored them for about ten minutes saying how the loose wire would trigger a surge of electricity and that would account for the high usage that had been recorded in the apartment. I insisted they switched everything off and then walk across the living room floor to see if the meter recorded any usage. It didn't, of course, and I assured them I had fixed the problem.'

Groshenkov nodded. 'So who is doing the monitoring?'

'I am doing it directly at my apartment. I am recording all the lines for twenty four hours each day. My machine will tell me if they contain speech. Do you want me to send the recordings to you or just contact you if I hear anything that you might find interesting?'

'There's no need for you to spend time listening to them. I'd like to receive those that have speech recorded each day. I might well hear something interesting that you would have considered irrelevant.'

'How long do you want me to do that?'

Groshenkov shrugged. 'Until I say you can go in and remove

the bugs. It may take some weeks or even months. Provided you insert new tapes into your machine each day and bring the appropriate used ones to me it should be of no great inconvenience to you.'

May 2016
Weeks Three and Four

Vasilis telephoned John. 'I asked my lawyer to have a look at my deeds for the hotel and he came up with the following information. The land was gifted to a Mr Iordonakis in 1946. He built a small house down there and then sold it a year later. The new owner, Mr Stammatakis, enlarged it to make a series of small rooms that he let out. He rather grandiosely called it called it a hotel. I bought it from him and made it into a proper hotel.'

'Who did Iordonakis buy the land from?' asked John eagerly.

'A family named Colonomakis. They still live locally and own a large olive grove. They also own that plot next door to mine apparently.'

'Do you know where they live?'

'Still up amongst the olive groves I expect.'

'Thank you, Vasilis. You have saved me a good deal of monotonous work trawling through the land registry.'

'Why is it so important for you to know where these people live?'

'I'd rather not say at the moment. I may be looking at the wrong family.'

'Is this to do with whatever you think might be illegal?'

'Not at present. You have nothing to worry about by telling me where they live.'

'What excuse are we going to have to visit these people?' asked Nicola as they drove up the dirt road amongst the olive trees.

'We'll say we've been talking to Evi. She asked if we had any news of them and wanted us to call to tell them that she was keeping well. I'm trusting the usual customary Cretan hospitality. Leave it with me. I'll do the talking.'

John parked to one side of the stone farmhouse. Additional rooms had been built on at one side and a woman looked out at them curiously from a window..

'I wonder if that is a Despina or an Adonia looking at us?' said Nicola.

'Only one way to find out,' grinned John. He waved at the woman he could see and strode up to the front door. 'I'll give her a minute or two and then I'll knock.'

The window opened and a woman looked out. 'Are you lost? Can I help you?'

John smiled widely. 'We're not lost, but I would like to know if you are a member of the Colonomakis family.'

'Yes.'

'Oh, I'm so pleased. That means we are in the right place.'

The woman frowned. 'What do you want?'

'I understand that Evi who lives in Pano Elounda is a distant relative of yours. She asked us to call but she was very vague about your location. All she could tell us was that you had a house above Elounda in amongst the olive groves.'

'Why is she interested in us? She and my grandmother fell out years ago. I hardly remember her.'

John gave a deep sigh. 'I think she is feeling guilty at having neglected you. Could we come in and talk for a short while? We don't want to intrude or be a nuisance.'

'I suppose so.'

Whilst waiting for the woman to come to the door John turned and looked at the view. The olive trees grew up the hill in the distance and the main road from Aghios Nikolaos could be seen at the summit.

'What a beautiful location,' he smiled as the woman opened the door to admit them.

'Come into the living room and have a seat. I'll be back in a moment.' She returned carrying a tray with two cans of beer, a jug of lemonade and a plate of biscuits. 'I didn't know which you would prefer. Help yourselves.'

Nicola poured herself a glass of lemonade and John picked up a beer.

'So what does Evi want to know? Is she hoping we are all dead and she is going to inherit our land?'

John shook his head. 'Not at all. She is rather a lonely old lady and I think she would just like to know who is married and has children. It would give her something to talk about to her friend in the village. She totally confused us as she kept saying that Despina had a daughter Adonia and then Adonia had a daughter called Despina. I finally realised that the family name had been carried down through the generations.'

'That's right. I am called Despina Eleni and my mother and my daughter are both called Adonia. I have a granddaughter called Despina Sotiria and she is at school.'

'Really?' Nicola smiled brightly. 'I wonder if our daughters know her? We have twin girls and they are at school locally. We'll have to ask them when we collect them later.'

'That would depend how old they are. Sotiria is at the senior school now.'

'So your family have lived here for generations. What wonderful stories the land would be able to tell us if only it could talk. You never considered selling and living a life of luxury down in Elounda or even in Aghios Nikolaos.?'

Despina Eleni shook her head. 'My great grandmother was adamant that the olive trees should never be touched. She insisted the land must never be sold for redevelopment. The olive trees are our inheritance and our income. We depend upon them. According to my mother it was bad enough when the government insisted on putting the road through between Elounda and Aghios Nikolaos. Her mother was desperate to stop them, but they took no notice of her. At least they paid her compensation for the lost trees. It was a shame they didn't want the land that was lower down.'

'Why have you never bothered with the area below the road?'

'The trees there always gave a poor crop. There is no great depth of soil and the wind and salt from the sea affects them. We decided it was better to concentrate our efforts on the land up here.'

'A friend of ours bought a plot of land down there to build his house. He wasn't very pleased when old bones were discovered and he had to wait until they were recorded and cleared away. He wished at the time that he had bought the plot next door that belongs to you and then more skeletons were found there.' As John said the words he recalled that one body had not been of the same age as the other skeletons. It completely destroyed his train of thought.

'I'm sorry, what did you say?'

'Just that there are old burial places all over the island.'

John nodded. 'You don't think of that possibility when you buy the land. It was fortunate that no skeletons were found on the land that had been bought by the government when they constructed the road.'

'There had been a footpath through the olive grove for as long as anyone could remember. It was the most practical place to put the road.'

'Good to know that sometimes the government sees sense. How do you manage at harvest time? It must be far too arduous for just your family to deal with.'

'We employ the locals to help. Even with our husbands helping it would be too much for us to tackle alone.'

'I suppose we should consider ourselves fortunate. There were mostly carob trees on my uncle's land and there was no money to be made from carob after the war. My father redeveloped the land to cater for the tourists.'

'A hotel?'

'No, he has self catering apartments with a small shop and taverna attached. It provides employment for all of us during the season and we spend the winter months repairing and refurbishing.' John replaced his beer can on the tray. 'I am so pleased to have met you. We'll be able to tell Evi that we came and you have a granddaughter. Is there anyone else we should know about?'

'My grandmother is still alive. She had a nasty shock recently and has not been the same since. She would not have been willing to meet you.'

'I'm sorry to hear that,' answered John politely. 'I hope we may be able to meet her when we come again. We must not outstay our welcome; I'm sure you have more than enough to do and we must return to collect our children from school.'

Nicola rose and extended her hand. 'It has been a pleasure to meet you. I'd love to come again and meet your granddaughter.'

Despina Eleni nodded. 'Well, you know where I am now.'

'So,' said Nicola once she and John were back in the car. 'Did you find out what you wanted?'

'More or less. From the door to the house you can see the main road as it goes over the hill. If that was the route of the original footpath you would see anyone approaching and I expect someone was watching continually for the arrival of soldiers during the war. They would have wanted to hide any food or valuables they possessed. She was obviously not going to talk about the skeletons that were found on her land recently. I need to speak to Vasilis's neighbour, Panayiotis about those. I wonder if that was the news that gave the old lady a nasty shock?'

'I think it would give anyone a nasty shock to find out that someone had been buried on your land.'

John nodded. 'I agree, but suppose you already knew the body was there and it was the shock of the discovery that disturbed her?'

'What are you thinking, John?'

'I've been concentrating on the soldiers and not considered the more recent body that was found. There's a chance that it could be Pietro's father.'

'Why on earth would he be buried there?'

'I don't know. We'll pass by Vasilis and Cathy's apartment on the way home and see if his friendly policeman is available.'

Panayiotis greeted them amiably, but refused Cathy's invitation to have a beer. 'I can't stay too long. I'm on duty this afternoon and it would be frowned upon if I arrived smelling of alcohol.'

'I'm sure we'll keep you no longer than a few minutes. We've just paid a visit to the Colonomakis family. I understand they own the land down by the seafront road along with the olive groves on the hill. What did they say when they were told a modern body had been found amongst the skeletons on their land?'

'Well,' Panayiotis scratched his ear. 'I thought the old lady was going to faint and her daughter was furious. She said the archaeologists had no right on her land although they had a permit giving them permission to investigate and excavate. I know they kicked up a fuss when the government insisted on purchasing some of their land to build the road down into Elounda. Once that had been completed they never went near the lower strip of land as far as I know and just left it neglected. I suppose they thought they had more than enough olive trees closer to the house.'

'That's what they said, although I thought olive trees were a valuable commodity wherever they were growing.'

'Those have not been looked after. The fruit is very small, probably not worth harvesting now. The trees would need attention from someone who would know how to revive them.'

'I'm hoping they will agree to sell the land to me,' said Vasilis. 'I am planning to approach the owners and ask if they would clean the area up a bit. It is just a rubbish tip at the moment. If they want to sell to me I'd make sure it was properly cleared and the olives could be added to my own crop each year. They could agree to clear it up and then not touch it. We really do not want it next door to us. I know stray cats live there and well meaning tourists leave food there for them. Before we know it we could have an infestation of rats or mice.'

Cathy shuddered. 'In that case it should certainly should be cleared up. We could ask one of the cat rescue people to catch the cats and once they were gone we could put down poison for the rodents.'

'I can't do that unless the land belongs to me. It would have to be properly fenced off so people did not allow their dogs on the land. I would hate to be responsible for poisoning someone's pet.'

Panayiotis looked at John. 'Was there anything else you wanted to ask me?'

'What's happened to the body?'

'It's still in the mortuary. I'm not sure how long they'll continue to make enquiries to try to find out his possible identity.'

'Was there nothing on him that would help to identify him?'

'Well, if he had a passport or driving licence originally that would have disintegrated long ago.

Once they feel they can do no more I imagine he will be buried in an unmarked grave.'

'I do hope he can be identified before that happens,' said John. 'Imagine finding out six months later that he was a relative and you had not been given the opportunity to hold a proper funeral for him.'

Panayiotis shrugged. 'It's nothing to do with me. Someone would have to come forward with proof that he was a relative. I'm sure if his identity does become known it will be in the local newspaper, possibly on the television news as well. You'll be sure to hear about it.'

John nodded. 'Of course. I'll keep an eye out for any news. Thank you for your time.'

'What did the Colonomakis family say about the body being found?' asked Vasilis as Panayiotis returned inside his house.

'We didn't mention it to them. We only remarked how unfortunate it had been for you to have to wait whilst your land was excavated. They shrugged off the skeletons saying human remains could be found almost anywhere on Crete.'

'So why did you go to see them?' asked Cathy.

'Oh, it was really just a social visit. They are distant relatives of the old lady, Evi, who lives in Pano. She wanted news of them and also to let them know that she was still alive.'

'So what do you plan to do now?' asked Nicola as they drove back home.

'If Marcus is willing and able to look after the taverna tomorrow morning I'll go back up there and have a look around.'

'Is he well enough?'

'I think so. In some ways Bryony breaking her ankle has helped. He became far more concerned about her and stopped thinking how he was feeling all the time.'

'Assuming Evi is telling the truth it would have been the Despina who was her husband's aunt who shot the soldiers. If Evi knew that and threatened to go to the authorities that could be the reason there was a falling out and she has not seen the family for years.'

John shrugged. 'Well if I cannot find any trace of them we will have to assume that Evi made the story up out of spite and there was a different reason that caused them to fall out. The soldiers would have used the footpath rather than walk through the olive grove and I want to see if I can find an area where it would be most practical to search.'

'Suppose they have guard dogs?'

'We didn't see any when we visited.'

'They may keep them chained up round the back.'

'I'm sure they would have barked when we arrived. Don't worry, Nick. I'll take Skele with me. He'll alert me to any guard dogs that might be around and he'll also be a good excuse if I'm accused of trespassing. I'll say he ran in and I followed to catch him and bring him back out.'

Nicola had waited anxiously for John to call her and say he was back at the taverna and once she had spoken to him she was longing to know how his visit to the olive grove had been. She had to curb her impatience until Yiannis was in bed and the girls were watching a cartoon

'So, tell me. What did you find out?'

'I parked in the viewing spot and then walked back down the road. I've never really taken any notice before but there's quite a high wall with a wire fence erected inside it. Further down, opposite another viewing spot, there's a gate. You can see there is a track between the trees and that must be where the trucks drive when the olives have been harvested. It would make sense to go through up there rather than drive back down to the house and then back up the hill to Aghios Nikolaos. There's probably another entrance higher up, but I didn't go looking for that today.'

'Did you actually go in?'

'I walked back to the car and collected Skele. He was able to go under the gate and I had to climb over. I just hoped that if I was seen they would think me too lazy to undo the padlock and chain. Once inside I walked between the trees so that I would be more difficult to spot and I didn't want to leave my footprints on the dusty road. I told Skele to 'find'. The poor dog had no idea what he was supposed to be looking for. He sniffed around the trees and kept looking back at me. I'd walked about three hundred yards into the grove keeping parallel with the path. Skele was all over the place, further ahead of me or amongst a row of trees above and he suddenly stopped and started sniffing around. I walked up two rows to where he was. He kept walking around the same area and sniffing the ground. He had certainly found something of interest there.'

'So what did you do?' Nicola asked eagerly.

'I had taken some metal bottle caps with me and I placed one at the base of each tree.'

'Why would you do that?'

'When I go up there with my metal detector I will be able to find the spot easily. I didn't want to tie anything to the trees saying 'this is the spot', but no one will take any notice of a bottle cap on the ground. Just to be sure I made a note of which row I was on and how many trees there were back to the wall.'

'So are you going back tomorrow with your metal detector?'

John shook his head. 'I'll have to wait until it's dark. If I pick up a signal I'll want to dig a small hole to find out the source. I don't think the Colonomakis family would be very amused to see me digging holes up in their olive grove.'

'I suppose you could ask their permission.'

'If they have nothing to hide they would still want to know why I wanted to investigate the land. I can hardly say that I believe there could be some soldiers' bodies buried there. If the men are there the family would certainly not allow me to dig and they might even move the bodies elsewhere.'

'So what will you do if you believe you have found traces of them?'

'I'll speak to Panayiotis. He'll know who to approach for permission to make a full scale search of the area.'

'What excuse will you give for not being at our evening meal?'

'I'll say I'm seeing Dimitris and not sure how long I will be with him. That will be true as I will be returning Skele to him.'

'I wish you were going to have Skele with you.'

'I wouldn't risk it. If they saw him they might shoot him thinking he was a stray.'

'They might shoot you!'

'I think that's hardly likely. They would probably accuse me of trespassing and possibly causing damage and hand me over to the police.'

'John, suppose you do find any evidence of the soldiers' bodies – do you think the family will be prosecuted for murder?'

'I don't see how that could be possible. The original perpetrators must both be dead. I can't see the authorities taking any action against the family now.'

As the sun went down John donned a black long sleeved T-shirt and black trousers before placing his metal detector, a probe, trowel and a torch in his car. He called to Skele who jumped inside with alacrity, anticipating another walk over the hills. John drove to Dimitris's and took Skele inside, where the dog sank down with his nose between his paws and glared at John balefully.

'What's wrong with him?' asked Dimitris.

'Because I brought him up in the car I expect he thought he was going to have a walk over the hill. He's just having a sulk. Once I've left and you give him his supper he'll get over it and be his usual self.'

'You don't think he's ill?' asked Dimitris anxiously.

'He's been fine all day. If you really become worried about him 'phone the vet and take him along.'

'They'll be closed by now.'

'Use the emergency number and then 'phone me, but I honestly do not think there is anything at all wrong with him.' John pulled gently at Skele's ears. 'I know you're just putting on the 'poor me' act. Behave for Dimitris and I'll take you for a long walk tomorrow.'

By the time John reached the viewing area on the road from Aghios Nikolaos to Elounda it was truly dark. He parked and walked cautiously across the road and down to where the gate to the olive grove was situated. He pushed his metal detector underneath, checked there was no traffic coming at that particular moment and climbed swiftly over the gate. He stood motionless behind an olive tree, partly to get his bearings but also to make sure that there were no dogs let loose in the grove at night. Once satisfied that he was safe he picked up the metal detector and walked up between the trees to the second row from the dirt path.

He counted the trees as he moved stealthily between them until he judged he should have reached the area he had marked with the bottle caps. Taking a last look round John placed the ear phones on his head and switched on the metal detector, swinging it carefully from side to side. There was no sound emanating from the ground where he was standing and he moved forwards a few steps until he was beneath the next tree.

The detector gave an indication that there was something metal in the vicinity and John switched on his torch and bent down. There was a metal bottle cap. With a pleased smile John moved the detector over towards the opposite tree and was met with the same result. He checked the other two trees where he had placed the bottle tops and they confirmed that he was standing where Skele had spent a good deal of time sniffing around.

John placed the bottle tops into his pocket and began to swing the metal detector from side to side. At first there was nothing, then a regular system of signals began to penetrate his ear phones. He switched off the detector and placed it on the ground beside him taking out his probe and running it over the earth where the sound had come from.

The signal continued and John took the trowel and began to dig at the area. The ground was harder than he had anticipated and he wished he had brought a fork with him to loosen it. Eventually he made a small hole and was able to insert the probe. This time the signal was even stronger and John enlarged the hole, placing the earth carefully to one side. The signal stopped and John realised he must have unwittingly removed the object. He ran the probe back and forth across the mound of loose earth and picked up the signal again. He held his torch in one hand and used the other to spread out the earth until he felt something hard and circular beneath his finger tips and shone his torch on his hand. The item was completely encrusted with earth and John scraped away at it with his finger nail until he could see some discoloured metal beneath. Still unsure of his find he slipped it into his pocket and moved to where he had heard the next signal.

Digging down again he found a similar object and added that to his pocket. Carefully he refilled the two holes he had dug and replaced the bottle tops beneath the trees. He was anxious to return home and examine his finds carefully. There was no reason for him to spend any longer up there until he was sure he had found some items of interest. He could always return and look again another night.

Nicola waited apprehensively for John's return. She dreaded finding the police at the door saying he had been arrested or even worse, shot as an intruder on the land. He tapped on their balcony window and she jumped in fright.

'Sorry, I didn't mean to startle you, but I'm a bit grubby. I thought it would be better to come here and clean myself up before Mum or Dad saw me and wanted to know what I had been up to.'

Nicola swallowed. 'You nearly frightened the life out of me. You could have warned me that you would come back round here.'

'I didn't think. I'll just take these dirty clothes off and have a quick shower, then I must 'phone Dimitris and ask if Skele is alright.'

'What's wrong with him?'

'I think he was just sulking as I didn't take him for the walk he was expecting. Dimitris was a bit concerned that he might be ill. That made me worried.'

'Did you find anything?'

'I'm not sure. I'll show you when I'm clean again.'

'Your Mum has saved you some supper as she didn't know what time you'd be getting back and if you would have eaten.'

'I'm pleased about that. I'm starving. I'll only be a few minutes.'

Dressed in clean clothes John called Dimitris and was assured that there was nothing wrong with his dog.

'You were right. He was sulking. Once you had left and I gave him his supper he was his usual self. I took him outside and threw his ball for him and if I hadn't called a halt we would still be out there. He's lying in his bed now having a wash. I imagine he will have forgiven you by tomorrow.'

John grinned at Nicola. 'Skele is fine.'

'Thank goodness. I know he is beginning to age but he should still have some years ahead of him yet.'

'I don't even want to contemplate that. Do you want to see what I found? I rinsed the earth off when I was in the shower room.'

Nicola nodded eagerly and John placed two brass buttons on the table.

Nicola's mouth formed a silent 'Oh' and she picked one up gingerly. 'Do you know what they are?'

'I think they are uniform buttons. I want to look at them under my microscope and then I'll photograph them and see if I can match them up with Italian army buttons. There could be some more up there as I kept getting a series of small signals.'

'Didn't you investigate those?'

John shook his head. 'I didn't want to be there for too long just in case someone had spotted the light from my torch and came to find out what I was up to. The ground is very hard so it takes a while although they were not that deep. Also, if they are from an Italian uniform the authorities won't thank me for digging around and disturbing evidence. Let's put these away somewhere safe and then I can go and get something to eat.'

June 2016
Week One

Mr Groshenkov listened to the tape recordings that Mr Anikov delivered to him each day and for the first three days there was nothing of any interest on them. He heard Svetlana saying she was going shopping and asking if there was anything the man wanted her to bring back for him. There was no answer so Mr Groshenkov had to assume the man had shaken his head. There was little conversation between them and the 'phone calls made by Svetlana were brief, no names being mentioned and usually just a string of instructions being given to the listener. Those made by her father were longer, but he seemed to spend most of the time listening to the caller and then replying 'Good' or 'Proceed as agreed' and the words gave no clue to the content of the conversation. Whenever the news was on the television it was listened to in silence and not commented upon when it finished. Groshenkov was becoming adept at fast forwarding the tapes as the couple appeared to spend most of the day in silence. There appeared to be little rapport between father and daughter.

When he heard Svetlana speaking to someone on her mobile and asking them to call the following day he had no idea if it was Ludmila who was expected but he called Borovich and told him someone was going to the apartment that morning

'Take a photograph of whoever it is and deliver it to me after they leave.'

When Mr Groshenkov listened to the tape the following day he was intrigued. Svetlana had answered the intercom and requested the visitor to come up to the apartment. Once there he was told he could sit down.

'I have something to show you.'

For a few moments there was silence, then Mr Groshenkov heard the visitor say that whatever he was looking at was a 'nice piece.'

'How much?' came the gruff enquiry.

'How much do you want me to pay you or how much is it worth?'

'How much is it worth?'

'Assuming these diamonds are real I would say in the region of one hundred and forty thousand roubles.'

'I can assure you they are real. I can vouch for the provenance. I expect one hundred and twenty.'

'You wouldn't take one hundred?'

'No. One twenty or I take it elsewhere.

'It's not stolen?'

'Certainly not. It is honestly come by as payment for a debt.'

'It will take me a day or two to get the cash.'

'That's no problem. Phone Svetlana to make an appointment when you have the money and I'll arrange for her to deliver it to you. She will expect to receive a brown paper parcel from you in return. There should be more of the same quality in a week or so.'

Mr Groshenkov wished he was able to see the item the man was being offered and contacted Borovich immediately.

'Who was the man who visited the apartments today?'

'I don't know, but I took a photograph as you had ordered, sir.'

'Then deliver it to my office.'

Mr Groshenkov studied the photograph carefully. He was certain the man was a local jeweller of dubious reputation.

Mr Groshenkov listened carefully to the next tape that Anikov sent to him. He clearly heard the man telling Svetlana to call Ludmila and instruct her to visit them the following day at eleven.

'Tell her I am ready to proceed but she must bring me the full amount.'

The conversation between Ludmila and Svetlana was brief, but he heard Svetlana confirm that Ludmila would be there the following morning.

Ludmila was elated after receiving the call. This must mean that a release date for Ivan was imminent. She checked the valuation certificate that she had from the insurance company and was certain that the value of her jewellery would be sufficient to satisfy Mother's fee. It would be a wise precaution on her part to obtain a photocopy of the document; it was likely that Mother would want to keep the original.

She arrived at the apartment promptly at eleven and was admitted immediately by Svetlana.

'Good morning, Mother,' she said nervously.

The man did not return her greeting. 'What have you brought for me?'

'Some jewellery that I hope you will be willing to buy. I haven't any more cash available.'

'Show me.'

From her bag Ludmila took out the boxes that she had removed from the safe at her apartment and passed them to the man. He opened each one and picked up a magnifying glass to examine the items more carefully.

'Where did you get them?' he asked.

'Evgeniy gave them to me over the years as presents.'

'Any receipts?'

'No, but I have the valuation that was given to me by the insurance company.' Ludmila passed him the sheet of paper with the description of each item and the amount of the estimated

227

value. Taking a calculator he pressed in various amounts and finally shook his head.

'With the amount I can expect to be paid for these it will not cover all the expenses.'

'Surely there must be sufficient,' gasped Ludmila.

The man shook his head. 'Such arrangements are expensive. Are you sure you have nothing else? What about the earrings you are wearing?'

Ludmila removed them from her ears and placed them in the palm of his hand. 'I truly haven't anything more. When will Ivan be back in Russia with me?'

The man showed his yellowed teeth. 'Once I have managed to dispose of these items to cover the final cost I'm sure he will soon be released. You will be informed.'

'Thank you.' Ludmila heaved a sigh of relief. It had been worth selling all her jewellery for the paltry amount Mother had given her to know that her brother would soon be back in Russia. 'How much longer do I have to be patient?'

'Two, maybe three weeks.'

When Mr Groshenkov listened to the tape he smiled in delight. Now he knew why Ludmila Kuzmichov had been visiting Svetlana Asimenikov and trying to raise money on her jewellery. He would contact Mr Propenkov at Russian Consulate in Heraklion and inform them that there was a scheme afoot to release Ivan Kolmogorov.

Once he knew that his information had been acted upon and the man was still being held securely he would ask the police to visit the address where the man Ludmila had called 'Mother' lived. He was sure now that it was a code name. No one would be suspected if they said they were giving a message to their mother or visiting her. The man obviously had undesirable associates and through him it might be possible to arrest a number of men who were under investigation by the police.

John looked at the buttons he had retrieved from beneath the ground under his microscope. They were discoloured, green and slightly rusty in places. He did not dare to clean them in case he caused further damage. Handling them carefully he viewed first one side and then the other, finally turning the microscope up to full magnification when he was able to make out some lettering on the reverse and a design on the front.

'Nick, come and have a look and tell me what you think this is.'

Nicola studied the button. 'Can you turn it round a bit? I'm sure there are some letters and they might be easier to make out if they were the right way up.'

With a pair of tweezers John moved the button around until Nicola told him to stop. 'I can see them now. There's a C, a bit I can't make out then I, N. There's another indistinguishable section then I, Z. Turn it a bit more, John.'

'There's an S, something else that I can't read and then ANO.'

'Does it mean anything to you?' asked John.

'Nothing at all. If I could read the other letters I might be able to make sense of the words. Let me see the other button.'

'There's no point. I've already looked at that and the lettering is impossible to make out. Let me turn it over. There's a design of some sort on the front.'

'I don't know what that is,' admitted Nicola. 'They could just be buttons that have dropped off someone's coat whilst they were working up there.'

John shook his head. 'I'm convinced they are uniform buttons. I'm going to photograph them and then I'll start looking on the internet to see if I can find out any information. Have you got a small box where I can put them for safety?'

John spent the evening looking up military uniforms and equipment on the internet. There were plenty of items for sale that the vendor claimed were genuine, but even when enlarged the design on the buttons was hard to distinguish.

'Why don't you contact Pietro and ask him what kind of buttons are used on Italian army uniforms?' suggested Nicola.

'Do you think he would know?'

'If he doesn't he'll have more chance of finding out in Italy than we have here.'

'What excuse do I give him? I don't want to say I've found some in the olive grove.'

'Just say you want to know what the buttons would look like if you did find any. These might be from a German uniform.'

John shook his head. 'They would be bound to have either a swastika or eagle on them.' He sighed. 'You could be right and they are buttons that fell off a workman's coat.'

'Contact Pietro and ask him,' urged Nicola. 'At least you'll know then if the buttons are of any relevance.'

It was four days before John received a reply from Pietro. He had been to the Military Museum in Rome and taken photographs of the uniforms that were on display. John enlarged them as much as possible, but still could not be sure that the buttons he had matched up with the photos.

'I'm going to try to clean one up and have another look.'

'Suppose you damage it?'

'I'll still have the other one. Has Mum got any brass cleaner in the kitchen?'

'I doubt it, we don't have any brass.'

'Have a look in Dad's 'mucky box'. He has all sorts of bits and pieces in there.'

Nicola returned with some silver polish. 'This is the best I could do. There's some chrome cleaner in there, but that might be rather corrosive.'

'I'm sure that will be fine.' John poured a small amount onto a cloth and began to rub it gently over the face of the button. 'That looks better already,' he announced. 'I'll have a go at the back now.'

'I'm sure that's a military button,' he announced finally. I'll rinse the polish off and then put it under the microscope again. You come and look. You're able to see more clearly than me.'

Nicola looked at him anxiously. 'Is that due to the blow to your head?'

'Probably. I don't normally notice a problem, but there again I don't often look through a microscope these days.'

'Maybe you should visit the optician. You might need glasses.'

'They wouldn't help when trying to look through the eye piece. The frames would get in the way.'

'I meant generally.'

John shrugged. 'I'll go when I have time or begin to notice a real problem. Have a look and tell me what you can see.' He placed the button carefully on the slide.

Nicola studied it carefully. 'I can see more of the lettering now. The last word is definitely 'MILANO'.'

'Can you make out anything else?'

'I think there are two 'Z's and possibly two 'I's. It occurs to me that the letters could be the name of the button manufacturers.'

'What makes you think that?'

'It's just a feeling I have. The uniform manufacturers are just going to order thousands of buttons. It would become too complicated for every regiment or battalion to have their name on the back of a button.'

John nodded. 'I think you could be right. Let me turn it over and see if you can make out the design.'

Nicola shook her head. 'I'm really not sure what it is. Why don't you send a photo of it to Pietro and ask him?'

'That might mean that he has to travel to Rome again.'

'I'm sure there must be someone locally who can tell him. Many people are interested in war memorabilia. It's worth sending an e-mail and a photo.'

This time Pietro replied promptly telling John that the design on the button was the Fascist symbol and asking where John had obtained the button.

'I really do not want to tell him,' frowned John. 'He could decide to come dashing back over here and start digging up the olive grove.'

'I don't think that's likely,' smiled Nicola, 'But I do agree that it would be better for him not to know the location where you found it.'

'Suppose I said it was in my Grandmother's button box?'

'Why on earth would she have kept a button like that?'

John shrugged. 'I suppose I could say I found it when I was using my metal detector up on the hill.'

'Well that would be nearer the truth. What are you planning to do now? Go back and see if you can dig up some more?"

John shook his head. 'I don't want to disturb the ground too much or I might interfere with evidence. I'm going to 'phone Vasilis and ask what time Panayiotis will be on duty tomorrow. I'll go to the police station and tell him the whole story.'

'Suppose he doesn't take you seriously?'

'I'll offer to show him the area and prove that there are more metal items below the ground by using the detector. He could then either agree that I dig some more small holes to see if there are any buttons or decide to ask for a professional examination of the area.'

'And if he still doesn't believe you?'

'Then I'll go back up there myself and dig around until I have conclusive proof.'

Panayiotis listened patiently to John as he related the details of Pietro's visit and his own subsequent investigation of the olive grove, finally showing him the buttons he had found.

'I'm not sure how I can get involved. You could be prosecuted for trespass by the olive grove owners for using your metal detector on their land.'

'I don't think they would have given me permission had I asked them. Assuming that the two ladies did shoot and bury the

232

soldiers they are both dead now. I'm not looking for a prosecution or anything like that. I just want to help Pietro.'

'Two uniform buttons are hardly proof that soldiers are buried there. They could have fallen from any Italian's uniform. If, and I repeat if, the bodies are there they will only be skeletons now.'

'I know and I don't want to be responsible for digging them up. I'm sure there are some more buttons up there and possibly their dog tags. If those could be found their identity would be known. Are you able to help me?'

'In what way?'

'If you came up to the olive grove with me tonight you could watch exactly what I am doing. If I found any more buttons or the dog tags you would know that the scene should be investigated.'

Panayiotis shook his head. 'I can't get involved with you digging about in their olive grove. I could lose my job.'

'I'm not asking you to do anything except accompany me. If someone from the house arrives on the scene you can then arrest me. Say you saw me up to something and came to investigate. I trust you'd let me off with a caution,' smiled John.

'And if you find nothing more up there?'

'Then I will give up and agree with you that the buttons just fell of a soldier's uniform.'

'Who else knows you are going up there with your metal detector?' asked Panyiotis.

'Only my wife.'

Panayiotis gave a deep sigh. 'I suppose I have to take your story seriously. It has always been known that the incident happened but no one has ever disclosed who the women were or where the bodies were buried. I'll come up there with you tonight, but only tonight. If you find nothing that's the end of the matter.'

John nodded. 'I'd really appreciate that and I don't expect you to grub around in the earth. You'll wear your uniform, won't you? They do need to know that you really are a policeman if you have to arrest me.'

'And if you find nothing I don't expect to hear that you've been going up there again.'

John shrugged. 'If there is nothing more found there's little point in me going back another time.'

As he drove home from the police station Panayiotis stopped at the viewing point down the hill towards Elounda. Although he was not sure if his superior officer would condone his activities he felt obliged to take John's story seriously until it was proved otherwise. He looked at the trees that grew there, some of them with a girth he would not have been able to span with his arms. He wondered just how old they were and how big they would have been during the war. Leaving his car in the lay by he walked a short distance down the road to the gate that John had mentioned. Even from across the road he could see that it was padlocked. That would mean he had to climb over it and hoped he would not ruin his uniform trousers.

It was dark when Panayiotis returned and found John was already there waiting for him.

'There are lights on up at the house, but no one around. Let's go up now in case they come outside later to eat.'

Silently Panayiotis followed John to the gate and watched whilst he slid his metal detector underneath and then climbed over. He held out his hand and Panayiotis took it to steady himself. He followed John up between the rows of majestic old olive trees until John stopped.

'This is the area,' he said quietly. 'I've brought some plant markers with me. Whenever I get a signal I'll put one into the ground. Once I've marked four or five I'll dig around and see what I come up with.'

Panayiotis nodded and watched as John swung his metal detector back and forth, forcing a plant marker into the hard ground at intervals. Finally John placed the detector on the ground and took his trowel and probe from his pocket. He bent down and dug a small hole, using the fork he had brought with him to break up the hard surface, then tested it with his probe before digging deeper with his trowel. When the probe no longer registered anything metal in the hole John ran the probe over the mound of earth and began to search it with his fingers. He examined a small metal object by the light of his torch, scraped at some of the mud that clung to it and finally held up a button to show Panayiotis.

John slipped the button into his pocket and began to search the next area he had marked and commenced digging another hole.

'Got it,' he said as he shone his torch on his next find. 'Thank goodness they were not buried too deeply or we could have been here all night.' He straightened up, a broad grin on his face. 'I'm sure these are dog tags. They are still on a chain. No need to dig any more tonight. I'll fill these holes in and we'll leave as fast as we can. I'll leave some metal bottle caps up here so you can find the area again.'

Panayiotis needed no second bidding. John filled in the holes, and stamped the earth down before leaving a plant marker lying beneath a tree and replacing the bottle caps haphazardly. As soon as he picked up his metal detector Panayiotis immediately began to make his way back towards the gate. He would be much happier once he was the other side of the fence and back on the public road.

'I think we ought to go back to the station,' said Panayiotis.

'Are you arresting me after all?' asked John.

'No, thankfully that was not necessary. I want to have a good look at those items you discovered. If you have found the dog tags I have to decide on my next course of action.'

John followed Panayiotis back to the police station in Aghios Nikolaos and was directed into a room at the back. Panayiotis spoke to the officer on duty and very soon two bottles of beer were delivered to them.

'Is this allowed?' asked John.

'I'm not on duty and you are paying me a courtesy visit. I don't think anyone could object to us having a bottle of beer. We're not likely to get drunk and cause trouble. Show me what you found.'

'I really need to give them a wash to get the dirt off. They'll probably be discoloured, but once they're clean you should be able to see enough to satisfy you that they once belonged to an Italian soldier.'

'Come with me. I'll take you to the Gents. There's a wash basin in there.'

John half filled the basin with water and then began to rub away at the button. 'It is the same design as the others. Rather a coincidence for a soldier to lose three buttons off his uniform all in the same area.' John raised his eyebrows quizzically at Panyiotis.

'Let me see.' John placed it in Panayiotis's hand and began to clean the dog tags.

'We may need a magnifying glass to see the engraving clearly,' John warned. 'I don't want to do any more drastic cleaning in case I cause any damage. Oh, no,' he exclaimed. 'It's come apart in my hand.'

'Give it to me.'

Panayiotis looked at the two pieces carefully. 'If I remember correctly the dog tags were designed to come apart. The idea was that if a soldier found a dead comrade he would take one half of the tag with the man's details on and leave the other half around his neck. That way his identity could be recorded and the bodies returned to relatives for burial. Clean the basin round and then we'll go back to my room and look at these properly.'

The items lay on a piece of paper in front of Panayiotis. 'The dog tags need to be professionally cleaned so we can gain as much information as we can about the soldier.'

'Can you make out the name?' asked John.

'I'm not sure. I think I can see a 'Z ' but it could be an 'S' and later a 'G' or maybe a 'C' There seem to be repeats of some of the letters, but I can't make them out..'

'Could it say Pietro Rossi?'

'Impossible to say.'

'So what happens now?'

'I'll place these items in the safe and I'd like you to bring the other buttons to me. I'll then refer the matter to my commanding officer and ask if a full scale investigation of the site can take place.'

'Suppose he refuses?'

'I think that's unlikely. It appears that a body is buried there and it would have to be unearthed to decide whether it was a modern murder or as we suspect dating from the war. I am relying on you not to mention this to anyone apart from your wife until I am able to advise you of the outcome.'

'I just hope that it's Pietro's grandfather that we have found.'

Yannis rubbed his hands together. 'What do you think of that, then, Marisa? I've sold the last Attic Ware amphora.'

Marisa nodded. If her brother was pleased then she was also. 'You'll have to buy some more now.'

'I'll have to check my stock first to make absolutely certain. I don't want to find any hidden away.'

John shook his head vehemently when his uncle suggested that some more amphora were ordered. 'No way are you to order any more. The whole idea of you having an exhibition outside is so that you gradually clear all your stock.'

'But I might have more orders,' protested Yannis.

'I'll take it off your web site and we can mark it as sold out. That might encourage people who are hesitating about buying something make up their mind. You have to be realistic, Uncle. How much longer can you sit outside and hope you make a few sales each week?'

'The summer has hardly started. I can certainly be out there until October.'

'I'm not talking just about this year. You're not getting any younger, Uncle. All the time you feel you can sit there and talk to customers that's fine, but will you feel like doing that next year or the year after?'

'I expect I will.'

'I hope you will, but there's no guarantee. If you order some more pots and you're no longer able to sit there and sell them there's no one who can take over and do it for you. We are all busy with the self catering and taverna.'

'Bryony could do it.'

'Bryony works up at Saffie's shop along with helping Mum with the housekeeping. You wouldn't be very pleased if you expected to have a meal only to find that Mum had been busy taking bookings and Bryony had been sitting out here.'

'I'm sure Nicola could manage to get me a meal.'

'Nick has the children to care for and she also helps out when we become really busy. You have more than enough stock to keep you going for this year and probably for some years afterwards. If you insist on ordering any more pots don't expect any help from any of us.'

'They're ceramics, not 'pots',' muttered Yannis.

'I think I've upset Uncle Yannis,' John explained to his mother when she asked why their uncle had retired to his room looking miserable.

'You did right by telling him not to buy any more stock. We need to finish clearing the spare room so I can get it prepared for Angelo and Francesca when they come next month. We can't expect them to be forever falling over boxes of pottery.'

John grinned. 'I'll tell him that we'll have to store any new stock in there and that they'll probably fall over them and break the contents.'

'That's not kind, John. If you say that he'll insist they are all moved into his room and there's hardly room to move in there now. I'll go and talk to him. I'll tell him we can order some more stock during the winter if necessary.'

'Just don't make him any promises, Mum.'

June 2016
Week Three

Ludmila moved the bookcase and took the chisel and hammer from the tool box. Try as she might she could not manage to insert the chisel between the frame of the safe and the door. Frustrated she sat down and wondered how she would be able to force it open. An hour later and after a number of further fruitless attempts she gave up and used her key. She looked at the open door and the solution came to her. She did not need to force it open, all she needed to do was cause sufficient damage so that it looked as if it had been forced.

The metal casing was stronger than she had realised and after hitting it as hard as possible she finally saw that she had made some dents in the casing. She pushed the door closed and it did so easily despite the damage. Once again she opened the door and began to hammer at the tumblers, seeing them gradually become distorted. The door would certainly not close now.

For a further hour she attacked the metal casing causing dents and scrapes and stood back to scrutinize the damage. She took up the hammer again and hit the door and tumblers until she was satisfied that the damage looked like an authentic attempt to break into the safe. She replaced the tools into the box and moved the bookcase back in front of the safe. She would have to plan her next move carefully.

John waited impatiently to hear from Panayiotis and was delighted when the policeman 'phoned. 'You'll be pleased to know that forensics have agreed to investigate the area. Of course, they wanted to know where I had gained my information and I had to tell them that I had caught you using your metal detector.'

'Am I going to be summonsed?' asked John anxiously.

'I think it unlikely that we will pursue a charge against you. You handed over to me the items you had found and they were not of any intrinsic value.'

'Have they told the Colonomakis family?'

'Not yet. There's paper work to be completed authorising them to dig up the relevant area. If they find nothing more then we will have to assume that the items you found were buried there and if there are any bodies they were buried elsewhere. They can't go digging up the whole of the grove.'

'The story as I heard it originally was that a woman saw the soldiers approaching and shot them. She and her daughter dug a grave and buried them. It's unlikely that two women managed to move two men to a totally different area and only buried a few buttons and the dog tags elsewhere. Has any information been found out from the dog tags?'

'I was waiting for you to ask. We have a name. Guiseppe Zingaretta engraved on the tags you found.'

'Oh!'

'You sound disappointed.'

'I am,' admitted John. 'I had hoped they would say Pietro Rossi.'

'Well, if two soldiers were buried there should be another set of dog tags somewhere close by.'

'I could go up again with the metal detector,' offered John.

'You're to do no such thing,' said Panayiotis sternly. 'Now I have informed the authorities I wouldn't want to explain to the land owners why you were there. You would very likely be prosecuted for trespassing and using a metal detector on their land without their permission. I want your word that you will keep away from the area.'

'I'm just worried that the family will get to hear that the area is to be excavated and move the bodies elsewhere.'

'At this moment we do not know if there are any bodies buried there and no one is going to inform them about investigating until the day they arrive to make a start.'

'Really? That's a relief. I might just keep an eye on the area to make sure the ground isn't disturbed.'

'No, John. Sooner or later you would be seen and they would want to know what your interest was on their property. It will be pretty obvious if the ground has been dug up and they could then have some awkward questions to answer.'

'When will the work start?' asked John.

'I can't tell you exactly, but I promise to let you know if they find anything up there.'

Ludmila opened her front door and chiselled out the lock, ensuring she damaged the frame at the same time and leaving splinters of wood on the ground. Finally she pulled the book case away from the wall and threw the books onto the floor. She looked at the chaos she had caused and felt satisfied.

With a last look around she picked up her shopping bag and left the apartment. She would ensure that she was noticed and remembered in the shops she visited by engaging the assistants in conversation and report the break in when she returned after an hour or so.

When the police arrived they were met by a distraught woman.

'I came home from shopping and this is what I found. Someone has obviously broken in. They have managed to open my safe and stolen all my jewellery. Please help me.' Ludmila collapsed on the sofa and buried her face in her hands.

Before Ludmila was permitted to return her apartment to an

orderly state she had to allow two policemen to investigate and photograph each room whilst she sat and answered the questions of a policewoman. She tried to be as vague as possible about the time she had gone shopping and the amount of time she had been away from the apartment.

'I'm not sure of the time, probably about ten thirty, maybe nearer to eleven. I called you as soon as I returned.'

The policewoman nodded sympathetically. 'Were you going anywhere in particular?'

'Only to do my shopping. I went to the supermarket along the road and also to the chemist and newsagent. The newsagent might remember me being there as I asked if he had a particular magazine. He took my name and address and promised to order it for me.'

'So you didn't have an appointment with the dentist or doctor that anyone else would have known about?'

Ludmila shook her head. 'I may have been seen leaving by another resident in the apartments but I can't imagine that one of them would break in and steal from me.'

'Rather risky for anyone to break in when they did not know how long you would be away,' observed the policewoman.

Ludmila shrugged. 'I can only think that someone had been watching my movements and knew roughly how long I spent out whilst shopping.'

'Have you noticed anyone hanging around?'

'I don't think so.'

'Now, your jewellery. Can you give me an idea of its value?'

'I have the certificate from the insurance company and photographs. Oh, I hope they haven't taken those.'

'I'm sure the company will have a record of the items and the value.'

'I wish I'd never removed them from the bank.' Ludmila shook her head miserably as she searched through a collection of papers that were stored in a drawer. 'Here they are,' she said at last.

'Why did you remove them?'

'It was inconvenient to have to go to the bank and ask for access and sign the necessary paperwork if I wanted an item to wear. I had a safe here that I thought was secure so I decided to place them in there. I never dreamt that I would be burgled.'

'Did you often wear the jewellery?'

'It would depend where I was going. I didn't have any on this morning as I was only going shopping.'

'I would like to take a photograph of the photo in your possession and another of the valuation certificate. There will be a description of the items on there and we can put out a notice to all the jewellers asking them to look out for anyone who tries to sell them.'

'Do you think you'll find them?' asked Ludmila eagerly. 'It's not just the value, they were also of sentimental value as they were gifts to me from my husband.'

'Where is your husband at the moment? Maybe you should advise him of the loss and ask him to come home to give you some support.'

'That's not possible at present,' Ludmila shook her head regretfully. 'He's working in America. I wouldn't want to worry him. If you are able to retrieve the items for me I'll put them back in the bank and not tell him about the break in. He'd probably come rushing back and that would mean he lost the deal he's currently working on over there.'

The policewoman shrugged. The woman's husband would probably berate her for removing her jewellery from the bank and that was why she did not want to inform him about the theft.

'Provided you are able to contact him if you should change your mind. We'll arrange for a locksmith to come and repair your front door so that you can feel secure again. There's not a lot of point in repairing your safe. I'll leave my 'phone number with you and if you are worried you can contact me and I'll ask someone to visit you.'

Ludmila smiled shakily. 'Thank you. I'm over the worst of the shock now. I just want to be able to clear up the mess.'

'There is just one other thing before we leave. We need to take your fingerprints.'

'My fingerprints? Whatever for? They are bound to be all over the apartment.'

'Of course, but if we find any that do not match yours we may well be able to match them to a known criminal. Would you like me to make you a cup of tea before we leave?'

Ludmila shook her head. 'No, thank you. I'll just sit here for a few minutes and then replace the books in the bookcase. Doing something positive will take my mind off the situation. Would one of your officers be kind enough to move it back into place for me?'

Ludmila showed the police out and sat back on the sofa. She would wait until she was certain they were not going to return to ask her any more questions and then she would make herself a cup of tea and replace the books.

'What do you think?' the policewoman asked her colleagues.

'Well, if that had happened to my wife I think she would have called me, even if I was on duty at the time.'

'Maybe she's frightened that her husband will blame her for taking the jewellery from the bank.'

'It was somewhat foolish of her.' The policewoman tapped the insurance certificate with her finger. 'We need to have this authenticated and if it's correct the jewellery was worth an enormous amount. I feel certain someone must have known it was there. They must have made a considerable amount of noise breaking the lock on the door and then gaining access to the safe.'

'We'll go back this evening and make some enquiries of the other residents. No one answered our knocks this morning.'

'Whoever did it probably knew that everyone else was out at work during the day. I'll go to the insurance company and see what I can find out from them. If they're no help I'll visit the bank and see what they can tell us.'

Mr Zavinalov telephoned Mr Groshenkov on the private number he used when reporting anything of note.

'I'm not sure what is going on. I followed Mrs Kuzmichov this morning and all she did was go shopping, her usual places. I was waiting to see if she was going to go out again later and the police arrived. They went into the building, but I have no idea which apartment they visited or the reason.'

Mr Groshenkov ran his hand through his thinning hair. 'Do nothing, but continue to keep watch as usual and report back to me if there is any more activity from the police. It may not be related to the investigation.'

The police returned to Ludmila two days later and she sat before them nervously.

'We have spoken to the other residents of this apartment block and they all say they were out during the morning; consequently they would not have heard anyone breaking in. We checked up on your insurance and it was confirmed that you indeed were the owner of the jewellery and also that the value was as stated. Unfortunately we did not find any fingerprints in the apartment apart from your own so we have to assume that the burglar wore gloves.'

Ludmila nodded. 'So what happens now?'

'We are distributing photos of your possessions to all the jewellers and they have said they will notify us if anyone tries to sell any of the articles to them. Of course, they may already have been sent away from Moscow and that will make them more difficult to trace. There is also the possibility that they will be broken up and sold for the value of the gem stones and gold separately. The thief may not try to dispose of them for a considerable amount of time and might even take them out of Russia thinking he could sell them elsewhere more easily.'

'It would be wicked if they had been broken up. They are unique designs, another reason why they are worth so much money. Am I able to claim on my insurance in the meantime?' Desperate though she was for the answer Ludmila did not want to appear too anxious.

'You can, but the insurance broker may insist that you wait a period of time before your claim is finalised. This is to allow for the items to be recovered. Of course, if the compensation is paid to you and the jewellery subsequently appears and is returned to you, the money you have received will have to be repaid.'

'Of course,' agreed Ludmila. 'I would far rather have my jewellery than the money,' she lied.

'Naturally. Items that are of sentimental value are far more valuable and cannot be replaced just by money.'

Ludmila nodded dutifully. 'When I feel I can cope I will visit the insurance company. At the moment I feel quite nervous about leaving my apartment.'

'I am sure the burglar will not return. In my experience it is very rare for a thief to return to the premises he has already robbed. He knows there is nothing more of value there.'

'That's a comfort, I suppose. I'd hate to come home and disturb him. He might be violent.'

'Would you be happier going to stay somewhere else for a few weeks? I'm sure we could arrange some suitable accommodation for you on a temporary basis.'

Ludmila shook her head. 'I have to put the incident behind me and continue with my life. If I decided to take advantage of your offer to go away for a while I would still have to return here eventually.'

'You are obviously a strong minded and courageous woman. Are you sleeping properly or do you need a doctor's prescription for a sedative?'

Ludmila managed a wan smile. 'I do wake up from time to time. I then get up and walk around to make sure I am alone and the doors and windows are locked. It can take me quite a long time to get back to sleep so maybe I should visit the doctor and ask for something to help me.'

'That would be a good idea. Once you have explained the circumstances to him I'm sure he will understand. Is there anything else we can do for you today?'

'No, thank you. You have been very helpful and comforting to me.'

'We'll be in touch if there are any developments,' promised the policewoman as she left.

Mr Zavinalov telephoned Mr Groshenkov again. 'The police returned yesterday and today Mrs Kuzmichov visited the insurance company who had insured her jewellery. I have a contact there and managed to find out that she is making a claim as her apartment was burgled and all her jewellery stolen.'

'So that explains the visits from the police. If you were out following Kuzmichov when the incident occurred did Lenishkova see anyone entering the apartment block?'

'She saw the couple who live below drive off in their car about twenty minutes after I went out. She said no one entered until Mrs Kuzmichov returned.'

Mr Groshenkov smiled to himself. Ludmila had obviously staged the break in and was planning to claim on her insurance.

John had given Panayiotis explicit instructions. 'I don't want you leading the police to the wrong area. Go in at the main entrance and walk up beside the wall until you come to the gate that we climbed over. From there you walk up past three rows of trees then move in amongst them. When you see the bottle tops you'll know you have found the correct area.'

The police pushed a wheelbarrow containing picks, shovels and trowels, followed Panayiotis up through the olive grove whilst two more officers went to the house to inform the occupants of the activity that was about to take place.

Eleni Despina folded her arms and glared at the policemen. 'You cannot do that. It is my land and I'll not allow it.'

'I'm sorry, Madam, but we are not asking your permission.'

'Why would you want to dig it up?'

'I'm not in a position to answer that for you, Madam. I was just asked to come here and advise you of the work that is commencing.'

Eleni Despina closed the door. She would go up into the grove and see if she could find out why the police were interested in her land. She walked into the living room where her mother was watching the television news and finishing her breakfast.

'I have to go out for a while, Mamma. I shouldn't be very long.'

'Whilst you're out can you get me some more of my indigestion tablets? I only have a few left.'

'I'm not going into the village at the moment. I have to go up into the olive grove. There are some people up there that I need to speak with.'

'It's too early for them to start robbing our olive trees.'

'I'm not sure what they're doing. I'll tell you when I come back.'

Eleni Despina removed her apron and marched up the path towards the wall that surrounded the property. Once there she saw there were two police cars and a van parked. At least they had not tried to drive their vehicles through the trees and caused any damage to them. She walked up beside the wall, peering through the trees for any sign of people, but it was not until she had continued past the gate that she saw movement. Yellow tape had been strung between the trees forbidding anyone to enter the area.

'What do you think you're doing? This is private property. Please leave immediately.'

Panayiotis went towards her. 'I believe our officers called on you and said that we were carrying out an investigation. We have been informed that there could be something of interest buried here. Should our information be incorrect the land will be left exactly as it was before we began our work and you will be paid compensation.'

'My husband will have something to say about this. I'm going to 'phone him and he'll come up here and stop you.'

Panayiotis shook his head. 'You may certainly call your husband, but he will be unable to stop us. The area has been cordoned off and no unauthorised person, not even you or your husband, will be allowed near the section. We will obviously carry out our work as quickly as possible and advise you of the outcome. You may stay and observe our current proceedings from a distance if you wish.'

Eleni Despina pursed her lips. There was obviously nothing she could do to prevent the excavation taking place. She watched as the hard ground was attacked with a pick axe, then the loose soil shovelled into a wheelbarrow and tipped in an area further away. Occasionally one of the men would bend and examine something that had been found and then discard it onto the spoil heap. Finally she turned away and walked back to the house.

'So what did you find out?' asked her mother when she returned.

'The police say they have been told there is something buried in the area and they have the legal right to dig. I can't stop them.'

'What are they expecting to find? Do you think a thief has buried stolen items there or could there be an icon hidden between the trees? That would be exciting. I've heard that they have been found in other areas where they were buried to prevent them from being stolen during the war.'

Eleni Despina's hand flew to her mouth. She had never believed the story that had been passed down through the generations claiming her great great grandmother had shot and buried soldiers during the war.. Could it possibly be true?

Panayiotis stood and watched as the men sweated and strained to remove the hard packed earth. They had removed their jackets and two of them had also taken off their shirts; all of them stopping frequently to have a drink of water. He wondered how much longer it would be before they found anything of interest; even a uniform button would add credence to his request that the area be investigated.

Finally an officer called for a halt in the proceedings. 'I don't think we should go any further. I've uncovered a bone.'

His fellow officers crowded round, trying to decide whether it had been buried by an animal and should be ignored.

Panayiotis took out his mobile 'phone. 'Before you go any further I think we need to have forensics up here. They'll be able to say if it belongs to an animal.'

'They'll not thank us for wasting their time.'

'I'd rather waste their time than ignore it,' replied Panayiotis. 'Dig around it carefully and see if you can expose more, but make sure you don't damage it.'

The officer who had first found the bone knelt back down and scraped away carefully with his trowel. 'If it does belong to an animal I certainly can't think of one that has bones this large.'

Reluctantly the other officers joined their colleague and began to trowel away at the earth higher up.

'It would make life easier if the ground was not so hard,' complained one. 'Can't we give it a good soaking?'

Panayiotis shook his head. 'Not unless forensics agree. Once they arrive and take over you'll all be relieved of duty for the rest of the day and be able to go home and shower.'

'My wife isn't going to be very pleased when she sees the state of my trousers.'

'They'd be worse if the ground was wet.'

'I just hope forensics arrive soon. My back aches from bending over and my knees are sore.'

Panayiotis ignored their complaints and watched carefully as the men trowelled conscientiously. More bones were gradually exposed and it became evident that they were of human origin.

'Whoever this was appears to have had three legs,' exclaimed a man.

'I think you could find there are two men buried there. Keep an eye out for any small items that might be exposed.'

It was a further hour before a forensics team arrived and Panayiotis was able to call a halt. 'All of you back home and you do not mention this morning's activities to anyone, not even your wife. You'll have to think up some excuse to explain your dirty uniforms.'

'Why don't we change at the station and take them all to the dry cleaners? We could say we had been out on manoeuvres.'

Panayiotis nodded. 'Good idea. You could deal with that, Tomas, whilst I stay here.'

By the end of the afternoon forensics had unearthed two skeletons, along with more buttons, two metal belt buckles and some dog tags.

'That's about it,' declared the scientist in charge. 'We've finished earlier than I had anticipated. We didn't have to dig as deeply as I expected. We've also dug around a bit further and can't find anything else relevant.'

Panayiotis nodded. He was convinced that it was the two soldiers who had been killed and buried by the family who lived at the olive grove during the war.

'I'll go down to the house and inform the woman that we have finished and arrange for a couple of men to be sent here tomorrow morning to fill in the ground.'

Despina Eleni watched Panyiotis approach with trepidation. She sincerely hoped that nothing of any significance had been found up in the grove. Her grandmother had been distressed when she had been informed that a body had been found down by the Causeway in the old olive grove there. She had spent most of her time since then in her room and Despina Eleni had heard her muttering prayers before the icon that hung on her wall. She was becoming concerned about her grandmother's mental stability and would need to speak to the doctor to see if there was a remedy.

Panayiotis took a seat in the kitchen and ran his hand across his head. 'I think you should also sit down, Madam. The news I have for you may come as rather a shock.'

Despina Eleni shuddered and sat down opposite Panayiotis. She hoped he would not notice that she was trembling.

'There is no gentle way I can break this to you. We have finished excavating the area in the olive grove that you visited this morning. I am arranging to have the ground filled in tomorrow morning. We found the skeletons of two men who had been buried there. Can you give me any information about how they came to be there?'

Despina Eleni touched the cross she wore around her neck and shook her head. 'I know nothing about them.'

'You never heard it mentioned that burials may have taken place up there?'

'It is not consecrated ground. Why should there be any burials there?'

'That is what we would like to find out. Is it possible that your mother or grandmother would be able to help us with our enquiries?'

'I'm certain they know of nothing that would help you.'

'I would like to speak to both of them, please.'

Despina Eleni shrugged. 'If you insist. I would ask you to treat my grandmother very gently. She is an old lady and has become very mentally fragile recently. She worries over the slightest thing.'

'You will be welcome to be with her whilst I speak to her. If you feel she is becoming too distressed I can return on another occasion when she is calmer.'

Reluctantly Despina Eleni rose. 'I will have to fetch them. My mother will probably be watching the news and my grandmother could be asleep. She often has a siesta during the latter part of the afternoon.'

Panayiotis sat unmoving until Despina Eleni returned. 'This is my mother, Evangelina Adonia. My grandmother is refusing to leave her room.'

'Very well. I'm sure when I have spoken with your mother you will be able to reassure your grandmother she has nothing to worry about when I talk to her.'

Panayiotis explained to Evangelina Adonia that in the course of the investigation carried out in the olive grove two skeletons had been found. 'Naturally we are very anxious to ascertain how they came to be buried up there. Are you able to help us at all?'

Evangelina Adonia shook her head. 'Burials have been found all over the island. Unless they had been unearthed when the trees were planted how would anyone know there were bodies buried up there?'

'When were the trees planted?' Panayiotis looked from one woman to the other.

'Goodness knows,' replied Despina Eleni.'Some of them are over two hundred years old.'

'You never heard anyone mention that burials had taken place in the olive grove?'

Despina Eleni frowned at her mother and then both women shook their heads.

'I would like to ask your grandmother. She may be aware of something that happened in the past.'

'I'm sure she knows nothing.'

'I would still like to speak with her. I have to report details of my investigation; who I spoke to and their response. I could be accused of not complying with my duties if I did not see her,' persisted Panayiotis.

'We'll tell her later. It is bound to upset her. She became very distressed when you called and said a body had been found on the lower land. She does not appear to have recovered from the shock. She is not her usual self; she spends a good deal of time in her room in prayer.'

'Has she always been a religious woman?' asked Panayiotis.

'Of course. We all attend church every Sunday.'

Panayiotis nodded. 'It would probably be advisable for you to break the news to her; less of a shock than seeing a policeman appear. Shall I accompany you to her room?'

Despina Eleni glowered at him, but knew she had to comply. She had no wish to be arrested for obstructing the police when they were carrying out their duty. She led the way up the stairs and tapped on the door.

'Grandma, are you awake?'

'Is it supper time?'

'No, I need to speak to you. May I come in?'

'Of course.'

Despina Eleni entered and Panayiotis pushed the door open wider so he could observe whatever took place between the two women.

'Grandma, there is a policeman here ...'

'The police? Whatever for? I've done nothing.'

'Of course not, Grandma. No one is accusing you of anything. They are just making some enquiries. They went up into the olive grove and dug up an area. They found some bones up there.'

'Bones? What kind of bones?'

'Old bones, but not as old as the ones that the archaeologists found in the prehistoric cemetery down by the Causeway. You obviously know nothing about them, Grandma, but the police have asked to see you.'

Despina Maria's hand went to her mouth and she clasped her cross tightly and began to mutter prayers. 'The sins of the fathers are visited on the children,' she said finally.

Despina Eleni turned back to Panayiotis who still stood by the open door. 'You understand why I say that my grandmother is unable to help you? The shock of the body being found on the lower land has affected her badly. I think her mind is becoming feeble.'

Panayiotis nodded. 'Thank you. I can report that I fulfilled my duties.'

'Well if you are satisfied now I would like to continue with my preparations for our meal. My husband will be home soon and after a day at work he will be hungry.'

'I can sympathise with him. I have had nothing to eat all day.'

'Then you will be relieved to get home also. I'll see you out.'

Panayiotis had hoped that he would be invited to stay and join them in their repast. Despina Eleni would have been bound to tell her husband about the skeletons and in the course of their conversation he may have heard something useful.

Upon his arrival at home he showered and changed from his uniform, pleased that he had not been expected to crawl around on the red earth and stain his trousers. He poured a beer and then 'phoned John.

'Yes?' answered John eagerly when he saw it was Panayiotis who was calling him.

'This is entirely unofficial,' Panayiotis warned him. 'The excavation took place today and the skeletons of two men were unearthed.'

John punched the air. 'I was right then. Who were they?'

'It's far too early to say, but some more buttons, two belt buckles and a set of dog tags were found with them.'

'They have to be the soldiers. Is one of them Pietro Rossi?'

'At the moment we shouldn't speculate. I'll let you know when I have any definite information.'

June 2016
Week Four

'I've finally found the perfect tiles,' declared Cathy. 'The floor tiles are larger and described as heavy duty, suitable for both inside and outside use. The wall tiles are exactly the same design and colour and come in two different sizes. We just have to send them details of the quantity we need of each and the colour code. They are rather expensive, though.'

Vasilis smiled. Cathy had a gift for always choosing the most expensive article without ever looking at the price tag first. The work at the house had virtually come to a standstill whilst he waited for Cathy to select floor and wall tiles. His original plan for them to move in July looked very unlikely.

'How much?'

'Well, the tiles themselves are quite reasonable, but they have to be imported from Italy.'

Vasilis raised his eyebrows. 'Italy? Don't they stock similar ones in Greece?'

Cathy shook her head. 'I have looked, and although there are some that look very similar they are not the same quality and they are not advertised as non-slip if they become wet. I'd be happy to have them throughout the house and if they're non-slip they could go outside on the patio as well. Come and have a look, Vasilis. If you don't like them I'll look for some different ones.'

Vasilis looked at the web site. "Sylvio Castiglioni Tile

Emporium". He scrolled down and looked at the illustration of each tile and the information. According to the web site the tiles could be made in various sizes, suitable for indoor and outside use and guaranteed to be slip proof. Samples could be sent upon request.

Vasilis sighed. 'I doubt that you'll find anything you like better. I suggest you send for some samples. If you're happy with them then I will be also. I'll ask Palamakis to look at them as well. If he agrees they're suitable I'll get him to measure up. If the order is large enough we may get a shipping discount.'

Ludmila waited anxiously to receive a telephone call from Svetlana asking her to call on Mother and finally hear that Ivan had been released. Provided she had received the compensation from the insurance company by then they would be able to leave Moscow and travel down to the Turkish border. They had friends in the vicinity and they would be willing to help them to enter Turkey. Once there Ludmila was convinced that they would both be able to obtain lucrative work that suited their abilities.

It came as a shock to her when she answered her door and found the police there again. She showed them in, hoping they would not be asking her any difficult questions.

'We're sorry to have to trouble you again, but there is a small matter we would like you to clarify for us regarding your burglary.'

Ludmila felt her throat go dry. Had they realised that she had been responsible for the damage and no burglary had taken place?

'You told us that your jewellery was in the safe.' Ludmila nodded and the policeman continued. 'Was all of your jewellery in the safe at the time?'

'Yes.'

'You are quite certain of that?'

'Yes.'

The policeman frowned. 'You see, an item matching the description on your insurance certificate and photograph has come to light in a jewellers. He insists that he bought it some weeks earlier from a woman who said she needed the money for her husband to have an emergency operation.'

'That was not me.'

'You did not entrust anyone to sell a piece of jewellery for you?'

'Certainly not.'

'Can you provide any explanation how the brooch could be in the possession of a jeweller before your burglary took place?'

'No.' Ludmila shook her head and clenched her hands together. She should have thought and not claimed that the diamond brooch she had given to Mother was in the safe amongst the other items. He must have given it to Svetlana to take to a jeweller. 'Could it be a replica?'

'We will obviously investigate that possibility. You are absolutely certain that it was amongst the jewellery that was stolen?'

Ludmila nodded. She could not change her story now.

'Well I'm sure the jeweller who examined the items for insurance will be able to attest to its authenticity. He would have a record of the weight and the cut of the diamonds.'

Panayiotis read the report sent to him from the forensic department. It confirmed the information that John had given him about two soldiers having been shot and subsequently buried. Both men had been identified by their dog tags, the Italian government would have to be informed and it would then be up to them to try to trace their relatives. He thought it likely that John would be able to speed up their enquiries when he told him the second body was that of Pietro Rossi.

John was delighted when Panayiotis telephoned with the news. 'Can I call Pietro?'

'There's no reason why you shouldn't. He'll have to contact the Italian government and they will probably want proof that the man was his relative.'

'Will he be able to claim the remains and have it sent to Italy for a proper burial?'

'Once the paperwork has been completed that should be no problem.'

'Will the Colonomakis family be prosecuted?' asked John.

'I don't think they will need to worry about that. It was a war time crime. The Italians will describe it as an atrocity and the Cretans will say it was a patriotic act of heroism. Whoever carried out the killing and burial will probably be dead by now so there is no one who can be brought to justice.'

'Do you think the current family knew about it?'

'It's possible, but we have no way of proving that unless one of them makes a confession. I think that is rather unlikely to happen.'

Pietro listened carefully to John. 'They're certain it is my grandfather?'

'One set of dog tags that were recovered were his. There can be no doubt that both soldiers were shot and buried in the olive grove.'

'I just hope their deaths were swift and painless. How were they found?'

'It's a long story,' smiled John. 'I don't want to tell you over the 'phone.'

'Will I have to come over and identify him?'

'There's nothing recognisable, Pietro. They are bones. Had their dog tags been removed there would be no way of knowing who either of them were.'

'Who was the other soldier?'

'Guiseppe Zingaretta apparently.'

'I've never heard of him.'

'The Italian government are going to be informed. I suggest you contact them and ask about the procedure for having your grandfather's remains returned to you in Italy. It will be up to them to try to trace the family of the other victim.'

'Provided I am given permission to take possession of the

remains I would like to come over and collect them in person. I'd like to meet you then and hear how they were finally discovered after all this time.'

'I'm sure all that can be sorted out between the government and yourself. I don't know the legalities. Let me know how you get on and I'll be pleased to meet you again.'

'I cannot tell you how grateful I am to you for your help.' Pietro wiped his eyes. He had not expected to have such an emotional reaction to the news.

Mr Groshenkov read the news that was e-mailed to him in disbelief. He had contacted Mr Propenkov and asked for Ivan Kolmogorov to be held in a secure unit as he was sure there was an attempted escape plan being put in place. Now he was told that two men had escaped the gaol and one had been shot dead.

He immediately called Mr Propenkov at the Consulate in Heraklion and asked for information.

'I'm not able to give you any details. There is an internal enquiry taking place to ascertain how the incident happened. Until that is completed they are keeping the information confidential.'

Mr Groshenkov sighed. 'Can you tell me anything?'

'As far as I am aware both men were being taken to Heraklion. They requested a stop en route to relieve themselves. As they were allowed outside the prison van one man ran and he was shot. The other escaped in a car. One guard suffered concussion and the other has disappeared.'

'So it was an arranged escape?'

'That is how it would appear.'

'Are you able to tell me their identities?'

'Not at this stage. The prison authorities are refusing to give any details to me.'

'When do you expect to know who they were?'

'As I said, there is an internal investigation taking place and until that has been completed no further details are being released to us. I am as anxious as you to know exactly who they were.'

Mr Groshenkov sighed in frustration. It was most likely that Ivan Kolmogorov had made his escape by car and his unfortunate companion had been told to run to distract the attention of the guards.

Vasilis examined the tile samples that had been sent to him from Italy. He made them wet and then trod on them whilst wearing leather soled shoes. He did not find his feet slipping. He held Cathy carefully whilst she repeated the experiment and she had no trouble keeping her balance.

'You do like them, don't you, Vasilis?'

'I think they are ideal for inside, but I'm not sure about using them outside. They could be very dazzling when the sun shines on them. I think we should have something out there that will not reflect the light.'

'I'll look at their web site again.'

'You could also look at some of the Greek web sites. You could see some that are eminently suitable and will not cost so much to be transported. I'll take these along to Palamakis tomorrow and ask his opinion. Provided he sees nothing detrimental that would cause a problem when they are laid I'll ask him to measure up and then I can put in a firm order. I'll need his advice. I don't know if the tiles should butt up against the appliances and cupboards or be laid beneath them.'

'Does it make any difference?' asked Cathy.

'Of course. If they are to butt up against them fewer tiles will be needed and all the appliances and cupboards must be in place.'

'I've decided on the appliances. I was going to ask you to order them this week.'

'Wait until I've spoken to Palamakis. I just hope the lift will be spacious enough for them to fit in. The delivery men will not appreciate carrying them up the flight of steps.'

'I've not decided on the colour of the work top yet,' frowned Cathy. 'When will that be needed?'

'Not until everything else is in place so you have plenty of time to make that decision. One thing at a time. Let me find out about the tiles from Palamakis and how he wants to lay them. It's going to be rather a large order and I hope they will have sufficient in stock. We don't want to be waiting months for them to arrive.'

Elena telephoned Marianne. 'I'm feeling really excited. I went to the real estate agents today and have viewed a house a second time that I think will be perfect.'

'Really? Where is it?'

'Not far away from here, but in an area where the properties are smaller. I thought about it carefully after I had viewed it the first time and then I asked to go back a second time. I wanted to make sure that if I am unable to climb stairs some time in the future I would be able to live on the ground floor.'

'Have you got a problem climbing stairs?'

'Not really. I have to take them slowly and be careful as I go down, but I wanted to make certain that I could convert the ground floor into an apartment if necessary. There's a reasonable sized kitchen with a large dining room and separate lounge. Across the hallway are three smaller rooms. I'll use two of them for storage at first but they could easily be converted into a bedroom and bathroom later. The third small room is already a cloakroom. Upstairs there's a bedroom at the front, two smaller ones behind and a full bathroom.'

Marianne frowned. 'Mamma you said you were looking for a one room apartment. Now you're talking about a house and thinking of converting it eventually into a ground floor apartment. That does not seem practical.'

'All the apartments that I looked at were in poor, run down areas or had been converted from a large house into very small rooms to make two separate living places. When I was in one of them I could hear the television that was on next door. I saw a couple of others that I thought had potential, but when I looked around the neighbourhood I did not feel happy with the neighbours I saw going in and out.'

'What was wrong with the neighbours?'

'They may all have been very respectable people, but there always seemed to be a collection of youths hanging around outside. They didn't approach me when I visited, but they made me feel very uneasy.'

'What about the neighbours in the new location?'

'It seems to be very quiet. Most the people in the area look well over retirement age. There's no one hanging around outside looking threatening.'

'Where are your amenities?'

'About as far away as walking into Elounda from your house. I wouldn't want to do that every day, particularly if the weather was bad, but at the moment I have my car. There's an area outside at the front where I can park it off the road.'

'What about the back yard area?' asked Marianne.

'It needs some attention, but it's not too big for me to cope with. When I've organised it I could have a summer house built so I can sit out there or I might have a conservatory added on, but that would mean entering it from the kitchen.'

'Mamma, please do not make any decision at the moment. If you decided to buy and then turned the ground floor into an apartment, what would you do with the upstairs? Would you want to let it and have people living above you? They could be a terrible nuisance.'

'I'd make sure I had someone quiet.'

'You couldn't guarantee that they would be. Why don't you continue to look around? I think you need to be closer to the amenities. You found the walk from us into Elounda quite tiring. Have you mentioned this to Helena?'

'I wanted to tell you first.'

'I wish I could actually see it,' sighed Marianne. 'You realise that whatever I say Helena will disagree with.'

'Of course she will.'

'Mamma, why don't you look a little further afield? You said some of the other apartments were more expensive but it could be worth paying extra to have exactly what you want and not have to think about conversions at a later date. You will tell us if you need some extra finance, won't you? We're having a good season so we would be able to help you.'

'I'm very grateful for the offer, Marianne, but you need to save your money for when you have a poor season or I you need some extra help with Marisa and Yannis in the future.'

Marianne laughed. 'Uncle Yannis is still besotted with his pots and sits outside every day with his exhibition. That was a brilliant idea that John had. It's given him a new lease of life and Grandma goes out and spends time with him. Before they would just sit around on the patio each day doing nothing. I don't think I'll need any extra help with them for a while yet.'

'What about Marcus? How is he now?'

'Virtually fully recovered. He does a full day's work most of the time, but Giovanni won't let him drive to the airport and back yet.'

'Was the information that I sent to John any use to him?' asked Elena.

'He says it was invaluable. I'm not sure exactly what he has been up to, but he is looking extremely pleased with himself. Why don't you ask him?'

'Not now. I have too many other things buzzing around in my brain. I just hope Andreas doesn't suddenly ask me to go up to New York.'

'You'll just have to tell him that it's an inconvenient time for you.'

'I couldn't do that. I promised I would give him any help that he needed. How are the children?'

'Fit and well and growing fast. Elisabetta and Joanna are doing well at school and Yiannis will be joining them in the Kindergarten in September. Nicola can't wait. He's such a live wire, into everything, an absolute replica of his father at that age.'

'I'd like to come over later and see you all again. I might even look for a little cottage like Andreas has. I don't really know why I am staying here. Helena's boys are grown and left home.'

'If that is how you feel you should certainly not purchase the house you have looked at. You could come here and look around and if you don't find anything you consider suitable you can look around again when you return. Think seriously about it before you tell Helena or progress with your current plans.'

Marianne heard her mother give a deep sigh. 'You're probably right, but I don't want to be a nuisance to you.'

'You're never a nuisance. Let me know if you want to come and stay and you'll be very welcome.'

'Maybe. I'll sleep on it and let you know.'

Marianne went in search of Giovanni. 'I've just had a 'phone call from my mother. She was terribly excited at first and told me all about a house she has seen and is thinking of buying. It sounds very nice but I'm not sure it's suitable for her.'

'If she is happy with it, what's the problem?'

'She's already talking about converting it into a ground floor apartment for when she can't manage the stairs. I didn't actually say as much, but that is a ridiculous idea. As we talked she asked after everyone. I think she's missing the children. She said she didn't know why she stayed in New Orleans and might look for a little cottage over here. I've told her to hold everything and come and stay with us.'

Giovanni raised his eyebrows. 'When did you have in mind?'

Marianne shrugged. 'Whenever she wants.'

'We have Angelo and Francesca coming to stay next month.'

'Oh,' Marianne bit at her lip. 'I'd forgotten that. I'm sure it will be no problem. My mother may decide not to come until the weather cools down.'

'Provided your sister doesn't decide to come with her. Vasi has refused to have her at his hotel and I'm certainly not allowing her to stay in one of the self catering units.'

'Knowing how well Mamma gets on with Helena she probably won't tell her that she is coming over here to stay for a while.' Marianne smiled. 'If Mamma does decide to buy somewhere to live here Helena will not be pleased and accuse me of influencing her.'

'Don't worry about it. Just wait and see what transpires. I think you're right to try to dissuade her from buying the property she told you about. Encourage her to come over here for a few weeks.'

'You're only saying that because you know how cross that will make Helena.'

Giovanni shook his head. 'Helena means nothing to me. Why don't you have a look around in Elounda and see if there is an apartment your mother could rent for a while and see how she likes living there?'

'Well, if she is here the same time as Angelo and Francesca that could be a good idea. They'll probably want to spend time with your mother and even take her out so they can spend some quality time with her. Having my mother around could be difficult. They might feel obliged to include her.'

Giovanni grinned at his wife. 'I can't see your mother being very happy with that. They'll spend all their time chattering away in Italian and she won't understand a word.'

Marianne aimed a mock blow at his head. 'Come to that neither will I.'

Elena sat and thought about her conversation with Marianne. Her daughter was right. She was foolish to buy another house at her time of life. She could convert her current house into a ground floor apartment if she decided to stay there. Helena would be furious if she backed out of the sale now, but she was prepared to face her wrath. For the present time she would mollify her by saying she was still looking for somewhere suitable. The excuse would be true. She wished she was more conversant with the internet so she could scroll through and see what was on offer further from New Orleans. She could go anywhere she pleased in Louisiana, but would prefer to stay in the area that she knew so well.

She would tell Helena that she was needed in New York by Andreas and arrange to visit him and ask his advice. Then she might well take Marianne up on her invitation to go and stay with them in Crete.

Vasilis listened to Palamakis's advice regarding the tiling that was needed in his new house.

'You should certainly have the tiles wall to wall and the appliances sitting on them. Should any of them need to be renewed at some time in the future they may not be exactly the same size as the current item it would mean you needed to find matching tiles; not only for the aesthetic appearance but also so the appliance was level. There is no necessity to have the tiles going back to the wall where you plan to have the fitted units and cupboards. The frames can be adjusted so that they stand level or the floor can be raised at the back with hardboard.'

Vasilis shook his head. 'I understand, but how many more tiles will I need? I don't want to find that I have a quantity left over; they are too expensive to waste.'

'Have you looked for similar ones locally to save the cost of importing?'

'Cathy is set on having these and although I have looked I cannot see anything here or in Athens that matches them for quality. At least I have dissuaded her from having them outside where the sun would reflect back from them.'

'Have you considered that they may make the rooms look cold during the winter?'

Vasilis waved his hand airily. 'I will get carpet for the lounge and dining area. That can be laid when the weather is cold and removed again in the summer.'

'Where will you store it? The carpet will be a large item and cannot be rolled up and left in a corner.'

Vasilis looked perplexed. 'We need an extra room.'

Palamakis chuckled. 'It's a bit late to think of that now.'

'So what do you suggest? '

'A storage area could be made beneath the steps. It would need to be fully waterproofed in case any rain was able to penetrate through the steps but you could use much cheaper tiles for the floor area.'

Vasilis nodded slowly. 'That sounds practical, but is it possible?'

'It will mean some extra work. Ideally it should have been thought about earlier.'

'I wish you had mentioned it earlier.'

'You did not tell me you planned to have carpets to store in the summer,' replied Palamakis immediately.

Vasilis sighed. 'I was too intent on installing the lift and making the interior safe for Cathy. Measure up for the tiles and let me know the quantity you will need. I was hoping we could move in next month. I'd prefer the inside to be completed before you start work on a storage area. It won't be needed until next summer.'

July 2016
Week One

'That's a coincidence,' Pietro had remarked when the request for tile samples arrived on his desk 'I was in that area a month ago. I wonder if the young man I met there knows who it is who wants the tiles.'

He would like to know more about the man who had now placed an order for such a large quantity. It would be practical to work out the cost of the manufacture and price the shipping separately and then ask for half the cost to be paid up front if the order was confirmed. He was not prepared to make the extra tiles that would be required and then have the order cancelled when the man received the final bill.

He had contacted the Italian War Office and been given permission by to collect the bones belonging to his grandfather and have them placed in an ossuary in his local cemetery. He still needed the authority of the Greek government to take them out of the country, but he had been assured that was just a formality and would be no problem. The bones were currently being stored in Aghios Nikolaos. Once he had permission to collect them he would arrange a visit to Crete and whilst he was there he would also call on John. He was curious to know how the soldiers had finally been discovered, but he still wanted to know the fate of his father. The young man might also know the identity of his customer.

Mr Groshenkov was dozing in front of the television when his mobile 'phone rang. Seeing that it was Borovich calling he was immediately alert.

'I thought you would want to know that a man has entered the apartment block where Svetlana lives.'

'Who was he? Do you have a description?'

'No idea. It was too dark to see him clearly or take a photo. He arrived in a taxi, a hat pulled well down over his face and he was carrying an attaché case.'

'Could he be a resident arriving home late from work?' asked Mr Groshenkov. 'What time is it now?' He squinted at his mobile phone to ascertain the time.

'Ten. I saw all the other residents arrive earlier. They are very regular with their working hours. Whoever he was visiting was expecting him as the door was opened immediately.'

'What time did he leave?'

'He has not come back out yet.'

'Did he go to the Asimenikov apartment?'

'I can't tell. Their curtains are drawn.'

'Keep watching,' ordered Mr Groshenkov. 'It's late for a social call. If a taxi arrives to collect him try to get a photo of him and the registration number of the cab. 'Phone me back however late it is. I'll 'phone Anikov now and tell him to be here with the tape first thing tomorrow morning. Judging from the previous ones I've listened to they run for twenty four hours.'

Ludmila was delighted when she received a message from Svetlana asking her to visit that morning. It must mean that Ivan was free. As she dressed another awful thought struck her. Maybe Mother had decided not to purchase her jewellery and wanted her to collect it. She wished she had asked Svetlana why Mother wanted to see her, although she thought it unlikely that Svetlana would have been forthcoming.

271

Mr Groshenkov received another telephone call from Borovich informing him that the man had not left the apartment block.

'You're sure? You didn't fall asleep?'

'Of course I didn't. I've been standing up all night,' Borovich yawned as if to add proof to his story.

'Make sure you stay awake and let me know if the man leaves.'

Mr Groshenkov waited anxiously in his office for the arrival of Anikov. The man was taking his time arriving although he had impressed upon him that he needed the tapes as early as possible.

'I was expecting you earlier than this,' commented Mr Groshenkov as the man entered.

'I was just about to leave when I heard the woman making a call. It meant I had to change the tape to bring you that one also.'

Mr Groshenkov nodded. 'Which is the one from yesterday?'

Anikov indicated the one that was completely full. 'If I hear any more today do you want me to contact you?'

'I'll let you know when I've listened to these.' Now Mr Groshenkov was in possession of the two recordings he was desperate to hear them and waved his hand towards the door indicating that Anikov should leave.

He inserted the first tape and fast forwarded it until over half was sitting on the used spool. He could go back and listen to it later if necessary. It was a further half an hour before he heard any conversation.

A phone could be heard ringing and was answered by the man with a brief 'Yes?' That was followed by the one word 'Good.'

Ten minutes later he heard the man speaking. 'Close the curtains, Svetlana. He shouldn't be much longer.'

Svetlana obviously did as she was told as he could hear the rattle of the curtains on the runners.

Another fifteen minutes went by before there was a ring at the bell and he heard Svetlana press the release button for the front door. Seconds later she opened the apartment door and admitted their visitor.

'You made it then,' he heard the man known as Mother say.

'Thanks to you. The organisation was perfect and I followed my instructions.'

'Good. You can sleep in Svetlana's room. She will use the sofa. Have something to eat and drink and then get some rest.'

'I need all of that. It was a long journey, but it's good to be back.'

'I'm pleased to see you, but you look exhausted. I'm longing to hear more tomorrow when you've had a good night's sleep. I've left a bottle of vodka beside your bed.'

'I'll enjoy that, but only have a glass or two. I won't appreciate having a hangover tomorrow.'

'I will be arranging for you to have a visitor.'

'That will be interesting.'

From then on the only sounds were of crockery being placed on the table and the man obviously eating.

Mr Groshenkov groaned in frustration. From then on the tape was silent, only slight sounds of movement recorded and finally Mother saying goodnight and Svetlana answering him. He selected the tape that was marked 'kitchen' in the hope of learning more.

Mr Groshenkov debated whether to listen to the earlier part and see if he could find out the identity of the man who was obviously sleeping in the woman's bedroom or listen to the one that Anikov said related to a 'phone call that had taken place earlier that morning.

He decided to listen to the phone call and return to the other tape later. He was delighted when he heard Svetlana ask someone to call at the apartment at eleven. Could it mean that Ivan had arrived and Ludmila would be going to meet him?

Mr Groshenkov immediately called Zavinalov. 'I need you to watch Ludmila Kuzmichov's apartment. Let me know as soon as you see her go out and tell Lenishkova to follow her.'

273

Mt Groshenkov's next call was to Borovich. 'There's a visitor expected at the apartment. Let me know immediately anyone calls and make sure you have a photograph.'

Vasilis read the e-mail from Pietro explaining that the quantity of tiles ordered were not currently in stock and they would have to be manufactured. He estimated that it would take no longer than two weeks for the required number to be made. Pietro quoted the cost, including the shipping and transportation from Heraklion to Vasilis's address. He ended by saying that before they could proceed he would have to be in receipt of half the cost and the full amount paid before the order was despatched.

Vasilis had expected the request. He debated challenging the amount that was being charged for the transport and then decided against doing so. If the man thought there might be a problem with him finally paying the full amount he could delay despatch. He needed Palamakis and his grandsons to progress with the laying of the kitchen area as soon as possible. The white goods Cathy had chosen were ordered and ready for delivery.

He e-mailed Pietro back immediately and promised to go to the bank the following day to make a transfer of the amount requested.

Ludmila, although desperate to get to Svetlana's apartment, thought it prudent to follow her usual routine and take the underground and then a taxi to the nearby road. She hurried along and pressed the bell excitedly. Mr Zavinalov had instructed Lenishkova to follow Ludmila and he called Mr Groshenkov.

'She's just left,' he announced. 'Lenishkova is following her.'

'Tell her to make sure she keeps out of sight. I don't want her to incur any trouble.'

Mr Groshenkov dialled the number for the main police station and asked to speak to Commander Osipenkov.

The receptionist stalled. 'Can you tell me who is calling, please. I could probably connect you to the appropriate department.'

'My name is Groshenkov. I am a Commander at the Ministry of Internal Affairs. This is an important matter and I wish to speak with Commander Osipenkov immediately.'

The line went dead and Propenkov looked at it furiously. Had he been cut off? A few seconds later he heard a man's voice on the line.

'Is that Commander Osipenkov?' he asked? 'It is Groshenkov here and I need to speak to him about an urgent matter.'

'That is me speaking. What is the problem?'

'As a Commander at the Ministry of Internal Affairs I am ordering you to take a detachment of men to the following address.' Mr Groshenkov waited whilst the man wrote it down and then checked that it was correct.

'What is the nature of the crime that is being committed?'

'I have reason to believe that a criminal who was being held prisoner in Crete has managed to escape and reach Moscow. This person could be a threat to security. It is also possible that there is another person there who is planning to receive some jewellery that has been registered as stolen.'

'Do my men need protective clothing?'

'That could be a wise precaution, but I don't think it will be necessary. It is essential that your men are there as soon as possible and keep out of sight until I 'phone you again. We need to catch these people unawares.'

Mr Groshenkov mopped his brow. If he was wrong in his suspicions he would very likely be demoted and accused of wasting police resources. If he was correct then he would be commended and his pension would be increased as a reward.

Mr Zavinalov called to say that Lenishkova had followed Ludmila on the metro, but when they reached the station the woman had taken a taxi and she had consequently lost her. Mr Groshenkov waited anxiously for a call from Borovich.

'A woman has just gone into the apartment building.'

'Keep watching,' ordered Mr Groshenkov and called the

police again. This time he was put straight through to Commander Osipenkov.

'I want you to wait five minutes and then order your men to go in. There's a fire escape at the rear and that needs to be covered. If the door is not opened voluntarily to them they must break it down.'

He would be interested to listen to the tape that Anikov would bring him the following day.

Ludmila entered the apartment, hoping that Ivan was there. As she saw who was there she gasped.

'Evgeniy!'

'Who were you expecting?'

Ludmila began to tremble. 'How did you get here?'

'Mother made some very satisfactory arrangements.'

'Is Ivan with you?'

Evgeniy shook his head. 'He met with an unfortunate accident.'

'What do you mean?'

'He was shot dead by one of the guards.'

'Shot? Why? How? He was supposed to make an escape.'

'So I understand and I was supposed to be the one laying in a field with a bullet through my head.'

'I didn't ask for that to happen. I only wanted Ivan to be free.' Ludmila's voice broke and the tears began to stream down her face. 'He can't be dead. Please tell me it isn't true.'

'Quite true. You're going to have to face life without your twin from now on,' smirked Evgeniy.

'I trusted you. Ivan told me you would help,' Ludmila spoke accusingly to Mother.

Mother shrugged. 'I work for the highest bidder.'

As a hammering on the door and shouts of 'Police. Open up,' were heard Evgeniy ran to the kitchen and opened the door to the fire escape only to be met by two burly officers who had their guns trained on him. Slowly he raised his hands and was escorted back to the living room.

Mother nodded to Svetlana and she made her way towards the door, but before she could reach it the police had forced it open and moved swiftly, a gun trained on each occupant. Ludmila was still sobbing whilst Svetlana stood silently, her face white and frightened as they were handcuffed. The man in the chair suffered the indignity of having both his hands and feet manacled and Evgeniy was pushed into a chair and restrained in a like manner.

Commander Osipenkov called Mr Groshenkov. 'My men have arrested four people, two men and two women, who were in the apartment. We are holding them for questioning, but I need information from you regarding the evidence you have against them.'

'The older man has been known to us for some time but we were unable to prove anything against him. Some questioning by your men could make him reveal the identity of his associates. The other man was responsible for people trafficking in Crete and serving a prison sentence there. His wife is trying to commit an insurance fraud for which she will be prosecuted.'

'And the other woman?'

'Nothing of a criminal nature is known about her at present, but enquiries could prove otherwise. I will hand all the information I have over to you and expect you to act on it accordingly.'

Mr Groshenkov rubbed his hands together with pleasure. He would call Anikov and ask him to deliver the latest tape recording to him immediately and then he would call Mr Propenkov and inform him of the arrests.

Elena 'phoned Andreas and asked if she could visit him in New York.

'I am rather busy,' he warned her. 'I won't have time to take you sight seeing.'

'I just want to talk to you.'

'Can't you do that over the 'phone?'

'If you have time to sit and listen properly to me.'

Andreas glanced at his watch. 'I don't have to meet with my publisher for another hour. Everything is progressing well. He is planning to have the book out in August.'

'I'm very pleased to hear that, Andreas, but that is not what I want to talk to you about.'

Elena proceeded to tell her brother about the house she had mentioned to Marianne and the reaction she had received from her daughter.

'Marianne is quite right,' said Andreas finally. 'It would be ridiculous for you to move to a house and then convert it into a ground floor apartment. You'd do far better to stay where you are and make the conversion eventually if necessary.'

'I've told Helena that she and Greg can buy this house from me. They already have a prospective purchaser for their property and she's pressing me to make a quick decision.'

'Why did you offer it to them? If you wanted to sell why didn't you put it on the open market?'

'Helena is being difficult. She says I need to be looked after and originally suggested that she and Greg moved in here with me.'

'Are you having problems living alone?'

'Not at all. I am managing perfectly well, although I admit to slowing down. I can't walk as fast as I used to and don't have as much energy as I had in the past.'

'That's natural. You're getting older. It doesn't mean you're incapable of looking after yourself.'

'I thought I should give them the offer to buy first. They would get a bargain as I would only expect them to pay the current market value, although it is probably worth more.'

'Tell them that you have changed your mind.'

'If I do that Helena will probably say that I am becoming senile.'

'So what do you want me to do?' asked Andreas.

'When I spoke to Marianne she suggested that I went over and visited them again.'

'That's an excellent idea.'

'That's why I want to come to New York and stay with you for a few days. I could tell Helena that you need some help with the book and then I could travel over to Crete from there.'

'Will you be confident travelling all that way alone? I won't be able to come with you,' Andreas warned her.

'Perfectly capable. I just need you to back me up in the subterfuge and not tell Helena my plans. You know the fuss she made when I refused to travel back with them.'

Andreas sighed. 'Of course I will, but there is one proviso. If whilst you are with me I come to the opinion that you are not able to make the journey alone then you do not go. You stay with me in New York until I am free to go with you.'

'When would that be?'

'After the book launch in August. I can't leave before then.'

Elena looked at the calendar. 'I'll arrange to come to you in two weeks time. Thank you, Andreas.' All she needed to do now was call Marianne and hope that if she visited in August rather than July it would be no problem for them.

Pietro read the official letter authorising him to collect his grandfather's remains from Crete at his convenience. He would have to take proof with him that he was legally entitled to receive them. He scratched his head. He had his grandfather's and father's birth and marriage certificates, along with his own birth certificate. He would phone the Army Records Office and check if they would be considered sufficient proof.

The Army Records Office was not particularly helpful. 'Now the identity of a soldier missing in combat has been confirmed and his next of kin informed it is out of our hands. You say you have received authority to take possession of his remains and bring them home to Italy so that should be sufficient.'

Still feeling uncertain Pietro called the 'phone number of the office in Aghios Nikolaos. Try as he might he could not seem to make himself understood and he could not understand the questions they asked of him. Feeling hopelessly frustrated he decided his only course of action was to call John and ask him if he could help.

John grinned at Pietro's discomfiture when he described his problem.

'Give me the 'phone number and I'll call them for you. I'll get back to you as soon as I have any information.'

Pietro was relieved when John called him back to say that the certificates and his own passport would be sufficient proof of the legitimacy of his claim.

'Make sure you get a withdrawal certificate from them. You don't want to be stopped at the airport for taking remains out of the country without permission.'

'How do I ask for that?'

'Contact me when you have an arrival date and I'll arrange to go with you. They could decide to be difficult as you cannot speak sufficient Greek to make your requests known.'

'Would you really? That would be such a relief. I can't make any arrangements for the next few days. I'm having to supervise a large order.'

'No problem. Let me know when you've booked your flight. Must go. I have a customer waiting.'

As Pietro finished the call he remembered that he had meant to ask John if he knew the identity of the customer who had placed the large tile order with his company.

Commander Osipenkov called Mr Groshenkov. 'I thought you would like an update on the arrests we made last week.'

'I certainly would. Were the tape recordings helpful?'

'They were. I'll start at the top with the old man who I understand is known in certain circles as 'Mother'. He insists he is just a business man and arranges the transport of import and export items. Apparently he is unable to go out to work due to his disability so conducts all the business from his home.'

'What is his disability?'

'He has two artificial legs.'

'Really! How did that happen?'

'Says he was injured when he was serving in the army. We've checked up on that and it isn't true. He was in the army for a while and is then listed as a deserter. He turns up again two years later in prison. It's my guess he had been living on his wits and committing petty crimes that caught up with him eventually.'

'So how did he lose his legs?'

'Prison brawl. He was working in the kitchen and a fight broke out. A pan of boiling water went over his legs. The guards dealt with the other inmates before they tended to him. He was placed in the infirmary but due to negligent treatment both legs developed gangrene. He was discharged from the prison and sent to the local hospital where both legs had to be amputated.'

Mr Groshenkov shuddered. 'How awful.'

'Plenty of other men have suffered injuries during their lifetimes but they have not all turned to crime for a living. He claimed he did not know that Evgeniy Kuzmichov was a criminal and thought he was a visiting business associate. The daughter says she just did as she was told by her father and I'm inclined to believe her. Ludmila Kuzmichov has confessed that she was trying to get her twin brother freed from prison and had given money and her jewellery to the old man who had promised to arrange his release.'

'So that was why she had been trying to raise money at the market and in second hand shops. That also explains why she staged a burglary at her apartment.'

'Not entirely. When the Asimenikov apartment was searched Ludmila Kuzmichov's jewellery was found there. The old man said she had given it to him to look after as she did not feel her safe was secure enough for such valuable items.'

'She should have left in the bank vault. What does she say?'

'She insists that it was payment to him so he could make the arrangements for her brother's release.'

'And her excuse for the bogus break in?'

'She said she was scared that when her husband was finally released he would find all her jewellery was missing and punish her. If she could convince him that it had been stolen she could avoid a beating.'

Mr Groshenkov laughed. 'Don't believe a word she says.'

'I don't,' Commander Osipenkov assured him. 'When Evgeniy Kuzmichov was confronted with the news that his wife's jewellery had been used to finance his escape he just shrugged and seemed unconcerned. He said he had no part in the escape plan; he just followed the orders given to him by the guard.'

'So what will happen to them now?'

'They are being kept in custody and I plan to have the tape recordings played to them. It will be interesting to hear the excuses they make to try to exonerate themselves or implicate each other. Rest assured they will all be charged and sentenced.'

'Even the girl who you believe to be innocent?'

'She must have had a fair idea of her father's business dealings. She's guilty by association. No criminal activities can be proved against her at present so she'll probably only spend a year or so in gaol. By the time their cases go to court I expect she'll have served half her sentence.'

July 2016
Week Two

Pietro telephoned John and asked if he could recommend a good, but reasonably priced hotel where he could stay for a week.

'My wife is coming with me. I thought once I had sorted out the formalities for the collection of my grandfather we could take the opportunity to visit some of the places in the area you had told me about.'

'Provided you are happy to stay in Elounda I know the ideal hotel. It belongs to a friend of ours. You'll be going up to Aghios Nikolaos so could spend a day up there looking around. Everywhere else I mentioned is easier to get to from Elounda.'

'Will I need a car?'

'It will be cheaper to hire one for a week and drive down than have a taxi and then hire one locally. You'll have to come over and have dinner with us one night.'

'I wouldn't want to impose on your family.'

'My uncle and aunt are visiting us so my mother won't even notice having two extra people to cater for. I should be free to go to Aghios with you on the Tuesday. I'll meet you at your hotel and follow you in on my bike. When you've completed your business you and your wife can stay there for as long as you want. I'll arrange for you to come to dinner on Wednesday if that suits you.'

'But you have visitors staying,' protested Pietro. 'My wife only speaks Italian.'

'They're Italian. She'll have no problem talking to them. Consider the arrangement made. I'll ask Vasi to contact you and confirm the hotel booking and I'll 'phone you there to arrange a time to meet on the Tuesday. Bye.'

As Pietro lost the connection he realised that yet again he had not asked John if he knew the man who had ordered the tiles. He must remember when he saw him.

By the time Pietro and his wife had collected the hire car and driven down to Elounda it was after mid-day.

'I feel quite hungry,' said Gabriella. 'Could we go somewhere for a snack? I'd really like a pizza. The hotel restaurant isn't open yet.'

'We could drive up to the village. There are bound to be places open up there or I could ask at reception if there is anywhere closer.'

The receptionist smiled. She was frequently asked the question. 'Walk to the end of the road and keep walking down by the sea. You'll find plenty of tavernas open who will be willing to serve you.'

'Do they have pizza?' asked Gabriella.

'They all have a very international menu available.'

'We'll walk, then,' decided Pietro. 'You ought to try some of the local food. I enjoyed most of it when I was here. A gyros is particularly satisfying.'

'I'll have pizza this afternoon,' said Gabriella firmly. 'I'll see what the restaurant at the hotel is offering tonight.'

Pietro looked across the bay as they walked along. 'It certainly is beautiful here. That island must be the one that John recommended I visited. I can ask him tomorrow and also about the other places. I didn't take much notice at the time. I was only interested in finding the churches and cemeteries.'

'Well now you can behave like a tourist. Have you seen that house there? It must belong to someone important.'

Pietro turned and looked. 'I haven't actually been along here before. Wait until you see the house where John and his family live.'

'Will I have to dress up when we go there?' asked Gabriella anxiously. 'I've only got two summer dresses with me.'

'I'll check with John tomorrow. We'll be in Aghios Nikolaos and that is a large town. I'm sure you could find something suitable there if necessary. We seem to have reached the tavernas. Start looking at the menus and decide which one to patronise.'

John called Vasi's hotel and asked for a message to be passed to Pietro Rossi saying he would be arriving at ten to go to Aghios with them.

Gabriella pulled a face. 'I was hoping he might be later so we could have a swim this morning.'

'There will be other mornings when we can do that. It seemed quite crowded down there yesterday; maybe we could find somewhere more secluded.'

'It seemed to be very rocky up by the tavernas. I wouldn't want to swim there.'

'There must be somewhere else where the tourists go. This beach is for hotel customers only. We can have a look down the other way and see what that area is like.'

'Better still ask your friend John. Is this him arriving now?' Gabriella asked as a young man drew up on a motor scooter.

'We're bound to be kept waiting at the office in Aghios Nikolaos. I'll ask him then.'

John looked surprised at Pietro's question. 'There's the Municipal beach. The local people use that one along with the tourists. If you walk along the road towards the Causeway there's a beach along there that never has many people on it. Why don't you use the beach at the hotel?'

'It looked quite crowded when we arrived yesterday.'

'You probably have to get down there straight after breakfast and book your spot.'

'We wouldn't want to be down there all day. Just for a swim in the morning and maybe another to cool down later.'

'The best thing is to make sure you have all your swimming gear in the car with you. That way you can stop if you see anywhere you fancy. The beach along at Plaka is good, but that also becomes crowded after lunch. If you want to find somewhere really quiet I suggest you drive over the Causeway and up towards the white house. Few visitors bother to walk that far for a swim. They usually visit the taverna over there and then walk back. Here we go, we're being called forward. Have your papers ready.'

Pietro did his best to follow the conversation that took place between John and the desk clerk. It seemed to be a long time before John asked him to produce his certificates.

'What was he asking you?'

'He just wanted to know how the remains had been found after all this time. He's going to photocopy the certificates and the letter of authority that you have to remove the bones from Crete, then he'll bring them out to you.'

'I thought he was being difficult about handing my grandfather over.'

'Not at all. You'll have to sign a form to say you have taken delivery of them and that's it.'

'I feel embarrassed now that I asked you to come with me. If that was all they wanted I should have been able to deal with that myself.'

John shrugged. 'No problem. They could have come up with a question that you were unable to understand. I suggest you lock the box in the boot of your car and take it up to your room later. It will be safe there, just don't forget to take it with you when you drive back to the airport. You'll need to have the official paperwork on hand when you arrive there,' added John.

'Will they put it through the X-ray machine?'

'Bound to. Make sure they know what it contains. It could give someone a rather nasty shock,' grinned John. 'I don't imagine they see a box of bones every day.'

Pietro and Gabriella arrived at Yannis's house on Wednesday evening. Pietro had pointed it out to her as they drove past on their way to Plaka, but there was little to see from the road.

'What does the notice on the gate say?' asked Gabriella as they arrived.

"It's advertising a display of ceramics. They're copies like the ones you can buy in the museum shops and belong to his great uncle apparently.'

'Is this really the house where that nice young man lives? Has he an apartment here?'

'Kind of I imagine. I told you that when I visited before I met other members of the family who live here.'

Feeling distinctly nervous Gabriella climbed out of the car. 'Is my dress alright?'

'You look lovely,' Pietro assured her. His wife had draped a pale pink silk scarf around her neck and replaced her gold ear studs with pearl earrings.

'They won't be in proper evening dress, will they?'

'I wouldn't expect them to be. Anyway, if they are you'll still outshine all of them. I was told to go around to the patio when I came before, but it seems rather rude to walk in unannounced.'

No one opened the door and John appeared from the patio. 'Come straight round,' he called. 'We're having some drinks and then Mum and Bryony will produce the food.'

Gabriella looked in amazement at the size of the patio. Two large tables were laid with plates and cutlery along with an assortment of small plates holding snacks.

'Come and be introduced. Angelo and Francesca are longing to meet you. You remember everyone else, Pietro?'

'I think so.'

'Then ask Marcus for a glass of whatever you fancy and then we can start.'

Pietro assumed that John meant they would start to eat but instead he tapped his glass and called for everyone to listen.

'I know my immediate family know how I found his grandfather's bones,' he said in Italian, 'but I've not told Pietro the whole story and I think Angelo and Francesca will be interested. We'll form a small group over here and the rest of you can continue to talk amongst yourselves.'

Pietro and Gabriella were ushered to one of the tables where Angelo and Francesca sat whilst Giovanni explained to Yannis and Marisa.

'I'll go and sit with them.' declared Marisa. She had hardly let Angelo out of her sight since he and Francesca had arrived.

John started by telling them about the visits his grandmother had made to the local villages to gather information for his great uncle and how it had been turned into a Christmas performance.

'I thought no more about it until Pietro arrived and told me that his grandfather had gone missing over here during the war. He visited us and it was whilst he was here that Nick remembered the shooting and subsequent burial of two soldiers that had taken place locally. I asked my Grandmother in New Orleans to tell me who had told her and then Nick and I visited the old lady. From her we learnt the likely location of the burials, although the olive grove is enormous.'

John realised that his small audience was listening to him intently. 'I took my dog up there and he showed interest in an area. I then went back at night with my metal detector and dug around a bit, finding two army uniform buttons.'

'So that's why you wanted the information,' exclaimed Pietro.

John nodded. 'I persuaded a police officer to return up there with me one night and we found another button and some dog tags. That was sufficient for him to request a full scale examination of the area. I am delighted to know that Pietro's grandfather has been found and can return to Italy to have the proper burial rights that he deserves.' John raised his glass. 'To Pietro's grandfather.'

Pietro felt his eyes grow moist and Gabriella squeezed his hand.

'You make it sound so easy, John,' commented Angelo. 'I'd like to hear more details from you later.'

Pietro raised his glass second time. 'I think we should drink a toast to John. I cannot thank him enough. If I could now find my father I would be a truly happy man.'

Marianne and Bryony began to bring plates of food out from the kitchen, putting a selection on each table. Although John filled his plate he managed to eat very little as he was continually plied with further questions about his investigation and discovery.

At the end of the evening John escorted Pietro and Gabriella to their car. 'There is someone I would like you to meet tomorrow. I'll come down to the hotel about ten and take you to his house.'

John left his bike at the hotel and climbed into Pietro's car so he could direct him and Gabriella into Elounda and to the turning where Panayiotis lived next door to Vasilis and Cathy.

Panayiotis opened his door as soon as they knocked.

'I thought you should meet Panayiotis,' said John. 'He's our local policeman and he risked losing his badge by coming up to the olive grove with me whilst I dug around. He doesn't speak Italian, but I'm sure he will understand that you are thanking him.'

'I certainly am.' Pietro seized Panayiotis's hand and pumped his arm up and down. When he finally released him he spoke rapidly in Italian and John listened in amusement as almost every other word was 'thank you'.

Panayiotis looked at John for help and took a step back from Pietro.

'Please tell him I understand. I'm only too pleased that he has had a satisfactory conclusion to his grandfather's mysterious death.'

'All he needs now is the answer to what happened to his father.'

'What do you mean?'

'His father came over here to try to find out what had happened and he disappeared without a trace.'

Panayiotis frowned. 'When was that?'

'Almost forty years ago if I remember correctly.'

'Forty years.' Panayiotis looked at Pietro. 'Ask him if he would be willing to give a sample of blood for a DNA test.'

'Whatever for? He has proved the remains are those of his grandfather by the dog tags and official birth certificates.'

'Just ask him. I'm thinking of something else.'

John shrugged and spoke rapidly to Pietro who looked puzzled by the request.

'I suppose so, if it's necessary. I could get it done when I return home.'

Panayiotis shook his head when John translated. 'I'd like it done here as quickly as possible. I'll call the clinic and put in an official request. If the request comes from me he won't have to pay.'

John spoke to Pietro who still appeared to be completely confused about having to confirm his relationship with his grandfather.

'I suppose I can. If I refuse I imagine this policeman friend of yours could arrest me and insist.'

'I don't think he'd go that far. I'll drive into Aghios with you and go to the clinic. You can take me back to the hotel to collect my bike afterwards.'

'Will we be long?' asked Gabriella. 'We had planned to go over to Spinalonga today.'

'We should be no more than an hour. You'll still have plenty of time.'

Whilst they were talking Vasilis opened his door and looked out. 'Are you visiting us, John?'

John shook his head. 'I needed to bring my friends down to meet Panayiotis. Now we are going to the clinic in Aghios.'

'Are they ill?'

'No, I'll explain to you later. How's the house coming on?'

'I'm expecting a delivery of floor tiles today. Once they're laid the white goods can start arriving.'

Panayiotis nodded to John. 'The clinic will take the blood test as soon as you arrive. It only takes a few minutes and the result should be through within a week or so.'

The visit to the clinic in Aghios Nikolaos took a little longer than had been anticipated due to the forms that Pietro was obliged to complete under John's guidance. The test itself was over in seconds.

'Is that it?' asked Pietro.

'All done. We'll go back to Elounda and the remainder of the day is yours.'

'By the time we've had lunch it will be too late to think about going to Spinalonga today,' said Gabriella.

'You could visit some of the other places I've mentioned and go tomorrow. If you're willing to make an early start I could take you,' offered John.

'Won't you have to be up at the taverna?' asked Pietro.

'I can ask Marcus to be there again tomorrow. He's almost fully fit now and pleased to feel he is being useful again.'

'Your father won't mind you spending time with us?'

'Provided the taverna and apartments are not neglected in any way my father doesn't mind who does the work. I'd only have to cancel our arrangement if there was an unexpected airport trip that I had to do.'

As Pietro negotiated the difficult turn down the hill to the sea front road John could see that the road was blocked by a large vehicle that was swinging pallets across to Vasilis's house.

'It will be better if you stop here and I'll walk along and collect my bike,' said John. 'I should be able to get through.'

'What's happening?'

'Vasilis's floor tiles being delivered. You'll be able to backup and turn. Good job we didn't arrive back any earlier or your car would have been blocked in until they finished.'

'They are my tiles,' exclaimed Pietro, reading the label on the side of the pallet.

'What do you mean?'

'That is the firm I work for. I received a large order from someone here and I kept meaning to ask you if you knew him.'

'He's the man who lives next to Panayiotis. You saw me talking to him this morning.'

'When are the tiles being laid?'

John shrugged. 'I don't know. Why?'

'I'd love to see how they look once they are in situ. Do you think he would allow me to go and look inside his house?'

'I expect the men will make a start on the work as soon as the delivery is complete. Should be something to see by Saturday. I'll call him and provided some of the work has started I'll arrange for him to meet you.'

Elena arrived in New York and took a cab to Andreas's publisher. He had excused himself from meeting her at the airport as he said it was vital he spoke with his publisher and lawyer before his book was finally launched.

'The film company I've worked with before are urging me to sign a contract that will give them a free hand to make any alterations they see fit if they decide on a film. I'm not happy to do that. They could make all sorts of changes that would destroy its integrity. I'm hoping we can come to an agreement, but it could take all day to finally thrash everything out. It would probably be best if you came here. If I've finished my business we can then go straight to my apartment or if not you can wait for me here. I can't leave you sitting in the airport cafe for hours.'

Now she sat in the comfortable waiting room, a plate of sandwiches and cakes in front of her and a young lady had offered her the choice of tea or coffee. She looked around; displayed on the walls were the paper covers of many of the books that had been published and become best sellers. Most of them she recognised and her brother's covers were amongst them. When she had eaten she would go and examine them more carefully.

It seemed an interminable time before Andreas eventually appeared, full of apologies for keeping her waiting so long.

'I was well looked after,' Elena assured him. 'Have you reached a satisfactory outcome?'

'I think so. They have agreed not to make any drastic alterations without consulting me first. I shall insist that they consult me on everything. They may not think an alteration is drastic, but I might. I'll check the wording of the new contract they are sending me. If I'm not entirely happy I'll continue to argue with them.'

Andreas finally seemed to remember that his sister was probably tired after her journey and be longing to arrive at his apartment and able to relax.

'I'll call a cab to take us to my apartment. Would you like to go out to eat later or are you too tired?'

'I'm sure I'll be up to going out to eat, but I do want to talk to you and a crowded restaurant is not really the place for serious conversation.'

'We'll talk before we go out, then you'll be able to enjoy your meal.'

Once home Andreas selected a bottle of wine and poured a glass for each of them. 'Now, tell me what is worrying you.'

'Am I doing the right thing by selling my house? Matthew and I were happy there. Somehow it seems disloyal to him.'

Andreas spoke gently. 'That was when Matthew was alive and your children were still around. You have a different life now. The house is too large for you to live in alone and it would be practical for you to sell and move to an apartment. Matthew would understand that.'

'I have looked for apartments, but so far I've not seen anything suitable. That was why I thought the house I had seen might be ideal.'

Andreas shook his head. 'I think that would be a very bad move. I suggest you go to Elounda and when you return you can look around again. You could find an ideal apartment has come on the market whilst you were away.'

'If I'm not over here I won't know,' protested Elena.

'You ask Giovanni or Marianne to access a property web site for the area. If you see something interesting you ask the agents to e-mail you details. They don't need to know where you are currently living. What is it that you really want?'

Elena took another sip of her wine. 'Company, I suppose. My current neighbours are out at work every day. They're friendly enough, but I don't feel I can go in to have a chat with them. I became used to having people around me when I was staying with Marianne and visiting the women in the villages. Marianne did say I could live with them and contribute to the expenses, the same as Marisa.'

'That's your answer, then.' Andreas poured himself a second glass of wine.

'I do enjoy their company and love being with the children but would I be happy living with them indefinitely?' Elena spoke wistfully.

'You could probably buy a cottage in Kato if you feel you want to live alone again.'

Elena smiled. 'I would not want to live in Kato. I'd find it impossible to walk up that hill with shopping on a hot day.'

'You could take a taxi.'

Elena shook her head. 'You were happy there because you were writing. I would like some social life.'

'The neighbours are friendly.'

'That's not quite what I mean. I like to be able to walk along the seafront, have my morning coffee in a taverna, go to the market, take a bus into Aghios or Plaka if I want a change of scenery.'

'So why don't you have a look around Elounda or Plaka whilst you're there and see if there is somewhere you could rent?'

'Everywhere will be taken during the summer months.'

'And once the season is over people will be more than willing to rent out an apartment for a bit of extra income. If you decided that you weren't happy you don't have to stay.'

'I suppose that might be possible. I don't know what Helena would say.'

'You do not have to explain your actions to Helena. I was expecting you to tell me she had chased you to the airport.'

'She was not at all pleased when I told her I was coming to visit you. She's far more concerned that they will lose the sale of their house and says they can always move in with me until I find somewhere suitable to live. I am certainly not prepared to have her and Greg living with me. They will just have to wait until I decide I have found somewhere else suitable to live.'

Andreas chuckled. 'She's going to be even more displeased when she hears you have gone to Elounda.'

'You do think I'm doing the right thing, don't you, Andreas?' Elena asked him anxiously.

Andreas nodded. 'You need some time away. Helena does not need you or the house. She has a very adequate house to live in. You're welcome to stay here with me, although I may well be out most days.'

'If you make me a list of museums and libraries and any other interesting places close by I'm sure I will be able to amuse myself.'

July 2016
Week Three

Panayiotis waited anxiously to hear that the DNA test he had arranged for the bones of the body in the mortuary was completed.

'I have another request now,' he explained to the technician. 'A man named Pietro Rossi left a sample of his blood to be analysed. If you would be good enough to check to see if the sample from the bones matches his sample you could have solved the identity of an unknown murder victim for us.'

'That should be no problem. I'll let you know the result tomorrow.'

Panayiotis turned the problem over in his mind. With the results of the DNA tests finally confirming that the DNA from the bones and that of Pietro Rossi were a match he felt he had no option. The Italian man had a right to know how and why his father had met his death. He would visit the Colonomakis family again and see if he could gain any information from them? He realised that if they were completely innocent of the crime he could be accused of harassing them.

Despina Eleni opened the door to him with a worried look on her face. 'What can I do for you today?'

'I would like to explain a rather difficult situation to you, Madam. May I come in?'

Grudgingly Despina Eleni led Panayiotis through to the living room where Despina Maria was sitting. The elderly lady looked at him with frightened eyes.

'I'll go to my room,' she announced.

'I would prefer that you stayed here and listened to what I have to say. I believe you may be able to help me.'

Despina Maria shook her head, but remained sitting in the chair.

'I would also like your mother to join us,' said Panayiotis to Despina Eleni. 'It could be easier if you were all together.'

Panayiotis waited until Evangelina Adonia joined them. 'Ladies,' he began, 'I realise that the discovery of the bodies of the soldiers in your olive grove must have come as a great shock to you. I believe you when you say you knew nothing about them being buried there. I have come to ask you about the other body that was discovered on your land down by the seafront.'

Despina Maria gave a groan and Despina Eleni looked at her sharply. 'My grandmother is evidently becoming distressed. It would be better for her to retire to her room.'

Panayiotis shook his head. 'I think your grandmother may have some information that can help me with the enquiry.' He looked at Despina Maria. 'Can you explain how the body of Lorenzo Rossi came to be buried on your land?'

'I didn't do it. I didn't shoot him,' protested Despina Maria.

'I am not accusing you of anything at this juncture, Madam, but I believe you may be able to tell me who did commit the crime.'

'My father,' whispered Despina Maria.

Both Despina Eleni and Evangelina Adonia looked at her in surprise.

'Please tell me the details,' Panayiotis spoke firmly.

'My grandmother had helped her mother to bury the soldiers in the olive grove. She was proud of the part they had played in resisting the Italian occupation and told me about it. When they were questioned by the Italian authorities they denied ever having seen them. Years later a man called and began to ask questions about them. He said he was looking for his father. My mother realised he must be the son of one of the soldiers. Again she denied all knowledge of them, but she was scared. She asked the man to stay whilst she went up to the olive grove to ask her husband to come to speak to him.'

'So why did your father shoot him?'

'He was protecting my mother. He may not have intended to kill the man, just frighten him into going away.'

'You were here when this happened?'

Despina Maria nodded. 'I was expecting Evangelina Adonia. My mother sent me into the kitchen when she returned with my father. I heard the shot and from the kitchen window I saw the man fall to the ground. My parents were horrified. My mother was crying hysterically. I didn't dare go out. My father called to me to take out the bottle of raki and I thought they were going to revive the man. I didn't know he was dead. My father took a long drink and then handed the bottle to my mother. After that they became calmer.'

Evangelina Adonia crossed herself. 'Poor mother. It must have been awful for you to witness that.'

Despina Maria shuddered. 'My father fetched the cart and between them they placed him on it and covered him with some sacks. When my mother came back inside she gave me a knapsack and told me to take it out to the back and burn it. That night, not long after I had gone to bed I heard noises outside and saw my parents pushing the cart down the track. I stayed at my bedroom window and eventually they returned. The cart was empty.' Despina Maria's voice broke. 'I suppose I should have told somebody, but they were my parents. I couldn't get them into trouble.'

'I understand,' said Panayiotis gently. 'Do you know what happened to the man after that?'

'I overheard my father telling my mother that she would have to help him as the body could not stay in the shed for very long or it would start to smell. The only sheds were in the olive grove that was down by the shore.'

'Why would they bury him there rather than where the soldiers were buried?'

Despina Maria shook her head. 'I don't know. Maybe the ground was not so hard down there.'

'Did you ever ask your parents for an explanation?'

'I asked my mother what had happened to the man and she said I was never to speak about it again to anyone. He had gone home.'

'So you kept the information to yourself all this time?'

'I had other things on my mind. Evangelina Adonia arrived two days later. She was earlier than anticipated and needed a good deal of care during the first weeks of her life. I put the other events out of my mind and devoted myself to her. I hadn't thought about the incident until you came here and said a body had been found down there.'

'No wonder you were so shocked,' said Panayiotis understandingly.

'Are you going to arrest me?'

'I have no reason to arrest you, Madam. You did not commit the crime.'

'So what will happen?' asked Evangelina Adonia.

'I will need to inform the Italian man that his father's remains have been located. I think he would appreciate knowing the circumstances as you have told them to me. I cannot imagine that any further action will be taken against your family.'

'Please, tell him that we apologise for the actions of our relatives. If he would care to call we would make him welcome and apologise in person.'

Panayiotis telephoned John and asked if he had a contact number for Pietro Rossi and would be willing to speak to him.

'What about?' asked John.

Panayiotis explained that he had ascertained the identity of the body in the mortuary. 'I think he will be relieved to know that his father has been located and should be able to return to Italy for a religious ceremony.'

'Do you know how he came to be shot and buried?'

'I do, but I will need you to explain to him and also to impress upon him that the police have closed the case.'

'Who did it?'

'I'll tell you when we meet. Ask him to return to Elounda and collect his father's remains.'

'He'll also be able to see most of the floor tiles in place at Vasilis's house. He was disappointed not be able to see them when he was here before.'

'Just arrange for him to come as soon as he can.'

'How was it discovered that the remains were those of Pietro's father?' asked Nicola.

'That was Panayiotis's brilliant idea. He asked for DNA samples to be taken from both men and compared. Perfect match. Apparently the Y-STR-DNA passes down through male line.'

'So who killed him?'

'Panayiotis says he knows, but he won't say anything until after Pietro has been told the facts. He wants me to be there at the time to translate so I'll be able to tell you when I return home.'

Pietro listened carefully as John translated Panayiotis's account of his conversation with the Colonomakis ladies.

'I have mixed feelings,' Pietro admitted. 'I feel sorry for the woman who witnessed my father's murder but if she had come forward at the time it would have saved my mother years of heartache and worry. If the perpetrators were still alive I would ask for them to be prosecuted regardless of their age. I feel very bitter towards them but I just have to accept the situation.'

'He could bring a private prosecution against the woman for withholding evidence,' Panayiotis had suggested.

Pietro shook his head when John translated Panayiotis's words.

'No, it's too late now. Nothing will bring my father back. It's best forgotten. At least I have closure on his disappearance and I can take him back home where he belongs.'

'They did offer to apologise to you in person.'

'I'm not sure of that would be a good idea. I would be rather nervous that they might shoot me,' Pietro gave a wry smile. 'I'll consider it. I did say I would be completely happy if I could find out about my father. Well, thanks to you, he has been discovered. I cannot ask for more.'

'Well, that was unexpected,' said Vasilis as he closed his mobile 'phone.

Cathy raised her eyebrows. 'Good news?'

'That was a call from Mr Propenkov at the Russian Consulate. You remember hearing on the news that two men had escaped from gaol when they were being moved to Heraklion and one was shot dead?'

Cathy shook her head. She did not listen to the Greek news as she was still unable to really understand the language.

'Apparently Mr Propenkov had Ludmila Kuzmichov's activities watched and he heard there was a plan to accomplish a prison breakout for her brother. When they broke in to an apartment in Moscow to arrest him they found it was Evgeniy Kuzmichov who was there.'

'Mrs Kuzmichov must be pleased.'

Vasilis chuckled. 'I don't think so. From what Mr Propenkov said she was expecting her twin brother; the man who had brought the refugees from Syria. He was the man who was shot whilst trying to escape. She was not at all pleased to see her husband. He has been re-arrested and will now serve the remainder of his sentence in a Moscow gaol.'

'Thank goodness you're no longer responsible for "The Central".

'It has nothing to do with the hotel, or me, for that matter. Mr

Propenkov just thought I might be interested. Apparently Mrs Kuzmichov has also been arrested and is being charged with insurance fraud.'

'What was she trying to claim for?'

'She staged a break in at her apartment and said her valuable jewellery had been stolen. It was found at the apartment where Evgeniy was arrested and the owner of the apartment insisted she had taken it to him for safe keeping.

'She would have done better to put it in the bank,' commented Cathy.

'Very difficult to stage a break in at a bank vault,' grinned Vasilis.

John opened the letter that bore an Italian stamp. As he had surmised it was from Pietro. Once again the Italian thanked him profusely for his help. His mother had mixed emotions regarding the discovery of her husband's body and he was making arrangements to have his remains returned to Italy. It would be necessary for him to visit Crete again to sign the legal papers to allow the transportation take place. He requested John's help again in completing the formalities, but it would be impossible for him to return before September as he had already used all his allocated holiday allowance.

He added that he and Gabriella had enjoyed meeting Angelo and Francesca and they planned to keep in touch. His one regret was that he had been unable to visit the house where the floor tiles manufactured by his company were being laid. He asked if John could arrange for him to visit the house and take some photographs that could be used in their advertising brochures.

He then continued with another request and John frowned as he read it. 'I have now decided I would very much like to meet with the family who were the cause of our family tragedies. They have apologised to me and I would like to tell them that I understand their actions and bear them no ill will. The past cannot be changed and I will now put it behind me and hope they feel able to do the same.'

'What do you think, Nick? Would that be a good idea?'

Nicola shrugged. 'I understand his motives, forgive and forget. Would the Colonomakis be willing to meet with him?'

'He's not planning any legal action against them. He could have asked for the old lady to be charged with withholding evidence.'

'That would have just been vindictive after all this time. Why don't you speak to Panayiotis and ask him to approach the family with Pietro's suggestion? Wait to hear from him before you reply. You would probably be asked to go along to the meeting to act as interpreter and you hardly want to become embroiled should there an acrimonious exchange of words.'

'That's true,' agreed John. 'I'll also speak to Vasilis and ask if Pietro may go and take photographs of his floor tiles.'

'When are he and Cathy planning to move in?'

'I'm not sure. I think Vasilis is waiting for the outside paving to be completed and the swimming pool installed.'

'Has he obtained permission for the pool?'

John grinned. 'Possibly, but even if he hasn't I'm sure it will be installed. Once it's in situ he'll probably be issued with a fine and that will be the end of the matter. It will be no different from all the other illegal pools and building additions that have been made over the years in the area.'

Giovanni returned from the airport having taken Angelo and Francesca to catch their flight back to Italy. They insisted they had enjoyed staying there and spending time with Marisa.

'We're not that far away, Giovanni. Mother isn't getting any younger and I'd like to visit more frequently now I've retired.'

'You know you're welcome whenever it suits you. Even if we haven't a spare bedroom available at the house I know plenty of people who would be more than willing to have you stay. I have one friend who is turning his big house into self catering holiday lets next summer. It will be far more sumptuous than our little self catering establishments. It's up on the hill behind Elounda, ideal for people who want to walk and also for photographers and artists. It's meant to be for groups of like minded people and will probably be rather expensive, but as he's a friend I'm sure I could get a reduced rate for you.'

'We'll bear it in mind. Come on, Francesca, we're at the airport.'

There was no response from Francesca and Angelo nudged her and raised his voice. 'We're at the airport,' and Giovanni winced.

He hoped that the next time they visited Francesca had finally given in and had hearing aids fitted. It had been very trying having to repeat things to her or remember to raise their voices when speaking to her. She had tried to say that her ears were affected due to the flight, but Angelo had confided in Giovanni that she had a problem but thought hearing aids would make her look and feel old.

Whilst Giovanni had been out Marianne had received a 'phone call from her mother.

'I've spent some time with Andrew and he says he can make my travel arrangements. I could leave New York on Monday, spend the night in London and catch a flight to Heraklion on Tuesday. Would that be convenient for you?'

'Of course. Just let us know your flight details and time of arrival and one of us will be there to collect you. Have you enjoyed New York?'

'I found it rather lonely. Andreas had warned me that he would be busy during the day and I would only be able to spend the evenings with him. He gave me a list of museums and other places I ought to visit. I enjoyed visiting the Empire State Building, but I preferred the museums. I found the National Memorial Museum on the site of the twin towers very moving, reminding me of that terrible day. Andrew took me to the Guggenheim Museum and it was nice to have a companion to share my thoughts and feelings about the exhibits. I have so many photographs to show you.'

'Have you told Helena that you are coming to Elounda?'

'Not yet. I thought I would 'phone her when I was in London. I don't want her coming to New York and creating a scene.'

Inwardly Marianne groaned. She would no doubt receive the full force of her sister's displeasure.

'Ask Andrew to arrange everything and then let us know when you plan to arrive. You have timed it well as Angelo and Francesca left today.'

'I'm sorry I missed them. I'm sure Marisa was delighted to see them and will tell me all about their time with you.'

'John is longing to see you and tell you all about his discoveries with his metal detector. He was instrumental in solving a crime.'

'What!'

'It's a long story and I'll let John tell you the details. It was due to you remembering who had told you about the shooting of the soldiers during the war.'

'Really? How are Evi and Maria?'

'Both well, and I'll take you up to see them whilst you're here.'

'I'm so looking forward to being in Elounda again and seeing you and the children.'

Marianne smiled to herself. She had an idea that her mother would not be anxious to return to New Orleans. She considered Giovanni's idea that she should look for an apartment that would suit her mother down in the village. She would ask Vasilis if he planned to sell his apartment when he and Cathy moved into their new house.

Ronnie opened the e-mail she had received from Luke in Australia curiously. She had not heard from him since they had e-mailed their thanks to her for painting the picture of Spinalonga and giving so much pleasure to his elderly mother.

'*Dear Miss Vandersham,*

I must ask you to forgive my long silence. My mother, understandably, became very dependent upon Ingrid and myself and eventually she no longer knew us and reverted to the past. Sadly she passed away three months ago.

Of course we had to arrange for her other sons to attend her funeral and it was somewhat time consuming and difficult to arrange a date when everyone could be together. As she had lived with us we were left to dispose of her belongings. To our surprise we found two large folders that contained her memoirs.

We had no idea she had been doing this to pass the time. I have read them, but I have no idea if they are a true account of her early life or a figment of her imagination. I wondered if you would be willing to read them and let me know if they are reasonably accurate? If you are able to spend the time it will be greatly appreciated.

Please let me know and I can photocopy all the pages and send them to you. Are you now living in your magnificent house in Kastelli? I will need the address where they can be safely delivered.

I would be grateful for a reply from you, even if you do not feel able to undertake my request.

Ingrid sends her regards.
Yours truly
Luke.'

Ronnie read the e-mail through a second time and showed it to Kyriakos.

'What do you think? Should I ask Luke to send the papers to me? I'm not sure if I will know if her accounts of almost a hundred years ago will be accurate.'

'You can always ask my mother.'

Ronnie gave him a withering look. 'You're mother will still have nothing to do with me.'

'She's a foolish old woman. You could ask John. If she is retelling the time she spent on Spinalonga he would know if her recollections were accurate.'

'I suppose there's no harm in saying he can send them to me. I know John and Nicola enjoyed translating Maria's diaries. They might find these papers interesting to read. I'll reply to him later and also say I am sorry to hear about his mother.'

To be continued .....